THE WIDOW

BOOKS BY K.L. SLATER

THE WIDOW
K.L. SLATER

bookouture

Published by Bookouture in 2021

An imprint of Storyfire Ltd.
Carmelite House
50 Victoria Embankment
London EC4Y 0DZ

www.bookouture.com

ISBN: 978-1-80019-913-2
eBook ISBN: 978-1-80019-912-5

To my loving husband

PROLOGUE

3 DECEMBER 2019

KATE

I stood at the edge of the field, flanked by two uniformed police officers. We were up at the Wadebridge estate, three acres of fields with a main house with a large garden and a row of five stone cottages that stood on the edge of the village of Lynwick.

The place my husband, Michael, had worked for more than twenty years.

A sheet of freezing rain arrowed down the back of my neck, trickling down my spine. My jeans were already soaked through and the raindrops dripped from the tip of my nose and my earlobes. I thought longingly of home, our house being just a fifteen-minute walk from here. The warmth of the log burner, curtains closed against the weather, and Tansy snuggled into my side as we read *The Ickabog* together for the umpteenth time this week.

In front of me was a different scene. My new reality. White tarpaulin sheets stretched high and wide across the middle section of the field, stark and clinical against the sludge and the moody skies.

Behind the screen, I could hear the guttural roar of the yellow digger, its dull black bucket plunging into the depths, forcing the earth to reveal its grim secrets. Powerful spotlights illuminated the area of police interest and the wide circle of land around it. The smell of damp, clogged earth stuck in my nostrils and throat, and I fought the urge to gag.

I turned away from the field to look at the people who were standing along the track – a public right of way that ran directly behind the row of cottages. They meandered in and out of their small, curious groups, standing and chatting for a minute or two before moving on. I recognised most of the faces that stared boldly back at me without acknowledgement. Locals who knew exactly what was happening here. People I used to consider friends and acquaintances who now found themselves unable to express their condolences. People we had lived peacefully alongside for years.

Now they'd braved the elements to come and watch our lives crumble as the drama unfolded, the small points of light cast from their phones dancing like sprites in the gloom.

Behind me: the press. The constant flashes from the cameras were distracting, and every few seconds I'd hear my name being called with a jarring, unwanted familiarity.

'Kate! Do you know what they're going to find here?'

'Who's looking after your daughter, Kate? Where's Tansy?'

My life was now an open book to these people, a free-for-all. I was no longer a human being. In their eyes I was subject matter. I was a headline, the star of a grim and gory story everyone wanted to read.

I didn't look their way. I didn't give any sign at all that I heard them calling out. I pulled up the collar of my old waxed jacket and shoved my bare hands into the pockets. The fingers of my right hand closed around a soft ball and my heart squeezed. Tansy's woollen mittens, left in my pocket from a few weeks ago, when we'd walked over here to bring her daddy his sandwiches and to forage for some yarrow for her flower press.

Stomach acid bubbled up into my throat and I closed my eyes

against what was to come, what my six-year-old daughter would have to face.

'Mrs Shaw? *Daily Mail*,' a man's voice called out, closer than the others. He sounded friendly, sympathetic. 'Did you have any clue at all about what your husband did? We can help you tell your side of the story. Put an end to all the speculation. What do you say?'

I didn't turn around. The rain pelted down harder, the biting wind scalding my cheeks, but I welcomed the discomfort. The sound of the digger filled my head with its relentless drone, every second bringing me closer to facing the horror that I dreaded and they all craved.

Then … a splutter, the powering-down of an engine and the noise suddenly stopped.

For a moment or two there was perfect silence. Then someone shouted from behind the tarpaulin sheet, a sound of alarm.

The gaggle of headline-hungry reporters behind me erupted, surged forward. Cameras flashed so rapidly it almost felt like daylight. Voices rose in unison, all shouting my name and vying for attention. Demanding answers.

Several officers formed a loose chain behind us to restrain the press.

'What's happened?' I whispered hoarsely to my escorts. 'Does this mean they've found something?'

Neither of the officers responded.

A few feet away, DI Price talked animatedly on her phone in a low, confidential voice. Before I could get her attention, she ended the call and dashed behind the screen. My sinuses were blocked solid and I had to drag air in through my mouth.

A hum of chatter rose up. 'Have they found something?' a man shouted from the track. 'Is it human remains?'

The radio of the officer to my right crackled and he stepped away to speak into it. Another spurt of crackling, but I couldn't decipher what was being said. I found myself praying silently: *Please God, don't let them have found her.*

But the air seemed drenched with a dark foreboding, and I knew it would be bad. Very bad.

The officer with the radio returned and whispered something to his colleague. The second man gave a low whistle. 'Jeez,' he said, shaking his head, clearly appalled.

'What is it? What have they found?' A wave of panic shunted up and gathered in my chest, choking me like smoke. 'I have a right to know.'

The officers looked at each other, and then one of them turned to me, his face impassive.

'You'll find out soon enough, Mrs Shaw. Don't you worry about that,' he said coldly, glancing at the reporters behind him. 'I can guarantee that by tomorrow morning, the entire country will be talking about it.'

ONE

KATE

The black sky lit up with whirls of dazzling orange, red and gold as the firework grand finale galloped toward its stunning crescendo.

I felt Michael slide his arm around my shoulders as we stared up at the night sky, and I allowed my head to fall against him.

The crowd oohed and aahed, everyone in sync as if they'd been rehearsing. My wellies were stuck fast in the mud and my feet felt like blocks of ice. But when I looked down at Tansy's awestruck little face, I wished I could preserve her expression forever. I felt the weight of my phone in my pocket but decided against taking a flash photograph and spoiling the moment. I'd taken so many photos on my phone, like it might slow down this life we all lived at breakneck speed. It didn't work. This year, time was rushing on like a runaway freight train. I'd go old-school instead tonight and file the memory away in my mind.

Due to essential work being carried out in the village, the parish council had combined the Halloween/Guy Fawkes night events and scheduled them early this year. Needless to say, it hadn't gone down well with the village stalwarts. But tonight, everyone had forgotten the inconvenience and we'd had a great celebration.

It seemed just weeks since we were strawberry-picking at a day out at a local fruit farm, and now here we were in October. Tansy had turned six this summer too, and she seemed to grow taller by the day. Taller and smarter and so caring. As I watched her at the centre of her group of little friends, dressed in her cute little witch outfit and making sure nobody stepped too close to the firework launch area, I swore there were times she had a wiser head on her shoulders than I had.

'I'll go and get us a coffee,' Michael whispered in my ear, and I smiled and nodded. Just what I needed to warm me up on this cold October night.

I looked around me at the sizeable crowd on the field. I knew every face, every name of every person I could see, and that was why I loved village life. After so many years feeling like I didn't fit in, I felt truly at the centre of our little community here in Lynwick.

'Mum, look ... the fountains!' Tansy pushed up the brim of her witch's hat, watching in awe as cascades of colour exploded, splitting the dark sky. 'They're beautiful!'

Before I could answer, someone tapped my right shoulder. I spun around, and my best friend, Donna, pressed her masked face close to me from my left-hand side. 'Boo!' she hissed with delight when I jumped.

'Donna, honestly!' She was like a big kid herself half the time. Her reddish-brown hair seemed to glow in the warm light of the nearby bonfire as she whipped off the hag's mask. Her striking dark eyes were sparkling with mischief, and with the cute sprinkling of freckles over her nose, I always thought she looked younger than her thirty-eight years.

'Great display, isn't it?' She regarded the lit sky, raising her voice amid the pops and bangs of the fireworks. We stood for a minute or so gazing upwards, until Michael appeared with

Donna's husband, Paul, and handed us each a coffee in a cardboard cup.

Paul was tall and skinny, with the sort of metabolism that allowed him to eat pretty much what he wanted without exercising. As a national sales manager for a kitchen company, he spent most of his time driving around the country. At six foot exactly, Michael was slightly shorter than Paul, but was more muscular, with wide shoulders and strong legs.

'I was trying to get Mike to come for a drink while you two lovely ladies looked after the kids,' Paul said, unable to keep the grin off his face. He loved winding me up, but he only managed to get me occasionally. These days, most of his silly comments were like water off a duck's back.

I looked at Michael and he winked at me. 'Don't worry, I've told him I'm strictly on dad duties tonight. I've even turned my phone off.'

It was music to my ears. Michael managed a local estate, and even when he was off duty, there always seemed to be some catastrophe that needed dealing with. I smiled and kissed his cheek.

'Maybe I'll turn it off more often if that's your response.' He grinned, sipping his drink. I laughed, but his comment did make me think. I probably wasn't as affectionate with him as I used to be.

'The kids are loving it,' I said, ignoring the thought. I nodded to Tansy and Ellie, who was Donna's daughter and Tansy's best friend. The girls, or the purple witch and the orange witch, as they called themselves tonight, had broken away from the main group of girls now. They had their witchy heads together, laughing as they unwrapped the toffee apples Paul had pulled out of his jacket pocket like rabbits from a hat. Suddenly Tansy let out a howl of protest as Ellie snatched her toffee apple away and pushed her own into Tansy's hand.

'You gave Tansy the biggest one, Daddy.' Ellie scowled, turning her back to finish unwrapping it. I waited for Paul or Donna to pull her up, but nothing was said.

Donna and I had been pregnant together, and so the girls were more like twins. They were in the same class at school, and went to drama and dance club together on Saturday mornings. But while Tansy was generous and liked to share, I couldn't help but feel that Ellie was the opposite. Whether it was at school or their club, her small face was always watchful, seeing who had what and judging if she was missing out. Woe betide us all if she found she was.

The final explosions of vibrant colour died away, and there was the inevitable disappointed groan from the crowd.

'Fancy a go on the hook-a-duck stall before it closes?' Michael asked, and the girls squealed in excitement.

'Let's see which dad wins a prize first, eh?' Paul, ever the competitive one, broke into a run towards the handful of pop-up stalls near the entrance to the event.

As the crowd began to break up, Donna squeezed my arm and leaned in closer. 'Those two seem to finally be mending broken bridges.'

I nodded, pleased she'd noticed. I'd asked Michael to make more of an effort with Paul when we were together with the girls. It had felt so awkward when they wouldn't even look at each other in the months following Paul returning to Donna after he'd briefly left her for another woman. I knew it was a big ask, but Michael had obliged 'for your and Tansy's sakes' and I loved him all the more for it.

'Listen,' Donna said, dropping her voice even though we were alone. 'Is there any chance you could pick Ellie up from school tomorrow? Paul's home, but he's going to cover for me at the café.' Donna owned a popular vintage tea room in the centre of the village. Occasionally, when she was pushed, Paul had been known to don an apron and help out there. She gave me a meaningful look. 'There's some ... *stuff* I need to check on while he's home, if you know what I mean.'

'Oh, I see.' My heart sank. I knew exactly what her coded words meant. She obviously suspected he was up to something yet again with another woman on his travels, and she wanted to go through his work diary, receipts log and laptop. She did this every so often, and she sometimes found a clue that gave her sleepless nights. Michael had been known to call Paul 'the love rat' behind his back. Gone were the days when I'd tried to convince Donna to demand better of him. Criticism of Paul always fell on deaf ears but it pained me to see her hurt and confusion yet again.

'Kate?' She stared, waiting for an answer. 'Is that OK?'

'Yes, sorry, no problem. She can stay for tea.' I took a sip of the tepid, bitter coffee. 'I'll drop her back at yours about six, if that suits?'

A shadow passed over her face. 'You will remember, won't you? There's nobody else to pick her up if you forget, and—'

'Donna, it's fine. I'll be there.'

The panic had settled into the creases of her mouth. It was totally understandable after what had happened to her as a kid, but it never seemed to lessen no matter how much time passed. Ellie was a child who hated being alone even for short periods, and I could see why. Donna had inadvertently infected her with her own fear.

'Perfect!' Her face brightened. 'Thanks, love.'

At that moment, Michael, Paul and the girls reappeared. 'Stalls are already closing up,' Michael said to disappointed groans from Tansy and Ellie.

'Never mind. It's not long until the Christmas lights turn-on. They'll all be back then and you can—'

A low, admiring whistle from Paul interrupted me, and we all followed his goggle-eyed stare. My heart sank when I spotted the object of his curiosity. I felt both sad and outraged on Donna's behalf, but as usual, her vitriol was reserved for the recipient of her husband's interest rather than Paul himself.

'Who invited *her*?' she seethed.

It was Zuzana Baros, the young, glamorous single mum who was a relative newcomer to the village and who had instantly got all the tongues wagging. She'd met Irene Wadebridge, Michael's boss, while working for the agency Irene used for her home help. They'd hit it off quickly, and Irene had offered her a job. 'She was looking for a permanent post and I was sick of having half a dozen different people coming here from the agency,' she told me.

'She's always up at the house,' Michael had remarked when I told him about it. 'One of Irene's tenants is moving out and she says she's going to offer the cottage to Suzy to rent.'

Then Tansy had mentioned that a new boy had started in her class – Aleks, who'd come over from Poland. Miss Monsall, her teacher, had assigned her as his class buddy. One day at the end of school when Tansy walked over to me, I saw a boy with black hair pointing at us.

His mum came over to introduce herself. 'I am Zuzana … Suzy … and I wanted to just say thank you to your daughter for helping Aleks, for being kind.' She looked down expectantly at him.

'Thank you, Tansy,' Aleks said shyly.

I wasn't sure what I'd expected, but Suzy was young – in her mid-twenties, making me feel ancient in my mid-thirties – and quite stunning by anyone's measure. I knew it was unfair of me, but I felt a frisson of annoyance that Michael would see her a lot while working. She seemed very nice, though, and told me she'd moved over to the UK from Poland a while ago hoping to make a new life here.

'Aleks and I were stuck in temporary accommodation and I found most jobs were for low pay and very long hours. But there is a big Polish community in the East Midlands and I got lots of advice online. Someone mentioned agency work, and I signed on and they sent me to help Irene. Now we have a nice new life at Wadebridge. Irene rescued us!'

That had been a while ago now, and I'd kept meaning to invite her to one of our village events, but I'd never really had a chance. I only seemed to see her at a distance.

She walked past us now, clasping Aleks's hand tightly and leaving behind a fragrant cloud of floral perfume.

'Jeez, not exactly appropriate attire for a few fireworks in a muddy field,' Donna remarked spitefully as she took in the younger woman's outfit.

Suzy was tall and slender, the perfect frame for the skinny jeans she'd paired with striking over-the-knee high-heeled boots. She wore a short faux-fur zipped jacket and her long blonde hair looked impressively sleek and unaffected by the damp air – unlike my own mop, which had already begun to frizz out of its restraining bobble, framing my face like a fuzzy dark halo. She wore a stylish pair of glittery horns on a headband in a nod to the occasion.

'To be fair, if I had a figure like her, I'd probably have worn the exact same thing,' I said wistfully, patting down my hair. I dropped my voice. 'Give her a chance, Donna, she's only been here a few months.' I called out loudly, 'Suzy!'

She stopped and turned, surprised to hear her name. 'Oh, Kate … and Michael, hi!' She flashed her perfect white smile.

'I don't think we've met. I'm Paul Thatcher.' Paul stepped in front of us and held out his hand, and Suzy took it. 'Anything you need, just let me … or Donna know, yeah?' It was painfully obvious he could hardly keep his eyes off her. Suzy faltered as Donna glared at her, and pulled her hand away.

Donna had never been very good at keeping her true feelings off her face. She'd taken an instant dislike to Suzy the first time she'd seen her outside school and had made it clear that she didn't want to include her in our mums' meet-ups for coffee each week. Now, with Paul so obviously taken with her, her eyes had narrowed to slits.

'Hi, Count Aleks!' I smiled at Suzy's son, trying to crack the ice. Aleks was tall for his age and with his pale skin and black hair, made an impressive vampire complete with black cloak and bloody dribbles at the corner of his mouth. He had equally dark eyes that really didn't want to meet mine at this precise moment. His lips twitched and he took a step closer to his mum.

'Say hi to Kate,' Suzy prompted him.

'Hello,' he murmured.

'We're having a Macmillan coffee morning next Wednesday,' I

said. 'Be great if you could come. It's at Donna's tea room, the Larder. You know it?'

'Yes ... I've been meaning to pop in. It looks so nice and welcoming.' She gave a hesitant smile.

Donna folded her arms and looked away. I wanted to nudge her so she'd stop acting so rudely, but Suzy would have spotted the gesture. I felt awkward stuck between the two of them.

'Well, you'd be very welcome,' I added, glancing at Donna and hoping she got the hint. No such luck.

'Oh, that's kind,' Suzy said. 'I ... I might do, thank you, Kate.'

'Everyone is welcome!' Paul boomed brightly, as if he'd got something to do with the organisation of the coffee morning.

Suzy glanced at Donna's stony expression and patted Aleks's head in its red wool hat.

'Well, we'd better get going. Someone is excited to have some ...' She hesitated, and grimaced. '... mushy peas? Did I get that right? I have to say, it sounds pretty revolting!'

'Oh yes, it's the law that you have to eat mushy peas on Bonfire Night.' I laughed.

'Ha! We will report back what we think. Bye, Kate, Michael ... and Paul.' She glanced again at Donna's blank face. 'See you!'

'Not if I see you first,' Donna murmured as Suzy walked away, her narrowed eyes tracking up from the other woman's heels to her long fair hair.

'Well, she brightens the place up a bit, doesn't she!' Paul said cheerfully to Michael. 'Bit of eye candy for you while you're toiling away up at Wadebridge, mate.'

'Paul! Have some respect, for goodness' sake.' I squeezed Donna's arm, aware that her eyes were glistening.

He didn't respond, too interested in watching Suzy disappear into the crowd. 'Very nice indeed.'

'Give it a rest, eh?' Michael growled, eyeing Donna's crest-fallen expression. Ellie moved closer to her mum.

'Just a joke! Christ, don't take yourself so seriously, man.' Paul grabbed Donna and pulled her to him. 'Why would I be interested in her when I've got a woman like this?'

Donna allowed herself to be kissed and hugged like a rag doll, but didn't respond.

'Come on,' Michael said stiffly, taking Tansy's hand. 'Time for us to get off home, Kate.'

I wasn't going to argue with that. We said our goodbyes and left the field. Michael was as angry with Paul as I'd ever seen him.

'That's it, Kate. I'm done with him,' he fumed as Tansy skipped ahead of us. 'If Donna wants to be disrespected like that with her daughter watching, then that's her lookout. But I'm not standing by and letting *our* daughter witness it.'

'I feel so sorry for Donna, but I could shake her at the same time,' I agreed. 'He's awful. And Suzy looked uncomfortable, too.' While all that was true, part of me understood that after what Donna had been through as a kid, Paul, dreadful as he was, was something consistent for Donna to cling to.

Irene Wadebridge was in her mid-seventies, a generous, gregarious woman who played a big part in our lives. Her land stood on the outskirts of the village. As well as the large detached main house, where Irene lived alone, there was a row of five stone cottages. Michael had started working there young, learning the ropes under Amos, Irene's husband. When Amos had died ten years ago, she'd appointed Michael as her property and land manager, and he'd been there ever since.

I worked as a temporary teaching assistant at the local village school, covering for sickness and listening to the children read mostly. Over the last year, the school had called on me to do more hours, which suited me as we needed the money. There was a restructuring taking place in spring next year and I was hopeful the additional hours might become permanent. Before Suzy Baros had become Irene's home help, I'd always tried to help Irene out with a few light cleaning and caring tasks in addition to my school work. I still collected her prescribed medication from the pharmacy in town and filled up her tablet boxes, each clearly marked with the day of the week. She was sharp as a tack mentally, but thanks to arthritis and sciatica, she often struggled with her mobility and needed a bit of assistance here and there.

Michael and I weren't exactly hard up, but we weren't awash with cash like Donna and Paul seemed to be. The holidays abroad and frequent meals out they took for granted were beyond our means most of the time. Ellie came to us for a sleep-over on alternate weekends, and Donna and Paul would often have dinner at an expensive restaurant in the city, though it was a sore point with Paul that Donna wouldn't leave Ellie for more than one night, even with us. When it was our turn for a free night, we usually plumped for a romantic meal and movie at home.

Donna knew we hadn't got much money spare, and to give her credit, she never flaunted the fact that they were well off, but Paul liked to. It had been Michael who'd told Donna that Paul was having an affair, and Paul had never forgiven him. He'd do anything to get at Michael.

It had always been well known in the village that Paul had a wandering eye. Over the years, his indiscretions had often been public knowledge, though most of them had been casual dalliances. Then one day three years ago, Michael had travelled out of town to see an important supplier at an upmarket hotel and had stumbled upon Paul and a young woman in the restaurant. Paul had his back to Michael and didn't see him, but as Michael walked by, he'd heard Paul charging the wine to 'our' room. On his return, he'd told Donna what he'd seen, and that was the end of any goodwill between the two men.

Paul had left Donna and Ellie and moved in with the young woman, who turned out to be his secretary. I'd nursed Donna through her heartbreak, and after about six months, I really thought she'd begun to turn a corner. Until Paul realised the grass wasn't greener after all. Donna had taken him back almost instantly, no questions asked. Her relief at being a family again was almost palpable.

Michael had really liked Paul as a friend, and they'd always got on well, but he had no patience with Paul's infidelity. 'What a prat,' he had raged when Paul left Donna. 'I've told him to his face he's an idiot, and do you know what he said? "I know, but I can't help it. It's not my head doing the thinking right now." He needs to keep it in his trousers.' After that, he had cut back on the amount of time he spent alone in Paul's company.

I loved it that Michael was such a devoted family man. He wasn't always out at the pub or the gym like Paul, and provided he didn't have to work, our weekends were spent together, just the three of us. It was the childhood I wanted for Tansy after my own turbulent and insecure upbringing. It was probably the most important goal in my life.

Donna took a different approach. Rather than demand better of Paul, she preferred to expend a great deal of energy keeping a watchful eye on him, which included making sure he stayed well away from the clutches of any woman who was remotely attractive. Still, you didn't have to scratch her tough shell very deep to find the open wounds of the past. Twenty-three years ago when Donna was fifteen, her younger sister, Matilda, had gone missing one day after school. Donna, who was two years older, usually met her and the two of them would walk home together. But that particular day, Matilda said she was staying a bit later to study in the library with a friend. Someone saw her leave the school building but she never arrived home, and she was never found. The police investigation was still officially open, but with a lack of new leads for so many years, it was clear the case was not a current priority.

Donna had blamed herself ever since, and unsurprisingly, she hated Ellie being out of her sight. Who could blame her for obsessing about security and safety after what had happened to her sister?

When she had first met Paul, he had been everything she'd thought she wanted. Someone strong to lean on, to feel safe with.

But it hadn't taken long for him to show his true colours and to keep breaking her heart again and again.

Harsh as that treatment must have been for her to take, I always got the impression that Donna found that behaviour easier to deal with than to risk being by herself.

TWO

21 OCTOBER 2019

The next morning, Tansy chatted all the way to school as usual. This friend had said this and that friend had fallen out with another ... I couldn't keep up. It was fascinating how nasty little cliques started at this age and progressed to full-blown ones in adulthood. That was when the idea occurred to me.

'Would you like Aleks to come for tea one day this week?' I said. 'He doesn't know many people, but I know you get on well with him.'

'Oh yes, Mummy!' She stopped walking and jumped up and down like she was on a little pogo stick. 'That would be so cool. I can show him my Sylvanian Families collection.'

'I'll ask his mummy later then,' I said, smiling.

The usual crowd of mums stood at the school gates. I approached the main entrance, nodding hello to virtually everyone I saw. Tansy ran over to join the kids and I fluffed up my scarf, shivering. Last night had been cold but dry, whereas this morning it had drizzled, and although it had stopped raining now, the air still felt damp and heavy.

'Hey, Kate!' Donna called, waving her arm in the air to attract my attention.

I picked my way towards her, through the parents scattered on the main stretch of wet pavement, then spotted Suzy alone on the other corner. As usual, she stood out amongst the rest of us because of how she was dressed. Everyone else wore dull colours, practical clothing choices in keeping with the weather. Lots of people had taken shortcuts across fields or were walking their dogs straight after the school run. But not Suzy. She wore a short skirt, opaque black tights and ankle boots paired with a cerise wool coat, belted tightly at her small waist. The glittery devil horns had gone and she'd pinned her hair up in a messy bun, a style that seemed completely unaffected by the elements and would have taken me at least an hour to try and emulate.

Every other parent was either talking to someone else or looking at their phone, but Suzy stared morosely at the floor, scuffing the pebbles under the sole of her heeled boot.

'Suzy, hi!' I veered off the path that led to my usual crowd and walked over to her. It was obvious she felt completely excluded, and it was in my power to do something about that.

She looked up, an alarmed expression on her face. 'Oh, it's you, Kate!' Her features relaxed into a smile.

'How's Aleks getting on at school?' I asked, thinking about Tansy's recent comments: 'Ryan wouldn't sit next to Aleks today in class, Mummy,' and 'Someone called Aleks smelly and got into trouble with Miss Monsall.'

'He is OK, I think,' she said hesitantly. 'He is quiet whenever I ask him, but I suppose it will take time for him to settle in, yes?'

I didn't want to add to her obvious tension by mentioning anything Tansy had said. But then if he was having problems in class, perhaps Suzy might welcome the chance to talk about it when she was more relaxed.

'I wondered if Aleks would like to come for tea tomorrow after school?' I said. 'He could walk home with us, then you could pick him up from our house at about five thirty and we could have a coffee and a chat. What do you think?'

She considered it for a few moments, then nodded. 'That is very kind of you, Kate. I think Aleks would enjoy it.'

.   .   .

'What did *she* want?' Donna demanded when I reached the group. 'You're the first person she's deigned to speak two words to around here.' A couple of the other mums stopped talking to listen in to our conversation.

'I just asked her if Aleks would like to come for tea tomorrow after school.'

Donna looked taken aback. 'What on earth would you want to go and do that for?'

'Why not? Tansy tells me they sit on the same table in class, so—'

'But Tansy and Aleks are hardly great friends.'

'That's not really the point, is it?' I said, smiling through my irritation. 'From the comments Tansy has made, I think he might be finding it difficult to make friends, so I thought I'd offer a helping hand.' I glanced around at the baffled faces. 'In fact, if a few of us did the same, he'd have a ready-made friendship group in no time at all. What do you think?'

Donna sniffed. 'Ellie said she's already tried to include him in playground games, and he just goes off and stands against the wall by himself.'

Another mum spoke up. 'Carter said their football bounced over, and instead of throwing it back, Aleks booted it in the opposite direction. He'll need to learn some manners if he wants the other kids to include him.'

'Oh, come on, he's six years old!' I shook my head. 'He's not only had to start at a new school, but he's come to a new country, too. That must be quite a culture shock. I think we need to cut him a bit of slack. Cut them *both* a bit of slack.'

Donna glanced at the other women before clearing her throat. 'I think what you've got to realise, Kate, is that Suzy hasn't been particularly friendly to people around here.'

One of the other women nodded. 'I tried to chat to her on Aleks's first day here, and she was so busy watching everyone else, I'm not sure she even heard what I said. It was quite rude of her.'

I thought about Suzy's startled expression when I spoke to her this morning. Was it possible she was feeling nervous about something?

'Me too,' another mother said. 'I asked her if she'd come over from Poland for work purposes and she changed the subject really quickly. She couldn't wait to get away! So unfriendly.'

I was stunned that they were being so judgemental. Suzy's English was excellent, but with an inevitable language barrier and her obvious and understandable caution about meeting new people, it seemed logical to me that she'd feel uneasy in the presence of a not exactly welcoming group of mums.

'I think it's a bit early to judge her so harshly.' I continued to try and make my point, even though it felt like I was losing their attention. 'Regardless of whether Suzy wants to make friends here, Aleks is just a little boy and we should all try and help him if we can.'

An uneasy silence enveloped the group. I was clearly in a minority of one. It was disappointing, but I'd tried my best.

Jill Chiltern, the senior teaching assistant, had asked me to cover for an absent assistant in Sycamore Class that afternoon. It was a lovely few sessions including PE and art and design, with the more serious literacy and maths lessons having been covered by the teacher during the morning.

The icing on the cake was to come at the end of school when Jill grabbed me for a quick word. 'There's a permanent position coming up in the new year, Kate,' she said. 'A bit of security and a pay rise for you, if you were interested.'

'That sounds amazing.' I nodded enthusiastically. 'I'm definitely interested.'

'Good. I'd encourage you to apply, then.' She smiled. 'I'll give you the heads-up when the advert's going out.'

I thanked Jill, and left the building to meet Tansy at the school gates with a spring in my step. There were no guarantees I'd get the job, of course. School vacancies had to be widely advertised and an interview process followed. But the fact Jill had said I ought to apply was a good sign in terms of letting me know she thought I was in with a chance, if I wanted to go for it.

The next day, Donna wasn't standing in our usual place at the end of school. Tansy came out of class holding Aleks's hand. My heart squeezed as she led him towards the gate, but as she got closer, I saw that she looked troubled.

'Ellie says she's not my friend any more,' she said when she reached me. She was putting a brave face on, but I could see she was upset.

'Did she now? And why's that?'

'Because I told her Aleks was coming for tea.'

I followed her gaze through the cluster of parents and kids to see Ellie and Donna standing on the far side of the gate, looking our way. Donna rolled her eyes, obviously getting earache from Ellie about the playdate, and moulded her hand into the shape of a phone. *Call you later.* I nodded and turned slightly away, blocking Tansy's view of them.

'Don't worry about that now. We're going to have a lovely time, right, Aleks?'

Aleks nodded doubtfully. He was watching Ellie and Donna, who had now turned their backs and were walking away with the others. My ears would no doubt be burning very soon.

I'd never thought to invite Ellie for tea too, because she came over regularly. Three could be a crowd when it came to kids, and I'd thought it would be nice for Tansy and Aleks to have some time together, to bring him out of his shell a bit. I also wanted the chance to get to know Suzy later without the peevish shadow of Donna looming over us.

We'd just got back to the house when Michael came in with a

small bunch of freesias, my favourite blooms. He held them out to me and leaned forward to kiss me on the cheek.

I inhaled the sweet scent of the flowers. 'What have I done to deserve this?'

'Just because you're you.' He squeezed my shoulder. 'Because I'm the luckiest man on earth to have you. Is that a good enough reason?'

I felt a glow of warmth inside. He always got me with his words. I heard other women complain all the time about how they felt neglected or taken for granted by their husbands. I could honestly say that Michael had always made me feel loved and very much wanted. It was the little things that meant so much. Leaving me a romantic note on the kitchen worktop, polishing my leather pumps for work without being asked, or running me a bubble bath and ordering me to take an hour with a good book in there when I'd had a bad day in class. 'They're beautiful, thank you,' I said.

'You're welcome. Hi, Tansy Pansy.' He bent down to kiss the top of our daughter's head, then ruffled Aleks's hair. 'Hey, big man, how's tricks?'

Aleks mumbled hello, and then turned his back. I hadn't realised quite how shy he was. I knew that he saw Michael regularly up at Wadebridge, but now he was acting as if he'd only just met him.

'Not in the mood for talking, I guess,' Michael joked, and winked at me.

'Why don't you three have a kick-about in the garden while I cook tea?' I said. 'You can play a bit of footie and then ...' My voice petered off as Aleks walked away and stood looking out of the window. I frowned at Michael, and he shrugged his shoulders, clearly as baffled as I was.

'It'll have to be another time,' he said. 'I've got to go back up to Wadebridge to finish off levelling the ground ready for the new paving in front of the cottages. Just wanted to bring my wife some flowers and say hi to the kids.' He nodded towards Aleks. 'But I know when I'm not wanted.'

'He's probably just feeling a bit out of it,' I said quietly as Tansy walked over to the window to speak to Aleks. 'Tansy said Ellie has been nasty about him coming here for tea and you know Donna, she wouldn't chastise her for anything.'

Michael tutted but didn't say anything. He had attended the same school as Donna and Matilda and remembered the traumatic affect Matilda's disappearance had caused in the community. 'It felt like a wave of shock and horror that swept over every single person in the village,' he'd told me when we first met. 'I knew Donna's face, but had barely spoken to her at school as we were in different friendship groups. But after Matilda went missing, everyone knew who she was. They'd stare at her in the street.' He'd told me Donna had to repeat a school year because of the upheaval and so I think Michael still cut her some slack because of that.

When Michael had left, Tansy and Aleks played nicely together, building Lego structures.

'You must see Michael quite a bit up at the cottages, Aleks,' I said as I walked past them.

He looked up at me. 'Sometimes, yes,' he said stiffly.

I wondered if he was nervous around men. After all, it was just him and his mum most of the time. It made me think about his dad, and, if they'd had a relationship, how Aleks felt about leaving him behind.

I made mini pizzas and potato wedges for tea, then watched as Aleks pushed the food unenthusiastically around his plate, nibbling bits now and again. I studied his posture, the way he hung his head, his shoulders drooping and his eyes dull. It didn't take a genius to work out this boy was suffering in some way. Suzy had said they'd come to England hoping to make a fresh start, but she hadn't volunteered any details about their old life and I didn't know her well enough yet to ask. Maybe he was missing his family back home, or perhaps it was the other kids being unkind to him.

'How do you like it in Oak Class, Aleks?' I said brightly. 'Miss Monsall is a lovely teacher, isn't she?'

'I got a star on the class chart for collecting up the reading books today, Mummy,' Tansy said, proud as a peacock. 'I told Aleks to help so he got one too, but he wouldn't.'

'That's amazing! Well done, sweetie,' I said, gently bringing the conversation back to Aleks. 'Sometimes it's hard to help when you feel like you don't know anyone, right, Aleks?'

He grunted and took a sip of his juice.

'But he won't *talk* to anyone, Mummy,' Tansy said with a sigh, as if he were a hopeless case who wasn't sitting right in front of us.

'Imagine if you had to go to a brand-new school in another country where you didn't know anyone. It's not always easy to make friends, Tansy.'

'In my old school, I had lots of friends,' Aleks suddenly piped up. I was surprised by his voice, steady and confident, and his English was excellent. Tansy looked at him, astonished, as if it was the longest sentence she'd ever heard him say.

'You must miss your friends,' I said softly.

He nodded but didn't reply. I wanted to ask him a whole bunch of other questions about his life back in Poland, but I didn't want to make him uncomfortable by interrogating him. I remembered one occasion when I was around a similar age. Mum had gone out on a drinking binge and hadn't returned to the flat by nightfall. It happened periodically, but this time, a neighbour we only knew slightly came to the door with a dish of stew.

'Are you all right, lovey?' she asked. 'I saw your mum go out earlier but haven't seen her come back yet.' She craned her neck to look behind me, into the house, then handed me the dish. 'Have you got a dad? I mean, is there anyone here looking after you?'

I was scared to talk because Mum had warned me about social services whipping me away and us never seeing each other again. But I also couldn't quite bring myself to rudely close the door on an adult. In those days, I was just plain scared about so many things.

The thought of Mum's fury if I let someone in when she was out was enough to bring me to my senses. I shut the door in her face. I stood very still in our tiny hallway, trying to get my breath back. The neighbour stood out there on the communal landing for a little while longer, and then, at last, she went away.

It taught me that what felt like helping to an adult might put a child under tremendous pressure. I didn't want Aleks to feel like that in any way.

'Well, you're making new friends now,' I said to Aleks. 'You'll soon have lots of new mates.' He looked so forlorn that for a moment I had to stop myself scooping him up into my arms.

Suzy seemed like a very good mum to me, and I felt sure she was aware of how he was feeling. I didn't know her well yet, but I hoped that would change and I'd be able to mention Tansy's comments about what was happening in class.

No child deserved to feel left out and alone.

THREE

ZALIPIE, POLAND

JAKUB

Jakub and Ana had met at school during rehearsals for the summer play. That had been the very start of it. A week later, they were eating lunch together and walking to and from school to their homes, which were close to each other. Five years later, nothing had changed apart from the fact that Jakub now kissed Ana whenever he had the chance.

Zalipie was a picturesque village made famous by its painted wooden houses. It was a place where everyone knew each other well. Where people did not lock their doors, and home-grown fruits and vegetables were left next to honesty boxes outside wooden gates at the end of small, neat gardens. Jakub fully believed he would spend his life with Ana, make the cutest babies and grow old together. That was the way things seemed to be playing out until they turned eighteen. Until Oskar Krol came back on the scene.

Oskar was in the same year as Ana and Jakub. He had attended the same school until the age of thirteen, when his father had landed a prestigious job at a major car factory in Krakow, a ninety-minute drive away.

There had been a typical celebration in the village park to send the Krol family on their way. Music, dancing and a scrumptious community buffet to which Jakub's mother had contributed smoked cheese and kielbasa. Oskar, however, was a shy boy and had sat in a corner alone for most of the evening, despite friends and family trying to coax him out to enjoy the fun.

A jolly time was had by all, but as was the way, within a few months, the Krol family had swiftly become a faded memory.

Then, on Jakub's eighteenth birthday, a handsome newcomer gatecrashed his party at the village inn. Jakub watched as the tall, broad stranger quickly gathered a gaggle of locals around him. Ana slipped her hand out of his and announced that she was off to the bathroom to powder her nose, but instead she headed over to the handsome young man. Time seemed to slow as Jakub saw their eyes meet. He could sense an energy sparking between the two of them, acting like powerful magnets that would let nothing get in their way.

He watched anxiously as Ana began talking and giggling with the man who seemed to be causing such a stir amongst the local girls, all of whom were hanging on his every word. He had envisaged her glued to his side during his birthday celebrations. Later, after the party, he had planned to walk her home and tell her about the meal he had booked for them the following week. He could barely believe his eyes when he saw the man slide his arm around her waist and whisper something in her ear.

He stomped over there to find the man was not a stranger at all, but Oskar Krol with a brand-new confidence that bordered on arrogance, no longer the shy boy who never joined in. They'd been the same height once, but now Oskar was a good four inches taller, with an impressive muscular physique that could only have been honed in one of those fancy gyms in the city that Jakub had seen online. Jakub felt slighted. He and Oskar had never been close friends, but they had understood one another, and he had never laughed at Oskar's geekiness like some of his classmates had.

'Hey!' he ventured. 'Long time no see. How long you sticking around for?'

'I'm back for good, man,' Oskar said, grinning down at Ana. 'Got myself a managerial position at the new car plant on the edge of town, and keys to my own house.'

Ana seemed impressed and completely entranced. She twirled a ringlet of hair around her finger and gazed up at Oskar with flushed cheeks. Unless Jakub was mistaken, she stood a little straighter, pushing out her small, firm breasts.

He battled an urge to take her arm and lead her gently away. He knew that would only make him look controlling and paranoid. After all, if he remembered correctly, Ana had barely noticed Oskar's existence back at school. And yet he was unrecognisable now from the weedy boy with glasses who had left the village five years earlier. He'd been no threat then, but now … Well, Jakub did not like the way Ana was looking at him. Not at all.

The new car factory had been up and running for six months now, and Jakub saw in the local newspaper that Oskar's father was on the board of directors. Hardly any young people their age had their own place. Most still lived with their parents, sometimes even for a few years after they married.

But things got worse. Within the week, Ana had ended their relationship because, she said, she needed time to consider what she wanted from the future.

'It's him, isn't it? It's Oskar,' Jakub raged, tears prickling at his eyes. 'I could see you were already in love with him on my birthday.'

'You are mistaken,' Ana said coldly, turning away from him. 'Oskar is just a friend. That is all.'

But within hours of Jakub and Ana's separation, news that she had been spotted walking with Oskar in the woods and that they had also enjoyed coffee together in a small café on the outskirts of town had reached Jakub's ears.

He felt as though everything inside him was becoming

unhooked. His head swam with the awful dread of losing Ana forever. It was a future he couldn't bear to contemplate.

Everybody had words of advice for him. Even, it seemed, Mr Kaminski, their lifelong neighbour, who was recuperating following a fall.

'She is young, my son,' he told Jakub. 'This boy, Oskar, he has cast a spell on her, but listen up, it will not last. The girl will see the difference between solid gold and a cheap imitation.'

Easy for Mr Kaminski to say, Jakub thought as he recalled Oskar's toned physique, his well-cut clothes and hand-made leather shoes.

'Be patient, Jakub,' his mother advised. 'Ana will come back to you. It is written in the stars that you two are meant to be together.'

So Jakub waited. Weeks, months and then a year passed. He would have waited longer still, perhaps even several years, but then everything changed. Ana and Oskar returned to the village after a few days away at the coast and announced that they were married.

'It will not last,' Jakub's grandmama predicted sagely.

His mother wrinkled her nose. 'Ana will see through this chancer before the year is out, I promise you that, my boy.'

But now their words fell on deaf ears. Jakub had been as patient as he was going to be, and he knew that despite what his mother and grandmama said, the time had come to face the truth. The truth that had been in front of him all along. Ana loved another man so much, she had made him her husband. She and Oskar would live together in his fancy cottage and build their new life and family there.

Jakub felt a resignation so complete, it gave him the courage and resolve to forge on with his own life. He would build his future in the village, be the master of his own fortune.

Sadly, it was not to work out quite so simply.

He had not anticipated Oskar strutting around the village for years as if he owned the place. He had not bargained on Oskar and his friends drinking daily outside the only tavern and heckling Jakub as he walked by.

'Hey, *idiota*, why so many bags?'

'It is Mr Kaminski's food shopping,' Jakub called nonchalantly. 'Perhaps you could offer to mow his lawn or mend his roof before the bad weather comes?'

'Perhaps we will just stay here with our good friend Zubrowka. Cheers!' Oskar held up his glass of the famous vodka before waving Jakub away. 'Run along and do your errands now, *idiota*.'

'Drinking in the middle of the day!' Jakub's grandmama shook her head when he returned home, long-faced. 'Ha, what happened to Oskar's fancy new job? Soon Ana is going to realise this man is no good. Soon she will beg for your forgiveness.'

Jakub blew out air. 'In my dreams only.'

'Ignore them all, *kochanie*,' his mother soothed, using the pet name she'd been fond of since he was a child. 'These immature boys, they have nothing better to do.'

But Jakub knew they were not boys at all. They were men, the same age as him, and most of them broad and strapping. He hadn't told his mother they had become intimidating and threatening towards him. Only yesterday, when he had emerged from the general store, he'd found his perfectly good bicycle wheel newly buckled. He'd looked around and seen Oskar and his friends sitting outside a nearby café, pressed together in a huddle, laughing.

On the way home, carrying the useless bicycle on his back, Jakub had wrestled with a wave of fury twisting deep inside him. For the first time in his life, he wanted to hurt someone. Anyone. He had placed his loyalty, love and trust in Ana and she had betrayed him.

Were all women like this? He had heard some of the older single men in the village say so and had always discounted them as bitter fools. But perhaps they were right after all.

That realisation had been the tipping point. He had stood Oskar's taunts for years. When he finally got home, sweating from the effort of carting the bike, he had realised that it was time. Time to leave his mother, his grandmama and his beloved Zalipie for pastures new. But to go where?

He glanced down at the newspaper his mother had folded and set on the sofa cushion. A headline screamed out:

Record numbers of Polish workers head to UK to make their fortune.

That was when the plan first began to form in his mind. He would go abroad and work hard. Soon he would become successful and far wealthier than Oskar Krol.

Then he would sweep back to Zalipie and show Ana the man he had become.

FOUR

22 OCTOBER 2019

KATE

The kids played really nicely, Aleks getting over his initial shyness and not a cross word between them, which made a change from when Ellie came around. She was forever complaining that Tansy wouldn't share or that Tansy had refused her a turn. Always Tansy. Never her.

Suzy arrived promptly at 5.30 to pick Aleks up. I opened the door and took a step back as she darted forward. She couldn't wait to get inside, her gaze sweeping up and down the street.

'Hi,' I said, leaning out of the door and looking around. 'Everything OK?'

'Sure. Everything is fine.' She glanced up the stairs as she heard the kids' laughter, chewing the inside of her cheek. 'How is Aleks? Is he all right?'

'He's fine. I hope you don't mind, but they've been so good and I let them have a few minutes on the Nintendo. I'll shout them down in five, though. Come through and I'll put the kettle on.'

'I cannot stay long,' she said hurriedly. 'I ... I've got some chores to do at the cottage.'

'I know the feeling,' I said, leading her through to the kitchen.

'If I don't tackle the ironing pile soon, one of us is going to get buried under it!' She hung back at the door. 'Sit down, Suzy. Tea or coffee?'

'Coffee is fine, thanks, no milk.' She perched on the small teal velvet sofa we'd bought in an effort to pretty up the drab wooden kitchen that was desperate for a refit. 'You have a lovely home.'

'Oh, thanks,' I said, filling the kettle. 'We've been here over ten years now and there's still lots to do. You never really finish trying to improve houses, do you? There's always something that needs doing. Still, I suppose you don't have to worry about that at least, with renting.'

Suzy didn't reply.

'How are you finding it up at Wadebridge?' I took out two clean mugs and spooned coffee in. 'Nice and quiet up there, I bet.'

'It is really quiet,' she agreed. She started chewing on a fingernail. Then faintly she added, 'Maybe too quiet.'

She fell silent and it got me thinking. About how it must feel to be stuck out on a limb, the stranger in such a close community. I busied about for a couple of minutes while the kettle boiled.

'You are a bit out of the way up there, I suppose,' I said after a while, carrying over our drinks and a plate of home-made shortbread from Donna's café. I placed them on the small table and sat beside her on the sofa. 'You must feel quite cut off from the bustle of the village, although I guess you see quite a bit of Michael while he's working up there.'

She picked up her drink, cradling it in her small, pale hands. Her nails were unvarnished and she wore no rings. She stared down into the mug. 'Sure, I see him around the place.'

'Will you be able to make the coffee morning next week, do you think?'

She hesitated. 'I don't know. I'm not very good at mixing. I don't really like busy places and ... I don't think Donna wants me to come.'

'It's not up to Donna, she's just providing the venue. We can always use another pair of hands if you fancy helping out rather than just attending,' I added, pushing the plate of biscuits towards her. 'You could help me serve the drinks. That could be a great way for you to get to know the other villagers.'

She glanced at the biscuits but didn't touch them. 'I get a little nervous around strangers. I mean … I came over here and I've met lots of new people, but that's different to spending time with people I don't know.'

It was frustrating, because I knew it would be the perfect opportunity to start breaking down those barriers. But I felt a strong underlying resistance from her and I didn't want to make her feel uncomfortable.

She pressed her lips together and looked down at her hands. 'Sorry. I know it probably doesn't make sense to someone like you, Kate. You're so confident and outgoing. Everyone knows and likes you.'

I laughed softly. 'It took me quite a few years to get to that point, I can tell you. I wasn't born here like Michael and Donna were so I didn't know anyone either. Still, it was easier for me to integrate than it is for you, I get that.' I sipped my coffee. 'You shouldn't sell yourself short, Suzy. You've had the guts to come to a new country and start a new life, just you and your boy. That's an enormous achievement that not everyone could manage.'

She gave me a grateful look and I noticed she hadn't taken more than a sip of her drink. It was going to take something stronger to get her to relax. I put down my cup. 'Fancy a glass of wine? I wouldn't normally drink at teatime, but we've got cause to celebrate.'

'We have?'

'Yes, we're celebrating you becoming a full part of Lynwick village life! That's a great thing to drink to.'

Suzy laughed. 'Well, I think I have a way to go yet, but yes, sure. I will have a drink with you.'

I fetched the bottle of Sauvignon Blanc that Michael had opened when we got back from the bonfire two nights ago, and poured us a couple of glasses. I carried them over to the sofa and handed her one. 'To a happy and fulfilling village life,' I said, clinking her glass.

'*Dzięki* ... Cheers!' She took a sip and smacked her lips in approval. 'This is good, thank you.'

'Now it feels like we're having a proper catch-up.' I grinned. 'You'll soon get in the swing of things around here. There's lots to do and take part in, if you're interested.'

'Thanks for making me feel welcome, Kate,' she said. 'It's been more difficult than I thought to fit in. Some people seem a bit wary of me.'

'Well, people have their own insecurities,' I said, thinking of Donna. 'But I hope we can be friends.' I looked up at the ceiling at the sound of loud music and banging feet. 'Sounds like our kids are getting on just fine.'

She laughed. 'Aleks was never as shy back home. He had lots of friends.' She took a sip of wine. 'We both did.'

It was the perfect chance to ask the burning question. 'Look, tell me to mind my own business, but I can't help but wonder why you decided to come over here if you were happy back home?'

She looked at me over her glass and I wondered if I'd pushed her too far, too soon. The wine had already warmed my throat and I'd probably relaxed into our chat a bit too quickly. 'Sorry,' I said. 'You must think I'm a nosy so-and-so. Forget I asked.'

'I don't think that at all, Kate. You are bound to wonder why I just turned up here. It was because of ... things that happened back home.' She took a breath. 'Just life, you know? I used to have a happy relationship, then it went wrong and I had to get away. I will not bore you with the details, but I came to the UK because I wanted to make a fresh start for myself and for my son.'

'Well, good for you,' I said, moving away from the close questioning. The 'fresh start' line was obviously her default answer. 'Sounds as if you've done the right thing for both of you.'

'I hope so.' She took another drink, this time quite a gulp. 'I have made enough bad decisions. I don't want to make any more mistakes.'

'Nobody knows anything about your old life here, so it should be easy to start afresh.'

She smiled sadly. 'I hope you are right, but life sometimes has a way of catching up with you, yes?' Her eyes flickered to her watch. 'I had better get going soon. It is getting dark out there.'

Her nervy demeanour had returned. Fidgeting hands and wide, darting eyes constantly on the lookout.

If I didn't know better, I might have thought she was really scared of something. Or someone.

FIVE

That night, Michael didn't get home from work until around eight.

'Sorry I'm late, love.' He kicked off his boots at the door and padded over to me in his socks. 'Got a late delivery of the paving slabs I'm hoping to start laying next week. I didn't want to leave them outside in the damp.'

'I've already eaten, but I can warm you up a pasty with a bit of salad?'

'Perfect, thanks. Is Tansy OK?'

'She's fine. Disappointed there was no Daddy story tonight, but I've told her you'll make it up to her tomorrow.'

Michael had FaceTimed Tansy before bed. He always made sure he did so if he got held up at work. And that happened quite frequently. If it wasn't late deliveries, Irene would often think of a pressing job in the main house that meant she had company for an hour or two longer.

I unwrapped a pasty and slid it into the oven on a baking tray. Then I fetched Michael a beer from the fridge.

'Just what I need, thanks, love.' He took a swig and looked at me, tipping his head. 'You OK? You seem worried.'

'I'm not worried exactly, but there was something I wanted to talk to you about. Something I think you should know. You'll probably just think it's me being paranoid.'

'Oh God, it's nothing bad, is it?' Michael looked up. 'My head feels like it's going to explode with everything in it right now. I've got the parish council on my back to organise the Christmas lights turn-on, Irene is badgering me about one of the cottage roofs and—'

'It's fine. It can wait,' I said quickly. He'd looked so tired these past few weeks. I'd asked him several times if anything was bothering him, and he'd just mentioned work things that had never seemed to faze him that much in the past. He wasn't sleeping well, either. A couple of times he'd got up and gone downstairs to make himself a drink, then fallen asleep on the sofa instead of coming back to bed.

I jumped when he kissed the back of my neck. I hadn't heard him come up behind me. 'Hey, why so nervous?' I turned around to face him and he put his beer on the side and wrapped his arms around me. 'I'm listening. What do you want to tell me?'

'Nothing! I mean it – it can wait, honestly.'

'No it can't, I can tell you're fretting about something.' His chocolate-brown eyes melted into mine. 'What is it?'

'It's Suzy. Something she said, earlier.'

'OK.' He dropped his arms and stepped back. 'What happened? Didn't the kids play nicely?'

'The kids were great, they got on really well. But there's something up with her, Michael. I reckon she's scared of someone, maybe from her past, I don't know.'

'Really? What did she say?' His brow furrowed.

'That's just it, she didn't say much at all. It was like trying to get blood out of a stone getting her to open up. She was acting really nervous and I kind of asked her outright if she was OK and ... well, she wasn't. She said stuff about her past catching her up with her ... I don't know, it was just odd.'

His eyes burned into mine. 'And that's all she said?'

'Yes, but I just got this feeling, you know? That something was wrong. I wanted to flag it up to you so you could keep an eye out up at Wadebridge.'

Michael blew out air. 'Sounds like a big leap in logic, Kate. Suzy's nervous and you think there's a security issue at the cottages.'

'When you put it like that, it sounds daft, but you didn't see her reaction.' I thought for a moment. 'I wondered if you'd noticed anything strange? Have you spoken to her much?'

'We've barely exchanged a few words. She probably talks more to Irene.' He held me close again. 'How about you stop worrying about other people and focus on this?'

He pressed his face to mine and we kissed, his soft, warm mouth covering mine. I closed my eyes, enjoying the feel of his muscular arms squeezing me tight. After speaking to Suzy and hearing about the troubled life she left behind, I felt so lucky.

Suddenly, I wanted to show him how much I cared. The feeling came out of nowhere. 'Let's go upstairs,' I whispered in his ear.

'What?' He pulled his face from mine and looked at me.

When we'd first met, spontaneous sex happened so often it didn't really qualify as spontaneous. We couldn't get enough of each other. Then, after a couple of years, things settled down a bit ... maybe a bit too much, if truth be told. But we did still have a healthy love life, just one that required more planning and that had become a little less active due to busy days and falling-asleep-in-front-of-the-TV nights.

Maybe things had got worse than I thought, because honestly, the shock on my husband's face!

'No need to look so horrified,' I said, trying to make light of his reaction. 'It was just a suggestion. Probably a silly one.'

'No, no. Not silly at all.' He leaned back just an inch or two, but it might as well have been a foot. 'I want you too, I really do. But it's just ... I'm totally whacked tonight. The slabs ... I had to move them all myself and—'

'It's fine,' I said, turning back to the oven, feeling mortified. 'Maybe you should speak to Irene again about hiring someone else.'

He opened his mouth and then closed it again. He'd been about to defend what amounted to Irene's refusal to get him more help. The job was a strange mix of paperwork and heavy labouring. When her husband had died, Irene had explained she needed someone to cover all bases, and Michael had been happy with that. In my opinion, he did too much, though. There had been one or two casual labourers. The last one who'd been there a couple of years had let Michael down, just failed to turn up one day, and he hadn't bothered to get a replacement. That had been about twelve months ago, now. 'More trouble than they're worth,' he'd said when I'd asked whether he was going to find someone else.

'Maybe tomorrow night?' He moved to the side of me so he could see my face. 'We can have a takeaway, maybe take a shower together. You know, like we used to do.'

'That sounds great.' The forced brightness of my tone scraped at my throat. 'It's a date.'

Michael nodded, grabbed his beer and sat down at the table. His shoulders looked broad and strong, and the back of his neck still had colour from the summer months.

I used to make more of an effort when he came home late. Shower, pop on a little make-up, brush my hair. Here I stood in baggy culottes and a shapeless tunic, my hair finger-combed back into a bobble. The last scrap of make-up had disappeared from my face hours ago. If I were him, I wouldn't fancy me either.

SIX

I woke on Saturday morning to Michael opening the bedroom curtains, a cup of tea already on my bedside table. The clock's digital display read 7.02.

'Mummy, Mummy, has Daddy told you where we're going?' Tansy whooshed into the room like a mini whirlwind clutching her favourite bedtime toy, Barnaby Bear.

I shuffled up into a seated position and picked up my mug. 'No. Where are we going?'

'White Post Farm!' She could barely get the words out above the fizz of excitement.

'Are we really?' I sipped my tea and eyed Michael.

'Yes, yes!' Tansy squealed with pleasure. 'How long before we go?'

'Not that long, so chop chop,' Michael said, chasing her out of the room. 'Go and put the TV on and I'll bring you some cereal.'

I heard footsteps pounding downstairs, then Michael reappeared. 'Sorry. I should've checked that was OK with you. I just felt guilty that I've missed a few Daddy stories in the last couple of weeks and with it being the start of half-term.' He sat on the edge of the bed. 'I don't mind taking her if you don't feel like a morning retch.'

It was a standing joke that the smell of farm animals made me gag. I avoided it when I could, but this was just what we needed, some time together as a family. Michael was stressed and working too hard and this could be the start of the three of us carving out regular time.

'A day out would be lovely,' I said.

Watching Michael and Tansy at the farm zoo was like balm to my soul: their closeness, the love they had for each other.

We laughed at the alpacas, screamed on the rides and ate too many doughnuts. Watching my big strong husband handling those tiny hamsters and rabbits so gently, teaching our daughter how to love and respect helpless creatures, touched me, drenched me in love for the two of them.

Tansy wanted to hold a lizard. Michael cradled it expertly in both hands before passing it over to her. Its beady eyes stared up at him and didn't blink once.

'He's got his eye on you.' I laughed. 'He's obviously got the measure of you.'

Michael tried to laugh, but it came out like a funny strangled yelp. A shadow crossed his face and his mouth opened, and for a moment I felt a spike of heat in my chest, so sure was I that he was going to blurt out something profound.

Then the moment passed. I breathed out as his smile softened and his shoulders relaxed. 'What?' I asked. 'What were you going to say?'

He looked at Tansy, who was gently stroking the scaly reptile. 'Just that I love you two more than life itself. I hope you know that?' he said softly, disarming me completely.

'Hear that, Tansy?' I laughed. 'Dad's getting all soft and gooey.'

Michael reached for my hand. Squeezed it hard. 'Never, ever let anyone tell you any different.'

.   .   .

Later, Michael put a very tired but happy Tansy to bed and read her a story while I cooked dinner. It was a simple meal but something a bit fancier than the pizza takeaway we'd usually have plumped for.

'Wow, my fave, spaghetti carbonara,' Michael said when he got back downstairs.

'And garlic bread,' I added, draining the spaghetti and adding it to the carbonara sauce.

'You're spoiling me.' I paused my stirring as he walked past and kissed me on the lips before heading for the fridge and reaching for a bottle of white wine. He took two glasses from the cupboard and nuzzled into my neck, sending goosebumps down my arms. 'I'll return the compliment later. You look gorgeous, by the way.'

I smiled, feeling warm inside. I'd been shattered when we got back from White Post Farm, but I'd made the effort to jump in the shower and wash my hair. While I soaped up, I thought about how keeping our love life fresh was really just a matter of effort. When we'd first met, I'd always made sure I looked good for Michael, even when I was tired, but over the years, I'd let tiredness win and had prioritised things like the ironing or making packed lunches for the next day.

After my shower, I'd unearthed a pretty set of pink lacy underwear. I'd splashed out on it last year from Marks and Spencer's new frilly range and could only recall wearing it twice. I'd defuzzed in the shower, and afterwards smoothed some vanilla body cream over my skin. Then I'd curled my hair and put a little lipstick and mascara on. All in all it had taken about forty minutes to spruce myself up a bit, and it wasn't just for Michael. I felt good about myself and the tiredness had receded.

Michael set the table and poured the wine while I served up the food. As I sprinkled on Parmesan, he raised his glass. 'To us three, to our happy little family.'

'Cheers.' I smiled, taking a sip of the crisp, fruity wine. 'What a novelty this is!'

'Sure beats egg and chips in front of the TV,' he said with his mouth full. He jabbed his fork towards the plate. 'This is amazing.' He chewed and swallowed, then picked up his glass again. 'I forgot to say. You'll never guess who came up to Wadebridge yesterday afternoon.'

I shrugged and twirled more spaghetti around my fork. 'Surprise me.'

'Paul.'

'Huh?' I stopped twirling and looked at him. 'Donna's Paul?'

'The very same. Must be about a year since he ventured up there. Came to ask me some advice about planting trees at the bottom of their garden. That's what he said, anyway, but you can guess why he was really there.'

'Suzy?'

He nodded. 'She came out to put a bag of rubbish in the bins and he made a beeline for her. They stood talking for a few minutes and then he left again.'

'Could you hear what they were saying?'

Michael shook his head and took a bite of garlic bread. 'I could see Paul working his magic, though, flashing his pearly whites, shoulders back, feet planted apart. Doing that alpha male thing that always seems to work so well on any females in the vicinity. Whatever he was saying was making Suzy blush and giggle anyway.'

I could picture what he was describing so clearly. When Donna first met Paul, I remember being charmed by his act, too. He was a good-looking man, but it wasn't just that. He had charisma, something intangible that could work a kind of magic.

Over the years, seeing how he'd treated my friend and the way he seemed to regard women in general as disposable distractions, his charm, for me at least, became seriously tainted.

'Poor Donna,' I said, laying down my cutlery and picking up my wine. 'He's never going to change. You should warn Suzy about him.'

'Ha! I think I'll leave that to you. I'm not going to get involved in all that malarkey.'

'I don't get it. Donna's such a strong woman in every other way, but when it comes to Paul ... I just wish she could find the strength to put the past behind her to the extent she refuses to put up with his games any more.'

Michael nodded but didn't comment. We ate in silence for a little while, a chill-out playlist threading discreetly through the room.

Then he said, 'I've been thinking about us booking a week abroad next summer. I saw some offers online, and if you pay now, it's only a small deposit. What do you think?'

I looked at him. 'Really? Oh Michael, Tansy would love that ... *I'd* love that!' I put down my fork. 'Are you serious ... I mean, can we afford it, do you think?'

'Absolutely.' He grinned, taking another gulp of wine. 'If we book now, it will give us plenty of time to save up, and it'll be something we can all look forward to. I'll take a week off work, and there'll be no coming back to sort out Irene's floods or leaks or power cuts. I'll be all yours ... and Tansy's, of course.'

'I can't wait!' I squealed, and he laughed and pressed a finger to his lips to remind me not to disturb Tansy. Elated, I jumped up from my chair and moved around the table to kiss him, and he pulled me onto his lap.

'That meal was wonderful, Mrs Shaw.' He pushed away his plate. 'But now it's time for dessert.'

'I can't wait.' I laughed as he scooped me up and carried me over to the sofa. I could hardly talk for giggling, the wine having relaxed me and warmed me up. Then mum mode suddenly kicked in. 'What if Tansy comes down? I don't want her to see anything she shouldn't.'

He thought for a moment. 'She's shattered, out for the count, but this will give us warning if she does.' He jammed a dining chair under the door handle before turning and advancing on me as he peeled off his T-shirt, revealing his honed stomach and biceps.

'Dessert looks delicious,' I said appreciatively as he reached the sofa and began helping me slip off my dress.

'And afterwards, I'll pour us another glass of wine and we can look at some holidays online. How's that sound?'

'Perfect,' I sighed as the dress came off and Michael began to plant soft, cascading kisses on my skin.

SEVEN

27 OCTOBER 2019

The Wadebridge land was located on the very outskirts of the village, just under a mile from our house and on the bus route to town. But if the weather was dry like today, I liked to take the long way round through the wood with its waterfall, a leftover from the cotton mills.

On Sunday morning, Michael went into work early. It wasn't unusual for him to work weekends. It had always been the kind of job that had no set days or hours. It drove me crazy at times but Michael took it in his stride.

Mid-morning, Tansy and I walked up to Wadebridge to visit Irene. Before Suzy came to work for Irene full-time, there were always bits I could do to help her out on the weeks the ever-changing agency workers hadn't been as thorough. Something as simple as running a cloth over the kitchen worktops, plumping up the pillows on her bed. That sort of thing. Now, though, I just collected her medication and visited for a chat and brought Tansy with me, who Irene loved to see.

Tansy skipped ahead of me, singing, naming plants she recognised. I'd walked in these woods with her as a baby, negotiating the narrow, bumpy paths with the pushchair, pointing out the different types of grasses and brambles, identifying birds by their whistles.

I was self-taught from library books. After school, I'd often linger in a little wood near our house in Bulwell – a town about five or six miles away from Lynwick – not wanting to go back to Mum if she was in the middle of one of her week-long drinking binges. She could get soppy and emotional, or her words could scar me like razor blades. And I never knew which side of her I was going to get. I used to think of the wood as my nature home and the birds as my friends. I made several dens, tucked away off the main paths. I got a thrill from hiding there, people walking by unaware, though their dogs gave me up so many times, bounding straight up and wrecking my set-up. Funny, looking back.

The village wood was a different place where I watched my daughter happy and free of the worries that had plagued my own childhood. Worries I'd make sure she would never encounter. It felt like a kind of medicine for that old hurt that had crystallised like ice deep down inside me, and I chipped a splinter or two of it away each time we came here and I saw my daughter's carefree demeanour. From the moment I'd held her in my arms a few moments after her birth, I'd promised myself I'd protect her always.

Suddenly Tansy stopped running and slowed her pace until she was by my side. 'Who's that?' she asked, her eyes trained on the trees to our right.

'Who?' I looked around.

'I saw ... There was a man. A tall man, he just ran through the trees. That way.' She pointed behind us, and a shiver of dread slid down my spine. I followed her finger but there was nobody to be seen.

'Are you sure?' I said faintly. 'I didn't see anyone.'

'He was there,' she said adamantly. 'He's gone that way now.'

'Maybe just a runner,' I said lightly, not wanting her to pick up on my discomfort. 'It's OK, there's no one there now.'

She stuck by my side for another thirty seconds, then slowly moved off in front again. Within a minute, she was singing and chattering away to herself once more.

I'd seen plenty of joggers in here before, but they didn't usually run in the close-set trees, preferring to stick to the path. I shrugged off the unhelpful thoughts. I'd walked in these woods for years. All the villagers did, and nothing untoward had ever happened. It was safe here. There was nothing to worry about.

Irene would be pleased to see Tansy. She spoiled her, always getting little gifts for her – maybe a craft set or a new book. I think she saw herself as a sort of substitute grandma. Tansy lapped up the attention. In the good weather, she loved being outside at Wadebridge with her daddy. It was a novelty for her to help him with gardening, maintenance jobs or a bit of paperwork in the office while I got things done in the main house.

As she skipped happily ahead now, I thought about Suzy and her visit to the house last Tuesday to pick up Aleks. I'd not been able to get her out of my head. Maybe it was just my imagination, but she'd seemed to keep out of my way at school after that. I had seen her there waiting for Aleks. She'd just waved and moved away before I could walk over to her and chat.

Now that Michael had told me about Paul sniffing around Wadebridge, I wanted to sound Suzy out. Give her a subtle warning about him if I could. Last week she'd fought not to show it, but it was obvious she was pretty nervous. The last thing she needed was to get tangled up with Paul and risk Donna's wrath. I thought it might be a good idea to talk to Irene about it if I could. Michael had said he thought Suzy might chat to her.

'Look, Mummy, the trees are naked! Their leaf clothes have fallen off.' Tansy's mischievous giggle trailed behind her like a ribbon as she ran ahead.

Although I was wrapped up warmly against the chill, I shivered when I passed the trunks of the silver birch trees she'd referred to, bone-like and skeletal. I sped up a little, my feet crunching on the hard ground. In the spring and summer this place was lush with verdant trees and nature-rich wetlands. It was equally beautiful in the winter months, but there was something about the stark black branches and the frozen water today that made me wish we'd taken the bus after all.

There was a sharp crack to our right. It had come from within the thick growth of trees there. Tansy stopped walking and we both fell quiet, listening.

'Probably just a small animal,' I said, swallowing down the lump in my throat. 'Come on, let's get a move on.' I took her hand and quickened our pace.

'Are you scared, Mummy?' Tansy looked up at me fearfully.

'Course not! It's just Irene will be expecting us, won't she? We're walking quite slowly and it's cold.'

She nodded and seemed happy with my explanation. I slipped my phone out of my pocket with my free hand and looked at the screen. No service in this part of the wood. But in a couple of minutes we'd near the edge and the signal would return.

I wasn't used to feeling unsafe around here. I hadn't actually seen anything myself, so maybe it was all in my imagination. If there was a man loitering around the woods, he'd soon be noticed. It was a popular place for the villagers, but then it was also a known walking trail and there were lots of out-of-town visitors. So not all faces were those of locals.

Out here in the woods and fields surrounding the village, there would be all manner of places for someone to hide out if they were trying not to be seen. No wonder Suzy felt nervous.

We emerged from the woodland and took the gently rising path up the hillside. My breathing returned to normal and I felt happy to be close to Wadebridge. Soon enough, the five cottages came into view. Three were used as holiday lets and would be empty until the Christmas/New Year week. Suzy rented one and Michael used the other. His cottage had not been renovated like the others. The window frames were still the old wooden ones and the front door needed a lick of paint. His office was on the ground floor, and he'd removed the kitchen to make more space. The upper floor held tools and equipment that had belonged to Amos and weren't used often, but that Irene wanted to keep.

'There's Daddy!' Tansy sang out, running ahead.

I saw movement at the office window. Michael was standing sideways on and not looking our way. He was on the phone, and I could tell from his body language and gestures – clapping his hand on the top of his head and pinching his nose – that he wasn't happy.

Tansy got there first, bounding up to the window and banging on the glass, calling out, 'Daddeee!'

'Don't shout when Daddy's on the phone, Tansy!' I reminded her.

I saw Michael smile and wave at her. As I got closer, he ended the call. He disappeared from the window and seconds later was outside.

'Daddeee!' Tansy exclaimed, grabbing his waist in a bear hug.

'Hey, how's my princess?'

'We walked through the wood. I saw a goldfinch. Mummy says they're quite rare around here.'

'No way! That's awesome.'

'There was a man in there, too. He was spying on us.'

'Tansy, don't exaggerate!' I rolled my eyes at Michael. 'We don't know it was a man.'

'It was! I saw him, Daddy.'

The good humour slid from Michael's face. 'Hang on, Kate. If there's some bloke hanging around, we need to know about it.'

Tansy let go of Michael and began to skip around the yard.

'I didn't see anyone.' I lowered my voice. 'Don't make a big thing of it – I don't want Tansy getting scared. It could've been an animal or anything.'

Michael looked unconvinced. 'All the same, I don't like it.'

'Suzy seemed so nervous when we chatted, I admit I felt a little jumpy in the wood. But I didn't see a man, so let's keep our imaginations in check.'

Michael nodded. 'Anyway, this is a surprise, you just turning up!' he said, kissing my cheek. 'You didn't say you were coming over.'

'How long have you been on your phone call?' I laughed. 'I texted when we left home.'

'Bloody contractors. I've been on to them for ages,' he said gruffly. 'They give you a date off the top of their head, then change their mind to suit themselves. I'm never going to organise the cement for laying the slabs at this rate.'

I looked towards the end cottage. 'Seen anything of Suzy and Aleks today?'

He shook his head, pushing his phone back into his trouser pocket. 'Haven't seen them.'

'Well, I'll leave you to it. I just thought we'd come and have a cuppa with Irene.'

Tansy ran off to the main house and I sauntered a little closer to Suzy's place. There were no signs of life, no lights on inside the dim interior. The upstairs bedroom curtains were closed, although I couldn't imagine she'd still be sleeping with a six-year-old bouncing around. I decided I'd pop over there again before we left for home.

EIGHT

Although the main house at Wadebridge was large and imposing, it was one of those places that looked much bigger on the outside than it felt on the inside. All the rooms were small, and there were lots of them. Dust magnets, I'd come to think of them, because Irene Wadebridge was a hoarder. Each one of the rooms was packed to the rafters with what I could only describe as *stuff*. There was virtually no worktop space left in the kitchen because the surfaces were neatly piled with cookbooks, torn-out newspaper and magazine recipes and Tupperware containers, most with mismatched or missing lids.

'Tupperware parties!' Irene had announced triumphantly when I questioned how she had acquired this many containers. 'Those were the days. None of those cheap supermarket versions here. These are all genuine Tupperware. Apparently there's a thriving second-hand market for them online.'

'Is that right? Well, I'm more than happy to get this lot onto eBay for you,' I offered. 'Think of the space it would free up.'

'No, no. I won't be getting rid of them. You never know when they might come in handy.'

Irene spent most of her time sitting in her chair with a small, ornate wooden box on her knee that she guarded jealously with all her small things in – reading glasses, headache tablets, lip balm and keys – all the bits that might get lost in the chaos that surrounded her. She remained steadfastly unconvinced to get more organised.

There were several reception rooms downstairs, a draughty conservatory at the back, an old-fashioned larder, and a downstairs loo you could just about squeeze into thanks to piles of boxes and bin bags full of shoes, most of which had belonged to Irene's late husband.

Amos had died over a decade ago, and last year I'd broached the awkward subject. 'I could sort through and find the shoes that are still wearable, if you like. I could take them to the charity shop and you'd have the satisfaction of knowing someone was—'

'No,' Irene had said shortly. 'I'm not ready to part with them yet. Just leave them be, please, Kate.'

The upstairs rooms were just as bad, crammed with ancient clothing and photograph albums not only from the recent past but from other generations of the Wadebridge family who had owned the land and built the cottages.

'Hello ... only me!' I called out as I knocked and stepped into the kitchen.

Irene shuffled through and I saw she was leaning heavily on her stick. She was a hefty woman with meaty arms and hands. Her hair was neatly set, with no trace of grey, courtesy of the mobile hairdresser who visited the house once a week. She had a friendly, open face and a pendulous double chin that wobbled when she walked.

Health-wise, she had good days and bad days and not much in between, particularly when it came to her arthritis and sciatica. I guessed today was a bad day.

'Hello, Kate. What super timing, I could just do with popping upstairs, if you could give me a hand.' Her face brightened when she set eyes on Tansy. 'Oh, you didn't say you'd brought a fairy princess with you!'

'It's *me*!' Tansy giggled coyly.

'So it is! Come and give me a kiss, and we'll see if I've got a bit of something for you.' Tansy obliged, leaning in and kissing Irene on her soft cheek. Slowly Irene moved over to the kitchen drawer and pulled out a bead bracelet craft set. 'How's this?'

'Lovely!' Tansy exclaimed, taking the gift from her. 'Thank you, Irene.'

'You can sit at the table and do that while I help Irene upstairs,' I said.

Tansy moved away, focused now on the brightly coloured beads.

'Did you see Michael as you passed the office?' Irene said as I helped her to the stairlift.

'Yes, but he seemed busy so I left him to it. Some contractor giving him grief, he said. I'd hoped to see Suzy but the upstairs curtains are closed in her cottage.'

This was my chance to steer the conversation around to Suzy's apparent nervousness.

'She's a very private person. Never has visitors,' Irene said confidentially. 'But she's proving to be indispensable to us here.'

To *us*? 'Oh yes? In what way?'

'Well, she's done some ringing around for supplies for Michael. She fits it around her duties in the house. Very efficient, she is. Very good.'

'She's been helping Michael?' I said, trying to keep the surprise from my voice. Michael hadn't mentioned her ringing the suppliers for him. In fact, he'd said they hadn't spoken much.

'She's one of those people who'll do anything to help out, if it's in her power,' Irene said approvingly.

She was painting a different picture to the nervous, isolated young woman who I'd spent time with on Tuesday afternoon.

'Aleks came to play last week, and when she picked him up she seemed rather withdrawn, if I'm honest. Do you find she's quite nervous?'

Irene waved her hand dismissively. 'She's just finding her feet. Coming over here was a big change but I can't criticise her work ethic.'

'Michael said he thought she was getting on fine helping you out in the house.' I didn't want to give the impression we'd been discussing it at home, so I kept my tone light and casual.

'Oh yes, she says she feels at home here. The three of us – myself, Suzy and Michael – we often have a cup of tea and a biscuit together mid-afternoon. Hasn't he said? She's such a lovely girl, I think she sort of looks up to him, asking so many questions about the place. So eager to please.'

I bet she is.

I turned to look through the hallway window. Michael was standing outside the cottages, on the phone again. He'd never mentioned their cosy afternoon tea habit. A feeling like indigestion spread in my chest. I wanted to march out there and give him what for. But I knew I'd do better to find out what I could first.

'He's been so busy lately,' I said, my eyes scanning his fit physique. He still looked as though he was in his early thirties, rather than approaching his fortieth birthday. 'He seems more stressed than usual. It's good of Suzy to help him out.'

The words nearly choked me but I managed to sound reasonably genuine, I thought.

Irene gave a soft chuckle. 'Don't take this the wrong way, but I think she's a bit soft on him. Every chance she gets, she's talking to him out in the yard.'

'I hope that's not the case. Not a very nice thing for me to be worrying about.'

A flush of indignation surfaced. I couldn't believe Irene had just said that, though over the past eighteen months I had noticed she'd become a little distracted and came out with the odd inappropriate thing, like when I'd worn a new top and she had offered an unasked-for opinion. 'Shows off your arms, and they're not really your best feature, are they, lovey?'

I'd been so shocked, I'd laughed, and when I'd told Michael at home later, he'd roared with laughter too before saying, 'Nothing wrong with your arms. They're very ... sexy arms.' And we'd both laughed again.

'Oh, you've nothing to worry about there, Kate.' Irene waved a hand dismissively. 'Michael thinks the world of you and Tansy. No roving eye in his head. You must know that.'

And I did. I did know that.

Which made it all the more strange that he hadn't mentioned any of these things to me. The cups of tea, the chats, her helping with suppliers … the list was getting longer, it seemed.

Later, I made a fish pie and steamed some vegetables. Tansy and I ate together and when Michael got home about seven, he was all smiles. 'Something smells good … some left for me?'

My conversation with Irene had been simmering on constant replay all afternoon and by the time Michael got home, I was struggling to contain a boiling-over of annoyance. I slammed about, setting the crockery down hard, jangling the cutlery. Michael looked up. 'Everything alright?'

It was the chance I'd been waiting for.

'No, actually, Michael. Everything is most definitely not alright.' I slid the baking tray back into the oven and turned to face him, hands on hips. 'I had an illuminating conversation with Irene earlier. She's been telling me the cosy little situation up at Wadebridge between you and Suzy.'

I expected him to start stammering, trying to talk his way out of a very awkward situation. But he sounded relaxed and genuinely puzzled. 'Huh? Are you joking?'

'I wouldn't joke about something like that.' I walked over to where he sat at the table. 'She said you take your afternoon breaks together and that Suzy is doing some work with you, ringing suppliers. That sort of thing.'

He made a noise of disbelief. 'Once! She rang the paving slab suppliers about the order being light. I'd been trying for over thirty minutes and had to get them shifted.'

'And the breaks … did that just happen once, too?'

He thought for a moment. 'Twice maybe. Three times tops.'

'But why didn't you mention it?' I felt ridiculously emotional when I thought about the stunningly attractive Suzy with her fancy clothes and slim figure. I felt panicked and lied to. My voice rose an octave. 'Why didn't you tell me you'd been with her? What did you talk about?'

'Hang on, hang on.' Michael pressed his hands in the air. 'Irene called me in as Suzy had made me a drink and I stood around for a few minutes and just had a general chat. Not me and Suzy on our own but with Irene there.'

'A general chat about what?' I forced myself to breathe a bit deeper but I could feel heat rising in my face.

Michael pulled down the corners of his mouth. 'The weather, the bit of landscaping I'm doing in front of the cottages. That's it. I swear, Kate.' I watched his face. He looked a bit more concerned now and his cheeks were flushed.

'Whenever I mention her, you act like you've hardly said two words to each other and yet it seems you see her quite a bit.'

'Only in passing. I can assure you there are no long and meaningful conversations!' He blew out air. 'This is starting to feel like I'm on trial and for what? Having a cup of tea in the vicinity of Irene's home help?'

'She's young, attractive ... most men would jump at spending time with her.'

'Well, I'm not most men.' He stood up and, grudgingly, I allowed him to pull me close. 'I'm a happily married man who's very much in love with his beautiful wife. OK?'

I wouldn't look at him.

'OK?' he persisted.

'OK,' I murmured. What he'd said seemed perfectly reasonable and yet I still felt put out about it. Put out and still on edge.

I didn't think Michael was lying per se, but there was something he was playing down, not talking about. I felt sure of it.

NINE

NOTTINGHAMSHIRE POLICE

DI Helena Price sat at her desk looking at the stack of ongoing cases and silently fuming. Detective Superintendent Della Grey had landed this thankless task on her out of the blue. 'Have a look through this lot with fresh eyes, will you?' she'd said flippantly. 'See if there's anything that looks promising. The old DI kept these on the back burner, but I'd like them thinned out a bit in the interests of our drive to improve community relations.'

Helena's predecessor had relocated, leaving an exciting promotional opening that Helena couldn't wait to jump into. But she was already beginning to think she'd been rather naïve. It had soon become apparent that nobody had asked the previous DI to clean up her ongoing case file list before she left, so Helena had inherited lots of these unsolved local cases that had been unofficially shelved because there wasn't much for them to go on.

Her DS, Kane Brewster, stuck his head around the door. 'Coffee, boss?'

'In a minute. Come through.'

Brewster hesitated. It was nearly eleven, and he was no doubt gearing up for one of his many snacks. 'Keeps up the energy,

ma'am,' he always said when gym bunny Helena raised a disap-
proving eyebrow at the chocolate, crisps and biscuits that littered
his desk.

He entered her office without enthusiasm and slumped into
the chair opposite.

'Don't look so down in the mouth, Brewster. You can help me
go through these files, then you're free to go and get your Scooby
Snacks.' She pushed the pile of folders across the desk. 'You read,
I'll ponder.'

He picked up the first folder and opened it. 'Looks like a series
of shop burglaries that occurred over a period of three months and
then stopped altogether,' he murmured. 'Till takings, sports stock ...
nothing major and nobody hurt. Hardly the case of the century.'
He closed the file and set it aside. Helena did not comment.

Next he opened a file with just three pieces of paper in it. He
picked up the first page and frowned. 'Disappearance of a Polish
man. Remember this?' Helena shook her head. 'His name was
Jakub Jasinski. He was reported missing by his family in Poland
about six months ago.'

She watched as Brewster leafed through the scant paperwork,
scanning the missing person report. 'Says here that according to his
mother, Jakub left Poland in the spring of 2012 to make his fortune
in England. Looks like she contacted the UK authorities to file this
report in April this year. He'd headed for the East Midlands area,
staying at various B&B establishments when he moved jobs and
had kept in touch over the years, albeit sporadically. But in 2018
all contact stopped.'

Brewster spoke matter-of-factly, but Helena was mindful of
Jakub's mother. Long forgotten by everyone else, but she'd still be
waking up every morning hoping and praying that this might be
the day she'd hear from him again. Sadly, in reality, nobody had
been doing anything meaningful to look for him.

Brewster scanned the last sheet. 'Looks like his calls just
stopped dead. She tried ringing around farms and factories in the
area who used casual labour, contacted the Devonshire B&B in

Sutton-in-Ashfield, his last known accommodation. She got nowhere with any of that and she hadn't made a note of the name of Jakub's latest workplace.'

'So what did we do?'

'Couple of officers asked around the Polish community, visited a few farms in the area. Got nowhere. Says here, "Transient workers move around the country all the time. Lots of them lose touch with home either by accident or on purpose."'

'They don't want to be found.' Helena thought out loud. 'The UK doesn't turn out to be the land of plenty they imagined it to be, and some people are just too embarrassed to admit they're stuck in a terrible job and awful living accommodation. Not the experience for everyone, but certainly for some.'

Brewster nodded. 'Reading between the lines, the follow-up inquiry looks a bit light. Half-hearted, really. Nothing to go on, you see. Takes up a lot of time and officer hours when you keep hitting a brick wall.'

Helena nodded. Someone up the ranks would have had to make the call that Jakub Jasinski wasn't worth the time and effort. It hadn't necessarily been as heartless a conclusion as it sounded. Trying to find a temporary European worker could easily turn into looking for a needle in a haystack, particularly if they didn't want to be found.

But she couldn't get Jasinski's mother out of her head. A woman stuck in another country, putting her faith in the UK police force to find her missing son.

'Let's give this one another go, shall we?' she said, putting down the sheet. 'Contact the press office to say we're opening up the investigation again. You can speed them up by drafting an article to rekindle some public interest in the case after all this time, particularly in the area's Polish communities. Ask them to get it into the local newspapers and online news and make sure you stress that all information will be treated as confidential.'

Brewster looked taken aback. 'It's been a whole year, boss. Not sure there'll be anything left for us to find.'

Helena pushed her chair back and stood up. 'Well, we won't know until we find out, will we? Come on, we'll start with the Devonshire B&B.'

'Eh?' Brewster stood up and pulled at his tie. 'I thought we'd have a break before we go. A coffee, maybe a snack.'

'You know what they say, Brewster, no time like the present.' Helena picked up her phone and headed for the office door, Brewster trailing a little breathlessly in her wake. 'And let's face it, it won't kill you to skip lunch.'

TEN

THE MANSFIELD SENTINEL

Friday, 1 November 2019

Nottinghamshire Police are set to reopen a local cold case. The investigation of missing Jakub Jasinski, who disappeared without trace just over a year ago, has so far thwarted local officers.

The family of Mr Jasinski have had no contact at all from him for the past twelve months, which they say is highly unusual and makes them fear the worst.

Mr Jasinski, now twenty-five, travelled to the UK from Poland in April 2012 at the age of just eighteen. He is described by his family as a loving, caring person who dotes on his family and who always kept in touch over the years he was away. Despite this, his heartbroken relatives have heard nothing from him since October 2018.

'This is just not like Jakub at all,' his mother, Janis

Jasinski, told the *Sentinel*. 'He has always made a special effort to keep in touch, but in the last year we have not heard a thing from him. No one has.'

Nottinghamshire Police, who are investigating his disappearance, say Mr Jasinski vanished without leaving any clues behind.

'We reported him missing about six months ago but we've heard nothing,' Mrs Jasinski confirmed. 'Just a series of dead ends from the UK police. My son seems to have disappeared from the face of the earth. We fear the worst, thinking that something may have happened to him or that he has perhaps fallen on hard times and is in desperate need of help.'

Detective Inspector Helena Price, who is leading the new investigation into Jakub's disappearance, said: 'This is an unusual case. Jakub appears to have just vanished without a word to anyone and we can find no signs to indicate where he is. We are appealing for Jakub himself to come forward and let us or his family or friends know he is all right. We know Nottinghamshire has a close-knit Polish community and we would urge anyone who has knowledge of Jakub's whereabouts to get in touch immediately. Their identity will be kept confidential.'

ELEVEN

10 NOVEMBER 2019

KATE

The village green was buzzing, a sea of warm coats and colourful woolly hats. Despite the usual grumblings about this year's earlier event scheduling, everyone had gathered for the annual Christmas lights event, and once again, the weather was on our side.

Michael and Paul were helping out near the tree, getting the wires sorted and making sure safety measures were in place to stop kids getting too close. While Donna staffed the drinks stall, I took them a tray loaded with coffee and mince pies.

'And an angel appears,' Michael joked, winking at me and taking a drink and a pie. 'Just what we need, Kate, thanks.'

Paul took a coffee but ignored the mince pies. 'Lovely, thanks, Kate ...' His voice trailed off and I followed his stare.

Suzy Baros walked by holding Aleks's hand. She wore a full-length black mac and a baby-pink scarf, hat and gloves. There was no doubt she looked striking. Paul didn't attempt to disguise his interest but I wondered what Michael privately thought to her style and panache.

'How's it going?' I said to Michael, and he rolled his eyes at Paul's obvious distraction.

'Yeah, good. We're nearly finished up here, and then—'

'Give me five, mate,' Paul said, pushing his cardboard beaker towards Michael. 'Just need a quick word with someone.' And he was gone. In the direction of Suzy.

'There's no hope for him,' Michael growled. 'I swear he's getting worse.'

'I'm going to have to try and speak to Donna about him,' I said. 'Shame Irene felt too rough to come tonight. It was her sciatica this time.' Secretly, I felt quite relieved she wasn't here. The last thing I needed was her making more off-putting observations about Michael and Suzy getting friendly.

Michael nodded. 'Irene's struggling a bit at the moment. I think. I might go up and check on her when the event is finished.'

'She's quite vocal, though,' I said. 'I'm sure she'd say if she needed any help.'

'Maybe.' He squeezed my hand. 'Catch up soon, yeah?'

'Fine, see you later.' The stuff we'd discussed about him and Suzy still felt like wire wool in my throat.

As I walked back to the drinks stall, the crowd parted slightly and I saw Paul heading back towards the Christmas tree and Michael.

Back at the stall, Donna and I handed out free tea, coffee and mulled wine as if our lives depended on it. I inhaled the smell of frying onions and sausages from the outdoor caterers who'd pitched up next to us, and felt a swell of happiness at being here with my family, with friendly faces all around us. My worries about Michael and Suzy had faded in the jolly atmosphere and now I couldn't wait for Christmas, especially with our holiday abroad to look forward to next year. It really felt as if life was getting better. If I could just get over Irene's remarks, I felt like Michael and I were becoming close again. And with the new job opportunity at school, maybe holidays were going to become a regular thing for us.

Tansy and Ellie were a blur, racing back and forth in front of the drinks stall. 'Mum!' Tansy called, waving her light wand every time she passed. I waved back in between customers, but Donna was distracted watching the girls. She'd already spilled a couple of drinks. 'I think we should tell them to stop running around like that,' she said. 'It's a big crowd and they could easily get lost.'

The tragic events of Donna's childhood still showed up every day of her life. Matilda's disappearance had affected her deeply, and understandably she was overprotective with Ellie.

'The girls will be fine,' I said gently. 'Everyone knows them here. Everyone keeps an eye on each other's kids.'

Donna nodded, but her brow remained furrowed. 'It's a Christmas lights event focused on families, but you always get one that wants all the attention.'

I looked over to see Suzy and Aleks walking back the other way. My buoyant mood faltered a little. I hadn't got the heart to tell Donna that Paul had scurried off to talk to her. Instead, I watched the crowd and soaked up the atmosphere. Folks were wrapped up warm, everyone smiling and glad to be there, frosty breath puffing like clouds as they chattered. Twangs from an electric guitar and little flurries of drumbeats started up on the other side of the green, where a local indie band were setting up ready to perform later.

Suzy and Aleks approached the queue as Donna disappeared, mumbling something about going to check on the girls.

'Hi, Kate,' she said, her eyes darting round as usual. 'I'll have a mulled wine, and an orange juice for Aleks, please.'

'Sure.' I noticed her perfectly applied eyeshadow and lip colour. She'd gone to a lot of effort for an informal event. 'How are you?'

'Good, I'm ... good. Thank you.' She faltered slightly under my gaze. 'I wondered if ... Would Tansy like to come to the cottage for tea after school one night next week?'

'I'm sure she'd love that, thank you.' I poured the drinks, Irene's words echoing in my head. 'Michael was saying you two were seeing a bit more of each other up at Wadebridge?' She looked at me. 'Always tells me all about your little chats.'

She swallowed. 'I ... I sometimes see Michael, yes, but—'

Aleks said something to her I couldn't catch above the noise.

'Not this time, Aleks. I haven't got my purse.'

His face dropped. 'What is it?' I asked.

'He wants one of the light things the kids all seem to have,' Suzy said.

I reached under the counter and pulled out a light wand. I might feel twisty with Suzy but I wasn't about to take it out on a little boy. 'Here, this one is spare, Aleks. Go and find Tansy and Ellie. They've got wands too.'

Aleks's face lit up as he took it. 'Thank you, Kate!' he said politely, and ran off.

'Don't go too far!' Suzy called after him, her words dissolving in the cold air. 'Thank you, Kate, that was really kind. I will pay you when I see you.'

I got the impression money was tight for Suzy, but she always looked a million dollars. I guessed she'd had a good life back in Poland. She'd accumulated quite a wardrobe.

'No need.' I waved her offer away. 'Irene was telling me you've been helping Michael out, ringing the suppliers. That's very good of you.'

Was it my imagination, or did her face flush? Hard to tell in the dark, but she looked uncomfortable. As if I'd uncovered something she'd thought I didn't know about.

'Oh, it was ... nothing really. Just a couple of phone calls. Michael is ... a good man. You have a good family man there.'

'Oh yes, I know that,' I said, forcing a smile. 'We're very happy.'

She picked up the drinks and took a step back. 'Well, I had better go and see where Aleks is. Maybe you and I could talk properly when Tansy comes to play.'

That took me by surprise. 'Yes, of course. Any time.'

'Good, that's good. I want to be honest with you, Kate. I ...' She shook her head. 'We'll talk next week, yes? See you.'

'Suzy, wait!' I looked around for Donna, hoping that she could do without me on the stall for five minutes. I wanted to know what Suzy had to say. I felt a bit sick. Did she mean the truth about her and Michael? I stood on my tiptoes to call her name again, but Suzy was already disappearing into the crowd, and I could see Donna's distinctive red beret bobbing around near to where the girls were playing. I looked over the heads of the villagers and up at the twenty-five-foot fir tree, currently a great dark shadow looming above the gathering, soon to dazzle us all with its glorious Christmas cheer.

Just a couple of hours earlier, and in the absence of anyone else daft enough to volunteer, Michael had climbed up a very long ladder propped against the side of the tree. Steadied on one side by the local butcher and on the other by a neighbour, he'd perched precariously at the summit threading a few more multicoloured lights up there, ensuring that the new angel with her glittering waterproofed wings would be fully illuminated.

After completing his onerous task, he had descended to a jolly round of applause and witty observations about risk assessments.

'Customers need serving, please!' Donna reappeared, waving a hand in front of my face. 'When you've finished contemplating the meaning of life, that is.'

'Sorry! I thought you were busy watching the girls.' I poured coffee into a cup and slid it across the table for the next customer to take. 'Just wondering how Michael managed to get back down that ladder in one piece.'

'Well, he's a far braver man than my Paul. Soon as they mentioned the word "volunteer", he scarpered off to speak to someone in the crowd.'

'Brave or daft.' I wiped up the spills. 'I'm not altogether sure which.'

I looked up and saw Michael rushing towards me.

'Irene just rang. Her downstairs loo is leaking. If it's a bad one, I might be a while, so I'll see you back at home later, yeah?'

'She struggles to get in the downstairs loo for clutter,' I

grumbled.

'That may be so, but it doesn't stop it leaking,' Michael pointed out.

I felt a rush of disappointment, and then resentment. We were minutes away from the lights being turned on, and Michael was going to miss it. I'd hoped to get some selfies of the three of us to mark the occasion.

'Surely it's not that urgent.' I scowled. 'She can wait another ten minutes until the lights are on.'

'I'd better not, Kate. If it's bad, it'll just mean more mess for me to clean up. Have fun, and I'll see you later.' He gave me a peck on the cheek and I felt like turning away. I was probably being childish, but Tansy was growing up so fast, and these events were memories in the making. Tonight was another one Michael would miss thanks to work.

I watched him thread his way back through the crowd of people now moving towards the tree en masse. Michael would do anything for anyone, but just lately, Irene was really taking the mickey. I'd noticed that whenever anything happened up at Wadebridge, it was always 'urgent' whether it was during his working hours or not. I hated the tendrils of distrust that had begun twitching since my recent conversation with Irene. Maybe there was another reason he was spending more time up there …

I pushed away the worrying thought. I was annoyed he hadn't volunteered the information about Suzy but still, I had to give him more credit than that.

I just wished it didn't feel like Tansy and I were always at the bottom of the pile when it came to his priorities. Sometimes, I felt like as long as Michael worked at Wadebridge, we'd be stuck in this stage of our lives.

I wanted more. More time together, enough money to have an annual holiday and to pay off the credit card. I wanted a feeling that we were progressing, moving on in our lives like other people seemed to do. I wanted it for me, for Michael and most of all, I wanted security and stability for our daughter.

TWELVE

The music from the speakers faded and the band struck up and played a clever indie rendition of Slade's 'Merry Xmas Everybody'. We had a sudden rush at the drinks stall, with everyone trying to get their mulled wine before the lights went on.

Donna craned her neck, looking this way and that.

'The girls are here,' I told her, pointing to them just in front of us, watching the band.

'I'm looking for Paul,' she said. 'He's supposed to be by the tree, but I haven't seen him since ... oh, there he is!' The relief was palpable in her voice.

The crowd suddenly fell quiet, and then a ten-second count-down started over the tannoy, with everyone joining in. When we reached 'one', the tree ignited with thousands of multicoloured lights, cascading its irrepressible festive glow down on the crowd. There was a cheer and a roar, and everyone clapped.

I sipped my warm mulled wine, savouring the spark of cinnamon and cloves on my tongue, feeling a rush of happiness. As a child, I'd had never had a proper family Christmas with Mum, but I always imagined this was what it should feel like. Although I was still disappointed that Michael wasn't with me, it felt right standing here in the centre of the village with everyone pulling together for the common good ... I felt like I belonged.

Tansy and Ellie appeared again, waving their light wands. 'Can we have some juice, please, Mummy?' Tansy sang out, her cheeks ruddy, eyes sparkling and bright.

I poured orange juice into two paper cups. 'Have you seen Aleks? I think he was trying to find you both earlier.'

Tansy shook her head and gulped at her drink.

Behind the girls the queue was building up again. Now that the lights were on, people wanted more drinks and mince pies. It was never-ending, and I seemed to be serving on average twice the number of people Donna was. She was too busy monitoring Ellie and Tansy and trying to spot her errant husband.

'Don't stray too far,' she told the girls as they wandered off with their drinks and light wands. 'Come back every five minutes to check in, and whatever you do, don't leave the village green.'

'Donna, they're fine. I know you live in constant fear but they're amongst friends. Let them have a little bit of freedom.' I laid a hand on her shoulder. I understood the tragedy that under-pinned her concern but I feared for Ellie's confidence, living under it twenty-four-seven.

'Easy for you to say,' she muttered, glancing up at the next person in line. 'What can I get you?'

The next twenty minutes passed in the blink of an eye. I didn't get a spare second as the villagers congregated around the stall, intent on getting their free drink and mince pie before proceedings wound down. But everyone was jolly, and it was pleasant to be chatting with the backdrop of the beautiful tree and the Christmas carols on repeat.

Fortunately, we could see both girls from our vantage point as they took part in a chasing game with a few other local children around the tree, so Donna relaxed a little. They were easy to spot with their day-glo light wands, but I couldn't see Aleks with them, or Suzy for that matter.

After a while, I picked up on a restlessness in the queue of people waiting for drinks. There was a growing audible murmur in the crowd, people looking at each other anxiously.

'What's wrong?' someone asked urgently.

Then someone else said, 'Who? Who's got lost?'

The music abruptly cut off, and I scanned the faces of the crowd, looking for a clue as to what the problem was. Then the tannoy burst into life again.

'Folks, we have a lost child here at the first-aid station. His name is Aleks, and he's wearing blue jeans and a navy puffa jacket with a red scarf. Could his mum come up here immediately to be reunited with him, please? Thank you.'

'Aleks?' Donna pulled the corners of her mouth down. 'Suzy's kid?'

I looked around the crowd, looking for Suzy's pale pink hat. 'They were here not long ago, talking to me.'

People started turning in the queue, talking to each other, scanning the faces in the crowd. We carried on serving for a while and then I started to sense an air of restlessness growing around us.

People were losing interest in the drinks and the lights and their easy, relaxed movements turned into a meaningful scanning of eyes with puzzled, concerned faces.

A couple of members of the parish council stopped near the stall and I overheard their conversation. 'Can't find the mother anywhere. Plenty of people have seen her but now, it seems she's disappeared into thin air. The kid's teacher is here. She's called his mum's phone but it's turned off.'

The other man frowned. 'If she doesn't show up soon, we'll have to call off the event, just in case. We have to be seen to be taking this seriously. We'll get the police involved quite soon.'

Donna's face paled. 'Oh God, it's happening again.'

'She can't be far away,' I said in what I hoped was a reassuring tone. 'She'll turn up in a moment, you'll see.'

'That's what they said about Matilda,' Donna said, staring into the dark. 'They said she'd be back, that she'd taken herself off somewhere and it would all be a false alarm.'

I stood on tiptoe and craned my neck. 'You sit down, have a coffee, Donna. Try not to panic.'

I poured her a drink and she perched on a stool, looking uncomfortable. Her eyes were trained on the girls, who, sensing the drama, were sticking closer to us.

After another ten minutes, there was another announcement over the tannoy. 'We regret the event is now closed. We still have Aleks Baros at the first aid tent. Could his mother, Miss Suzy Baros, please make her way directly to the tent to collect him. Thank you very much, everyone.'

Donna stood up. 'I can't just wait here. I'll take Ellie to Paul. I'm going to go and help look for her.'

I scanned the area again, hoping to spot Suzy, who was probably frantically searching for Aleks. I pulled my phone out from under the counter and called Michael.

He picked up on the second ring. 'Hi, Kate, I've just got here, I'm—'

'Suzy Baros is missing,' I said quickly. 'They've stopped the event early.'

'What?'

'Suzy's gone missing!' I said again, a little sharply, then, 'Sorry. It's just mayhem here. Poor Aleks is on his own in the first-aid tent. I'm going over there in a minute. Can you check she hasn't come back to the cottage?'

'Yes, course. Hold on, I'm right near there.' I heard his footsteps scuffling, his quickening breath. 'Place is in darkness,' he said, knocking on the door. 'It's all locked up. I'll check round the back.' I heard him walking again, his breathing slightly laboured. 'She hasn't just nipped to the shop or something?'

'I haven't spoken to anyone in charge yet. They just announced that they had Aleks, who was lost, at the tent and now everyone's looking for her.'

'And she's just disappeared?'

'They can't find her anywhere and she'd have mentioned it to

Aleks if she was going somewhere, I'm sure,' I said. 'She'd never leave him alone like this.'

Michael groaned. 'The cottage is locked up around the back too. No lights on anywhere. I think it's safe to say she isn't here.'

'You've got a master key for the cottages, haven't you? Can't you check inside?'

He hesitated. 'Not really, not without a good reason.'

'Like the fact she's gone missing, you mean?'

'It's an invasion of privacy, Kate, unless the police ask me to.'

'Well, that might not be very long.' I ended the call, irritated, then walked around the stall out into the crowd.

Donna appeared again, a worried expression on her face. 'There's no sign of her,' she said, a little breathlessly. 'I've just been over to the first-aid station. Paul's in there, and the kid – Aleks – he's just sitting there staring into space. Wouldn't say a word to me.'

I untied my apron and dumped it on the table. 'I'll go and see if he's OK. You stay here with the girls.'

Donna nodded, not taking her eyes from Ellie, who was still with Tansy, waving their light sabres near the tree.

I walked off towards the first-aid station. A group of teenagers ran by, pushing into people and laughing, high on adrenaline. Oblivious to the concern all the adults were feeling.

When I reached the small tent, Paul was standing inside like a sentry on guard. 'He's OK,' he said curtly, obviously displeased to see me. 'Best not to make a fuss, in my opinion.'

Aleks looked smaller, as if he'd folded in on himself. He clutched his light wand like his life depended on it. When he saw me, someone he recognised, relief flooded his face.

'Hi, Aleks, are you OK, love?' I crouched down next to him and slid my arm around his shoulders. 'They're looking for your mum now. I'm sure she'll be back very soon.'

He sniffed, rubbing at his already sore eyes. 'Where has she gone?'

'That's what we're trying to find out. We're checking that she hasn't gone back home or something. Did she not say she was popping off somewhere?'

He shook his head.

'Where were you when you last saw her?'

He pointed to the edge of the green. 'We were standing there and I wanted to be closer to the Christmas tree when the lights turned on, so I ran over there, and when I came back, she was gone.'

'We've asked him all this, Kate.' Paul frowned. 'This will just stress him out more.'

I ignored him. 'Did you see your mum speak to anyone before she got lost, Aleks?'

He thought for a moment, and looked at Paul. 'I can't remember,' he said, dropping his head. 'I only wanted to see the tree.'

'It's all right, Aleks,' Paul said pointedly. 'You're not in any trouble.'

'Of course he's not in trouble.'

'Maybe you should stop questioning him like he is, then.'

I shot Paul a withering look before turning back to Aleks.

'Don't worry, I'm sure your mummy will be back here soon. I'll sit with you until she gets here. Would you like that?'

'There's no need.' Paul objected. 'I can—'

'Yes,' Aleks said, looking relieved. 'I'd like you to stay, Kate.'

A couple of hours later, the village green was swarming with police. Michael had now returned and had hastily put together a search team.

'I checked the cottage again before I left, but it's still locked up and in darkness,' he told me. 'She's definitely not there.'

The police had set up a small inquiry tent on the green, and officers were moving around and speaking to people, asking anyone who'd seen Suzy at the event to report what they remembered.

I kept thinking about Suzy's cryptic comments about why she'd left Poland, and her nervous manner. It was hard to explain it to someone else. It had just been my take on it. I hoped she was OK and not in any danger. I didn't know her well, but I felt convinced that she wouldn't leave Aleks behind, whatever the reason might be.

A group of uniformed officers walked by and I overheard that they were heading for the woodland that skirted the edge of the village.

'This is starting to feel really serious,' I said to Michael when he came over.

'Hopefully she'll turn up,' he said. 'The police want me to take them up to her cottage before we start the search around the village. I'll call you if we find her.'

When I got back to the first-aid tent, a couple of women were standing with Aleks. He turned and said something to one of them. 'We're from social services,' she said, holding up her ID lanyard. 'I know Aleks is new to the village and a gentleman called Paul Thatcher said he and his wife were happy to take him in tonight. But Aleks tells us he knows you and someone called Irene?'

'Yes, Irene Wadebridge is their landlady.' I moved closer. 'Are you OK, Aleks?'

His dark eyes looked up at me, and I could see flecks of panic sparking in them.

'I don't want to go with Paul or those ladies,' he said quickly, tapping his fingers on his leg. 'I want to stay here with you until they find my mummy.'

I turned to the social worker. 'I'm happy to take him home with me tonight until things are sorted,' I said. 'I work at the school, so I have all the appropriate safeguarding checks. You can speak to the head teacher if you need to.'

She took a phone out of her handbag. 'It's kind of you to offer,' she said. 'Let me make a couple of calls and see if I can get that approved.'

I sat down next to Aleks. 'Don't worry,' I said. 'Everything will be OK.' But I had an uneasy feeling stirring in my gut.

. . .

I sat with Aleks and the girls while the social workers made their calls. Donna kept the drinks stall open for the benefit of the large search team, but she closed up eventually because of getting Ellie home.

She came over to say goodbye and I stood up and moved away from the kids to speak to her. 'He's coming back with us,' I said.

'What?'

'Just for tonight, until they locate Suzy. I couldn't see social services take him and it was kind of you and Paul to offer, but he's so upset and he knows us a bit better.'

'We haven't offered to have him!' Donna frowned.

'Well, the lady from social services said Paul had offered,' I explained. 'Which was good of him.'

'Trust Paul! But poor lad. I feel for him,' Donna said. 'Well done you for volunteering to have him, Kate, he knows you all well.' She hesitated. 'But have you thought what's going to happen if they don't find Suzy tonight ... or tomorrow?'

I shrugged off her comment. I felt confident Suzy would turn up, having had some sort of crisis that had prevented her from getting back to Aleks.

Later, at home, I found Aleks some red Christmas pyjamas someone had bought for Tansy last year that were still a bit too big. I made Tansy and Aleks some hot chocolate and got them ready for bed. They were both exhausted. I was so busy fending off Tansy's whining about the pyjamas *she* wanted to wear and the biscuit *she* wanted with her drink, I didn't think anything of Aleks's quietness. Then I looked at him and saw tears streaming silently down his face.

'Oh sweetheart, come here.' He resisted at first, then he sort of melted into my side.

Tansy's eyes were wide and startled. 'What's wrong with him, Mummy?' she said fearfully.

'He's sad, Tansy. The way you'd be sad if I got lost.'

She crept to the other side of me and huddled in. 'It's OK,

Aleks,' she said. 'You can stay here with us until your mum gets home.'

We sat like that a while, then went upstairs. 'I'll be in very soon,' I told Tansy, and took Aleks into the spare room, where I tucked him in tightly.

'I want Wojtek.' He sniffed, starting to cry again.

'Who?'

'Wojtek, my teddy bear.'

'I promise we'll get him for you tomorrow. Michael can pick you some stuff up from the cottage. But tonight we all need to get some sleep, OK? Tomorrow is a new day.'

He nodded sadly, and closed his eyes.

'Don't worry, Aleks,' I whispered as I kissed his forehead. 'We'll find her.'

Afterwards, I went to Tansy's bedroom. We stood at her window and watched the torches flitting around like lit matches in the fields that framed the outskirts of the village.

'Nobody's giving up,' I said. 'Your daddy is out there looking for Aleks's mummy with lots of other people.'

'But what do you think has happened to her?' Tansy said in a small voice. 'Where has she gone?'

'I don't know, sweetie,' I said carefully. 'But if anyone can find her, Daddy can.'

She nodded, looking reassured. I tucked her into bed and went back downstairs.

I'd started to doze on the sofa when Michael texted me at 11 p.m.

We're calling it a day. No sign of her anywhere.

I put down the phone and sighed, my heart heavy when I thought about the distraught little boy upstairs. How could anyone just disappear into thin air in a village where everyone knew each other?

It didn't make any sense at all.

THIRTEEN

Michael got home just before midnight. 'Jeez, what a night.' He looked dog-tired, heavy shadows under his eyes, his body still sprung with tension.

'Aleks is asleep in the spare room,' I said as I pulled myself off the sofa to make him a hot drink.

'What?' Michael looked up from unlacing his boots.

'Yeah, I offered to have him because we're just about the only people he knows well. Paul offered but Aleks wanted to come here. That's OK, isn't it?' He stared at me, and I felt moved to defend myself further. 'I was worried about him, Michael!'

'I'm worried about him too, but ... well, I can't help wondering if he'd be better off with professionals looking after him.'

'Social services, you mean?' I said, horrified.

'No ... well, maybe. It's just that they'd know what to say to him. While his mum's missing, I mean.'

'I know I'd want someone from the village to look after Tansy if I went missing,' I said, dropping a tea bag into a mug. 'Someone she knew.'

'I know, and you're right.' Michael went back to unlacing his boots. 'It's just that there's no sign of Suzy and now we've got the boy here ...'

'Aleks.' I poured on boiling water and got milk from the fridge.

'Yes, we've got Aleks here and that adds pressure because it means we're right in the centre of it all whether we want to be or not.'

I took a teaspoon and sloshed the tea around a little too vigorously. Dark brown liquid splashed over the lip of the cup onto the worktop.

'I did what I thought was right, Michael. I didn't think about the inconvenience to us if Suzy wasn't found right away.' I plonked the mug down unceremoniously on the table in front of him.

'Don't be like this, Kate.'

'Like what? You're the one being unreasonable. Is giving temporary shelter to a distressed child really one step too far? Even Paul found it in his heart to offer.' I knew I was being unfair. He was clearly shattered, but the words were out before I could stop.

'We hardly know them, that's all I'm saying. And we need to think about the effect all this is going to have on Tansy.'

'Teaching her kindness to others, you mean?'

'Look, I've got something to tell you.' His face sagged. 'They searched Suzy's cottage and found my keys on her kitchen worktop.'

'Your *keys*?'

He nodded. 'My second work set, for the mower, the storage shed, the gates. Stuff like that.'

What was he saying?

'Why were your keys in Suzy's cottage?' My voice emerged thin and strained.

He looked away. 'It sounds stupid ... but I don't know!'

My breathing quickened, panic squeezing at my throat. 'Are you trying to tell me you've been there with her? Is this a confession?'

'God, no! I honestly don't know how the keys got in there, Kate. You have to believe me.'

'If your keys are in there, you must have left them,' I said quietly.

'No! I haven't been in the cottage since … since I repaired the tap earlier in the week, and I've used the keys after that.'

'You told the police this?'

'Yes, but …' He dropped his head into his hands. 'I could tell they didn't believe me. I wanted to let you know in case they speak to you and it comes out.' He looked up. 'I wanted to be the one to tell you. I want you to know.'

'It sounds like you're covering yourself,' I said quietly. My hands were tingling.

'No, Kate.' He stood up and moved over to me, grasping my fingers. 'If I'd gone in there alone and found the keys myself, I'd still have told you, because it doesn't make sense.'

'What did the police say about it?'

'Well, they were surprised, I think. But I told them the same as you, that I didn't know how they'd got there.' Frustrated, he blew out air. 'It's the truth, I swear.'

A quiet fury began to seep into my chest. 'You know Suzy much better than you let on, don't you?'

'What? No, I don't know her well at all.'

'The breaks you took together, the cosy little afternoon teas. You damn well do!' My outburst was ill-timed, but still. He should have told me this stuff before.

He raised his hands in a sign for me to calm down, which only infuriated me more. 'I mean, yeah, I see her up at Wadebridge sometimes, and Irene asked her to call some suppliers for me, but I don't *know* her as such.' His cheeks coloured up slightly.

We were going around in circles. But I was in a dilemma. I'd known Michael seventeen years now, and he wasn't a liar. He valued the truth, always had. Which was why none of it made any sense.

'Michael, I don't know what to think. All I know is that Suzy is missing, her son is distraught, and now the police probably think you have something to do with it.'

'I swear to God, I don't know where she is, Kate.' He looked at me from panicky eyes. 'But one thing I do know is that it's not good news they can't find her with such a comprehensive search. I mean, where could she be?'

The awful possibilities silenced me for a moment.

'Kate, please ... we're OK, aren't we? We'll get through this.'

I felt puzzled about the keys, suspicious and scared about what it might mean. I felt these things all at once, the emotion bearing down on me like a steam press.

I said, 'I'm going up to check on the kids,' and walked out.

After I'd checked on Tansy, I looked in on Aleks in the spare room. He was fast asleep, his straight, fine dark hair brushed off his smooth forehead, his eyelids fluttering as if he was caught in a dream. I felt a pull inside. He shouldn't have to experience this kind of fear and loss at such a young age. If only he had a father we could contact, but from the little Suzy had said on the matter, he was probably the reason they'd left Poland in the first place.

And then I felt that same tightening inside again. The sharp clutch of loneliness and fear that came from being young and scared and on your own. That feeling that you weren't safe and it was only a matter of time before your life blew up.

I'd promised myself my own daughter would never feel that way. All I could do was hope the police believed Michael's plea about the keys. Even though I was having problems believing him myself.

FOURTEEN

The next morning I was woken at 6.30 by Michael's phone pinging with a text. It was Irene, to say there was a heavy police presence up at Wadebridge, and could he possibly come in early. I left him getting his work stuff together and went into the bathroom.

I had a quick wash at the sink and splashed cold water on my face. I'd shower later, but for now, I didn't want to disturb the kids with the noisy hot water tank.

Downstairs, I was surprised to find Tansy and Aleks already up and in the living room, sitting together in front of the television sharing the warmth of a fleecy blanket.

Tansy looked up at me. 'Aleks woke up and he'd had a nasty dream about his mummy, didn't you, Aleks?' He nodded forlornly. 'So I brought him down to watch television.'

'That was a good idea, sweetie,' I said. I wondered how she'd got so grown up so quickly. 'How are you feeling, Aleks?'

'Have they found my mum yet?' he said.

'Not yet, but we're hoping there might be some news today.' I leaned forward and squeezed his shoulder. 'Now, who'd like some toast and juice?' I had to try and keep his spirits up without blindly telling him everything was going to be OK, because I didn't know that. Nobody knew that yet.

At seven o'clock, there was a knock at the door. A quick glance through the spyhole revealed two uniformed police officers on the doorstep. I glanced back into the living room to ensure the kids were still distracted by the television, and then opened the door.

'Sorry to disturb you so early, madam,' one of the officers said. 'We're conducting door-to-door enquiries following the disappearance of a young woman yesterday. Can we ask you—'

'I have her son here,' I hissed, checking over my shoulder before turning back to him. 'I have Suzy Baros's son staying here and I wouldn't want him to overhear any details.'

'Oh, I see,' the officer faltered.

'Everything OK?' Michael came downstairs, dressed in his work gear.

'They want to ask us some questions about Suzy, but I'm worried about it upsetting Aleks,' I told him. A picture filled my mind – the knock on the door all those years ago when I was a kid, the police officers standing there and me hiding behind the sofa, terrified what they were about to tell me about where Mum had been for the past week. Me lying about her drinking and her finding the car keys I'd hidden ... feeling responsible for everything bad that happened as a result of that.

'Come through to the kitchen,' Michael said to the officers. 'We can close the door while we talk.' He squeezed my hand. 'Do you want to check on the kids, Kate, and I'll take the officers through?'

I nodded, grateful for Michael thinking on his feet. I closed the front door, then went back into the living room. Tansy was munching on her toast, her gaze glued to the TV, but Aleks was pushing his breakfast around his plate, his eyes glazed and unfocused.

'I need you two to stay in here for a little while, OK?' I said as casually as I could, but Tansy was sharp as a knife.

'Why? Who came to the door, Mummy?'

'Police officers,' I said. 'They need to speak with me and your dad, so stay in here, please.'

'Is it about my mum?' Aleks looked up, his expression landing somewhere between hope and fright. 'Have they found her?'

'Not yet, Aleks, but they're asking lots of questions and finding out lots of important information that we hope will help find her.'

Wordlessly he turned back to the television. I blew a kiss to Tansy and closed the door. Then I walked into the kitchen, closing that door behind me too.

FIFTEEN

The officers were both male. One tall and thin, in his late twenties, the other about ten years older and on the portly side.

'I'm PC Turner, and this is PC Jenkins,' the tall one said, flashing ID.

'Can I get you both some tea?' I asked, thinking Michael probably hadn't thought to offer.

'Thank you, but no,' Turner said briskly, earning himself a scowl from his colleague. 'We have a lot of houses to cover.'

We all sat down at the table, and Jenkins pulled out a notebook and pen. 'Now, I'm assuming that if you have Suzy Baros's son staying here, you know her well?'

Michael looked over at me.

'Not really. Her son is in my daughter's class, and Suzy has been over here for a coffee. We're not best friends or anything. I've been trying to get to know her a bit better.'

'Trying?'

'She's quite a private person,' I said carefully. 'I think she finds it difficult to open up to people.'

'Why do you think that might be?'

I hesitated. Should I tell them she'd hinted that she'd come over to England to escape problems in Poland? This wasn't the time to keep information back.

'I got the impression Suzy was unhappy for various reasons at home in Poland.'

'Really? What did she say to make you think that?'

'She said she was hoping to make a fresh start. Leave her problems behind.'

'What sort of problems?' the other officer asked.

'She didn't say.'

'Suzy lives in one of the Wadebridge cottages. She's Irene's home help,' Michael said suddenly. 'I'm Irene Wadebridge's property and land manager, so I'm up there every day.'

I noticed a clear gear change from both officers. They sat up a little straighter, shuffled to the edge of their seats as they made the link. 'You helped organise the search last night,' one of them said. 'Your keys were found in Miss Baros's cottage?'

'Yes,' Michael said carefully. 'As I explained to the officers at the time, she must have found them lying around the site and took them in for me.'

'And how long have you worked for Irene Wadebridge, sir?'

'Ten years in my current position,' Michael said easily. 'But I worked with her late husband for ten years before that.'

'I see. Can I ask what your duties are?' Jenkins said, scribbling away.

'A bit of everything, really. A full range of duties connected to the cottages and land. I take care of the small maintenance jobs, but if there's bigger stuff needs doing, I'll get the necessary quotes and use local companies, if I can. I cut the grass, but we have a gardening company for the planting and weeding.'

Turner said, 'So I take it you must also know Suzy Baros personally, Mr Shaw?'

Michael glanced at me. 'Like I said, she's a tenant in one of the cottages.'

'Does that involve you having contact with her on a daily basis?'

'Not every day, but inevitably there have been occasions when we've spoken.' Michael sounded polite, but I detected a slight irritation.

'Could you give us some examples of your recent contact with Miss Baros, sir,' Jenkins said, writing something down.

'Also, exactly when you last saw her,' Turner added rather curtly.

I swallowed. This was starting to sound like proper police questioning. Was this the point where we should ask if Michael needed a lawyer? I was getting the uncomfortable feeling of being the last person to know what had been happening. I clasped my hands together and sat forward.

'Nothing to worry about, Mrs Shaw,' Jenkins murmured, noticing my tense manner. 'This is all part of the door-to-door, just routine enquiries.'

Michael gave me a quick nod to show he was OK with it, and I sat back.

'Let's see.' He looked up at the ceiling while he organised his thoughts. 'I saw her a couple of times last week, just to wave hello to while I was out and about.' An image of Suzy in her tight jeans and high boots flitted unhelpfully in and out of my head. 'I was at her cottage last Monday afternoon to fit a new washer on the kitchen tap.'

'And how long would you say you were in there, sir?'

Michael pulled down the edges of his mouth. 'No more than half an hour. It was a straightforward job.'

'And did you have a chat with Miss Baros while you were there?'

'We ... passed the time of day,' he said, a little stilted. 'She made me a drink.'

I felt a now familiar stab of discomfort. He'd mentioned the tap but not the fact he'd spent half an hour with Suzy in her cottage that day.

On top of that, Michael had clearly decided not to tell the police about their cosy afternoon cuppas and the fact she'd been ringing suppliers and no doubt relaying that information to him. If I was a cynical sort I might think he was feeding various people – including me – different stories depending what suited him.

'And while you were attending the repair,' Turner ventured, 'did Miss Baros say anything that led you to believe she was thinking of taking off anywhere?'

'No,' he said quickly. 'If that were the case, I would've spoken up last night, instead of helping to organise a full-scale search until nearly midnight.'

Jenkins ignored Michael's swipe. 'You were on the village green last night with everyone else?'

Michael nodded. 'I didn't see her at the Christmas event last night. I was busy with the organisation of it.'

No mention of leaving early to go up to Wadebridge. I felt my throat tighten.

'Fine, I've got all that down. Thank you,' Jenkins said, tapping his notepad. He turned to me. 'Same question for you, please, Mrs Shaw. Apart from last night, when was the last time you saw Suzy?'

'Aleks came over to play after school recently. Suzy picked him up, but she didn't stay. She had to shoot off to do something or other, I forget what. I was running the drinks stall at the Christmas event last night and she came by to ask if my daughter would like a playdate next week up at the cottage.'

'What time would that have been?'

I thought for a moment. 'It was before the lights were turned on at six. I'd say maybe fifteen minutes before that.'

'And you and Mr Shaw were together all night apart from the search?'

'Well, Michael was round and about doing stuff for the event and I was running the drinks stall, but yes. We were there all the time, apart from …' My words petered out.

'Apart from?' Jenkins echoed, looking from me to Michael. I'd slipped up.

'I had to leave just before the lights were turned on,' Michael said, as if it were no big deal. 'Irene Wadebridge rang me to say her downstairs loo was leaking.'

'I see,' Turner said, his eyes narrowing. 'So at the point when Suzy Baros's absence was discovered, you had already left the event, sir?'

'Yes.'

'What time did you arrive at Wadebridge?'

Michael thought for a moment. 'About six thirty. It took me slightly longer because I had to call at home for some of my tools. Mrs Wadebridge will be able to vouch for my movements.'

I didn't look at him. He'd never mentioned popping home before going up to Wadebridge, and as far as I knew, he kept his tools in the cottage or his van.

The officers asked a few more general details about village life, the number of events there'd been in the last month and suchlike. 'Thank you both very much for your input. Someone will be in touch if we need to follow up,' Turner said to Michael as they left.

We stood in the hallway for a minute or two.

'Christ, that was a bit heavy.' Michael blew out air and pinched the bridge of his nose. His face looked damp and hot. 'You dropped me in it at the end when you mentioned that I'd had to leave. Made it sound like I'd purposely not told them.'

'I said it without thinking, but why didn't you tell them yourself?'

'It slipped my mind. So much was happening last night.'

'I can't see how you forgot that Irene summoned you about the leaking toilet. You never mentioned you'd hung around talking to Suzy on Monday after fixing the tap, either,' I said, trying and failing to keep the accusation out of my voice.

'I didn't spend time there as such, I was mending her tap, that was all.' He threw up his hands. 'I must do half a dozen repairs a week on the cottages, and I wouldn't dream of boring you with those either.'

'I know, but ... Irene reckons she's sweet on you.'

'Oh come on, Kate. Irene's got nothing better to do with her time than make up silly stories.'

Easy to try and discount Irene's opinion, but we both knew it was the fact that Suzy was a young, attractive woman that was making me so annoyed. I tried to avoid sounding jealous and petty, but it wasn't easy. It gave me a small insight into how Donna must feel about Paul. 'With Suzy being new to the village and keeping herself to herself, I thought you might have found out something interesting, that's all. I'd told you she seemed nervy about something or someone.'

'It was just a "how are you settling in" type of chat. Nothing deep and meaningful to report, Kate, or I'd have told you. You know that.' He draped his forearms over my shoulders. 'You are a silly goose at times.'

I felt myself bristle. Michael could defend himself all he liked, but Suzy had gone missing last night, leaving our sleepy little village in shock. Anyone else might have thought it a good idea to mention to their wife that they'd spent time at her cottage a few days earlier. I wasn't the only one surprised at the revelation. The police had seemed taken aback too.

'I didn't know you'd come home before going up to Wadebridge,' I said. 'What tools had you left here?'

'I thought I'd left my blue toolbox in the porch, but I checked and it wasn't there. When I went back to the van, I saw it was in there after all, hidden by a dust sheet.' He pulled at his bottom lip. 'Have you ever thought about joining the police, Kate? You're starting to sound like them.'

I rolled my eyes. 'I'm going to keep Tansy and Aleks off school today,' I said, feeling relieved that there was a simple explanation about the tools. 'There's no way Aleks is going to be able to concentrate on his schoolwork, and it won't do Tansy any harm to keep him company until Suzy is found.'

Michael pursed his lips. 'Sounds like an executive decision has been made.' He gave a wan smile. 'I'd better get over to Wadebridge. Irene will want a full report on what's happening. It'll kill her that she's missing all the drama because of her sciatica. She's usually the first to arrive at a village event.'

'Michael! We're not talking about the village fete here. A woman is missing and I get the feeling you should be worried about that more than most.'

'What do you mean by that?'

'I mean you work where she lives and the police are already curious about how your keys came to be in her cottage. You didn't even tell them about your afternoon chats and the fact she'd been helping with suppliers. You're right about one thing, this is big drama. Unfortunately, you're right at the centre of it.'

He looked at me, a strange expression on his face. I thought for a moment he was going to say something but he shook his head, almost to himself, and turned away.

He popped through to say goodbye to Tansy and Aleks, then kissed me on the cheek before he left. 'Have some faith in me, Kate,' he said softly. 'I need you to totally believe in me because if you don't ... why will anyone else?'

'That sounds a bit cryptic,' I said, my mouth suddenly dry. 'What are you trying to say?'

'Nothing.' He smoothed a few stray ponytail hairs from my cheek. 'Just that I need your support while the police are up at Wadebridge sniffing around. It's stressful, that's what I'm saying. The way they try and make more of things. Do you understand?'

I nodded, but I wasn't sure I did. Not really.

Michael left the house smiling, but underneath the surface, I could feel a new, unresolved tension sitting between us. The man who came home to give me flowers and who'd been so attentive lately seemed a million miles away right now.

I really wanted that man back.

SIXTEEN

IRENE

Irene Wadebridge stared out of the front-room window at the beech hedge Amos had planted all those years ago to give them some privacy from the cottage tenants. The copper leaves turned and twisted in the wind as if they were trying to work their way loose. The cottages had been built for mill workers in the nineteenth century, and were sturdy but cold, no matter what the season. Several had developed damp problems, and Michael had devised a rolling remedial programme he continued to work on.

There had been a whirlwind of activity up at Wadebridge all morning. Police and forensic officers had been on site since the early hours, and Irene understood that door-to-door enquiries were being carried out back in the village. She'd had to allow them full access to Suzy's home and the surrounding grounds too. It was like something on the telly.

Numerous police officers and other officials had wanted to speak with her. Irene had taken her involvement, as the owner of Suzy's cottage, very seriously indeed. The efficient senior officer, a DI Helena Price, had explained that there was a clear and rigorous procedure that must be worked through and that Irene was an important part of it.

Using her walking frame, which got her around the kitchen slowly but safely, she had made the officers countless cups of tea and coffee, and had lined water and juice up on the worktop for anyone who wanted a cold drink. It wasn't easy with her arthritis, not to mention the painful sciatica that flared up with alarming regularity – both conditions she'd never had while Amos had been alive – but she hadn't minded doing it. It was reassuring to be able to contribute, even in this small way, to the process of finding out exactly what had happened to that poor girl.

The village had only recovered in recent years from the disappearance of the schoolgirl, Matilda, so she wasn't surprised when Michael told her the villagers were in a quandary to have another unexplained vanishing occur in such a small place.

The uniformed officers, who all looked to Irene as if they had just left school, were a friendly bunch. They seemed very grateful for the refreshments and to be allowed the use of a cottage bathroom.

Sadly, their efforts had so far drawn a blank, and DI Price explained that everyone would decamp back to the station to regroup and strategise, which Irene thought sounded rather impressive.

She stared out over the hedge toward the cottages. Amos would be turning in his grave at the thought of something untoward happening in dwellings owned by his family for generations. There were no holidaymakers at this time of year, although she had taken a couple of bookings over the Christmas period. The place felt quiet and empty without all the police activity, and she was already missing the unofficial updates the grateful officers had given her when they came in to get their drinks.

Still, Michael was here again now. He'd looked weary, and had explained that Kate had taken young Aleks in for the night, which Irene thought admirable. 'She's keeping Tansy and Aleks off school today,' he'd added. 'I know it's hard on the boy, but I would've thought it best to keep things as normal as possible.' When Michael confided in her like this, Irene felt a warm glow spread through her chest. 'I mean, we don't know where Suzy is.' He looked out of the window at the fields beyond. 'Who knows how long it might take to locate her?'

There were a few moments of silence until Irene, who hadn't got any children, said, 'In my experience, once you start keeping little ones at home, it's very difficult to convince them to go back to school.'

Michael gave a grunt of agreement. His phone rang and he moved outside to take the call.

Irene stood up. Predictably, her bones protested. She supported herself by holding on to the windowsill, from where she had a clear view of the end cottage that Suzy rented. She had started as just another home help from the agency Irene had used for years but had swiftly proved she was the best one. She'd jumped at the opportunity of a full-time position when Irene offered her a direct job and had resigned from the agency, telling them she was moving out of the area. When Suzy told Irene about the cramped B&B they were living in, she'd offered her the cottage. Suzy had signed a twelve-month contract and moved in five months ago. Irene had already got used to having her and Aleks around.

For a young woman, Suzy was surprisingly insular. For the first couple of weeks of her tenancy, Irene had seen little of her or the boy when she was off duty. Then she'd invited them over for a cup of tea and a piece of cake, and that had been the start of the two of them popping over to the house more regularly.

When Suzy had an appointment in town one weekend, Irene played board games with Aleks for a couple of hours, and it had gone on from there. Suzy would pop into town to the supermarket to do her shopping and take a list of a few things Irene needed herself, and if it happened to be the school holidays or out of school hours, Irene would watch Aleks.

It soon became clear to Irene when she saw the cheap white

bread and endless tins of beans nestled amongst her own organic chicken, prawns and branded goods that the young woman had scarce funds. But she was a proud girl and she'd already told Irene that her mother had raised her to be frugal and hard-working and Irene had admired her staunch spirit.

Suzy seemed interested in Wadebridge and how things ran here. Irene enjoyed taking her through the mechanics of the place and the history of those who had worked there. She always got the impression that lots of the villagers assumed she didn't have an overview because she wasn't a hands-on owner. But they were mistaken. She'd wager there wasn't a thing happened up here that she wasn't aware of. She even dealt with the online bookings in the summer months. She might've just turned seventy-five, but she still had her wits about her, even if her body was letting her down.

Three weeks ago, she had asked Suzy if she had the time to help her sort out her over-stuffed wardrobes and the half-dozen old suitcases packed with clothes that were taking up space. Kate was always badgering her to do so, but she wanted to feel in charge of her own possessions. Kate would have her old clothes bundled in black bin bags and be heading to the dustbin with them before Irene had a chance to consider each garment carefully.

'Of course,' Suzy had said without a second thought. 'It is my pleasure to help you.'

Irene had asked Michael to bring down the dusty old suitcases from the attic and Suzy had made a start while Aleks was happy in front of the TV with the Marvel colouring book, crayons and snacks Irene had provided.

Upstairs, Suzy had oohed and aahed when she'd set eyes on Irene's old Biba pieces. Some garments hadn't seen the light of day for fifty years, when Irene had been in her early twenties and had been quite the girl around town.

Suzy's eyes were popping. 'This clothing is classed as vintage now, Irene. Did you know you can sell them for good money on eBay?'

Irene had laughed. 'Goodness, I knew I was getting on a bit, but *vintage?* That makes me sound really past it!'

Suzy had been mortified, her hand flying up to her mouth. 'Oh, I didn't mean to upset you, Irene, I'm so sorry. "Vintage" is a fashion term, you see, and—'

'I know, I know. I was just joking, dear girl!' Irene reassured her, realising that her cheeky sense of humour had somehow got lost in translation.

Suzy's pretty features relaxed then and Irene had insisted she pick a couple of pieces for herself. She tried on a skimpy gold knitted top with her jeans and a pair of chunky platform shoes that Amos had branded 'clodhoppers' and that Irene could only remember wearing once.

Michael had popped in looking for his keys and oh, Irene had watched his face when Suzy walked in all dressed up like that. It had given the term 'eyes on stalks' a whole new meaning!

Still, in Suzy and Michael, Irene knew she'd struck gold.

Michael kept the cottages maintained and organised the landscaping of the gardens and surrounding fields. He'd come over late on Christmas Eve last year when the boiler had gone out, and he was familiar with all the stringent health and safety and legal requirements. He was crucial to the management of the place, and although Irene would never tell him as much, he probably did the work of three or four people. It was an arrangement that worked well, seeming to suit Michael as much as herself, and she made up her mind that she'd protect it at all costs.

SEVENTEEN

SPRING 2012

JAKUB

When the plane landed at Stansted airport, Jakub walked down the aircraft steps zipping up his fleece against the biting wind. If this was a taste of England's spring, he had better adjust his expectations.

Jakub prided himself on his internet research skills. He had joined an online forum, where he'd found a plethora of advice from Polish nationals who had successfully made new lives for themselves in England. Using this excellent resource, he'd already established a couple of useful contacts, one of them a man who came from the next town to Zalipie. He'd told Jakub there were established Polish communities in the East Midlands area, and had given him a couple of places that were large employers of casual labour.

Jakub had heard the rumours of Polish girls at these places, many of them friendly and looking to make a connection with a boy from the motherland. He could usually spot a Polish girl before she opened her mouth. There had been a few on the plane. The way they looked, their style ... that unspoken way they seemed to recognise his nationality too. He'd tried to ignore the twist of fury that shot through him at the flirtatious glances, the fact that they were here and wanted him but Ana was back home in the arms of another man. He had nowhere to put the anger, so he swallowed it down.

He had pre-booked a National Express coach ticket from Stansted to Nottingham, with one change at Leicester. After a never-ending wait in passport control, he boarded the coach and braced himself for the four-and-a-half-hour journey. To Jakub, this journey represented the start of him making his fortune and winning back Ana.

Something had happened inside him, like a switch flipping, since Ana had left him for Oskar. It had loosened him up. Nothing much mattered any more, and it had made him feel a little dangerous. Women seemed to pick up on that.

There had been a couple of girls since Ana. None of them had come anywhere close to her, of course. Jakub had found a new attraction to more unavailable girls, the ones who weren't looking for a man or who actively discouraged his interest. It was a little screwed up, he knew. But he didn't care. He didn't care about anything but getting Ana back. He dreamed about her day and night and she took up every minute of each waking hour. He was a man obsessed and there was nothing he could do about it.

The Hollies bed and breakfast accommodation he'd booked online for the first week was located in a market town called Sutton-in-Ashfield, which was conveniently located about twelve miles north of the city of Nottingham.

The place was basic but clean. He shared a large room with another Polish national, an older man called Ludwik, who had no family and who had lived in the north of the country.

Jakub showed him the two factories that had been recommended online, and Ludwik had screwed up his face.

'These are OK if you want to breathe in stale air while you

work sixteen-hour days,' he said scathingly. 'No windows, few breaks. You might as well be in prison, yes?'

Jakub grimaced. This wasn't the picture he'd painted in his head of his new life in England. 'I heard they have strict laws here about the number of hours one can work.'

Ludwik laughed. 'On paper, for the benefit of the health and safety inspectors, of course! In reality, it is a different story my friend. Unofficially, they will offer you twice the working hours, with the extra paid at a much lower hourly rate but in cash. Nobody likes this but everyone does it for the money.'

'If there is no choice in the matter, then that is what I must accept to make a start.'

'If you want my advice, find a small farm that is hiring. Also long hours and hard work, but anyone who likes fresh air and a sense of freedom would just wither away and die in one of those godawful factories.' Ludwik chewed the inside of his cheek. 'I am hoping for a good opportunity myself soon. I can feel my luck changing and soon I will leave this house and get my own place. You should do the same.'

Ignoring the advice he'd been given, the next day Jakub went to the first prospective employer on his list, a packaging factory that had numerous mentions on the forums as a place that always needed cheap casual labour. When he got off the bus, he had to walk for miles to the sprawling concrete building in the middle of nowhere. His thin T-shirt and frayed denim jacket offered little protection against the biting wind, and his worn leather shoes finally gave up the ghost when the heel came detached from the upper, letting in damp and grit and flopping about as he walked.

He followed the signs to reception and registered his details before sitting in one of the screwed-down plastic seats, his sock sopping and uncomfortable. There were three other young Polish men in the waiting room, but they didn't acknowledge each other. They sat in silence for twenty minutes until a disinterested middle-aged man called them through together and gave them a short tour around the shop floor.

Jakub stood aghast for a moment when they first entered the factory. The noise of machinery assailed his ears, making it difficult for him to think straight. So many bodies busy working, lifting boxes, loading assembly lines. No time for chatting or even noticing that anyone had entered their working area. He could not see the other side of the room, so vast was the space.

His eyes gravitated to the walls. No windows, just like Ludwik had predicted. He breathed in the warm, electrically charged air and made his excuses. Working from dawn to dusk in a place like this would kill him, kill the hope he had inside of making his fortune and winning back Ana. That hope was all he had in life, and he knew instinctively that he had to keep it alive at all costs. Otherwise he might as well be dead.

He would go back to the B&B and research the area, and tomorrow he would take his chances with finding work as a labourer on a farm, as his knowledgeable roommate had suggested.

EIGHTEEN

11 NOVEMBER 2019

NOTTINGHAMSHIRE POLICE

The Devonshire B&B was a tired-looking three-storey semi on a run-down street near the centre of town. Helena noted a peeling sign in the front window announcing *Vacancies*, and another next to it that boasted *Shared Rooms Available*.

'A shared room in a B&B?' Brewster grimaced. 'Wouldn't fancy that.'

'I suppose some folks don't get a choice,' Helena remarked.

Brewster tried the front door, but it was locked. 'Sign of the times,' he murmured. He rang the bell.

A large man in his early thirties with greasy brown hair came to the door. He wore a *Star Wars* T-shirt and baggy jeans that tucked under a protruding belly. His mouth was full of something that caused escaping crumbs to tumble onto his chin. He didn't speak, but continued chewing and raised his eyebrows at them instead.

Brewster flashed his ID. 'DI Price and DS Brewster, Nottinghamshire Police,' he said briskly. 'We'd like to speak to the owner of the establishment, please.'

The man continued to chew. Eventually he swallowed, wiped

his mouth with the back of a large, pale hand and said, 'That'll be my sister, Pat, but she's out shopping.'

'How long is she likely to be?' Brewster asked.

'Who knows? I reckon it'll be too long for you to sit and wait.'

'Perhaps you could call her, ask her to return?' he suggested.

'Nah, she ain't got a phone, has she? Reckons they rot your brain.' The man laughed, displaying teeth that were badly in need of dental attention.

'Right, well, we'll step inside just briefly if that's all right, Mr ...?'

'Carter. Dean Carter.'

'If we can come in, Mr Carter, perhaps you could help us in your sister's absence.'

Carter blinked and led them through an entrance hall that smelled faintly of damp and featured a brown and orange patterned carpet with peach Artex walls. It was a three-storey property thanks to an attic extension, and the stairs led up directly from the lobby. He showed them into a large room on the left that seemed to serve as a communal lounge. There was a television on which a video game had been paused, a clutch of mismatched armchairs and, at the far end, a small bar with optics and a couple of stools. It reminded Helena of the B&B in Blackpool she'd go to with her parents as a kid, to see the illuminations in the winter months. That place had held an air of excitement and possibility, she remembered. This house seemed shrouded in faint melancholy.

'How many rooms do you have here?' she asked.

'Six. All doubles and shared but one,' Carter said, stuffing his hands into his pockets. 'We've got one spare but it'll be snapped up before long. I thought that might be an enquiry when you rang the bell.'

Brewster took out his phone. 'Do you know this man, Mr Carter?'

Carter squinted at the photograph on the screen. 'Oh yeah, that's ...' He clicked his fingers repeatedly. 'That's whatshisname.

Jakub! That's it. Your lot came round here ages ago asking after him.'

'We're looking at the case again,' Helen said. 'What can you tell us about Jakub Jasinski?'

'I know he left without settling his bill,' Carter said shortly. 'My sister was fuming about that, I can tell you. But I don't have much to do with the guests, didn't bother me.'

'Any small detail you might remember could help,' Helena said.

'All I know is that he shared a room.' He looked up at the ceiling. 'His roommate's still here. Pawel. He might be able to help you.'

Brewster perked up. 'Is he up there now?'

Carter looked longingly at the TV. 'I'm not sure. We don't keep tabs on 'em.' He tilted his chin and frowned. 'He's second floor, first door on your left – room 2A. Go on up if you like.'

They climbed the stairs, passing a small window on the right, the sill crammed full of chipped Royal Doulton ornaments. Ladies in their finery.

'The higher we go, the more it smells like cooked cabbage,' Brewster complained, earning himself a poke in the back from Helena.

Brewster rapped on the door of room 2A. Helena heard a shuffling sound from within and thought the walls must be paper thin. When the door opened, a dishevelled man of around sixty, thin and pale with an unshaven face, said simply, 'Yes?'

Brewster went through the introductions again and Pawel invited them inside without hesitation. Helena braced herself, but the place was spotless. Worn and tired, certainly, but the window was open and the surfaces were uncluttered. The room was larger than she had expected, but she still struggled to imagine living here day in, day out.

Brewster explained that they were looking for information about Jakub Jasinski, and Pawel smiled sadly. 'He was a nice boy and I missed him when he went. We shared this room.' He pointed to a large old-fashioned oak wardrobe against the far wall. 'His bed used to be there, but when he left, Pat let me have the room to myself. This is the only room for a single person in the house,' he said proudly. 'But I hope to move on soon myself. I am hoping for the right opportunity ...' He paused, looking thoughtful. 'Meanwhile, the time passes so quickly.'

Helena said, 'Pawel, I know you've spoken to the police before, but we wondered if you could—'

'Me? No, no. Cops have not spoken to me before, only to Pat and that layabout brother of hers.'

Helena looked at Brewster, who shook his head in disbelief. A man went missing and officers didn't even speak to his roommate? It bordered on negligence.

'So, it's a while ago now, I know, but could you tell us anything you remember about Jakub? Anything he said to you that might give us a clue about what happened, why he suddenly left without a word?'

Pawel walked over to the window and stood with his back to it, gripping on to the windowsill either side. 'He had so many dreams and plans. Like lots of young Polish men who come over here. Sadly, most of them find out very quickly that this is not quite the land of milk and honey they had hoped, no matter how hard one works.'

Helena nodded. 'And what were Jakub's plans?'

'The usual.' Pawel sighed. 'To work hard, make his fortune. But he did not come from a place of greed. He wanted to regain his self-respect after a romantic disappointment back home. He dreamed of going back as a wealthy man to show her what she had missed.'

'I see,' Helena said. 'Jakub's mother said that in the last communication she had with him, he told her he was happy in his work and he'd been stable there for a couple of years. Unfortunately, she didn't make a note of his workplace as there had been so many over time. Do you know where it was?'

'Sorry, he never mentioned the name of the place.'

'And where did Jakub say he was going when he left?'

'He didn't. I had to return home for a week or two as my sister fell ill. When I came back, Jakub had already left.'

'Before you went home, did you notice anything different about him? His manner, his routine? Anything that might indicate he had problems?'

Pawel shrugged. 'He wasn't around that much so hard to know his normal self, but ... he did ask me not to mention his name if anyone came looking here.'

'Who did he mean?'

'I wasn't sure at the time. He just said I was to pretend I did not know him. He asked Pat to do the same thing and she agreed. She said she was used to doing that.' Pawel frowned. 'One day a big guy came by.' Pawel indicated a foot above his own head with a flat hand. 'He said he was looking for his friend, Jakub Jasinski. Pat wasn't in so it was left to me to speak to the man. I didn't like the look of him. Sly eyes. I told him I'd never heard of Jakub.'

'Did you by any chance get this guy's name?' Brewster asked hopefully.

'Sorry.' Pawel shrugged. 'I wanted to get rid of him, not strike up a conversation.'

Brewster said, 'Did you inform Jakub that someone was looking for him?'

'Yes. I described him and ... I don't know, something about his face losing colour ... I think he knew who this person was. But he gathered himself and said he did not recognise him.'

'So when you came back from your trip home, where did you assume Jakub had gone?' Helena asked.

'I thought maybe he had gone back to Poland. Maybe it was his family he didn't want to find him, or maybe he went back there between then and now. Who knows?'

Helena said, 'Jakub seemed close to his family. I called Mrs Jasinski before we began to investigate the case again to check Jakub hadn't turned up back in Poland but she said not.'

Pawel nodded. 'People come and go, moving place to place,

trying to find the happy life they came here for.' He looked down at the floor, his face sagging.

Brewster handed him a card. 'If anything else occurs to you, no matter how small, please do get in touch. We'd be very grateful.'

They thanked him and moved towards the door.

Outside, Brewster took a call from the station.

'Righto,' he said. 'Sounds interesting. Cheers, bud, leave it on my desk.' He looked at Helena. 'Information called in by a member of the public, boss,' he said. 'Fancy a McDonald's before we head back?'

NINETEEN

KATE

The school's head teacher, Collette Greer, called me mid-morning. 'I've been talking to social services, and we think, under the circumstances, it might be best for Aleks to come into school.'

'Oh! Yes, of course. I thought it might be a bit much for him, worrying about his mum.' As a teaching assistant, I probably should have known better and checked with the school before making a decision. 'I kept Tansy off to keep him company and ... Sorry. I'll bring them both in.'

'No need to apologise. I know everything was up in the air last night,' Collette said. 'But as you know, it can be better to distract children rather than give them too much time to dwell on distressing matters.' She hesitated. 'As I understand it, there's still no sign of Ms Baros.'

'Not yet,' I said. 'It doesn't seem the police have very much to go on.' *Except for Michael's keys being in her cottage when they shouldn't have been.*

'I think social services will be in touch shortly regarding arrangements for Aleks,' she said. 'It must be stressful for you trying to cope with his emotional state.'

'I don't mind, really. But thanks for calling. I'll bring the children in after lunch.'

In the living room, the news was not received well.

'But you said we could stay home and play here,' Tansy said crossly when I told her to get ready. 'Aleks wants to wait here until his mummy comes back, don't you, Aleks?'

'Yes,' he agreed.

'Tansy, enough,' I said sternly. I looked at Aleks. 'If your mummy is found while you're at school, you'll be brought straight home to see her, OK?'

He nodded.

I took them into school in time for the afternoon registration, and Miss Monsall called me at afternoon break.

'Tansy and Aleks are fine,' she said. 'I just wanted to put your mind at ease, as I thought you'd be worrying.'

'That's good of you, thank you,' I said, breathing out again. 'I've been thinking about Aleks since I dropped him off.'

'He seems to be coping quite well,' she said. 'Tansy, on the other hand, is ... Well, she seems to be in protection mode and she's managing to fall out with everyone who so much as looks Aleks's way.'

'Oh no. She ... she's just worried about him, I think. She's a good friend.'

'Of course.' Miss Monsall hesitated. 'Sadly, Tansy and Ellie seem to be at loggerheads. Nothing serious, just some unkind words, a bit of backbiting. I thought you could talk about it when she gets home.'

I clenched my teeth. Ellie could be such a spoilt little brat, jealous if Tansy didn't give her all her attention. 'Thanks, I will,' I said. 'I'll also have a word with Donna and ask her to rein Ellie in a bit.' It was time Donna admitted that her little angel could also be a dominating diva at times.

'Oh no, sorry, I didn't make it clear. Ellie has been in tears because Tansy has been unkind. She's told Ellie not to go near Aleks or she'll hit her.'

The anger drained from me in seconds, and I gripped the phone hard as I heard myself make appropriate shocked noises. When the call had ended, I just stood for a moment, thinking it through. Tansy wasn't a bully, and she didn't usually go around threatening people, especially her best friend.

She must be feeling stressed and responsible for Aleks in some way. Had I somehow subconsciously placed that burden on her young shoulders?

TWENTY

NOTTINGHAMSHIRE POLICE

Helena shrugged her jacket off and draped it over the back of her desk chair and yawned. It was all systems go now the Baros woman's disappearance had landed on their plate. She'd woken in the early hours and ran through the little they knew so far until it was time to get up at six.

'So, Brewster, what's the latest on the Baros case?'

Her colleague ran a hand through his thinning red hair. Helena spotted a mustard stain from his impromptu McDonald's on his shirt. She chose to ignore it. She'd never seen him leave the station without something or other smeared on some part of him.

'Not much. The problem is, boss, we know nothing about her. No Facebook, Instagram or anything else along those lines.'

'It's not escaped my notice that she's a Polish national like Jakub Jasinski,' Helena murmured, glancing at a printout one of her team had left on her desk. 'But there's a thriving Polish community in Nottinghamshire, so that might not mean anything in itself.'

'It's as if she just landed here from Mars,' Brewster added. 'This is someone who didn't just want a fresh start like Jakub did. She's gone to great lengths to excise anything that went before.'

'We've got Immigration tracing her address in Poland, but until that comes in, we have nothing at all?'

Brewster shook his head regretfully. 'Absolutely nada. The only person who knows anything at all about her is the boy. Her son, Aleks.'

Helena referred to her notes. 'And he's staying with friends?'

'Yes, he's staying at the Shaws' house. Shaw's wife, Kate, is fully police-checked and is apparently well respected in the village, and their daughter is in Aleks's class at school.'

'Hmm.' Helena tapped her pen on the desk. 'Aleks is the obvious place to start. I'll contact Kate Shaw and tell her we want to speak to the boy.'

'OK ...' Brewster dragged out the word, sounding unconvinced. 'He's only six years old, so we'll have to tread carefully.'

'I'm aware of that, Brewster. We'll ask Kate Shaw to stay with him as his responsible adult so he feels supported. It might be worthwhile speaking to the school, also.'

'Perfect. I can book a room at the station and get him in here.'

Helena sucked in air. 'No, no, that won't do at all. We'll need to speak to him in a place he's familiar with and feels relaxed. Maybe at the family home where he's staying?'

'Right, of course. I'll see what I can do.'

Helena busied herself with paperwork. Brewster left the office and after a few minutes, he reappeared with two coffees. He placed one on her desk, then pulled a pack of Mini Cheddars out of his pocket.

'Any luck?' He tore open the packet and offered it to her.

'No thanks, Brewster.' She watched as his chunky fingers delved greedily into the pack. She picked up her phone and waved it at him. 'I've just got to get Kate Shaw on board with it. You can take those back to your desk.'

But before she could press the call button, Brewster was back, his eyes wide. He waved a piece of paper at her. 'This is the info called in earlier, boss. Anonymous caller on an unregistered phone.' He held up the message written by the desk clerk. *If you're interested in finding Jakub Jasinski, ask Michael Shaw at Wade-bridge, Lynwick.*

Helena put down the phone and took the paper. 'This is Kate Shaw's husband, right? Lives in the house where young Aleks Baros is sheltering?'

Brewster nodded. 'He's the property and land manager up at Wadebridge. Uniforms spoke to Shaw as part of the door-to-door and he answered all their questions. But they felt his wife was surprised to hear about contact he'd had with Suzy. Visits to her cottage that he hadn't mentioned to her, plus his keys found in there.'

'I fear your Mini Cheddars are going to have to wait, Brewster. The press will slaughter us if they discover we left Suzy Baros's son in the care of a man who we'd had a tip-off about.' She stood up and slipped on her jacket. 'Detective Superintendent Grey needs to know about this right away.'

TWENTY-ONE

IRENE

When Amos had first died, over ten years ago now, the villagers had rallied around, bringing Irene home-cooked food and staying for a cuppa and a chat. But people had their own busy lives and their interest soon waned.

She'd hired part-time carers from agencies to help, but they weren't invested in the job and most of them had poor English and couldn't provide the daily companionship she craved. It was just a means to an end for most of them, and they skimped on their duties and couldn't wait to get away at the end of each shift.

Meanwhile, Michael stepped up without being asked. The general maintenance jobs on the cottages were kept on top of and there were no complaints from the regular tenants back then and the glowing reviews of holidaymakers continued. But Michael was working the same part-time hours as he had when Amos had been alive.

One night, lying awake in bed because of pains in her legs, Irene realised that she hadn't seen a soul all day long. She thought about some of the decisions she'd made over the years. The way she'd neglected making friends because Amos was her world and she was his. Having each other had been enough for both of them. But now the years had just evaporated, leaving her alone with no children, and riddled with ill health.

But her mind was intact, and that was the main thing. Nothing got past her. Nothing ever had.

Amos had been old-school, like his father before him. He'd never been a financial risk-taker and had shied away from the stock market. Instead, he'd salted away large sums in a standard investment account. The sort where you had to give a minimum of three months' notice to withdraw, or lose a disproportionate amount of interest. Yet Irene couldn't deny that his obsession with saving money had paid dividends, and his nest egg for a rainy day had been growing impressively.

In that light-bulb moment, she had realised that, far from having nothing, she possessed what most other people craved: money. She had copious funds and nothing to spend it on.

That was how it had started. The transformation from a life lived entirely alone to Irene Wadebridge's embrace by the great and good of Lynwick. She made regular generous donations to the parish council, including sponsorship of the village's floral planting and various events like the Christmas lights turn-on. Her generosity brought many invitations: to sit in on the parish council committee meetings, to join a new book club run by the village ladies' group, to sponsor a reading award at the local school and present attendance prizes at the end of term. Someone would visit the house most days of the week regarding village matters. Others would just drop by to see how she was doing. They would partake of a cup of tea and a slice of cake, and it was only when they made a move to leave that they might remember some good cause they needed her help with.

When her health had taken a downturn and she became less active on the village scene, Irene tried not to think about the reasons why her visitors quickly dropped off. In her quiet moments it seemed fairly clear that people had made the effort not because they liked her, but because they liked her money.

She had known Michael Shaw since he was a small boy. Amos and Michael's father, Gus, had been close business associates, and Irene knew Michael to be a hard worker because of his years as Amos's assistant at Wadebridge. So she'd offered him a position as property and land manager for a generous remuneration package that rivalled even Nottingham city's rates.

Of course, Michael had snapped her hand off. Irene smiled to herself as she recalled his gratitude. It had been a good decision. Michael was the son she'd never had. He was always up here, even outside working hours. He was her first port of call if she needed help in any way, and she'd never known him to complain.

When Michael got married, just a few years before Amos died, Irene had gotten friendly with Kate right away. When Tansy came along and in the absence of any grandparents, Irene relished her time spent reading to her and doing arts and crafts.

At key times of the year – Easter, summer and Christmas – Irene would put something extra in Michael's pay packet. 'Think of it as a small bonus,' she told him if he protested. She went to the Shaws' on Christmas Day and Easter Sunday. She received invitations to Tansy's school play, her ballet and tap show. If she needed Michael or Kate, they would come at the drop of a hat, no questions asked.

Irene stretched and shifted in her chair. Her perennially aching joints had kept her awake longer than usual last night. With the new anti-inflammatories Dr Kendall had prescribed last week, she now took a total of six tablets twice a day. The medication took a surprising amount of time to organise, and she felt grateful that Kate took care of it.

She pushed the walking frame away from the armchair and let her head sink back into the cushion.

'Where have you gone, Suzy?' she whispered into the silence. Michael had told her that Kate was taking care of Aleks, but it wasn't the same as being at home, in the place you were used to, and the boy had already experienced so much upheaval in his life. Irene decided she'd speak to Kate and ask her to bring him up here to visit so she could comfort him. He loved playing Monopoly, a version of which he'd enjoyed back in Poland, and Irene had started to show him some simple card games, like Snap, which she enjoyed as much as he did.

Irene was desperately worried about Suzy, but she couldn't tell the police what she knew about Michael. Besides, she couldn't be certain that it was even connected with Suzy's disappearance.

What a mess it all was.

When she read some of the traditional fairy tales to Tansy, she sometimes tacked on a nicer ending so her little charge didn't become upset. The story itself remained the same, with just a little tweak at the end.

That was what she had to do now if the police questioned her again. The only thing that made any sense at all was for her to forget that she'd ever seen anything in the first place and skip that bit of the story.

TWENTY-TWO

KATE

Donna's tea room was called the Larder and was situated in what used to be the old post office in the centre of the village. She had opened it six years ago when the postmaster and his wife had retired and moved away.

'It's always been my dream to run a vintage tea shop, and this is my chance,' she'd told me excitedly when Post Office Counters announced they were closing the branch permanently – despite fervent protests and a widely circulated petition. With Paul's full support, she had snapped up the Grade II listed premises when it became available for rent.

She employed a small team of part-time staff. A couple of students and a handful of local people. Between them, the café's opening hours of eight until five each weekday were covered, with the students working the weekends. I'd been known to step in and help her out if she had staff off sick, if I could fit it in with my own work.

Donna was a woman of contradictions. She was confident and forthright in village matters but could transform into a jumpy, nervous woman whenever she thought Ellie was in danger, which was really most of the time. She clung to Paul as if she couldn't survive without him. I understood she felt insecure because of her past, but it stuck in my craw that Paul exploited that weakness when it came to his infidelities. I'd tried so many times to talk to Donna about it but she'd always pushed me away.

I walked into the Larder and, as always, took pleasure in looking around at the pretty, traditional tea room. It highlighted another of Donna's contradictions. She was quite a practical woman when it came to her largely monochrome wardrobe and her love of Nordic-style interiors, and these preferences were reflected in the look of her home. So when she'd initially shown me a board of fabrics and colours she was considering for the tea room – ice-cream colours and delicate florals – I'd been pleasantly surprised.

A whole bunch of us, friends and family, had got stuck in at weekends and transformed the dusty, dated post office space into this Laura Ashley-esque oasis on a budget. It hadn't been a chore at all. We'd had drinks and snacks and music, and generally had a great time!

Small white wooden tables and matching chairs were draped in white tablecloths, and all bore tiny pink blossom vases with fresh flowers in. The main wall was of exposed brick softened with tiny white fairy lights. A local joiner had knocked together some rustic shelving from reclaimed wood from the post office counter and storeroom. These were now stacked high with a collection of quirkily mismatched bone-china cups, saucers and side plates that Donna had sourced mainly online. Along the other wall was a counter displaying delicious home-made cakes from a local bakery under huge glass domes. Next to that, a couple of vintage Welsh dressers with stocks of sugared almonds, artisan biscuits and speciality teas for customers to purchase, the shelves artfully trimmed with pink and lemon flag bunting. Donna had managed to rescue the original wooden floor by back-breaking hours spent sanding and varnishing it. The overall result was a delightful space to enjoy a brew and relax. Needless to say, it had proven extremely popular with villagers and visitors alike.

After the call from Miss Monsall, I'd texted Donna and told her I was on my way over. I didn't say why.

She appeared from the back. 'Sit down, Kate, and I'll bring us some tea. I'm just getting straight after the lunchtime rush.'

I sat at a table near the window. Donna brought over a plate of lemon curd shortbread that I resisted for all of thirty seconds. I'd just taken a bite when I felt my phone vibrate in my pocket. I snatched it out and answered the call with a full mouth. 'Hello?'

'Mrs Shaw? My name is DI Helena Price, Nottinghamshire Police. Are you OK to talk for a moment or two?'

My armpits instantly felt damp. I glanced at the counter, where Donna had begun preparing our drinks. Hastily I swallowed down the shortbread. 'That's fine, yes.' I kept my voice upbeat. 'How can I help?'

Donna glanced across as she poured our tea from a big silver pot. She'd sensed my slightly formal tone.

'I understand you have Aleks Baros staying with you currently while his mother is missing?'

'That's right.' Michael's concerns whirled in my head. He'd want me to use this opportunity to enquire what they intended to do if Suzy wasn't found soon. But I said nothing.

'How is he bearing up?'

'Not great, as you can imagine, but he's getting there,' I said. 'He's gone to school today.'

Donna frowned as she tried to make sense of my words.

'That's good. We'd like to speak to Aleks as soon as possible. Obviously social services will have to get involved again if his mother isn't found, but for now, after school tomorrow would be perfect if you could accommodate us and—'

'I ... yes, tomorrow is fine.' I felt a bit put on the spot.

'Great, let's say four p.m. then.' She took a breath, but didn't pause long enough for me to answer. 'Are you happy for us to come to the house and for yourself to remain in the interview as Aleks's appropriate adult? If not, I could ask his head teacher, see if someone from school wanted to attend.'

I hesitated. 'Well, I—'

'Aleks needs to be as comfortable as possible, you see. It could make all the difference.'

It made sense. 'Yes, OK then. I'll do it.'

We said our goodbyes and I sat staring at my phone. I knew Michael wouldn't like the police at the house again, but what could I do?

Donna came over with the tea. 'Everything OK? I couldn't help overhearing your conversation, and you sounded a bit stressed.'

'Everything's fine,' I said, reaching for the pretty Royal Albert cup and saucer in front of me. 'Nice to catch a bit of peace with you in here.'

'I can see everything *isn't* fine.' She began to chew a fingernail. 'Look, Kate, if you know something, you need to tell me. I don't want Ellie in any danger if there's a maniac loose out there.'

'Donna, calm down. That was just the police saying they want to interview Aleks.'

She stared at me for a moment, then, seemingly satisfied that I was telling the truth, she picked up her own cup. 'This is my worst nightmare. Brings everything back. Matilda vanishing into thin air, everyone coming up with theories, everyone suddenly Hercule Poirot.'

'It must be awful for you.' I reached over and touched her arm. 'What's the general consensus about what happened to Suzy?'

Donna blew on her tea before taking a sip. 'I've heard various scenarios, but the current favourite seems to be that Suzy just got tired of village life and the fact that she didn't really fit in, and simply took off.'

'That's ridiculous,' I said, biting into a biscuit and catching crumbs in my hand. 'Aleks is Suzy's world. She'd never just leave him behind like that.'

Donna shrugged, pulling down the corners of her mouth. 'Like I say, it's just what people are surmising. Paul reckons she looks the sort to just take off. He was scathing about her, actually. Said,

"What can you expect of a woman who dresses like a tart even for the school run?"' Her cheeks bloomed with approval of his misplaced criticism.

'Oh, I think that's a bit harsh, Donna!' Injustice burned in my throat at Paul making such disparaging remarks when he'd been following Suzy around like a panting dog.

I could see her chest rising and falling as her breathing became heavier. 'Harsh maybe, but that doesn't mean it's not true. I know it's early days, but after a massive search and a door-to-door, nothing's turned up yet, has it? She seems to have just done a moonlight flit.'

'I'm not sure how. She didn't drive, and Michael said the police had mentioned checking with the local taxi firm, who said no cab had been ordered.'

'Bus?' She bit her lip.

'I think someone would have seen her waiting at the bus stop, don't you?'

She looked at me over her cup, dissatisfied with my lack of agreement. 'Well, what do you and Michael think?'

'We just don't know.' I sighed. 'Michael is ... I don't know, he seems a bit low at the moment. I think he feels like the police are suspicious of him because he works up at the cottages.'

Donna's eyes widened. She placed her cup back on the saucer. 'Why, what have they said?'

'It was just the routine door-to-door visit. They were quite probing, and he was ... unnerved, I think.'

'They've accused him of knowing more than he's letting on?'

She was instantly interested, and who could blame her? We'd been friends a long time and I trusted her not to gossip, but I still found it difficult to discuss our personal business. It felt disloyal to Michael somehow. But Donna was like a dog with a bone. She'd studied my face and had seen something.

'Look, don't say anything to anyone, but ... the police searched Suzy's cottage and found Michael's work keys in there.'

'What?' Her eyes widened. 'Had he been in there?'

'No, no. Nothing like that. He swears he doesn't know why they were there, and that's what he told them.'

She picked up her cup again. 'Even so, the police must view it as suspicious.'

'When the officers came for the door-to-door, it was the way they questioned him more than what they asked,' I said. 'The fact that he works for Irene Wadebridge seems to be a dead weight around his neck. Since then, he says they've been hanging around the cottages. He's been told to expect a more thorough search of the surrounding land soon, and he reckons they'll want to speak to him again.'

'That's awful. It's bringing it all back, that horrible feeling of being both desperate for, and dreading, information at the same time.' Donna pressed her fingers to her chin. 'Do they think ... I mean, do they suspect there might be something gruesome to find up at Wadebridge?'

'Who knows?' I gave an involuntary shiver. 'But I feel really bad for Michael. He's completely innocent but feels guilty by association, you know?'

'Hmm. I suppose it's natural for the police to be asking questions, though, isn't it? Especially when they found his keys in her cottage. Young, attractive woman, older married man ...'

I stared at her. I felt shocked and affronted. 'I can't believe you said that, and I'll thank you not to repeat it, Donna. That's how nasty rumours start in a small place like this.'

She sniffed and sipped her tea. 'Sorry if I've upset you. I'm just saying what people around here will think. I can't sleep for all this trouble. I don't want to let Ellie out of my sight.'

'Well, that's precisely why we should be careful what we say. I'm probably to blame for Michael feeling like he does too, with taking Aleks in.'

'Aleks isn't your responsibility, Kate.'

'I know that. I offered him a safe place with people he knows rather than some faceless social services placement.'

'It's a massive commitment, though, you must admit it.'

'Yes! But I'd do the same for any child. I'd take Ellie in without hesitation if you went missing.'

'And I'd take Tansy in,' Donna shot back. 'But our girls are best friends. *We're* best friends. You hardly know Suzy and Aleks.'

'And yet Paul offered to have him at your house.'

'Well, Paul says he didn't offer. Not in as many words, he just showed concern for where the boy was going to be taken.'

The lady from social services had told me herself that he'd offered but seeing as Donna didn't approve, it sounded like he'd done his usual number and denied everything.

'Well, anyway, it might not be for much longer. The police are coming over tomorrow to speak to Aleks, and then if Suzy is still missing, social services might have to get involved again.' I traced around the rim of my teacup with a fingertip. 'I admit I've probably bitten off more than I can chew, but I thought it was the right thing to do at the time. Michael thinks the same as you, that we should stay out of it.'

'You've got a good heart, Kate. But when are you going to realise you can't save everyone single-handedly?'

I flinched. 'Have the police interviewed you and Paul?'

'Our door-to-door was very quick. No awkward questions from the police,' she said a little smugly.

'Did Paul tell them he'd spoken to Suzy?' The words were out of my mouth before I could stop them.

'What do you mean?'

It was too late to back out now, and besides, this could be important. 'When I took drinks over to Michael and Paul by the tree last night, Paul bolted off to talk to Suzy as she walked by.'

'I don't believe that.'

'I was there, Donna. I saw him.'

'Well, he must've had something to ask her, or perhaps she'd left something behind near the tree, or—'

'Why do you let him treat you like this?'

Her mouth dropped open and she stared at me. 'What are you talking about?'

I'd crossed a line and I knew it. Through her refusal to discuss his affairs and the way she absolved him of any responsibility, Donna had let me know in no uncertain terms that Paul's behaviour wasn't up for scrutiny. And I'd fallen into line. Well, no more. Yes, I was discovering things about Michael that were shaking my faith in him. But Donna was more than happy to point those out to me, and I would do the same to her about Paul.

'The way he ogles other women in front of you, in front of Ellie. The way he's had affairs and you've just taken him right back without a—'

'Enough!'

'Have you thought about the message you're giving Ellie as she grows up, that it's OK for men to treat women that way? What if—'

'I said *enough*!' Her teeth were bared aggressively, but her eyes were wide and scared. 'It's none of your business. It's nobody's business but ours.'

'If that's how you feel about it, then fine,' I said, purposely dropping my voice against her rising anger. 'I just wanted to—'

'Well, don't. Don't "just" anything, OK? Keep your nasty little opinions to yourself.' A tear trickled down her cheek and she wiped it roughly away with the back of her hand. 'Me and Paul, we have something good. We have something worth fighting for, and he loves me. I know he does. It's nobody's business. Not yours, not anyone's.'

'Understood.' I took a step back. 'I'm sorry you're so upset, Donna. I care about you and Ellie.'

'I don't comment on your marriage, do I?'

I looked at her.

'Gone a bit quiet now ... Nothing to say?'

'We're talking about Paul's infidelity. Michael hasn't been unfaithful.' Despite my loyalty to my husband, my heart drummed against my chest wall. All the things I'd discovered lately that he'd failed to tell me. Was I in any position to criticise Donna?

She put down her cup and it made a sharp *ching* on the saucer.

'Kate, what's got into you? I know it's a difficult time with

Michael feeling the heat, but there's really no need to take it out on me.'

'I'm not taking it out on you. I'm just asking if Paul had mentioned he'd spoken to Suzy! It doesn't take much for the police to become interested in a perfectly innocent person. That's the point I was trying to make earlier.'

Donna nodded slowly, regarding me with fresh caution. 'They're just doing their job, though. They found Michael's keys inside Suzy's cottage ... that would be considered a clue.'

'It looks suspicious, but Michael said he knows nothing about it, and I believe him.' I looked down at my hand and saw a pile of broken biscuit crumbs beneath my fingers. 'I didn't mean to upset you, Donna. I know this brings everything back for you. I can't imagine how it feels to lose someone in this way. But that's why I felt so bad for Aleks, you see.'

'When you texted to say you wanted to talk to me, I thought it was for a specific reason, not just to have a go! But anyway, let's just agree to differ on things.'

'I'm sorry, I got distracted.' I clamped my hand to my forehead. 'The reason I came over was because of the kids. Tansy and Ellie.'

I told her about the call from Miss Monsall.

'I'm really sorry Ellie got caught up in it all, but it's a tough time for Tansy right now, too. She's being overprotective of Aleks, and who can blame her?'

'Me, I can blame her!' Donna's eyes darkened. 'Making Ellie cry at school? That's unacceptable, and actually' – she pushed her chair back and stood up – 'it's not really Tansy's fault, is it? It's *your* fault. You're also overprotective of Aleks, and Tansy has clearly picked up on that. She's turning into an interfering little—'

'Hang on! Ellie's also a little madam at times and you need to admit it, Donna.' Her observation of my need to protect and feel responsible for others hit home. But that was just me. What could I do about it? Everyone had parts of themselves they had to just accept and get on with.

'Ellie hasn't dumped Tansy in favour of some kid who's been in the village just two minutes, has she? Fortunately Ellie has lots of other friends. I'll be asking Miss Monsall to sit the two of them apart from now on.'

'Oh, come on, that's just—'

Donna leaned forward, her eyes gleaming, her jaw set. 'You're blind to any of your family doing anything wrong. Maybe I'm not the only person who's gullible about their husband's excuses.'

'What are you talking about?'

Donna stalked off to the counter and I stood up.

'Hey, you can't say something like that and just walk away!'

'You told me yourself ... Michael's keys in Suzy's cottage. That's a bit worrying, wouldn't you say? I've got stuff to do now, Kate, and not sleeping is driving me crazy. I'm beginning to think this village is cursed.'

The tea room door chimed and three customers came in, all mums from school.

'Hey, Kate, hi, Donna,' one of them sang out.

'Excuse me.' I headed for the door and stepped outside into the cold, damp air. After Donna's comments, my mind was swimming with all sorts of possibilities. Part of me was aware that I was turning into exactly the sort of person I'd criticised her for being. After what Irene had told me about Michael's cosy breaks with Suzy, and the police discovering his keys in the cottage, I was beginning to wonder if Donna was right and I was being incredibly naïve just accepting his excuses.

I decided to talk to him tonight. Pin him down until I got the full truth of the matter.

TWENTY-THREE

Later, I got to the school with just a minute to spare, and skirted around the group of mothers that included Donna.

'Is my mum back?' Aleks said as soon as he and Tansy reached me. I saw Ellie stalk off in the opposite direction towards Donna.

'Not yet, sweetie. But the police are working really hard to get her back home.' I watched him deflate in front of me and felt a squeeze in my chest.

'Ellie's been horrible to Aleks today,' Tansy said, glaring down at their group. 'She said she's not my friend any more.'

'Oh dear,' I said. 'Not again.'

On the way out of the gates, I looked over to catch Donna's eye and offer a smile, but she'd turned her back and was talking animatedly to the other mums. Nobody acknowledged me.

I took the kids straight back to the house and decided to say nothing to Tansy for now about the upset with Ellie. Both she and Aleks looked tired and a bit down. I made their tea and let them chill out watching television and then playing computer games, but when I went through to get something, Aleks spoke up.

'When can I go home, Kate?'

'Soon as they find your mum, Aleks. I know it seems like forever to you, but it's only been a day.'

'Why hasn't she sent a message?'

It would've been so easy to lie to him, but I wasn't going to do that. 'I don't know. I'm sure she would if she could. But we're hoping to hear something very soon.'

Glumly he went back to his game, and I knew he'd found no comfort at all in my vague words.

When Michael got home from work, late as usual, the kids were already in bed. He looked wretched. His face sagged and he moved slowly, almost lumbering.

'I'm going up for a shower,' he said, greeting me with a kiss on the cheek that I didn't return. 'Wadebridge has been crawling with cops. They've searched the woodland again and all of the cottages, not just Suzy's.'

'Have they questioned you about the keys again?'

He frowned. 'Not yet, but they probably will.' I could see the stress lines settling in around the corners of his eyes.

'What does Irene think about it all?'

'It's a bit weird, but I think she's enjoying the attention and the company. She's worried about Suzy but seems to have blind faith that she'll turn up. Doesn't seem to realise the seriousness of the situation, or the fact that the police are trying to get their claws into me.'

I felt sure that couldn't be the case. Nobody, not even Irene, liked having police intervention on their property. I wanted to discuss the stuff that was bothering me, but there was something else to tackle first.

I told him about Miss Monsall's call. 'Sounds like Tansy has been a little Rottweiler to the other kids. She's always been protective of her friends, but I said I'd have a word when she gets home. I haven't done so yet because they'd clearly had a tough day.' Michael said nothing, but his face was like stone. 'I went to the tea room to speak to Donna and she was really defensive. I challenged her about Paul treating her badly in front of Ellie, and she implied I was naïve about *you*.'

He busied himself slipping off his work jacket and hanging it up, instead of tossing it on a chair like he usually would. 'In what way?'

'She didn't elaborate, but I felt like she was implying you were involved with Suzy Baros's disappearance. I suppose that was the crux of it.'

'I hope you know that's rubbish!' Michael cried out. 'Utter rubbish! It doesn't take much for folks around here to start talking and before you know it, you've got a kangaroo court on your hands.'

'I agree and I said as much.' I sighed. 'But there seems to be more and more stuff in the "things I didn't know" pile, Michael. Stuff you've been keeping from me. Tea breaks with Suzy, the fact that Irene reckons she's sweet on you. The keys.'

He groaned. 'Please don't tell me you believe Irene. It's all in her head! Honestly, she must be losing her marbles.' He grabbed my upper arms. 'I love you. Got it? Even if I have a cup of tea with Irene and a tenant one day, I love *you*. I haven't got a clue how those keys got there. I do tend to leave them around as they're not my most important bunch. But I hadn't been in her cottage for days and I'd used them since. I told you all that!'

If his goal had been to make me feel better, he'd failed, yet it was in my nature to give him the benefit of the doubt. To believe in him. I decided to finish my news. 'There's something else. The police called me this afternoon. They're coming here tomorrow, to the house, to speak to Aleks.'

'You see, this is what I meant, Kate. This is what I was worried about.' He fell quiet a moment, collected himself. 'Having the kid here has just put us all in the spotlight, got people's tongues wagging. Do you think you could speak to someone about getting him a temporary foster family or something?'

'You'd seriously want me to do that?' DI Price had already broached the subject but Michael didn't know about that. This wasn't like my caring husband. He seemed uncharacteristically panicky. I had absolutely nothing to hide from the police, but what about Michael?

'Without Aleks here, we'd be just another village family,' he said, in a placatory tone. 'Instead, it feels like we're in the thick of the investigation.'

'The detective said social services will be in touch about taking Aleks, if you must know. But it's not him being here that's causing their increased interest in you. It's the fact you work up at Wadebridge! You were always going to be involved, Michael, whether you liked it or not.' I tried to bite my tongue, but it didn't work. 'You cosying up in Suzy's cottage wouldn't have done you much good, either.'

'That's not what happened. How many more times?' He squeezed his eyes shut. 'I can't stand this, it's like waiting to be shot. The coppers are biding their time, but they're after me, I know it.'

He was starting to sound paranoid, completely overreacting. Unless there was more stuff he wasn't telling me.

'Look, why don't you have that shower and then come downstairs and we'll talk. We can—'

There was a knock at the door.

'I'll get it,' he said and headed for the hallway.

I heard voices, and then the door closed and the voices continued. I rushed into the hall and stopped dead.

'Hello, Mrs Shaw,' DI Helena Price said pleasantly. DS Brewster nodded.

'They've got some questions for me,' Michael said, his voice flat. 'We'll go into the front room.'

'The kids are in bed,' I said, walking towards them. 'I'll come in too, if that's OK?'

'That's entirely up to Mr Shaw,' Brewster said. 'Sometimes people prefer to speak to us in private.'

We all turned to Michael. He looked alarmed for a second, and then nodded. 'Course.'

The detectives both declined drinks and we all sat down.

'Just some things we need tying up,' Brewster said easily, taking out his notebook. 'There's the matter of your keys being found on the kitchen worktop of Suzy Baros's cottage the night she went missing, Mr Shaw. Anything else you'd like to tell us about that?'

I glanced at Michael, but he didn't look back at me. He stared straight ahead. 'I have no idea how they got there,' he said simply.

'Where do you usually keep them?'

'I don't really have a set place for them. I attach my main bunch of keys to my waist, but the second bunch, the ones you found, they're used less often. They're usually in my office, or in the main house if I'm doing something there and forget to pick them back up.'

'Might you have been doing something in the cottage and forgot to pick them up in the same way?' Brewster said. Price looked at me and I averted my eyes.

'I hadn't been in the cottage for about a week. I replaced a washer on the tap there, as I explained to the door-to-door officers. I've used the keys since then, so I know I didn't leave them there that day.'

Brewster made a note.

I watched my husband carefully, saw tiny pricks of perspiration on his upper lip. Was he telling the truth? I thought so, but I couldn't say for sure.

'We looked into Jakub's connection to Wadebridge and it seems highly likely he was there at some point as a casual worker.' Price took a piece of paper out of her bag. 'Earlier today, the team received an anonymous call claiming to have some important information.' She read from the paper: '"If you're interested in finding Jakub Jasinski, ask Michael Shaw at Wadebridge, Lynwick."' She looked at Michael. 'There appears to be a growing trend of people going missing from your workplace. Who is Jakub Jasinski, Mr Shaw?'

'I've never heard of him,' Michael said firmly.

'Let me help you out. Jasinski is on our missing persons list,' Brewster said. 'He disappeared from the East Midlands area over a year ago, by all accounts. His family back in Poland are understandably worried and are desperate to trace him.'

'That's as may be, but I can't help them, I'm afraid.'

I sat there mute and shocked. Jakub was a casual labourer who'd worked at Wadebridge for a couple of years. Michael had said he was a good worker, but one day, about a year ago, he hadn't turned up for work, and Michael hadn't seen him since. Why on earth would he lie about that?

I chewed the inside of my cheek. I dared not look at DI Price, who I knew was studying my face.

'Does the name mean anything to you, Mrs Shaw?' she asked, her voice clear and cutting.

I froze. This was the moment I either told the truth and got Michael arrested, or lied to the police for the first time in my life.

'Kate has nothing to do with Wadebridge operations,' Michael said confidently.

'I don't,' I agreed, my heart thumping so hard I began to feel queasy. I wanted to protect him. I wanted to be honest. The conflict between the two cut me like a knife.

'Do you employ many casual staff on Wadebridge land?' Brewster pressed him.

'Sometimes we have, in the past,' Michael said gruffly. 'But I haven't had any help for a long time.'

Brewster nodded. 'Well, should you suddenly remember you do know Mr Jasinski after all, be sure to let us know, sir.'

TWENTY-FOUR

When the detectives had gone, I rounded on Michael.

'What the hell did you lie to them for? You know full well who Jakub Jasinski is, and you know he worked up at Wadebridge.'

'Leave it, Kate.' He grabbed his wellies from the mat at the back door. 'I need some space.' He stomped out into the dark and started pacing up and down like a madman.

I pressed a switch and the outside lights illuminated the small garden. I watched him from the warm, dry kitchen. Five minutes after he'd gone out, it started to drizzle. When he showed no sign of coming inside, I called to him, but he waved me away without looking up.

I knew something was wrong. I could see it in his slightly wild eyes, his lack of appetite, the way he'd disappeared into himself so that I now felt I couldn't reach him. Being raised by an alcoholic trained you in spotting the signs of trouble that others might miss.

The pattern following one of my mother's binges was always the same: the guilt and shame, the resolve to get help and stay off the drink. For a brief time, I'd get a glimpse of the tantalising normality most of my classmates enjoyed. Things like having my mum at home when I got home from school, sitting together to eat tea and talk about our day, watching a movie on television with popcorn and soft drinks.

But always, just as I allowed myself to consider the possibility that this time things could be different, the signs would start again. Always discreet and almost unnoticeable at first. Her restlessness, her inability to concentrate. The way that during a conversation her eyes would gradually become unfocused, as if she were yearning to be somewhere else. And yet she'd swear there was nothing wrong. She'd swear she hadn't touched a drop. That's how she'd ended up in the car that day ... because I wanted so badly to believe her when she said she hadn't been drinking. I let her take the keys and drive away. I went against my instincts just as I was doing now.

I watched Michael pacing almost manically in the rain now. He didn't seem to notice that his hair was sopping wet, his wellies tramping the lawn into a mud bath. My instincts said something was very wrong.

I pulled on my own wellies and coat, grabbed an umbrella and went outside.

Suzy's disappearance was getting to him. It was getting to us all. Little Aleks was the one who was suffering most. But it felt like there was one thing after another to tie Michael to Suzy Baros. So far, he was sticking to his story about the keys. I felt uncomfortable about it, but I had to accept she might have found them lying around outside somewhere and picked them up to give him the next day. Naïve, maybe, but it was circumstantial. It didn't mean he had anything to do with her disappearance.

Michael's first instinct, ever since I'd known him, was always to help if others needed him. He seemed to take pleasure in making people's lives easier. During our fifteen-year marriage, he'd been a thoughtful and loyal husband. He adored our daughter and had always managed to make time for us both, even though he often spread himself too thin. He cared about Irene and – admittedly, to my irritation at times – would come out at the drop of a hat if she needed help. He could never have been described as a sly or underhand man, because he just wasn't. Which made recent events and observations so incongruous. I didn't quite believe them, but they were too serious to ignore.

'You can't let it get to you like this,' I said, throwing my hands up. 'You can't start lying about things that can probably be checked out. Why *did* you lie?'

He stopped pacing and looked at me. '*You* knew the truth, but you didn't say you knew him, did you?'

I was speechless. It seemed so unfair when I'd kept my mouth shut to save dropping him in it.

I took a step back, my heart pounding against my chest. I looked at my husband, his square jaw, his strong, wide shoulders, his dependability. We'd always been so solid together. Now it felt like he was turning on me.

'What do you think they'd have done if I'd admitted I knew Jakub? They'd tear me to pieces to get their conviction. That's how they operate.' He took several steps forward. 'They're closing in on me, Kate. I can feel it. They keep finding excuses to come up to Wadebridge, and after finding those keys, they can smell blood. It feels like it's only a matter of time before they pin something bad on me. Something really bad.'

The rain came down harder, sheeting at me at an angle and defying the umbrella. The collar of my jacket felt sopping against my neck, and I adjusted the brolly so he could see my face again. We looked at each other for a long moment.

'Have you got anything to do with Suzy Baros's disappearance, Michael?' I asked.

'No.'

'I want the truth, no matter how bad.'

'I've done nothing wrong,' he said solemnly. 'You have to believe me, Kate, because if they manage to get enough dirt to stick, they could even pull you into all this as well. Say you lied to protect me. What would that do to Tansy? We could lose everything, including our daughter.'

.   .   .

While Michael was in the shower, I rang Donna's mobile.

It rang for a while and I thought she wasn't going to pick up. Then she answered in a surly tone. 'Kate. Hi.'

'Hi, Donna, listen, I just wanted to say sorry for having a go at the tea room. I'm stressed, Michael's stressed, the kids are stressed. We're living in a bit of a nightmare here.'

'If anyone understands how you're feeling, it's me,' Donna said. 'But I'm not going to deny you upset me today. Attacking Paul, and then justifying Tansy making Ellie cry. She was still in a state when she got out of school. Have you spoken to Tansy about it?'

'Yes,' I lied. I couldn't stand animosity with Donna on top of everything else that was happening. 'She knows she's done wrong and she's going to apologise to Ellie tomorrow.'

'Right. Well, let's put it behind us then. How's Aleks?'

'He's confused, upset. Everything you'd expect really, though he doesn't say much.'

'When are the police coming to speak to him?'

'Tomorrow, after school. They're coming here, to the house.'

'Give me a ring afterwards, let me know how it goes,' she said. 'Maybe we can have a get-together after school one day this week.'

I could have done without it, frankly, but I wanted to get back on an even keel.

'That would be great. Thanks, Donna.'

When I put the phone down, I felt as if I'd gone a bit cap-in-hand to her, but if that was the price I had to pay, then so be it. That was what being friends was all about, wasn't it – give and take. And I needed Donna. I needed her friendship and support to get through this tough time.

I mean, things were bad enough right now, but who knew what was around the corner?

TWENTY-FIVE

12 NOVEMBER 2019

NOTTINGHAMSHIRE POLICE

DI Helena Price stared out of the window as Brewster drove through the pretty village in a marked police car, the only car available. Lynwick was well kept, with small shops and interesting landmarks like ancient stone crosses and small channels of water that ran either side of the main road, which were known locally as 'docks'.

As the car slowed and turned off the main road into a smaller side street, she noted the curious glances, people commenting and pointing. Nothing went unnoticed in a place like this, and yet it seemed that a young woman had somehow disappeared at a busy event without anyone seeing a thing. In Helena's experience, small, claustrophobic places could either be a blessing in disguise, in that people saw everything, or a barrier that outsiders, including the police, were unable to break through. She hoped the former observation would apply this time.

As they pulled up, Helena leaned forward to get her first look at Kate and Michael Shaw's house. It was a modest detached home, neat and stone-built, with a small front garden. Quite unremarkable in this village, which boasted several impressively large houses with plenty of land.

It was Kate who answered the door. She was a tall woman, with dark hair pinned up at the back and escaped tendrils framing her pleasant, open face. After introductions, she led Helena and Brewster into the hallway.

'Do we have to wait for someone to come from school?' Kate asked.

'No. I spoke to the head teacher at Lynwick Primary and we decided we'd just keep it low key, the least people here the better,' Helena said.

'Aleks seemed very nervous when I said you were coming to chat with him,' Kate said, dropping her voice to little more than a whisper. 'He doesn't say much even to us, doesn't show much emotion, even if we mention his mum. It's quite worrying really.' She looked at Helena. 'You might be wasting your time here, I'm afraid.'

Helena nodded. 'That's always a possibility, but we'll see.' Children often did not behave in the way adults thought they should in times of trauma. Adults tended to release emotion and display visual signs of worry and grief. Some children were the opposite to that and completely closed up, like an oyster shell. It was a way of protecting themselves when they felt vulnerable and exposed.

Kate led them through to the living room, where Aleks sat waiting. His hair was very dark, almost black, and his skin was pale. Dark circles underscored his hooded eyes. He didn't look up when they entered the room, but chewed furiously on the inside of his cheek. When they moved closer, he crossed his hands in front of him. Essentially another safety barrier.

'Hello, Aleks, I'm Helena Price. I'm a detective leading the investigation to find your mum. This is Kane Brewster – he's a detective too.'

'Hi, Aleks,' Brewster said warmly, crouching down at the side of his armchair. 'I'm here to try to help. We want to get your mum back here, where she belongs.'

Kate Shaw smiled and nodded at Aleks reassuringly. The boy shuffled closer to the other arm of his chair, subconsciously trying to get as far away as possible. It was a normal reaction Helena had seen before.

She stood up and walked over to the chair facing him. 'Aleks, I know you're very upset and worried about your mum.' She sat down. 'I want you to know my team are doing everything they can to find her, OK?'

'Yes,' Aleks said in a small voice, steepling his fingers together in front of him.

'I've come to see you today because there's something else we can do to help find her. Something only you can help us with.' Aleks glanced at Kate and sat up a little straighter. 'I have a few questions I need to ask you. Nothing difficult or upsetting, but things that could help us find your mum. Do you understand?' The boy slumped a little. 'It doesn't matter if you don't know the answers, and if you want me to stop, then you just have to say and we'll leave. Do you think we might have a little try?'

Aleks knotted his fingers together securely and frowned at the shining white knuckles that popped up.

Kate Shaw said helpfully, 'I'll be sitting here with you the whole time. What do you think?'

Aleks looked at Helena and Brewster, then back at Kate. He gave a single nod.

'Well done,' Kate said. 'Your mum will be so proud you did this brave thing.'

'Thank you, Aleks.' Helena moved on swiftly before nerves got the better of him. 'Now, I know you and your mum came here to the UK from Poland. That's where you lived before?'

He nodded.

'It must have been difficult for you to leave your home,' she said softly.

'I was sad to leave my friends and Banjo, my rabbit.'

'Of course.' She nodded. 'And your mum, she must have missed her family.'

Aleks shifted in his seat. When children of this age hesitated to communicate, it wasn't always, Helena found, because they didn't have the answers. It could be they had been told to stay quiet by an adult.

She waited. The house felt silent and cool. The light outside was dropping and cast the room in a dull bloom.

'She missed her friend,' Aleks said.

'Which friend is that?'

'Petra.'

'Ah yes,' Brewster confirmed, as if he knew who he was referring to. 'You saw a lot of Petra, yes?'

He nodded. 'She worked with my mum at the bakery and sometimes she'd bring cakes for our picnics.'

Helena grinned. 'You lucky thing! And that was the bakery in …' She looked up to the ceiling as if she were trying to recall the place name. Aleks watched her. 'Hard for me to remember Polish place names. I think it's in …'

'Tarnow,' Aleks said.

'Tarnow! Of course.' Helena stuck her index finger in the air. 'Thank you, Aleks.'

Brewster wrote something down. 'Aleks, could you tell us your address back in Poland? It's really important we know exactly where you lived there because—'

Too late, Helena threw him a warning look.

'No!' Two pink spots glowed on his pale cheeks.

'It's OK,' Helena soothed him. 'Remember, you don't have to talk about anything that makes you feel uncomfortable.' Aleks nodded and folded his arms. 'But you know, it would be really useful to know your address back in Poland, because then, if your family are worried about your mum not contacting them, we can let them know you're all right.'

'I can't remember the address,' he said stiffly.

Helena knew the child was reluctantly responding with clearly rehearsed dead-end answers. Aleks had probably been told by his mother to issue this stock reply if asked any details about their life in Poland. That was why it was important to avoid direct questions like Brewster had asked, and take an indirect approach instead.

'Aleks,' she said softly, waiting until he looked up. 'Sometimes when adults tell children to keep quiet about something, it's because they're feeling scared too. Maybe your mum told you to say you can't remember because she was afraid of people finding something out.'

He shifted, his face reddening.

'We're going to find the address soon, because of the forms your mum filled out to get her passport,' Brewster said gently. 'It could just save us some time if you could tell us now.'

He looked slightly alarmed.

Helena continued. 'There's no need to be afraid, because all we want is to help you. We want to find your mum as soon as possible and bring her back home. If you can trust us with this information, it will really, really help us.'

Aleks looked her in the eye, and Brewster poised his pen above the notepad. Then he spoke, his voice clear and confident as if he were reciting the lines of a poem.

'I can't remember our address, and all our family have moved away now from the village we lived in in Poland.'

Frustrated, Brewster put down his pen and looked at Helena, who seemed unfazed.

'That must have been very tough on you,' she said evenly. 'When you came here, to England, you got to know some new people. People like Tansy and Kate.' Aleks glanced over at Kate, and she smiled at him. 'Then there are your friends at school, your teacher, and I know your mum gets on well with Irene Wade-bridge, too.' Aleks nodded, seemingly relieved to be off the subject of Poland. 'Anyone else I've forgotten, any new person in England who Mum saw a lot or spoke about?'

'Michael,' Aleks said, looking brighter as if he'd suddenly remembered a detail. 'Michael came over to the cottage a lot.'

Kate Shaw stood up as if she'd been slapped. 'That's not right! I mean ... he just came to the cottage to mend a leaking tap, didn't he, Aleks?' she stammered.

Aleks's eyes widened as he sensed he'd said something wrong. Helena moved over to him, her body acting as a shield between him and Kate Shaw. She held up a hand to the other woman. 'If we can just let Aleks speak, please, Kate. You'll get your chance to say something afterwards if you wish.'

'But ... he's made it sound as though Michael is involved in—'

'Mrs Shaw, please! We will discuss this privately,' Brewster said pointedly.

'When you say Michael came to the cottage a lot, Aleks,' Helena said, still standing with her back to Kate, blocking Aleks's view of her, 'what sort of things did he do there?'

'He just mended the tap, that's all,' he said breathlessly, his eyes darting around the room.

There was a new tension in the air. Helena could feel the nervous energy rolling off Kate Shaw. Kids were great conduits of adult stress without even realising it themselves. The evidence appeared in their body language and their reluctance to speak. Aleks had clearly picked up on Kate's anxiety. His focus was now on backtracking, trying to make amends for what he'd said.

'He mended the tap, we know that. And the other times he came over, what did he do then?' Brewster said carefully, mindful not to lead Aleks's reply in any way.

'I don't think he went over there apart from that,' Kate said, earning herself another warning look from Helena.

'Aleks?' Brewster tried again, ignoring the interruption. 'When Michael came over to the cottage, what sort of things would he do? Did he chat to you and your mum?'

The boy pressed his lips together and folded his arms, and Helena knew then that he'd closed down completely. There was really no point in going any further.

She turned to Brewster. 'I think that's as far as we can take it today.'

It had always been a risk having Kate Shaw present, but it had been Helena's hope that she would calm and reassure Aleks so he might open up a little more. Instead, she had inadvertently managed to undermine the trust that Helena and Brewster had tried so hard to establish with him. In his mother's absence, Kate was the boy's key adult, and he'd naturally want to avoid upsetting her at any cost.

Helena took a breath to smother her irritation and smiled tightly.

'Any idea where your husband is this afternoon, Kate?' she said carefully. 'There's something we'd like to speak to him about, today if possible.'

TWENTY-SIX

Michael Shaw contacted them within the hour. Brewster put the call on loudspeaker as he offered to come to the police station.

Helena raised her eyebrows and gave him a thumbs-up.

Brewster said, nice as pie, 'See you here soon then, Mr Shaw.'

'Now there's a turn-up for the books,' Helena said, leaning back in her seat and tapping a biro on her teeth. 'Usually have to drag them in here kicking and screaming.'

'Makes sense if he wants to keep whatever he's going to say quiet.' Brewster pulled a face. 'I'm not saying it'll be a full-on confession about abducting Suzy Baros, but I bet you he's been a naughty boy and tried it on with—'

'Thank you, Brewster,' Helena interrupted him with a roll of her eyes. 'Best if you keep your sordid imagination to yourself.'

Brewster opened a packet of shortbread biscuits.

When Michael Shaw arrived, he looked clean and fresh, like he'd just stepped out of the shower. Helena noted his smart-casual look. Jeans, plain black tee, a trendy utility jacket and black suede pull-on boots. She and Brewster had made several visits to Wade-bridge, and each time they'd seen or spoken to Michael up there, he'd worn paint-stained dungarees or baggy patched jeans with a waxed jacket, cap and work boots. It was a surprise to see how well he scrubbed up. She could quite imagine a young woman like Suzy finding him attractive if she'd seen this side of him. It was interesting.

Brewster said, 'We'll be recording our chat for posterity, but it's not a formal interview as such. You've volunteered to talk with us here at the station because you said you wish to keep the inquiry separate from your work and home life, is that right?'

'That's correct, yes,' Shaw replied, lacing his hands loosely in front of him.

Helena began. 'Are you aware that earlier today we spoke to young Aleks Baros at your home?'

'Yes,' he said shortly, and Helena noticed his fingers locking a little tighter together.

'In general conversation it was suggested that you may have been a regular visitor at the Baros cottage,' Helena said easily. 'Did you visit Suzy and Aleks there on several occasions?'

Shaw cleared his throat. 'It's my job to keep the cottages maintained and in good running order, so yes, I'm often around that area, tinkering with this and that. I had to repair a tap last week, and I think Suzy offered me a drink.' He swallowed, and Helena imagined his throat was probably dry with nerves. 'Yes, she did. We had a cup of tea and a chat.'

'A chat about what, exactly?' she asked.

'About how she was finding village life, how her son was settling into school. My daughter and young Aleks, they're in the same class. They're friends.'

'Yes,' Helena said.

'What about the other visits?' Brewster pressed. 'We know all about that pesky leaking tap now, but we're also under the impression you popped round there on several occasions over the months Suzy Baros was living in the cottage. On occasion, you might even have left something behind ... such as the keys officers found in the initial search.'

Shaw thought for a moment. 'I might've put my head around

the door to ask if she wanted the hedge cutting. As for the keys, I've said again and again that I've no idea how they got there.'

'I see,' said Brewster, clearly unconvinced. 'What else did you put your head around for?'

'It's hard to think. I'm busy all day up there. There's hardly a minute spare.'

Helena spotted a flush creeping up from the neck of Shaw's T-shirt.

'We've plenty of time, Mr Shaw.' She smiled. 'Can we get you a glass of water? You look rather … warm.'

'I'm OK.' He pulled at the collar of his jacket. 'I'm used to being outside in the fresh air, that's all it is.'

'You were telling us about your visits to Suzy Baros's cottage,' Brewster reminded him.

'Like I said, it's hard to—'

'Don't play these games, Mr Shaw. You don't want us thinking you're trying to hide something from us, do you?'

'I'm not! I'm not trying to hide anything. It's just …' Helena could hear him breathing heavily. His hands were now balled into loose fists. 'You keep asking when I've been to the cottage, but you don't ask anything about her and how she—' He bit down on his tongue, clearly flustered at having said too much.

Brewster was on him like a terrier, leaning forward in his seat. 'About how she …?'

'Nothing. Forget it.'

Brewster smiled disingenuously. 'Ah see, it doesn't work like that, Mr Shaw. You trip yourself up and we notice, and then you have to spill the beans. They're the rules.'

'I didn't trip myself up,' Shaw said tightly, his cheeks flushing. 'I just meant that you lot seem to think she was a meek little thing, but she wasn't.'

'Really?' Brewster fixed him with a cold stare. 'What was she like, then?'

'She was … feisty. Determined. She got it into her head I had something to hide, which was ridiculous, because I haven't! Got anything to hide, I mean.'

'What exactly did she think you were hiding?' Helena chipped in.

'Information about some Polish bloke who she said worked at Wadebridge, I don't know.' Helena and Brewster exchanged a glance. 'She kept going on at me about it, finding me in the yard or when I was out on the ride-on mower, insisting I knew something. I got fed up of it. In the end, I told her I'd get Irene to end her tenancy, and she turned nasty. She threatened to tell my wife I'd been coming on to her.' He stared at his hands, and for a moment Helena thought he looked beaten. 'I swear I didn't touch her. I would never do that.'

Helena nodded to Brewster. This informal chat was fast becoming something else entirely.

Brewster indicated for Shaw to stop speaking. 'This interview is now going to be conducted under caution. I must tell you that you do not have to say anything, but it may harm your defence if you don't mention when questioned something which you later rely on in court. Anything you do say may be given in evidence.'

Shaw sat forward. 'What? What's this? Why—'

'You're not under arrest, you're free to leave at any time and you're entitled to have a solicitor present if you want,' Brewster continued. 'Do you understand?'

'Yes,' Shaw said curtly. 'I don't need a solicitor because I've done nothing wrong.'

'OK, Mr Shaw, let's continue,' Brewster said. 'So, what exactly did Suzy Baros tell you about the Polish man?'

TWENTY-SEVEN

MICHAEL

When he came out of the police station, Kate was ringing him. He picked up.

'Michael, what's happening? You've been gone ages, I've been—'

'It was terrible, Kate. I thought they were going to arrest me there and then. They're convinced I've got something to do with Suzy's disappearance ... and Jakub's too. I don't think it'll be long. They said they might call me back in later today.'

'What? Hang on, I thought it was just a few questions.'

'Their attitude changed once they'd got me there. They interviewed me under caution.'

'They tricked you! Can't you—'

'I love you, I hope you know that,' he said, the words cracking as he spoke them. 'I love you, and I love our daughter more than the world. You have to believe it.'

'Of course I believe it!' He heard her voice rise as she started to panic. 'Michael, what's happening?'

There were a few beats of tense silence before he said, 'I never meant for this to happen. For things to get out of hand like this.'

'Michael, what are you saying?'

He couldn't speak for fear of blurting out the terrible truth.

'Are you coming home?' Her voice sounded high and tight like something was about to snap. 'Leave your car there and I'll pick you up. Just tell me where to come.'

'I'm OK, Kate. I need some time. I'm going for a walk and I'll be home soon. Remember what I said. I love you both. No matter what.'

He turned off his phone, desperate for time to think. He couldn't go straight home, because the walls felt like they were closing in on him. Being under suspicion for Suzy Baros's disappearance was bad enough, but Jakub Jasinski ... If they found out what had happened, revealed his lies, it would be curtains. And if they went out snooping around on the land, they *would* find out. They'd know everything. How could he have believed he could get away with it? He felt trapped. There was surely no escape now.

He walked up the road to a small row of shops and stood there by a regal oak tree that must have been over a hundred years old. The shame of everything coming to light would finish Kate. If suspicion fell on her it would be disastrous. At the very least they'd have to move out of the village. Tansy would lose her little friends. And all of it would be his fault. He dropped his head and pinched the top of his nose. The thoughts swirled around in his head. What to do, what to do ...

His body jolted, his eyes blurring and his head filling with noise that made no sense. He lost his balance and stumbled out into the road, arms flailing, and the lorry he'd seen approaching at speed from the bottom of the road was on top of him before he could blink. An enormous red vehicle with a matt-black grille and two sets of chrome headlights that momentarily blinded him. There was no chance of escape, no way of minimising the impact. Just the relentless blast of a deafeningly loud horn as his head exploded into a myriad of bright lights and he flew gracefully into the air before hitting the cold asphalt with a heavy, blunt thud.

Time slowed. Michael's snapped bones folded beneath him as

if they were made of cardboard. Acute pain sparked in every millimetre of his body before a wave of numbness followed, enveloping him like an icy sleeve. His eyes flickered open as the driver jumped out of his cab, his face a pale mask of horror peering down at Michael from above.

So this was what dying felt like. This was what it must have felt like for …

The words were an electric shock that crackled through his mind, leaving silence and darkness in their wake.

Other motorists and passengers stopped to offer help. Someone barked, 'The ambulance is on its way.'

Memories flashed before him like the last few seconds of a firework display, so colourful and real. His mother's face as a young woman, the school yard where he'd broken his leg as a ten-year-old. His beautiful daughter. For a glorious moment, Tansy was right there with him, hovering above him, reaching out. Then just as quickly she was gone again and his fingers fluttered into the cold, thin air.

Kate would be waiting at home for his return. He could picture her now at the window, staring fearfully and hopefully towards the road. The first time he'd seen her, she'd been just seventeen years old with no idea of her own beauty. Standing outside the college waiting for the bus. Slender and tall, with long raven hair that almost reached her waist. A sleek mane that shone blue-black in the sun like a rich ebony curtain.

He'd attended college one day a week as part of his job training up at Wadebridge. The course had been useful to him but the real win had been in meeting Kate.

His mind wandered back to the village. To the Wadebridge cottages. *Oh dear God. No.* How long would it be before they found out? Before the shadow he'd fought to contain finally revealed itself?

'I'm so sorry, Kate,' he whispered out loud. 'I never wanted it to come to this.'

The truck driver bent closer, cupping his hand to an ear. 'What did you say?'

Michael closed his eyes, his mind clogging with the urge to tell his grisly secret. He'd battled hard against it, but now it would finish him, and Kate would have to deal with the aftermath. Tansy would grow up with the taunts of others ringing in her ears.

The final dregs of life began to drain away like the last trickle of light before dusk turned to nightfall, He felt glad of it, did not want to live any more. He did not want to witness what came next.

He had been forced to live with both sides tangled together inside him. There was no space in this world for good and bad existing together. People couldn't cope with it. You were a good person or you were a bad person. Period. People liked to know exactly who they were dealing with.

He could hear the sirens now, but they were faint.

He became aware that there was a small circle of people standing around him, looking down. The faces drew closer and then faded out again, like someone twisting a telescope in front of his eyes. He heard someone say, 'Is he conscious?'

Don't go out there, he told Kate silently as a thick, velvety silence floated down on him like a final curtain. *Forgive me. Look after our girl.*

Then Michael Shaw closed his eyes. Soon, all that would be left of him in this world was that hidden, shameful part of him his beloved wife would soon discover.

TWENTY-EIGHT

KATE

Michael had sounded strange on the phone. His thoughts and words had been fractured and not like him. It was obvious the police interview had not gone well. I wanted him home so I could make sure he was OK.

I called him again, but his phone was turned off. He'd said he was going for a walk, so it could be poor signal. I left a message.

'It's me again ... Is everything all right? Let me know if you want picking up. Come home and we'll talk.'

Tansy looked up with a faint frown from where she and Aleks had set up a toys' picnic. 'Where's Daddy?'

'He's just popped to the shop. He'll be back soon, sweetie.'

She returned to her picnic, clearly satisfied that all was well, but Aleks did not look away from me. He fixed me with those dark, knowing eyes and did not return the weak smile I gave him.

Michael had been gone ages now. Too long. Something must have delayed him, something beyond his control. I willed my phone to ring. Imagined him cursing under his breath and saying, 'Don't worry. I'm only five minutes away from home.'

But the phone didn't ring, and the churning in my stomach intensified.

Up until the last couple of weeks, our life had been uncomplicated. Some might say predictable. But I'd always liked the routine, the certainty of what would come next. I still found it reassuring after my turbulent years with Mum.

Silly things made me feel good. Waking at six o'clock to tea that Michael had made me before leaving the house for work. Tansy's school routine. The chats with the same people at the school gate. Knowing each and every face I passed as I walked through the village. Being part of the school staff; the library there. Walking over to visit Irene, my heart still fluttering after fifteen years of marriage when I caught sight of Michael working outside, in his element. Meeting Donna for a coffee for our Friday morning round-up of the week. Before things had changed, I'd loved it all.

And now it had been more than an hour since I'd spoken to Michael, and he still wasn't home. Something wasn't right. I felt sure of it.

I rang the police station.

'Hi, my husband, Michael Shaw, has been talking to detectives at the station. Can you tell me if everything was OK when he came out?'

'Hold on, please,' the woman said officiously and I heard papers being shuffled. 'Michael Shaw has left the station now.'

'Yes, I know that. He called me, but he sounded strange. That was over an hour ago and he's still not home.'

'Sorry, all I can tell you is that he's left the premises.'

Useless! They were so bound up in their silly rules, they didn't care about people's well-being. I ended the call, steeped in fury.

Tansy appeared in front of me, arms folded, a concerned expression pasted on her face. 'Mummy, is it time for my bath yet? When will Daddy be home?'

Michael always made an effort to make Tansy's bath time great fun. I'd smile at the howls of laughter that reached me downstairs as they flicked water at each other or made bubble cocktails together using brightly coloured plastic cups.

'We might have to skip your bath tonight, sweetie. Daddy's going to be back a bit later now.'

Aleks watched us, saying nothing. It would be less worrying if he was crying or demanding to know if his mum had been found. His skin looked dull, and he had no energy about him. Maybe Michael had been right and he would have been better off with a foster family, people who hadn't got all this stuff going on.

That set off the recurring thought: where *was* his mother? There were lots of questions being asked and the police seemed particularly interested in Michael. But what progress were they making? I had an uncomfortable feeling that the investigation was fairly static at the moment and he was their only suspect.

Tansy regarded me suspiciously. 'Why is Daddy so late?'

'He's been delayed. Listen, why don't you and Aleks pop up and get your pyjamas on, then we can all read a nice story together. How's that?'

I was surprised when Tansy nodded, placated by the offer.

'Is that OK with you, Aleks?' He looked blankly at me. 'Pyjamas and story time?'

'I want my mum,' he said, so faintly I could barely hear him.

I moved closer to him and squeezed his hand. 'I know you do and I know it's really, really hard right now but we're going to get through this together. We will.'

His soulful dark eyes met mine for a moment before he pulled away and followed Tansy upstairs.

When I heard them padding about in the bedrooms, I picked up my phone and googled local traffic news to see if there had been any major accidents between the police station and here. Nothing. I put down the phone and sat on the sofa in the kitchen. The log burner was down to its last smouldering embers, but I felt too distracted to tackle it. I closed my eyes briefly, willing the back door to fly open and Michael to stomp inside, complaining how long the journey had taken him. But the kitchen remained eerily silent.

After a while, Tansy and Aleks returned, dressed for bed. Tansy was clutching Barnaby Bear. Aleks had his own teddy bear and pyjamas after the police had allowed Michael to go in and get some of his stuff from the cottage.

Tansy held up a book. 'I want *The Magic Porridge Pot* tonight,' she said, a touch grumpily. 'It's Daddy's favourite and he always puts on a funny voice when he says: "Stop, little pot, stop."'

'Right.' I nodded. 'Well, I'll try my very best to fill Daddy's story shoes. Let's all sit on the sofa, shall we? Come on, Aleks, you too.'

I tossed another log on the fire and the three of us curled up together with the book. I'd just opened it when the doorbell rang. I jumped like I'd been prodded with a live wire. The kitchen was at the back of the house, so I couldn't see who the caller was from here.

'Is it Daddy?' Tansy rushed out into the hallway, leaving Aleks on the sofa. But I knew it wasn't Michael because he'd have used his keys.

'Tansy, come back here. Let me go, please,' I called out. She stopped in her tracks and turned around, startled by my sharp manner. I couldn't help it. I was full of dread and I didn't want her to hear anything she shouldn't. 'Sit back down next to Aleks, there's a good girl. I'll be back in two minutes.'

I shut the kitchen door behind me and walked briskly to the front door just as the bell rang again.

Calm down. Breathe.

It could be something simple, like Michael had lost his phone and had sent someone to let me know he'd been delayed. That theory exploded when I looked through the peephole and saw the two detectives standing there. DI Price and DS Brewster. A tall woman with short black hair and black-rimmed glasses stood behind them. A hard knot popped into my throat. I opened the door.

'Hello, Mrs Shaw, may we come in?' Price said, her voice clear and calm. She indicated the others. 'You know DS Brewster and this is a family liaison officer, PC—'

'Has ... has something happened? My husband, he ...'

'We'll need to step inside, if that's all right, Mrs Shaw,' Brewster said quietly.

'I ... The kids are ...' The words faded away and I found I couldn't speak at all. My breath felt ragged and insubstantial.

'Mummy, who is it?' Tansy's voice called out nervously behind me. 'Is it the police?' I spun around, my eyes darting to her pale little face and Aleks standing beside her, silent and wide-eyed.

I stepped back so the officers could come in, and crouched down, placing my hands on my daughter's shoulders. 'Listen to me, sweetie. I need you and Aleks to go upstairs to your bedroom and put the television on. Keep the door closed until I call for you, OK?'

She stared in awe at the police officers. DI Price smiled and wiggled her fingers at her. Tansy didn't wave back. 'I want Daddy,' she said, her bottom lip trembling.

'Have they found my mum?' Aleks whispered.

'Not yet, Aleks,' Price said kindly. 'But we're still doing our best to look for her.'

'Aleks's mummy is missing and now Daddy's gone too,' Tansy wailed.

I stood up and spoke in a firm but kind voice. 'Tansy, I need you to be a brave girl so Mummy can get this sorted out. Go to your room with Aleks, please. The quicker Mummy can speak to the police officers, the quicker we can find out where Daddy and Aleks's mum are. Yes?'

Tansy gave a single, unconvinced nod and reluctantly headed for the stairs, Aleks trailing behind.

I looked at the officers. 'Please.' I indicated the living room door. 'Let's go in here and sit down.' I waited until I'd heard Tansy's bedroom close before joining them.

'What's happened?' I demanded, the words nearly choking me. 'Is this about Michael?'

'I'm afraid your husband has been involved in a road traffic accident, Mrs Shaw,' Price said softly, her eyes dropping to her hands.

'Oh no, but I checked if there had been any accidents. Is he ... is Michael OK?'

She only hesitated for a second or two, but it was enough to warn me there was bad news coming. I heard the television blaring music upstairs, the kids' feet stomping through the ceiling.

'I'm so sorry to have to tell you that Michael was hit by an articulated lorry just over an hour ago on Oxclose Lane,' she said carefully. 'Paramedics attended the scene and tried their best to save him, but sadly he passed away in the ambulance on the way to the hospital.'

TWENTY-NINE

My wails filled the kitchen, cracking through the stagnant air like a whip. I bit down on my tongue, remembering the kids upstairs. The FLO rushed past me, returning with a glass of water.

'My daughter ... I don't want her to hear this,' I said. 'Not yet.'

'Take a few sips.' The FLO handed me the water. 'Try to breathe. Slowly, in and out. That's better.'

'What happened?' I whispered, gripping the glass. 'I mean, how did it happen?'

Price said, 'The local Roads Policing Unit together with the Collision Investigation Unit are gathering information. The lorry driver told officers Michael seemed to step out into the road, straight into his path.' She hesitated. 'If it's any comfort at all, officers at the scene believe it all happened very quickly. Your husband probably didn't have time to even register what was happening.'

Michael was gone. Snuffed out in the blink of an eye. 'The lorry driver, are they ...'

'The driver is badly shaken but unharmed,' Brewster confirmed.

'Yes, but ... you can't just take his word for it.' I imagined the lorry driver lying through his teeth, trying to worm his way out of trouble. 'What if he was looking at his phone? You hear about that all the time.'

'Rest assured we don't take anyone's word, Mrs Shaw,' Helena said quietly. 'Among other checks, the other driver's mobile phone and other electronic devices will be screened to make sure they weren't in use at the time of the accident.'

'In addition to searching for any witnesses, measurements, photos and 3D images will be taken,' Brewster added. 'The truck will be fully examined for mechanical defects or other evidence that may confirm exactly what happened.'

If Michael had stepped into the path of a lorry, then it followed that it couldn't be the driver's fault. But why was he so distracted? I thought about his agitation in the garden, how I'd challenged him for lying about not knowing Jakub Jasinski.

'What did you say to him at the police station?' I asked accusingly. 'He sounded troubled when he called me afterwards.'

'He certainly left there with some things to think about,' Price said.

'Like what?'

'Now's not the time to discuss that, Mrs Shaw,' Brewster said gently. 'The dreadful news we've had to impart is enough for you to take in.'

'Where is he? Can I see him?'

'The hospital will be contacting you shortly when they're ready for you,' he said diplomatically. I knew exactly what he meant. Michael's body would be a mess. I shuddered at the horror of it.

Price cleared her throat. 'I'm so sorry to have to share these distressing details, Mrs Shaw, but you will need to contact a funeral home, who will collect your husband's body from the hospital after the ... the post-mortem, and they'll take him into their care.'

I buried my head in my hands. I couldn't get Michael's face out of my mind. I kept thinking what they'd said about the accident. The lorry driver had said it looked as though he'd just stepped out into the road. I knew he was worried, but ... The walls pressed in closer, the room seeming to spin. Why hadn't I seen the warning signs?

'Mrs Shaw?' Price's voice was kind. 'Is there someone we can call? Someone who can come over and sit with you for a while? It's such a terrible shock and I know you have your daughter to think about.' She glanced back towards the hallway, and the stairs beyond.

'I just ... I need some time to process what's happened.'

'Of course.'

I stared into space, my fingernails digging into the arm of the sofa. Michael must have been so tired he'd become unable to focus. Was that why his concentration had lapsed in that crucial moment? Or was it worry? I'd probably never know for sure.

'Is there anything else we can do for you, Mrs Shaw?' the FLO asked as they all stood up. 'I could make you a cup of tea before we go?'

'No. Thank you, but I can do that.' I looked around helplessly.

Price handed me a card. 'Please don't hesitate to contact us if you need anything at all,' she said. 'We'll be in touch as soon as we know more.'

A few moments after the front door closed, two small figures clad in colourful pyjamas appeared.

'Come over here.' I held out an arm and Tansy ran to me. It was all I could do to stop myself from choking. Aleks followed her, but lingered by the arm of the sofa.

'Where's Daddy?' Tansy said, nestling into my side. 'What did the police lady say? What's wrong with your eyes?'

'We're trying to find out exactly what's happened.' I tried to smile.

'Has he gone missing, like my mummy?' Aleks's words hovered above us all like small storm clouds.

Tansy began to whimper. 'Daddy's not missing too, is he? When will he be back?'

'Shh, come on now, let's not start talking like that.' My voice was going to crack at any moment. I was desperately trying to keep it together.

Tansy looked up at me. 'Why did the police come?'

'They had to speak to Mummy about something.'

Her fingers twisted together. 'About Daddy?'

'That's right.' I struggled to keep my voice level. 'We're just trying to find out where he is.'

'Ring his phone!' Tansy said hopefully, sitting bolt upright. 'If you ring him, you can ask Daddy when he's coming home.'

'Come on now.' I shuffled to the edge of the sofa, knowing that if I tried to stand up, my legs would fail me. 'Can you be a really big girl and go back up to your bedroom with Aleks? I'll be up soon to read you both a story.'

Tansy screwed up her face and rubbed her eyes. 'Can't I stay down here with you?'

'It's just ... Mummy has a headache, and I need a few minutes to think about what the police officers said.'

'Why do you need to think about it?'

'Well, because they said lots of things and I'm trying to remember them all.'

'Hurry up and remember, Mummy,' she whined as she stood up reluctantly. 'I want to find out where Daddy has gone.'

'It's OK, Tansy, the police will find your dad and my mum too,' Aleks said kindly, and I wanted to pull them both to me and cry into their soft hair.

What should a good parent do at a time like this? We didn't know where Aleks's mum was yet, but I was essentially lying to Tansy, pretending Michael was still OK, still out there somewhere. Yet to tell her the awful truth ... it felt beyond me. And Aleks being here and listening to everything I said when his mum was already missing ... It was a nightmare. It had to be done in the proper manner, when I felt calm and resolved. It had to be done in a way that was the least traumatic for our daughter.

Tansy loitered around the door, sulkily rubbing at a mark on the wall.

My right foot began tapping the floor. I couldn't seem to make it stop.

Michael's face kept flashing into my mind and disappearing again. There was a tide of emotion pushing to escape from my chest, but I couldn't let that happen, not while the children were here. I craved space. To release this spiralling grief before it choked me.

'Up you go, there's a good girl,' I said, as firmly as I could manage. She glared at me and stormed out into the hall. I heard her stomping up the steps in protest, Aleks trailing in her wake. 'I'll be up very soon,' I called out guiltily.

My heart ached and my head pounded as I thought about how I was going to tell Tansy that her daddy wouldn't be coming home. I sat staring into space for a while, thoughts of the accident swirling in my mind. What if there was some connection between Michael's death and Suzy's disappearance? What if Michael had killed himself because he'd done something terrible and couldn't face us?

I dropped my head into my hands. The house already felt so empty without him. I glanced over at the painting Tansy had done for him at school only last week. It showed Michael at work on his red ride-on mower. The sun was shining, and there were lots of colourful flowers and even the row of Wadebridge cottages behind him.

'This is my favourite one yet, Tansy Pansy!' he'd announced, and her face had split into a neon-bright smile at the in-joke. Every piece of art she brought home was Michael's new favourite. 'This little masterpiece is going on the fridge door.'

I looked around the kitchen. Traces of him were everywhere. His canvas work jacket hanging over the back of a chair, his steel-toed work boots with trailing laces by the back door, and his reading glasses on the table next to the newspaper. His half-empty coffee cup still sat next to the sink. I traced my finger around the edge and touched it to my lips.

I heard Tansy's television come on upstairs. She must have turned it up to full volume in protest, as I could hear the cartoon voices loud and clear. I couldn't stop my hands from shaking. I felt cold to my bones. I stood up and walked towards the log burner, my head full of one endlessly repeating thought:

How on earth was I was going to manage without my Michael?

THIRTY

I didn't feel up to looking after Tansy and Aleks. I just wanted to curl up in a ball somewhere dark and quiet. I knew I had to call Donna. I had nobody else.

I picked up my phone, and for a moment I couldn't remember what I needed to do. I opened up my call list and jabbed a finger on a contact. Donna picked up after two rings.

'Hi, Kate, can I call you back? I've just put Paul's tea on and—'

'Michael's gone,' I whispered. 'He's dead, Donna.'

'*What?*'

'He went out and ... and ... A lorry ... The police came here to tell me. He's dead.'

'My God, no!' She fell silent for a few seconds, and then she called out to Paul, 'I've got to go, can you come in here, babe?' She muffled the phone and I heard her speaking urgently in a low voice. 'OK, Kate, I'm on my way. I'll be at yours in five minutes. Get the kids' stuff together. They can have a sleepover with Ellie tonight.'

She ended the call and I sat staring at the wall. I felt numb. Spaced out.

'Mummy!' Tansy yelled from the top of the stairs. 'When are you coming up?'

'I'm coming up now,' I mumbled under my breath. Michael was going to come home and read them both a story. He'd put them to bed and then come downstairs and pour us some wine. We'd talk about the police interview and he'd tell me everything would be fine, and I'd say I was sorry for thinking the worst and …

Someone was shaking me. 'Mummy, Mummy! What's wrong? Why are you talking to yourself?' I refocused, saw Tansy's tearful eyes and worried expression.

'It's OK, darling, you and Aleks get your coats and shoes on. You're going to stay at Ellie's house tonight.'

'What?' She punched her hands to her hips. 'We're already ready for bed!'

'Can I go back to the cottage?' Aleks said hopefully.

'No. No,' I said vaguely. 'Get ready.'

'What's wrong with your mum?' I heard him whisper.

'Grab your coat, Tansy,' I said, pulling myself together. 'Aleks, you too. Put them on over your pyjamas. It will be fun.'

'It won't be fun because Ellie doesn't like Aleks,' Tansy said crossly, folding her arms. 'She might not let him play in her bedroom with us.'

There was a knock on the door and Donna walked in. She headed straight for me and embraced me. It took every ounce of my resolve not to collapse sobbing into her.

'The kids don't know yet,' I whispered into her ear.

'OK, kids, grab your stuff. I'm taking you to my house and then I'm coming back to look after your mum, Tansy. She's not feeling too well.'

'Donna, please. I don't want to ruin your night, there's no need to come back.'

'I'm coming right back here,' she said firmly. 'Paul will sort the kids out.'

'I'll manage, I'll …' I couldn't seem to focus, to finish my thoughts. Michael's face filled my mind in technicolour.

I grabbed on to a chair and squeezed my eyes closed.

'Mummy?' Tansy ran over and pressed into my side. 'I want to stay here and look after you.'

'Just go with Donna for tonight, sweetie. I feel ... very tired and a bit sick. Can you do that for me?'

She nodded slowly, her eyes flitting across my face, looking for clues that everything was still OK.

'I will stay here,' Aleks said slowly. 'I don't want to go to Ellie's house.'

'Get your shoes on, please, Aleks,' Donna said briskly. 'Everything will be OK, I promise.'

I pushed a few things into a bag and kissed Tansy, and they left. When they'd gone, I sat down, feeling strangely devoid of emotion. It came and went like the tide.

It only seemed like minutes before Donna was back again, but when I checked the wall clock, I saw that over half an hour had passed.

'The kids are fine. Paul just got back but he knows what he needs to do to get them into bed. Tell me everything.' She sat down next to me and held my hand.

Carefully I relayed the facts. It was important to me that she knew everything, and it was a relief to speak openly, without worrying about the children overhearing.

'Michael had been at the police station. They'd asked to speak to him again and he said it would be best to go in to show willing. When he came out, I phoned him, asked him how things had gone. He seemed ... a bit down. He didn't want to talk about it and said he wanted a walk before he came back home and we'd talk then.'

Donna gripped my hand.

'I knew something wasn't right when he hadn't come back home within an hour and hadn't texted me or called. I didn't know what to do, and then those two detectives came. They said he was hit by a lorry and ...' I looked down at my hands. They were shaking, and I tucked them under my thighs. 'They tried to save him, the paramedics, but he died. In the ambulance. On the way to the hospital.'

'Oh Kate. I'm so, so sorry,' she said softly.

I could see the scene playing out in front of me as if I'd witnessed it with my own eyes. Michael flying up into the air, blood and brains on the grille of the lorry. His lifeless eyes staring out into the sterile emptiness of the ambulance ...

'All I keep thinking is how I'm going to tell Tansy he's gone,' I said.

Donna embraced me, held me tight. 'Don't torture yourself about that. She doesn't need to know this very minute.'

I pulled away. I couldn't bear the closeness. I wanted to get Tansy back and run away from it all.

Donna sat back. 'The police ... did they say it was the lorry driver's fault? Was he looking at his phone perhaps and didn't see Michael?'

I stared ahead, glassy-eyed. 'They said the other driver told them it looked like Michael just stepped out into the road.'

A moment of silence. Then Donna said, 'He didn't see the lorry coming? That seems unlikely. Are they looking into exactly what happened?'

I closed my eyes and imagined for a moment that Michael hadn't gone out. That Suzy hadn't gone missing and there had been no police interview. He would still be alive. He'd come up behind me, wrap his big, strong arms around me without a word and kiss my neck. I could almost feel the goosebumps now, as if he were pressing against me.

'Kate!' Donna gripped my arm hard, shaking me. I snatched it away and rubbed it. 'Sorry, but ... you scared me.' Her voice softened. 'I'm going to call the doctor, OK?'

I didn't answer, because I didn't care.

Dr Kendall lived in the big white house at the top end of the village. His old-fashioned surgery was an extension at the back of the house. Michael used to joke that it was the last place on earth you could still get an emergency appointment with a GP without wrestling with some awkward receptionist. I stared into space, listening as Donna spoke confidentially into her phone, as if she didn't want me to hear.

'That's right, he died in the ambulance and she's … she's acting strangely. Just not like the Kate we all know. She seems absent. She's not making much sense. I think she might be in shock. I wondered if … Oh, yes, thank you. I'll look out for you.' She ended the call.

I folded my hands into my lap and looked at her blankly. 'How am I going to tell Tansy she's never going to see her daddy again?' I said.

THIRTY-ONE

15 NOVEMBER 2019

The three days after Michael's accident, it felt as if my life had been torn to shreds. I'd been thrown into a new world of inquests and police investigations. Endless phone calls, emails, informing me, guiding me through the nightmare that was Michael's death, on top of the shock and trying to come to terms with the fact that he'd gone. That we would never see him again.

Legally, someone had to identify Michael's body soon after the accident. I loved him so much, I wanted to be the one to do it, but I'd felt massive resistance inside. What would he look like following the accident? I was terrified that would be my final memory of him.

'Paul will go,' Donna said firmly when I confided in her. 'He's done it before for his uncle and he's already told me: anything you need, you've only to let him know.'

Even amid the slight haze of Dr Kendall's medication, I felt relief and gratitude. The police had located Michael's car parked on Beckhampton Road, close to the station. Paul had collected it using the spare keys and put it in our garage.

In Suzy's absence, Irene had been forced to get a new home help. As luck would have it, a local lady I knew vaguely, Doris, was looking for work. Irene's sciatica seemed worse than ever, but for about a week, I couldn't bring myself to visit her. Wadebridge had so many memories for me, I honestly thought it would tip me over the edge if I went up there. She sent an enormous bouquet with a lovely message of sympathy. I knew she'd miss Michael terribly. He'd taken care of everything at Wadebridge since Amos had died. I didn't know how she'd manage to replace him.

Tansy and Aleks stayed with Donna, Paul and Ellie for the first few days and I still hadn't told Tansy her daddy had gone.

Donna and Paul were doing such a great job, filling the kids' time with activities, crafts and the Disney Channel. Tansy was upbeat, and although she asked about Michael, she was full of Ellie's new Barbie motorhome, and their visit to Water Meadows, a local indoor water park. Donna had a chat to Ellie and now she and Aleks seemed to be getting on fine, which was a relief. I worried about them missing school but Donna was adamant it was only three days and the best temporary solution under very difficult circumstances and that she would speak to the head teacher.

I went over to the house a few times, and on Friday afternoon I took Tansy out for a walk into the woods we loved so much.

'Let's stop for a moment,' I said when we reached a bench about halfway through the wood. 'It's lovely here. What can you hear?'

It was a game we often played, where we'd close our eyes and take turns naming a sound: a bird singing, the rustle of leaves, the sound of the distant passing traffic. Tansy closed her eyes and lifted her face to the sky. 'I can hear ... a mouse running in the hedgerow,' she said, smiling to herself.

'What else?'

'I can hear ... the trees whispering to each other and a fairy singing under a toadstool. And I can hear Daddy on his mower up at Wadebridge.' She opened her eyes and the smile evaporated. '*Is* Daddy up at Wadebridge?'

I reached for her hand. 'Remember when we were waiting for Daddy to come home and the police came to the house?' She nodded fearfully. 'The reason Daddy hasn't come home is because he was in an accident that day.'

'An accident?'

'Yes. Daddy was crossing the road and a lorry hit him. And … it's very sad, because Daddy died.' She stared at me so steadily I felt unnerved. I wondered if she'd understood what I was trying to tell her. 'So you see, darling, Daddy won't be coming home again. He's gone to heaven now.'

'Daddy has died?'

I held both her hands. 'I'm so sorry, Tansy, but yes, Daddy has died and somehow, you and me, we've got to carry on without him.'

She looked away, stared into the trees. There were no tears.

Silently I led her to the tinkling stream that flowed through the wood. She and Michael would launch flowers into it, then run to the end to see whose flower had won the race.

'Pick a flower for Daddy,' I told her, 'and set it free in the stream like he loved to do.'

She bent down and plucked a vibrant red campion, before crouching down and cradling the flower in her palm. I gazed at the crown of her golden hair, the smooth purity of the back of her neck. She kissed the flower. 'Love you forever, Daddy,' she whispered. Then she lowered her hand into the water and let the current take it. 'I miss you so much, Daddy. I hope you can see me up there in heaven.'

I bit back tears. 'I'm so proud of you. Your daddy will always be with us, looking down, watching and keeping us safe.'

Her bottom lip trembled, and finally the tears began to roll silently down her cheeks. 'Has Aleks's mum died too?' she said.

That weekend, Miss Monsall, Tansy's class teacher, paid me a visit at home.

'This is a life-changing time for you and Tansy,' she said softly, after giving me her sincerest condolences. 'It's so important that we, as her school, get it right in order to minimise the stress and upheaval for both of you.'

I nodded. Tansy's education was one of the thousand worry strands swirling slowly around in my head like seaweed. 'What do you suggest?' I asked.

'There are really no hard-and-fast rules because every child is different. Saying that, in our opinion it's best to get Tansy back to school as soon as possible.'

'It feels too soon,' I said quickly, a wash of dread travelling through me at the thought of Tansy crying alone at break time.

'I understand. But school is familiar to her and could have a stabilising effect at a time like this. We think she may find comfort in routine. It might help her realise that some things remain the same, even when so much around her is changing.'

'What about Aleks?' I said, shocked that I'd forgotten him for a moment.

She held up a hand. 'Please don't worry about Aleks. The head teacher is speaking to social services. You looking after him was only ever a temporary situation, as I understand it, and there are decisions to be made. It's Tansy we need to talk about today.'

I sighed. 'What you say makes sense, but … I don't know. It feels cruel to send her back so soon.'

'Of course. But when so much is happening at home, school can give respite to a child.' She pressed her lips together in a sympathetic smile. 'Look, Kate, you know your daughter better than anyone, I get that, but Tansy enjoys school, and it strikes me that she might appreciate having her friends around her. We'd offer her full support, of course, and she'd have access to the school counsellor as well as a break-out room where she can go for space and quiet time if it all gets a bit much.'

'I can't bear to think of her having to put on a brave face just to get through the day,' I said, my voice cracking. 'I know it's not the right solution, but I just want to keep her here, for us to hide and make the outside world go away.' I covered my eyes with a hand

and rubbed the bridge of my nose hard. I could feel the pain slicing away at me, raw and relentless.

'That reaction is completely understandable,' Miss Monsall said kindly. 'But in terms of what's best for Tansy, getting her back to a routine where she's fully supported and among her friends and school family is crucial.'

'But ... kids can be cruel, can't they? What if—'

'We have systems in place for these very challenging events in our pupils' lives, Kate. It's also an opportunity for the other children to learn empathy and how to relate to a classmate who is grieving. Rest assured we'll handle all that.'

'I ... I know you're right. It's just hard.'

'I know that. It must feel like the hardest thing in the world.' She stood up. 'I'll leave you in peace now. Just think about it, and have a little chat with Tansy if it helps, although children don't always know what's best for them and she may even feel guilty about leaving you at home alone. But you decide and then let me know.' She placed a small card on the table. 'That's my personal mobile number. Feel free to call me if I can help in any way.'

I walked her to the door, and when she was gone, I sank to the floor and sobbed, because I knew that what she'd suggested was the best thing for Tansy and the worst thing for me. And I hated myself for even having that selfish thought.

Donna and Paul were my lifeline. Paul cancelled a weekend work conference and stayed at home to look after the girls while Donna and I chatted at my house. I felt so awful for the things I'd said to her about him.

We talked about Michael. She made me endless cups of tea and sat and listened so patiently while I offloaded all my feelings, my worries and troubles.

Then, when Tansy came back home, Donna and Paul kept Aleks at their house and arranged a meeting with social services there.

On Saturday night, Donna popped over to see me again. She told me gently, 'Social services have found temporary foster care for Aleks.'

'Oh no, the poor kid.' I closed my eyes. 'I wanted to spare him that. Couldn't we manage between us?'

She shook her head. 'Like they said, with everything that's happening here, he's not getting the specialist care and attention he deserves. You and I, we need to be able to focus on Ellie and Tansy's well-being. We're just not trained to help Aleks in the way he needs while his mum is missing.'

I hung my head. I knew on one level that it made sense, but I also knew this was going to be so stressful for Aleks. It was exactly the situation I'd tried to save him from. Michael's voice echoed in my head. He'd said it wasn't right, but I'd gone my own sweet way, wanting to help and probably making things worse.

'He's in good hands,' Donna continued. 'DI Price is personally overseeing his temporary foster care.'

'He's suffered so much,' I said sadly. 'I wish there was something I could do to help.'

'You mustn't feel guilty, Kate. Social services wouldn't let you keep him right now anyway. He's traumatised already, and this latest sad news is too much for him. He needs stability. I really do think it's for the best.' She stood up and embraced me before walking towards the door. 'I'll get off now. Try and get some rest and I'll call you tomorrow.'

'Donna?' She looked back, her hand on the door handle. 'Thank you so much for everything you've done these past few days. Please thank Paul for me too. I don't know what I'd have done without the two of you.'

'You don't have to thank us. I know you'd have been there for me just the same if Ellie and I had needed help.'

I realised that her face looked strained, her eyes troubled. 'How are you coping with what's happening?' I asked. 'Suzy's disappearance, police all over the village ... I know it must be bringing it all back, how you suffered with Matilda.'

She tried to paste a brightness onto her face but her features crumpled slightly. 'Not great, if I'm honest. I'm jumpy, snappy with Paul and he's suffering too. Michael's death has really affected him. I can't sleep. It feels like my worst nightmare is taking hold of my life and ripping it to pieces, bit by bit. I'm just grateful Mum doesn't know what's happening.'

Donna's mother had advanced dementia and had been in a care home in a nearby town for the past three years. Her dad had died a few years after Matilda disappeared. 'From a broken heart,' her family had insisted when he suffered a massive heart attack close to Christmas. Donna visited her mum a couple of times a week, but she'd confided in me a few months ago that she'd started to dread it. 'Mum talks non-stop about Matilda, and it's getting worse,' she had told me. 'She's constantly asking when she's coming home from school. Other times she thinks I *am* Matilda.'

'I'm so sorry, Donna.' She was helping me so much and yet I couldn't do a thing to ease her burden. 'It must be heartbreaking to see your mum like that.'

'You have no idea,' she sighed. 'And on top of everything, I think Paul is messing around again.' The mask slipped and her eyes filled up. 'We were arguing and he told me he wants a divorce.'

Donna had found me the number of a reputable funeral director in the next town. I called them on Sunday morning, feeling vague and absent. It was a state they were obviously used to, as the woman on the end of the line guided me expertly through the procedure.

'We can take your husband from the hospital into our care,' she said, her voice quietly respectful. 'We can get him ready for you to visit in the chapel of rest.'

Get him ready. 'Yes.' I shuddered. 'Thank you.'

'If you want me to come with you to the chapel of rest, I will,' Donna offered when I called to tell her about my appointment.

'No. Thanks, Donna, but it feels like this is something I need to do on my own. It's hard to explain.'

A moment of silence on the end of the line then, 'No need. I understand. But just so you know, the offer is there. You're not alone, Kate, remember that. We will be strong for each other.'

I nodded and thanked her. 'I'm not much cop right now, but I'm here for you too,' I told her.

When the call ended, her words echoed in my ears. *You're not alone.* But my husband, my soulmate, was dead.

And that made me feel very alone indeed.

I arrived at the funeral home later that morning. A petite woman in her forties in a dark suit and crisp white blouse walked towards me from behind the reception area.

'Mrs Shaw? Welcome to Dignified Goodbyes.' She shook my hand, her soft brown eyes crinkling at the edges. 'My name is Marilyn and I'll be taking you through to see your loved one shortly. Can I get you a cup of tea, coffee ... or we have a water dispenser behind you, if you prefer?'

'I'm fine, thanks,' I said, my heart thudding so hard it was making me feel queasy.

'Then please, come this way.' She led me through the reception into a hushed carpeted corridor with dimmed lighting. Piped music played so quietly I couldn't identify a melody, just a discreet flurry of melancholy notes. Marilyn glided slightly ahead until we reached a polished mahogany door with a dull bronze sign that read *Chapel of Rest*.

She rested her fingers on the brass handle and turned to face me.

'Mrs Shaw, we at Dignified Goodbyes are so very sorry for your loss.' She lowered her eyes. It felt like a performance, but I appreciated the gesture. 'Please, take as long as you need. I'll see you back in reception, up the corridor to the right.'

I nodded, and she pressed down the handle and opened the door, moving back so I could enter the chapel.

I stepped inside and closed the door behind me. The room was cool, with upholstered chairs dotted around the walls. The windows were shallow and long and set horizontally around the top of the room in order to let in light but also afford complete privacy. To the far left was an alcove with the curtains pulled back to reveal Michael's body. I stood by the door, taking in the cream-coloured walls, the artificial plants, the low coffee table with leaflets bearing details of various funeral packages. I felt frozen. I just couldn't move.

I closed my eyes and took some controlled breaths, in and out, counting to five each time. My heart didn't slow its beat and I didn't feel any less sick. When I opened my eyes, my dead husband was still waiting for me in the alcove.

Robotically, I stepped forward ... one, two steps ... further into the room but facing the opposite wall, not the alcove.

Come on, I berated myself silently. *You have to do this. The longer you wait, the worse it will be.*

I slipped my handbag off my shoulder and placed it on one of the upholstered chairs. Then I turned to face the alcove, walking forward until I reached him.

It didn't look like Michael, lying there so cold and lifeless. His skin was dry and strangely creased, like parchment. His eyes were closed, his mouth very slightly open. They'd turned his head away from the room, buried it in white satin folds. The sheet covering him had been pulled up to his chin.

I didn't want to think about why there was so little of him on show.

'What happened, Michael?' My voice was barely more than a whisper, but it still sounded too loud in the hushed space. 'How could you not have seen the lorry coming?'

Was it possible he'd wanted to die because he'd done something awful, so awful he couldn't bring himself to admit it to me? I could never openly accept that because of Tansy. He'd thought the world of our daughter. He'd adored her, worshipped the ground she walked on. She couldn't have a future tainted by such a horrendous fact.

But what if he'd seen it as a way to protect her?

I shook my head to dispel the awful thoughts. Even if the police interview hadn't gone well, nobody threw themselves in the path of a truck because of that.

I looked at the soft sheen of the satin fabric next to his face. A face I hardly recognised. Whatever had made him Michael Shaw was no longer there. There was just a husk of who he used to be.

'Oh dear God, Michael,' I whispered. 'I can't believe you're gone.'

I reached out my hand to touch his face, and my fingers shrank back involuntarily.

I wanted to touch him ... but then I didn't want to touch him.

My body pulsed with emotions I could barely name. So many feelings knotted and tangled together. Sadness, anger, fear and shame.

Anger that he hadn't come straight home and talked to me about what the police had said.

Sadness that my daughter would grow up without her daddy to love and protect her.

A powerful mix of fear and shame that somehow awful secrets might come out and I'd be left to account for it all.

Back in the reception area, I was relieved to see there was nobody else there.

Marilyn immediately put down her paperwork and rushed forward.

'Is everything all right, Mrs Shaw? Can I get you a glass of water?'

'No,' I said. 'Thank you.' I felt desperate to get out of the place now. 'You said on the phone that there would be paperwork to sign?'

'Yes, of course, I have it here, ready for you.' She placed the documents in front of me, explaining the purpose of them, and I signed each one without taking in what it was for. 'Is that it?' I asked after the final one.

'That's it,' she confirmed. 'And now you can take this with you.' She held up a sealed plastic bag containing some items. There was a signed label on there. 'The hospital sent Michael's belongings.'

I took the opaque ziplock bag without looking at it.

'Thank you,' I said, walking to the door.

'Take care, Mrs Shaw,' she called after me. 'We'll be in touch regarding the other arrangements.'

They used a secret language here in this subterranean world of death that nobody wanted to experience but that we all had to face at some point. It was a language where words pertaining to death and loss could not be overtly voiced. There were 'arrangements' instead of a funeral, 'your loved one' instead of the body, 'at rest' instead of dead. I appreciated their consideration, but somehow it made the forbidden word 'death' loom even larger in my mind.

I stepped out into the street. People walked past oblivious, absorbed in their own thoughts, looking at their phones or talking to each other.

I wanted to scream at them that Michael was dead. I wanted them to hurt as much as I did. It felt like I was walking a tightrope, and it was only a matter of time before I came crashing down to hit rock bottom.

When I got back home, I walked in and stood for a few moments in this cool, quiet house that a few mornings ago had been a hive of activity. Michael searching for his car keys, the television on in the other room, me calling out to Tansy to hurry up or she'd be late for school. Now there was only a deathly silence, a reflection of the emptiness in my life.

I put the kettle on and grabbed my handbag, pulling out the plastic bag from the funeral director's containing Michael's things. I upended it on the table. His car and house keys fell out, his wallet, some loose change and his phone.

It was out of charge so while I made a drink, I plugged it into the charger we left on the kitchen worktop for convenience. I sat on a breakfast bar stool and waited until the Apple icon flashed on and the phone screen lit up with a miniscule charge on the battery. I left it plugged in and held it up until the face recognition function failed so I could tap in Michael's passcode. We knew each other's codes. They were the same … our wedding anniversary.

The phone vibrated indicating a passcode error so I tried again, tapping the digits in again, taking more care this time. It failed. Michael had changed his passcode without telling me the new one.

I shivered, goosebumps popping up all over my arms. It felt so significant that he would do this. I thought for a moment and realised the last time I'd accessed his phone was the day we went to the coast in the summer holidays. He'd hoisted Tansy up onto his shoulders and I'd wanted to take a picture with his phone. I'd tapped in the code and he'd laughed. 'You don't need to do that – the camera icon is on the lock screen.' But I'd done it anyway and the phone had opened.

Somewhere between the end of July and the day of his death, he'd seen fit to change it for reasons I can only think were suspicious. I tried his birth date, then Tansy's and, finally, my own but of course, none of them worked. If he'd so obviously wanted to keep me locked out, he'd hardly have used dates that were familiar to me.

I put the phone down and pressed the heels of my hands over my eyes. A level of knowing rose up steadily inside me like dirty floodwater. He'd been having an affair with Suzy Baros. It had to be that. Everything fit: the cosy chats, her 'helping' him with suppliers, his keys in her cottage, Irene saying she was 'sweet' on him. And now, the ten-year-strong passcode on his phone had been changed.

The stuff he'd said to the police raced through my head. The things he'd told them, the things he'd left out. And then something he'd said hit me straight between the eyes. Something he'd said to the police officers who carried out the door-to-door enquiries the morning after Suzy's disappearance. He'd told them he'd left the Christmas lights event early but called home first.

'I didn't know you'd come home before going up to Wadebridge,' I'd said. 'What tools had you left here?'

'I thought I'd left my blue toolbox in the porch, but I checked and it wasn't there,' Michael had said easily.

I rushed over to the sideboard and grabbed the family laptop, sitting on the sofa with it balanced on my knee. I opened up the Ring doorbell app and scanned down the video clips. Every time something activated the camera, usually one of us leaving or arriving home, a courier or the postman, the Ring camera captured a bit of live footage. You could have notifications every time it happened but I'd soon tired of that. It was amazing how many things set it off. A cat, a spider, a passing car.

I saw the camera grab memory was almost full but luckily there were around the last three weeks of captures still on there. I scrolled down until I found the correct date: Sunday, 10 November 2019.

I scrolled down to early evening and there we three were, leaving the house together for the Christmas lights event. I let out a small, plaintive cry for what we'd lost. Our little family decimated. I skipped through the next two activations: a leaflet drop and a dog sniffing at the end of our small front path. The next thing the camera had captured was me returning to the house with Tansy and Aleks, my face looking tired and drawn with concern. Finally, Michael returns at nearly midnight, scowling, his eyes hooded and dark.

He hadn't returned for the toolbox and looked inside the porch as he'd said. He'd lied to the police officers and he'd lied so convincingly to me, too.

I grabbed his car keys and went out to the garage. I snapped on the bright overhead lights that illuminated Michael's three-year-old black VW Golf. I unlocked it and opened the boot, pushing away a pile of blankets to reveal the blue metal toolbox I knew he kept in there.

It was the sort that opened out wide at the sides with a selection of segregated trays inside. I levered the double-hinged lid and pulled the sides out. The small top tray sections were filled with screws, nails, cable ties, that sort of thing. I lifted those trays out and saw that in the larger trays underneath, recognisable tools such as screwdrivers, pliers and small hammers were neatly lined up like soldiers. I kept going until I got to the bottom section of the toolbox where bulkier items were kept. I pulled out rags and a can of WD-40 and there, nestling in the corner, was a small silver phone.

My shaking fingers closed around it and I brought it out into the light. I recognised this phone. Small and silver with a peeling sticker on the back featuring a red heart and the words *Tęsknie za Tobą*.

This was Suzy Baros's phone.

I closed the boot, turned off the lights and took the phone back into the house. I sat back down on the sofa, my whole body shaking. The tremor in my hands was so bad I couldn't hold anything for a few moments.

I got up, poured a glass of water and sat back down, cradling it in my hands. I gulped down half of it and set it on the small side table.

I looked down at the Android phone on the cushion next to me. I could see a button on the top that I assumed turned it on. I pressed it and, as I'd expected, nothing happened. The device appeared to be out of charge. I took it over to the kitchen worktop but could instantly see the charging port was wider than the iPhone charger. Then I had a thought.

I ran upstairs to the bedroom and grabbed my Kindle charger from the bedside table. Back downstairs, I tried it on the phone and it was a match. I paced about waiting for it to gather enough charge to turn on.

I tried to organise my thoughts, tried to think of a single reason, a single excuse why my husband would have buried the phone of a missing woman in his toolbox and I came up with nothing. There was no reason at all apart from the obvious fact that he had done something very, very bad.

After about ten minutes I pressed and held the top button and the screen lit up. I had to battle the urge to throw up. I was expecting texts, maybe lurid, maybe angry, between Suzy and Michael.

Words appeared on the screen and I pressed the return key and a couple of arrows. But nothing would shift the phrase that read: *Factory reset complete.*

Someone had erased all the data from this phone.

I put the phone down again and stared into space.

I'd be the most naïve wife on earth if I continued with my assertion that he was the truthful, loyal man I'd loved for seventeen years. So what was I thinking, now? That Michael had had an affair with a woman who'd gone missing … or that Michael had been having an affair and was responsible for her disappearance?

Everything I now knew pointed to the second assumption. The evidence was overwhelming and yet part of me still railed against it. I feared the moment I believed the worst about Michael, I'd start to completely unravel.

My eyes focused on the colourful family portrait on the wall opposite. A big canvas print of the three of us last Christmas, a photo taken by Donna in front of the log fire when our two families enjoyed a meal out at a local pub. Michael's arm around me, his head inclined lovingly towards mine and Tansy standing in front of us both, her cheeks flushed with happiness. We looked so happy, a perfectly contented family. The way I wanted to remember us.

Fear trickled into my veins, lacing my blood with ice. I couldn't let that memory and others become forever tainted for my daughter. Who knew how it would affect her in the future, the way people regarded her, if her father was found to be a murderer?

Yet the only way I could protect her from that was to conceal the new evidence I'd uncovered and lie through my teeth to the two detectives.

It could only be one or the other.

THIRTY-THREE

18 NOVEMBER 2019

On Monday morning, Tansy was very quiet as I helped her get ready for school. As Miss Monsall had suggested, we'd had a chat last night when I'd put her to bed.

'I do want to see my other friends, Mummy,' she said sadly. 'I want to see Polly and Jasminder again. But I don't want to leave you on your own because you'll be sad now Daddy is dead.'

I tried not to flinch at her easy use of the word. 'Of course I'll be sad. You'll be sad too,' I said. 'But Daddy wouldn't want us to be like that, would he? What would he say?'

'Chop chop, off you go,' Tansy said miserably, quoting one of Michael's favourite sayings whenever something needed doing.

'That's exactly what he'd say.' I cuddled her close. 'And so that's exactly what we must do. Chop chop, off to school, and soon I'll go chop chop, off to work.'

That had seemed to satisfy her, but her mood was different this morning. As was mine. I was constantly having to push away the terrible thoughts about Michael and what he'd done with Suzy Baros in order to keep calm for Tansy.

'I feel like nobody will want to be my friend now,' she fretted as she squeezed toothpaste onto her brush.

'That's just not true, sweetheart,' I said gently. 'You've got Ellie and Aleks and lots of other friends in class.'

We'd telephoned Miss Monsall last night to tell her that Tansy would be coming into school on Monday morning. 'The whole class is looking forward to seeing you, Tansy,' she'd said. 'We've really missed you.'

Tansy had listened to her comments doubtfully. 'Who will I sit next to?' she asked.

'Exactly the same people you did before.' Miss Monsall had explained that she'd kept Tansy's chair vacant so there would be normality upon her return. 'Everyone knows you've had some very sad news.'

Tansy had looked unconvinced but stayed quiet.

'You're a really brave girl going back to school,' I said now, as she rinsed toothpaste from her mouth. 'Daddy would be so proud of you.' I made a point of mentioning Michael all the time at home. I wanted Tansy to feel the presence of her father in the house and know she could talk about him at any time.

'I'm a bit scared, Mummy,' she said in a small voice. 'But I do want to see my friends and Miss Monsall.'

'That's my girl.' I kissed the top of her head, then crouched down and gave her a tight hug. 'I'm sure once you get into class you'll feel happier being with your friends.'

She nodded and disappeared into her bedroom to get dressed.

I felt nervous on her behalf, but I was desperate for her to get some normality back. I had a lot of faith in Miss Monsall's ability to oversee her successful return to school.

I needed some normality back in my own life too, but that still seemed an awfully long way off.

We left the house wrapped up warmly in our woolly hats, gloves and scarves. We turned off the high street and set off walking up the slight hill. The school sat at the top, looking down. An old Victorian building with new UPVC windows and electric gates.

Soon I would have to think about coming back to work. I'd had a conversation with my supervisor, the senior teaching assistant, and she'd told me to take my time. But I was already craving some normality to at least try and keep my mind busy and away from melancholic thoughts about Michael.

Despite the gates being open, lots of parents and kids had congregated around the entrance instead of walking through to the classrooms. Two minutes before the bell, they'd start to gravitate there, but for now, there was the weekend to catch up on.

As we approached, I noticed a subtle muttering of conversations behind hands and a turning of heads to look our way.

I ignored the stares, but they puzzled me. A few people stepped forward as I walked through the throng to say how sorry they were about Michael. I thanked them and moved on before they could say anything else.

'Mummy, there's Ellie and Donna,' Tansy said. Her hand tightened in mine.

Ellie spotted Tansy too, and she immediately ran up, bless her heart, and took her hand. 'Come on, let's go and see the others.'

I breathed a sigh of relief. Donna said, 'Relax, Kate. Why don't you come back to the tea room with me and I'll make you a cuppa?'

I realised she probably wanted to talk about her own problems with Paul. But the tea room meant more people to face. More curious stares and mutterings and I had to avoid telling her what I'd found. It was too serious.

'I really need to get back home. There's still so much to sort out.' My heart thudded and my scalp felt hot and irritated under the woollen hat. I'd never had a panic attack, and this was nowhere near the one I'd seen Donna have when we were in an amusement arcade in Nottingham last year and she thought Ellie had gone missing. But I still felt anxious and stressed out. I wanted to get away.

'If you need me, I'm here, OK? We'll meet for coffee soon if you feel up to it.'

I nodded, not trusting myself to speak, and Donna went back

to the group of mums I'd been a core part of only days before. I looked over, and one or two raised a hand, but most didn't meet my eyes.

The atmosphere here felt very odd. I wasn't sure why. Maybe it was me who'd changed, who was perceiving people differently. Maybe people just had so much drama to talk about. Suzy Baros missing, Michael's death ... who knew?

As I neared the gates on my way out, a woman in her late forties approached me. She was plump, with a kind face and waist-length hair that she'd secured in a low ponytail. Then I caught sight of the child following her.

'Aleks!' I cried, and held out my arms to embrace him. He didn't react.

'He's not in a great place, I'm afraid,' the woman said, holding out her hand. 'I'm Janet Hanson, Aleks's foster carer.'

'Oh, hi. How is he?' Aleks was still hanging back. 'He looks like he's lost weight.'

'It's always a difficult time while they settle in somewhere new.'

Aleks glanced at me and looked away again. He blamed me for breaking my promise to look after him. I could feel it. Yet it was far worse than that because I now knew that Michael was responsible for taking his mother away.

'It's been such a terrible situation. We took Aleks in and then ... my husband died and—'

'Yes, the social worker said. I'm so sorry.' She patted Aleks on the head. 'My husband and I do a lot of work like this with the local authority. Short-term placements for children in difficult circumstances.'

I looked at him. 'Oh Aleks, I'm so sorry this has happened. We miss you.'

Still no reaction. I felt like such a witch. I had the power to put an end to this situation, to tell the police what I knew about my husband. If I did that, I'd be traumatising my own daughter. There were no winners here. Somebody had to lose.

'He'll come through,' Janet said. 'It just takes time.'

'Have they got any further in their investigation, do you know?' I asked.

She got what I meant. 'No. Apparently no new leads.' She glanced at Aleks and said, a little more upbeat, 'Hopefully, there'll be something soon.'

'Yes,' I said faintly. 'Let's hope so.' And then I turned and walked away before I burst into tears.

On the day of the funeral, the sky was overcast, but at least it was dry.

Downstairs in the hallway, there were some flowers, a few cards. I picked them up to see who they were from. Donna and Paul, Irene and a lovely hand-tied bouquet from school with a card from the children. I opened the cards. When I walked into the kitchen, Donna was making tea.

'Hey, everything OK?' she said, walking over to the fridge to return the milk. She looked pale and thinner than I'd seen her for a while. All this upset bringing what had happened to Matilda back with a vengeance and the ongoing problems with Paul would be taking its toll.

'Yes,' I said vaguely.

She stopped what she was doing and looked over at me. 'It's a very difficult day, I get that. But you look ... a bit strange. You've been strange for a while.'

'I'm ... struggling with stuff a bit.' I could feel the pressure bubbling up inside me. The need to speak to someone.

Astute as ever, Donna said, 'Is there anything you're not telling me?'

I hesitated and she was on me. 'What is it, Kate? I can tell there's something serious.'

'Michael told the police he called at home after leaving the Christmas event early to head to Wadebridge. There was some time not accounted for.'

'Yes?' she said faintly.

'I checked the Ring doorbell video and he didn't. He didn't call home first.'

Donna frowned. 'Why would he lie about that?'

'I don't know. And ...' I bit my lip. I couldn't tell her about finding Suzy's phone in his toolbox. I just couldn't.

'And?'

'The funeral home gave me his belongings. He'd changed the passcode on his phone.'

'Well, that doesn't mean anything in itself,' Donna said blithely. 'I don't know what Paul's is. Never have.'

'We kept the same one for ten years. Our wedding anniversary date.'

'Kate, listen. Don't beat yourself up about this stuff. Michael has gone, sadly, so you can't ask him. It could be something and nothing. You need to conserve your energy to get through today.'

She wouldn't say that if she knew about the phone I'd found. 'People around here think Michael did something to Suzy, I know it.'

'You don't know it, you just think it because you're upset.'

'Nobody from the village has even been round to the house. It just feels odd. Like they're keeping away from me, you know?'

Donna looked away.

'What?' I pressed her. 'What are you thinking?'

'Nothing. Just that sometimes people don't know what to say, I guess.' She sounded doubtful.

'Maybe it's because they think I know something about Suzy going missing. Do you think that's true?'

'I don't know, Kate,' she said with a sigh. 'I just know it's a mess.'

She looked weary, as if she just wanted to sleep for a month.

'Listen to me banging on. How are you?' I changed the subject. 'How's things at home?'

'Oh, you know.' Her voice sounded flat, and she turned her back. When she opened the fridge, I could see a couple of home-cooked meals in there in strange, unmatched dishes that didn't belong to us. 'I brought you some food over.'

'Thanks, Donna,' I said. I knew she was avoiding talking about her own problems. 'Why are you convinced Paul has someone else?'

She sighed. 'You know, if I tried to explain, you'd think I was mad. It would sound like nothing to someone else, but I know him. I know his ways.'

'I'm listening,' I said.

'He keeps finding reasons to go out in the car. Says, "I'm just popping here, popping there, I'll be back in an hour or so." He used to wear his baggy old sweatpants and Crocs to go to the shop but now he's smarter. Smells nice.' She smiled at me. 'It's nothing, I know. But it's something. It's definitely something.'

'Has he said any more about the divorce?'

There were a couple of moments of silence. Usually, she'd snap at me for raising the subject, not wanting to discuss Paul's wrongdoings. But she could hardly do that today.

When she replied, she sounded almost flippant. 'He didn't mean it, I'm certain. We had an argument, see. I accused him of all sorts and he shot back with "If you really have such a low opinion of me, then we might as well get divorced." He hasn't mentioned it since and so I'm pretending it never happened. I'm hoping it was just something said in anger.'

We sat and drank our tea at the kitchen table. I drew circles with my index finger in a tiny puddle of water in front of me. The house was silent. We hadn't sent the girls to school, and Paul had offered to take the day off and look after Tansy and Ellie at their house.

With careful consideration, I'd decided not to put Tansy

through the funeral. I'd kept having a recurring dream where I was standing there, holding her tiny hand in front of her daddy's coffin. Tears were streaming down her face as I kept trying to convince everyone he was an innocent man. How the police had got it wrong. If I took her today, it would be something she'd remember forever and I didn't want that. I wanted her to remember all the good times with Michael. After speaking to her teacher and to Donna and Irene, I thought it was best, and anyway, we'd already had our own little service in the wood to send her daddy to heaven.

Irene had telephoned yesterday to let me know her sciatica had eased enough that she'd be coming to the funeral.

'That's good news. Michael would have wanted you there,' I said gratefully. 'Is there still a lot of police activity up at Wadebridge?'

'A few officers came up yesterday sniffing at this and that,' Irene said. 'I watched them from the kitchen window, and they stood there for ages, looking out at the fields and pointing this way and that before they went away again. It all seemed rather futile. I honestly think they're clutching at straws now. Before they left, I tried to pin them down on the progress of the investigation. They wouldn't say much, but it was fairly obvious to me they're still convinced they're going to find some new lead.'

My hands started to shake. I pushed them under my thighs.

We'd expected to wait a bit longer to bury Michael because of the coroner's investigation into the accident but luckily it had happened quicker than expected due to the driver having to return to his native Belgium. Following the inquest, and the lack of witnesses or CCTV footage, the coroner had recorded 'accidental death' on his death certificate and released his body for burial.

Last night, I dreamed about my husband lying cold in the mortuary. Crude black stitching covered his chest and stomach. His eyes were stitched up too, and he cried out, trying to open them.

I'd woken in a sweat, sat up in bed panting. I'd been making a conscious effort to push away the thoughts that were gathering like a tsunami with each passing day. Like the distinct possibility that Michael had thrown himself into the road deliberately, in a moment of pure panic. Whether the police had been on the brink of finding new evidence like I had done myself.

Every minute of every day, the decision presented itself repeatedly in my head: *Do I lie and conceal evidence or do I tell the truth and face the consequences?* The trouble was, there weren't just consequences for me. My six-year-old daughter would suffer for the sins of her father and that's what kept me quiet for now.

I'd laid out my clothes for the funeral in the spare room. After showering, I went in there and closed the door. I dried my hair and smoothed it back into a neat bun before securing and spraying it. After that, I applied foundation, blusher, mascara and a nude lipstick. It felt wrong to make the effort now that he'd gone. I put on the tiny diamond studs he'd bought me when Tansy was born that I'd always saved for best. I slipped on my underwear and opaque black tights, and finally the black shift dress I'd had in the back of the wardrobe for ages but had never had occasion to wear.

The dress bagged around my hips and stomach. I didn't know exactly how much weight I'd lost since Michael had died, but everything I wore was beginning to feel loose now.

I slipped on a black jacket and slid my feet into kitten-heeled black suede court shoes. Then I sat on the end of the bed and waited.

My stomach lurched when we left the house. There were one or two of the older villagers on the street who bowed their heads in respect. I felt my eyes stinging. There had been a couple of funerals these past five or six years where people had stood out on the street to show their respects, tossing cut flowers at the hearse. Michael knew everyone in this village. He'd done favours for nearly all of them over the years. Where were they now? I felt less concerned for his legacy than for the reason why they'd stayed away. Had the pernicious rumours started in earnest? It would only be a matter of time before the police got to hear of it, if so. Donna nudged me and handed me a clean tissue.

For now, I'd kept the Ring doorbell footage and I'd buried Suzy's phone under blankets and towels in the drawer beneath the bed. But I had to make a decision on what to do and soon. Either get rid and perpetuate Michael's lies or come clean regardless of the consequences.

The limousine crawled behind the hearse carrying Michael's black wicker coffin. I sat in the back with Donna as we made our way to Mansfield Crematorium, about seven miles away, a fifteen-minute drive. I just wanted to get out of the village. Behind us, another car carried Michael's sister and her husband, down from Scotland. In the seventeen years since I'd known my husband, I'd only met his sister twice. Once at our wedding and once after Tansy was born. When we said hello I could barely look her in the eye.

When the cars had passed through the entrance of the crematorium, the funeral director got out walked in front of the vehicle, his top hat bobbing up and down like a macabre parody.

I wondered how Tansy was. I felt I'd done the right thing in not putting her through this. It wouldn't have been right.

Donna didn't speak, and I was glad. She knew I needed space. I reached over and squeezed her hand and saw she had tears in her eyes. I didn't think they were for Michael. This would be bringing back painful memories of Matilda and underlining the heartbreaking fact Donna has never been able to lay her beloved sister to rest.

I felt a sudden urge to blurt out what I'd found, to share the terrible burden. But she looked so sad, I knew I couldn't add to her grief.

I took the small mirror out of my handbag and checked my face. Despite the make-up, my face was pale and haggard. My swept-back hair looked darker than ever against my skin, and the black clothing seemed to absorb any remaining light like a sponge.

I barely recognised the woman looking back at me. It felt as if something had changed inside me on a cellular level. As if something had hardened at my core. Perhaps it had.

After the service, we went outside. I watched as they lowered Michael's coffin into the ground. In that moment, the transformation inside me felt complete.

I was no longer the wife of a man I realised I'd never really known.

At the age of thirty-four, I was officially a widow.

THIRTY-FIVE

SUMMER 2018

JAKUB

Jakub sat in the field on a canvas chair, eating his sandwich and looking up at a cloudless, blue sky. He was in the English country-side, the birds were singing and he had found a good place to work here at Wadebridge. Finally, he was living the life!

Granted, he hadn't made his fortune yet, far from it. But that wasn't really the point now, because his anger with Ana and Oskar had dissipated somewhat. Still, he called home less and less these days. His mother insisted on updating him on what Ana was up to, describing the impressive new house she and Oskar had moved into. He always came off the calls with a heavy heart and he couldn't afford that, not when it took all his energy to keep positive and optimistic for his own future.

He'd been back to Zalipie, Christmas 2012. He'd attended the church service with his family and seen Ana there with Oskar. His heart still ached for what might have been but nevertheless he still loved Ana, so he'd been pained but relieved to see her happy. He'd matured so much in a short space of time and he felt glad he'd had the opportunity to come to the UK. He'd never have done that if he and Ana had stayed together, and now he knew she had never loved him. Not really.

Afterwards, as he'd stood outside waiting for his mother, he'd come face to face with Ana. He'd expected her to scurry away, pretend she hadn't seen him, but she didn't.

'How are you, Jakub?' she'd asked, seeming genuinely interested.

Jakub had opened his mouth to brag about his new life, but he couldn't follow through. He couldn't lie to Ana, not then, not now, not ever.

'It is lonely, it is hard work, but I get through,' he'd said. 'It is a life I did not think I would be living, but who knows what is in store for us, hey?'

'Walk with me,' she'd said. 'Just a little way.'

'But Oskar is—'

'He has already left to be with his friends and his mistress. Vodka.'

Ana had looked right at him, and for a moment, a shadow passed over her beautiful face and something clouded her eyes.

Could it be regret? Then it was gone, and Jakub scolded himself for wishful thinking.

The tiny white church sat at the edge of sparse woodland and he followed her as she took the path that wound around the outside of the trees. They talked about the village, the people, carefully avoiding any mention of what used to be their lives together. No mention of their abandoned hopes and dreams.

As they skirted the back of the church, Ana suddenly grabbed his hand and pulled him towards an old woodshed that Jakub and his friends had used as a hideout as children.

'What ... Ana, no!'

She giggled at his shock and pushed the rickety, creaking door shut behind them. It was very dim in here but not quite dark thanks to the holes in the roof, the splits in the wooden door.

'Ana, we shouldn't—'

'Ssh.' She'd planted her soft, strawberry-scented lips on his and pressed her slim, taut body against his. God, how he'd missed her. He knew it was madness, that they could never retrieve what they had together but ... for now, he was prepared to forget that.

The urge to have Ana again rose in him with the strength of a hurricane. He pinned her up against the crumbling brick wall of the woodshed as they pulled at each other's clothes. Their powerful lust was tempered only by the looming shadow of so many unspoken regrets and thoughts of what could have been.

As quickly as it had started, it was over but Jakub didn't want to let her go. Ana stepped away from his tender embrace and pleading eyes. She adjusted her clothing, patted down her hair and stepped quickly outside.

'This was a mistake,' she whispered, her eyes darting around the trees. 'We must never allow it to happen again.' And then she was gone, leaving only her sweet scent and ghostly kisses on Jakub's skin.

Since Jakub had arrived in the UK, a lot had happened. His plan to look for work on local farms instead of in the soulless factories had faltered at the first hurdle. He'd been unable to find any casual labouring in the fields. A fellow Polish immigrant had told him why he was having problems.

'They all want experience, my friend. It's a catch-22 situation. They will not employ you until you know what you are doing, and yet you can't get this experience until someone gives you a chance.'

'What do you suggest I do?' Jakub had asked him, hopefully.

'Well, for a start, you should stop telling the truth.' The man had grinned. 'You don't have to outright lie, but just embroider your experience a little. For instance, I'm assuming you have done a little gardening back in Poland?'

Jakub pulled a face. 'My grandmama's allotment, that is all.'

'Perfect!' He grinned. 'So when you are asked, you can say you have experience in cultivation and growing vegetables, yes? General labouring and harvesting, too. This is some of the truth.'

Planting a few carrots and pulling up a handful of potatoes for a stew was an awful long way from the truth, but Jakub understood well enough what the man was trying to say.

For a long time, he drifted from job to job. Then one autumn, he heard from another Polish man about a local farm expanding their operations and needing labourers who could start right away. Greet Farm was located in Southwell, a minster town about fourteen miles north-east of Nottingham.

Jakub made the seventy-five-minute bus ride there and walked the remaining three miles out to the farm. The farmer was a gruff man with a double chin and at least a week's growth of whiskers, who had an unnerving habit of constantly looking at his watch as he spoke.

'Got any experience?' he barked when Jakub explained that he was looking for a job.

'Yes, lots of experience back in Poland,' Jakub said, praying that the heat he could feel channelling into his face did not betray him. 'Cultivating the land, growing vegetables, harvesting.' The farmer narrowed his eyes and scratched his bristly chin. 'You can see I am big and strong. I do not tire easily like some. I am not afraid to work long into the day until the job is done.'

That seemed to do the trick.

'I'll give you a two-week trial,' the farmer said grudgingly, already losing interest and moving away. 'Minimum wage, paid weekly but no accommodation. Starting tomorrow, be here for sunrise.'

Before Jakub could thank him for giving him a chance, he was already striding off, yelling into his phone about a late delivery.

Jakub stayed at Greet Farm for ten months and carried out just about every farming task possible. So when the farmer told him regretfully that his planned expansion wasn't working out and he needed to downsize, he was in a far better position to land himself a new job.

Wadebridge wasn't a farm, rather a few acres of land with some properties located on the outskirts of a pretty village called

Lynwick. Jakub had heard two of his workmates at Greet Farm chatting, discussing how they'd heard that the manager there was very laid-back. 'If you work hard, he stays out of your hair,' said one of them. 'Trouble is, he's very particular. If your face doesn't fit, he's not interested. I know how to get round a man like that, though. I'm going over there this weekend to spin him a clever tale about how talented I am at working alone in the fields.'

Jakub hadn't a clue if he himself had the kind of face that might suit the manager, but he had every intention of finding out, and he would make sure he got there well before the weekend.

The next day, he skipped work and travelled over to Wade-bridge. It was quite a walk through the woods and up a steep hill from the village where the bus had dropped him off. He walked across the yard to a row of cottages, to see if he could spot anyone, but there seemed to be nobody around. At the main house, he knocked on the door. Nobody answered, so he knocked again.

He was about to turn away when movement at the window caught his eye. He peered closer and caught sight of an old woman.

'Hello?' he called out. 'I'm here to ask about the job.'

There was no response, and when he stepped closer to the glass, he saw that the woman had disappeared. He cupped his hands around his eyes to cut out the reflection and peered in. He could see an armchair, an empty grate and a scratched wooden table.

'Oi! What do you think you're doing?'

He spun around, alarmed by the aggressive demand. A broad, muscular man of around forty was headed straight for him, his hands balled into fists.

'Sorry, sorry!' Jakub said quickly, holding his hands up. 'I knocked on the door and I thought I saw someone. I shouldn't have looked through the window, it was very rude of me.'

His servile attitude seemed to stop the man in his tracks. His muscled frame reminded Jakub more of a security guard than a land manager.

'What do you want?' he barked.

'I am here about the labouring job. I've taken two buses and walked for miles, so I was hoping to speak to someone about it. I'm very sorry this is our first introduction, Mr ...'

'Michael Shaw,' he provided, but did not offer his hand.

This man did not match the laid-back descriptions Jakub had heard mentioned, but his stance relaxed a little and he studied Jakub closely, as if he were trying to get the measure of him.

'I have been employed on Greet Farm at Southwell for the past year, but now Mr Greet is downsizing and I heard you may be hiring.'

Shaw relaxed his hands. 'Oversaw the Greet Farm expansion, did you?'

Jakub had just been a farmhand. He hadn't overseen anything. He thought about the bluster of the man who'd been discussing the job, his assertion that Shaw liked his workers to get on using their own initiative. But there was something about Shaw that made him reconsider.

'I merely assisted Mr Greet, I cannot claim any more than that, sir.'

Shaw laughed. 'I know Dan Greet and I know what a control freak he is. So I know that you've given me an honest answer. I've already had a handful of time-wasters here claiming there's nothing they can't do. Come on, I'll show you around.'

Jakub got the job and was happy at Wadebridge. Michael quickly trusted him with lots of duties, and Jakub was delighted when his wages were increased. But he stayed away from the main house. It became clear to him that Irene, the owner, did not like him. She acted strangely whenever he waited outside in the yard for Michael. She'd watch from behind the curtain, and if he waved or tried to communicate in any way, she'd move quickly away without saying a word.

One day, his courage ran high and he mentioned the subject to Michael. 'I am sorry if I have offended Mrs Wadebridge in some way,' he said, placing his hand over his heart to show his genuine concern.

'Don't worry about her. She's just cautious, doesn't like anyone sniffing around the place. But I know I can trust you, right?'

'Of course.' Jakub nodded.

'Ask no questions and we'll tell you no lies.' Michael had winked and Jakub had nodded and smiled knowingly.

But he hadn't a clue why they seemed to be nervous here and he didn't understand his prospective boss's cryptic comments. What did it matter, anyway? He planned to do his job, keep his head down and try to forget about the life he thought he'd be living at this point in time.

THIRTY-SIX

KATE

The day after the funeral, I watched as DI Helena Price walked up the short front path with DS Brewster. I guessed she was in her mid-thirties like me, and I wondered how she managed to be so confident and able to deal with whatever situation she came across. Tall and slim, she had brown wavy hair that grazed her narrow shoulders. She wore black trousers, flat shoes and a loose olive-green jacket. Everything about her felt no-nonsense and transparent. No sign behind her eyes of the tangled emotional mess that I saw in my own reflection. Brewster was older. Short and stocky, his red hair beginning to recede. He wore a dull grey suit, a shirt and grubby tie, and carried a phone in his hand.

Their feet crunched the gravel on the path and the very air in the room seemed to thicken as they drew closer, my heart thudding in time with their footsteps. Why were they here?

'Hello, Mrs Shaw,' Price said, making an effort, I thought, to keep her voice level. 'We wondered if we might have a quick word?'

The ground seemed unstable beneath me, my head swimming.

'Mrs Shaw?' She darted forward. I couldn't seem to stop my

legs shaking. 'Are you OK? Here, lean on me. Come on, let's get you inside.'

'I'm OK,' I said, forcing myself to stand up straighter.

In the kitchen, I sat on a stool. 'What is it you want?'

She hesitated. 'We wondered if you'd mind answering a few questions concerning the time leading up to your husband's death?'

My face still felt numb with grief and shame and a thousand other negative emotions. I had to silently repeat her words to myself before they made sense. 'What sort of questions?'

'Did you notice any changes in Michael's behaviour?' Brewster ventured. 'In his mood, his routine ... anything that seemed out of the ordinary?'

'Yes to all of those,' I said, feeling weary with exhaustion. 'Wadebridge has been crawling with police and Michael had felt under suspicion. He was worried word would get around the village that you lot were implying he might have had something to do with Suzy Baros going missing. The discovery of his keys in her cottage had especially unnerved him, because he genuinely didn't know how they'd ended up in there.'

My heart ached and my head pounded. I wanted them gone. The lies stuck in my throat like pieces of gristle.

'Let me explain, Mrs Shaw. As you know, DS Brewster and I are heading the investigation into Suzy Baros's disappearance. We're also looking into the disappearance of another Polish national, a man called Jakub Jasinski, whom your husband claimed not to know. Does that name mean anything to you?'

I was on the spot. Should I lie to back up Michael's interview, or should I tell the truth? I knew the whole situation would get worse if they found out I'd lied. But I had Tansy to think of. It was bad enough her losing her daddy, never mind the police trying to implicate him in Jakub's disappearance.

'Mrs Shaw?' DI Price prompted me.

I decided to land somewhere in between the truth and a lie.

'Michael must have been confused by your barrage of questions, because I'm sure I remember a labourer called Jakub who worked up at Wadebridge for a couple of years.'

'My, that's some confusion, to forget someone you've employed for two years.'

I ignored her sarcasm. 'Michael had said he was a good worker, but one day he didn't turn up for work and that was it, they never saw him again. I'd hardly call it a disappearance, though. Michael always said the casual labourers tended to be transient. They often moved around the country.'

I felt breathless with the act. I needed to slow down and breathe.

Brewster cleared his throat and checked his notebook. 'Your husband claimed not to know the name. He didn't seem to remember Jakub and yet now you're saying he worked closely with him for two years. I'm asking myself why that might be.'

'I've no idea,' I said. I felt suddenly cold. I glanced at the wood burner and saw that the warm embers were gone now. It was completely dead. 'He probably simply forgot. He sees a lot of people, has a lot on up there.'

'Right,' he said, his voice hollow with disbelief. 'The fact remains that two people have now gone missing from the place your husband managed, Mrs Shaw.'

'Yes,' I said. 'I know.' I couldn't say another word without choking.

'It's most unfortunate timing, having to come here like this with your husband's funeral only happening yesterday, but we have to find a resolution here. Do you believe Michael could have taken his own life because evidence was stacking up against him?'

'No!' I had to force myself to stay in my seat. 'I don't believe he did that.' I couldn't allow Tansy to grow up with the knowledge her father had taken his own life because he couldn't face his crimes. And I didn't believe he had. *I didn't.*

Price studied me for a few moments and then they both stood up. 'Please don't hesitate to contact me if you think of anything once we've gone,' she said. 'Should you think of anything we might find of use, be sure to let us know, Mrs Shaw. I'm very sorry for your loss but I must remind you that you have an obligation not to hamper this investigation by keeping information from the inquiry. Doing so could be seen as withholding evidence, which is a very serious crime.'

'You've made yourself crystal clear,' I said tersely.

Why did I get the feeling it might not be too long before I heard from them again? I shuffled to the edge of my seat.

Price put up a hand. 'We can see ourselves out. Take care, Mrs Shaw.'

From behind the curtain, I watched them walk down the path. A small draught of cool air kissed my hot face. I could hear the pebbles crunching beneath their feet as they slowed to a stop and got into their car.

It was drizzling but there were people sauntering by the house, staring at my visitors. Then a woman suddenly aimed a camera in my direction and took some photographs. Press. I felt sick. Exposed and vulnerable.

Only when the detectives had disappeared down the road did I breathe out fully. I waited for the tears to come, but my chest felt clogged and raw. Nothing was real, least of all the fact that Michael was dead.

Michael and I had shared everything, or so I'd thought, but he had a whole other life I knew absolutely nothing about.

I sat down. The walls felt like they were closing in. I felt overwhelmed.

All my life I'd tried to do the right thing by everyone I knew. Help out when I could, go the extra mile and, most importantly, love and support my family.

But the rising panic inside told me I couldn't keep this up. Something had to give and the moment of truth was coming. I could feel it.

THIRTY-SEVEN

30 NOVEMBER 2019

On Saturday, Tansy and I walked up to Wadebridge. Before we got off the main road, we saw several villagers we'd known for years. People who suddenly had to take out their phone, or cross the road. People who hadn't the decency to ask after the welfare of a six-year-old girl, regardless of their feelings about Michael or myself.

I held my head high and distracted Tansy with chatter about what movie we'd watch together later. Still, I could feel the tendrils of pressure and awful possibility creeping up into my chest like knotweed. The village was turning against us.

We took the path through the wood, but the skipping girl who identified songbirds was gone. She walked morosely by my side, clutching my hand almost fearfully. Her eyes stared down at the dirt track at her feet, not up at the trees and the sky.

The mystery man flittered into my mind. Tansy being certain she'd seen someone and me telling her she was mistaken. But I didn't dwell on that for long because the bright little star at my side had dimmed. Making her feel safe was my priority now.

'It's all going to be all right, you know,' I said softly. 'You and me, we're going to get through this.'

She said nothing and we walked on. Then, 'Do you think Daddy is up in heaven now, watching us walking?'

'I'm certain he is,' I said, pushing unhelpful thoughts about Michael aside. 'He'll always be watching over you. When you feel lonely or sad or afraid, just close your eyes and you'll see his face like he's here next to you.'

She looked up at me. 'But I'll just be imagining that. Like I imagine being at my Sylvanian Families picnic. It's not real.'

'It's ... different,' I said, hoping I wasn't saying the wrong thing. 'Daddy was real, you see, and you have a special bond with him that nobody can ever take away.'

'And the bond lets me see him?'

I was making things worse. Too complicated.

I stopped walking and crouched down in front of her, taking her mittened hands in mine. 'You can talk to him any time you like in your head. You see, your daddy loved you more than the world, more than the universe, and love never dies. It never, ever dies.'

'You're squeezing my hands a bit hard, Mummy,' she said solemnly.

'Sorry.' I loosened my grip. 'It's hard to explain how you can feel someone is still with you when they've gone to heaven, but you'll see. OK?'

She nodded, still looking a bit confused.

I stood up and we started walking again.

Tansy said, 'Ellie said she heard her mummy and daddy talking and her daddy said my daddy had a girlfriend ... and that it was Suzy, Aleks's mum.'

I stumbled slightly and steadied myself on a nearby tree.

'No. That's not true. Listen to me, Tansy.' Her eyes looked so blue and forlorn. 'Your daddy hadn't got a girlfriend. He had me and you and he loved us more than anything. No matter what nasty things people say. OK?'

Was this what people in the village were saying? That Michael was seeing Suzy and he must have had something to do with her disappearance? They didn't know about the evidence I'd found. For all I'd revised my opinion on Paul, it sounded as though he was far from being a true friend to us. I felt as though the villagers had turned against me, too.

I reached for my daughter's hand and began to walk. One foot in front of the other. *That's all I have to manage for now*, I told myself. I kept having to defend my daughter's father, who was also a man I wasn't sure I knew any more. The events of the last few weeks … Irene's comments about him and Suzy, the police finding his keys in the cottage, the witness who said he'd stepped out into the road, the Ring door video footage, the phone business … all this had shaken everything I'd ever believed about him but there was no space to think it through. I felt like events were flashing by at breakneck speed and it was making me very nervous and very tense.

'Ellie is my bestest friend,' Tansy said as she walked. 'And I like Aleks too, but he said he doesn't want to play with us any more. He just stays on his own looking sad.'

The cottages came into view on the brow of the hill, and my heart jolted, like it might stop at any moment.

'Who's that in the field, Mummy?' Tansy frowned as a middle-aged man walked up to the ride-on mower and climbed astride it.

'I don't know. We'll ask Irene.'

There would never be a time when I didn't come here and think about Michael. Everything I saw reminded me of him. His office, the fields he loved to walk around at the end of each day, surveying the land for broken fences or patches of grass that needed attention. The dilemma was that Irene lived here and she was a dear friend who'd cared about him too, and without Michael and Suzy around, I knew she'd be struggling. So I had to make the effort.

When we reached the house, Irene was sitting on the sofa listening to a radio discussion programme, one of her legs propped up on a footstool. I sat down opposite her and she turned the volume right down.

'The sciatica is better but the arthritis has started up again in my left knee,' she grumbled. 'It won't leave me alone, I've hardly slept. Tansy, sweetheart, come over here.' She patted the seat cushion next to her and Tansy obliged. Irene opened her wooden box and handed her a small Amazon package, earning herself a smile.

'I'll make us a nice cup of tea,' I said, shuffling to the edge of my seat.

As Tansy opened the parcel, Irene looked at me. 'How are you both?'

'Oh, you know,' I said, settling back again with a sigh. 'Managing to get through. I'm not quite sure how. Who's that out in the field?'

'That's a local farmer who knew Michael,' she said sheepishly. 'He kindly offered to help until I can sort things out here. I'm sorry you had to see him there, Kate. It must have brought back memories but I'm not trying to replace Michael.'

'No need to apologise,' I said. 'You can't afford to let the place slide, and Michael wouldn't have wanted you to. He poured his heart and soul into Wadebridge and he'd have hated to think you were struggling.'

'Thank you, Kate. It's a weight off my mind to know you're not offended.'

Tansy held up a Play-Doh set. 'Look, Mummy, there are heart stencils with it and everything.'

'That's lovely! Irene spoils you.'

'Nonsense. She deserves to be spoilt.' Tansy started to open the cellophane wrapper. 'I remember only too well, back when Amos passed, it helped getting the funeral behind me. But then you feel the gaping hole they leave behind more than ever. It's not easy. None of it is easy.'

'There just seems to be a mountain of stuff to sort out. Financial, insurance, notifying everyone from the local council to the bank ... Every day I think of a hundred more jobs I need to do.' *Plus the rest of it I can't talk about ...*

Irene nodded. 'You'll get through it. Don't expect too much of yourself. If you want me to help with your to-do list, you've only to say. And Tansy is always welcome up here, you know that. Have you heard how Aleks is doing?'

'He's OK. They've found him a new foster family. The woman introduced herself to me at school and she seemed nice enough.'

'That's good, I do miss seeing him around. I wanted to say, I'm here for you too, Kate. Any time you want to talk about Michael, or just to get things off your chest, you've only to say the word.' She looked at me pointedly. 'I really mean that.'

'Thank you. I ... There is something that's bothering me.' I glanced at Tansy, aware that just because she didn't look like she was listening, it was no guarantee that she wasn't. 'The detectives called at the house again.'

'Oh, really?' Irene looked surprised.

'Hmm, I was taken aback too. Anyway, they wanted to ask me if I'd noticed anything different about Michael – his mood, anything like that. I said he'd been down and seemed worried and that it was no wonder because he'd felt a bit hounded by the police.'

'Quite right,' she agreed. 'And for no other reason than that he worked here at Wadebridge.'

'Exactly. But then ... then they told me they were investigating another missing person. Jakub Jasinski.'

Irene hesitated. 'How odd.'

'Yes, I thought so. I told them he worked here as a labourer for a couple of years and that he just didn't turn up for work one day. That's what happened, isn't it?'

Irene was quiet for a moment, then she said, 'I can't recall, dear. Michael dealt with the casual labourers, as you know. I knew nothing about that side of things.'

But Jakub had been around for a long time. He was always out in the fields but I'd seen him enough to know who he was, so Irene *must* remember something.

'Michael told the police he didn't know a Jakub Jasinski,' I said.

'I asked him why he'd lied and he said it was because they'd never leave him alone. But now I'm wondering if there was more to it than that.'

'Well, if I were you, I'd stop your wondering right away.' Irene regarded me steadily. 'Don't give yourself anything else to worry about, Kate. Trust me, you're better off developing a touch of amnesia like me. That way nobody can catch you out.'

I thought it was a strange response. 'Are you saying you've told the police you can't remember who Jakub is, too?'

'Do you know, I've quite forgotten who's asked me what! Now, shall we have that cup of tea?'

THIRTY-EIGHT

NOTTINGHAMSHIRE POLICE

DI Helena Price hunched over the desk while Brewster flicked through documentation screens on the computer sent by UK Immigration.

'So this is what we've got. A timeline of Jakub Jasinski's arrival into the UK, various sightings, any interaction with public services, GP, stuff like that. He headed up to the East Midlands and that's where the trail stopped, in terms of the earlier investigation.'

Price frowned. 'No use of credit cards, mobile phones?'

He shook his head. 'Casual workers from Europe mostly don't bother with bank accounts. They deal in cash, at least until they settle somewhere. Their first priority is usually securing some kind of income. Now Kate Shaw has confirmed that he was at Wadebridge, when Michael Shaw and Irene Wadebridge claimed not to know him.'

'I think it's time to put on our wellies and have a scout around there.'

Brewster nodded and clicked on to another screen. 'I was hoping you might say that. We've a nice, solid lead from the drone exercise the specialist team carried out. I've taken the liberty of creating a visual format on this map. By anticipating the coordinates, I can—'

'In English please, Brewster.'

'I've drawn a circle around the areas that may be of interest to us.'

'Better. And what did you find?'

He pointed to the map. It showed the area known as Wadebridge, with an overlay of pale grey in the shape of a circle.

Price peered at the screen and wrinkled her nose. 'Looks like quite a big area.' She could almost anticipate the super's reaction. Asking her to present evidence as to why digging up Wadebridge seemed like a good idea.

Brewster reached for the mouse and hovered over a pin towards the centre of the circle. He clicked and the map increased in size. Price saw a representation of patchwork fields with a building in the centre. Brewster nodded to the screen. 'The drone footage reveals some interesting possible disturbances to the ground. This field right here. I'm wondering if there might be more than Jakub Jasinski's disappearance to interest us up there.'

THIRTY-NINE
1 DECEMBER 2019

KATE

The next day, I let Tansy watch a Disney film while she ate break-fast – it was Sunday after all – and told her to come and get me when it came to our favourite scene. I sat on the edge of the bed, staring into space, torn between keeping the Ring footage and Suzy's phone to myself, or telling the police everything. I lost track of time and was shaken out of my trance state by Tansy calling up the stairs.

'Mummy, it's the bit where Jasmine flies on the magic carpet.' She sounded half-hearted, as if she hadn't the energy to shout.

Startled, I jumped up off the bed and made for the door. I felt guilty I'd just left her downstairs.

I rushed downstairs and ground to a halt at the bottom. There was a white envelope face down on the mat.

'Mummyy!' Tansy yelled. 'Come. On!'

'Coming ...' I called back in a high sing-song voice.

I picked up the letter and turned it over in my hands. Printed in neat block capitals was my name:

KATE SHAW

I slid my finger under the seal and ripped it open. Inside was an A4 sheet of plain paper that had been precisely folded. The contents of the letter had been typed.

FAO Kate Shaw

There are a large group of people in this village who believe you know what your husband, Michael Shaw, did with that poor young woman.

The reputation of this village is being ruined. Increasing numbers of people – and now the press – are landing here every day to try and find out what happened and help solve the mystery.

We have solid reasons to believe YOU KNOW EVERYTHING. For the sake of your daughter and for the preservation of our village life, PLEASE SPEAK UP. Do the right thing and tell the truth.

And then go. Please go away and find a home somewhere else.

You are no longer welcome here.

Collectively,
Lynwick Village Residents

I crumpled the letter and released it, as if it were poison on my fingers. It fluttered to the floor. They really believed that Michael had harmed Suzy Baros and that I had information and was protecting him. I felt outraged until I realised that's exactly what I was doing.

What were the 'solid reasons' they thought they had? Nobody knew about Suzy's phone but me. And if the villagers suspected my involvement somehow, were the police just one step behind? And who had Paul been gossiping to about Michael having a thing going on with Suzy? I was going to have to speak to Donna about it and I could guarantee it wouldn't go down well.

Tansy appeared in the hallway, her little arms folded, her mouth pursed with impatience. This tiny girl who needed me now more than ever.

'Mummy, when are you going to ... oh! What's this?' She dashed forward, her hand outstretched to the crumpled ball of paper at my bare feet.

'Leave it!' I yelped and she jumped back, snatched back her hand, startled. 'Sorry, darling, it's ... it's just rubbish. Don't touch it.'

Tansy shrank back and I saw how much more nervous she'd become. She had a new fear of the unknown, a newly developed expectation that bad things could happen.

'Sorry, it's OK. No need to be scared, it's just ... let's go and watch Jasmine fly, shall we?'

She took my hand and we walked back into the living room. She set the movie playing again and kept glancing at me to see if I was paying attention. My face told her I was, but my mind told a different story.

That note had been well-written. It had been considered and thought through. These were not people who threw bricks through windows or posted dog mess through the letterbox. They were far cleverer than that, but their words were just as lethal and damaging as any physical act of aggression.

My daughter and I were surrounded by them. Once people who we'd lived happily amongst but that now wanted us gone. I'd been party, in the past, to the insidious ways they achieved what they wanted. I'd heard about the secret meetings organised when a neighbouring village wanted to share use of the village hall. The way certain actions were planned but no minutes or attendance recorded. They had consulted private legal advisors a few years ago when the then head teacher of the primary school put forward a proposal to change the timings of the school day. The school governors voted unanimously against his plans and six months later he tended his resignation, 'to pursue other interests'.

These were people who did not come out and speak their truth. Instead, they preferred to work covertly behind the scenes, using their imagination and contacts to reach their desired outcome. And it usually worked.

I could probably hazard a reasonable guess at who the people behind the note were. Mums at school, members of the parish council, prominent business owners in the area. But I'd never know for sure. I'd never know if the person making me a sandwich in the local bakery was someone who was part of the village 'collective' who'd signed that letter. And that made Lynwick a dangerous place for us to be and a toxic place for Tansy to grow up.

I don't know. Maybe if I was outside looking in, I too would find it hard to believe a wife could be so gullible and unsuspecting. I might suspect she was protecting her husband in some way.

I snuggled in close to Tansy's warm little body, desperate for comfort. Our daughter, full of goodness and kindness. *To the best daddy in the world*, we used to write in all Michael's birthday and Father's Day cards, because it had been true. I'd believed that with all my heart, but now I couldn't get past all the evidence that was stacking up. I felt the weight of all the questions and difficult conversations that were still ahead of me, bearing down.

After the film, I fixed Tansy a glass of milk and a biscuit, and she settled down to draw Princess Jasmine flying away on her magic carpet.

I sat down at the kitchen table with a coffee, my head in my hands, allowing myself five minutes of hopelessness. I kept thinking about Suzy and Jakub, the fact that they'd both been at Wadebridge, the fact that they were both Polish ... the fact that Michael had known them both. And still, it made no sense whatsoever.

. . .

Donna and Ellie came over mid-afternoon. Soon, the girls were playing with a tea set and Tansy's soft toy brigade while we sat at the breakfast bar. I made coffee and set the biscuits Donna had brought with her on a plate.

'Are you feeling OK?' Donna narrowed her eyes as she regarded me with concern. 'I can see you're troubled, and no wonder. You're grieving.'

I nodded. 'Just being up at Wadebridge yesterday for the first time without Michael there. It was so ... odd. So strange.'

'It never goes away. You just have to learn to live with it.' She looked away, towards the light of the window. 'Even now, I wonder if we'll ever be able to find Matilda and put her to rest. Losing her will stay an open sore until we find out what happened. I pray we can do that before Mum goes.'

I wrapped my arms around her. 'The police have been again,' I whispered in her ear. 'They're gearing up the investigation into Jakub Jasinski. He was a labourer who worked at Wadebridge. Michael told me he'd left about a year ago with no explanation, and although they haven't said as much, the police seem to think foul play may have been involved.'

'No! Are you saying they're putting Michael in the frame for *his* disappearance, too?'

Again, the urge to confide in Donna about finding Suzy's phone surged up in me, looking for a way out. I felt so desperate to unburden myself, but I couldn't do it without finally sealing the suspicions about Michael. I fought it back down inside.

'Michael lied to them. I was there when he said he'd never heard of Jakub, and Irene is also being cagey about him, says she can't recall his name. I'm really scared Michael had something to do with him going missing.'

I reached into my pocket and pulled out the letter from the villagers that I'd flattened out and refolded. 'This was pushed through the door earlier.'

Donna scanned the contents, her eyes widening and then darkening with anger. 'Do you know who wrote this? They have no right!'

I shook my head and signalled for her to keep her voice down in front of the girls. 'I'm sure I can guess some of the people behind it, just as you could. What bothers me are the "solid reasons" they refer to. Imagining what's being said is worse than actually knowing.'

'I can't imagine how you're feeling, with even more trouble landing at your door like this. I can see your pain, and I can see how it's affecting Tansy.'

I heard myself speak before I could censor it.

'Donna, I wanted to let you know that Tansy was so upset the other day. Ellie had said she'd overhead you and Paul talking. She told Tansy he'd said Michael had a girlfriend and it was Suzy.'

'Oh no.' Donna paled. 'No. That's not right, Kate, Ellie must've got confused. I'd absolutely remember if he'd said something like that.'

And there it was, strong as ever. The old denial that Paul could possibly do anything wrong. I knew for a fact Ellie was too young to make something like that up. She'd heard it and then innocently repeated it to Tansy. That much was obvious, but really, what was the point in arguing about it? And there was the small detail that Paul was dead right. I couldn't deny it any longer after the new evidence I had uncovered. And yet ... there was something inside, some tiny thing – you could call it naïve, or just plain stupid – that was forcing me to hold on to a wisp of hope that Michael was innocent of all wrongdoing.

Is that what we all did when our backs were up against the wall ... cling on to the tatters of what we wanted, *needed*, to continue to believe? If we'd spent years investing ourselves, our entire lives and those of our children in the integrity of someone, did we fall apart too if that person was found to be a stranger ... a monster in our midst? If Michael had committed atrocious crimes, then I'd been living that lie, too.

I glanced over and watched my daughter, absorbed in play yet far from the happy-go-lucky girl she'd been before. There was no doubt about it, Tansy was struggling with the death of her father. That would only be made a hundred times worse if the police found that something bad had happened to Jakub as well as Suzy.

And if they became convinced I knew something ... well, it didn't bear thinking about what could happen.

FORTY

IRENE

Irene had just woken up from a pleasant ten-minute doze when Doris bustled through and told her there was someone here to see her.

'It's those two detectives,' she whispered. 'I said you were resting and could I help, but they said they really needed to speak with you because you own the land.'

'That's all right, Doris,' Irene said, not remotely agitated. 'You can bring them through. Offer them some tea.'

Doris nodded and disappeared. Irene sat back and took in the view of the garden and the fields beyond. Doris was doing a good job in Suzy's absence. She was a hard worker and dependable and looked to Irene for guidance in every aspect of her work in the house. It was most satisfying, and it occurred to Irene that perhaps she should have gone for a more mature lady as a home help before now. The younger ones just brought trouble, it seemed.

She looked up as Doris led the two detectives into the room. She'd spoken to these two before a couple of times, helped them with general queries. But Michael had been at her side then.

'Hello again, Mrs Wadebridge.' DS Brewster was larger than

life and a little too bold for Irene's liking.

'Nice to see you, Mrs Wadebridge.' DI Price smiled and nodded behind him.

'Please, sit down,' Irene said. 'What can I do for you?'

They sat, and Price folded her hands neatly together. 'As you know, Mrs Wadebridge, we've been working hard on investigating the disappearance of Suzy Baros.'

'I do indeed know that.' Irene nodded. 'But not had much luck in finding her, as I understand it.' She saw Brewster wince.

'Well, we think that might be about to change,' Price said. 'We're also very invested in solving the disappearance of Jakub Jasinski, who we believe worked here as a labourer for a considerable length of time.'

'As I've said before, Michael dealt with all that,' Irene said firmly, picking up her cup.

Brewster leaned forward. 'We wanted to ask you about that particular detail, Mrs Wadebridge. How were the casual labour paid? Were they on the payroll, or was it a more ... informal arrangement?'

'Again, that was Michael's domain,' Irene said regretfully. 'I'm sure I don't know what I'm going to do without him.'

Brewster nodded. 'Well, we're here today to tell you about an exercise we've carried out remotely using the police drone.'

Irene looked at him blankly.

'Are you familiar with drones, Mrs Wadebridge?' Brewster's voice softened a little. 'Would you like me to explain to you what they are?'

'If you mean one of those unpiloted aircrafts that can carry out a number of procedures ranging from delivery of packages to assisting in police and military operations, then no. I think I'm up to speed, thank you,' Irene said mildly. 'You have to have a licence to use them, apparently.'

She noticed DI Price attempt to smother a smirk.

It had to be said that Irene didn't see much of the world outside the village these days, but she did listen to informative radio programmes and read the newspapers to keep up to date with what was going on. She had several papers delivered daily, from high-brow publications that stuck to the salient facts through to the more playful editions that kept her abreast of the latest celebrity news and what was good to watch on television.

It never failed to amuse her how people – especially men, it had to be said – seemed to assume she needed everything explained in a simple, drawn-out manner. Despite her having lived, in some cases, twice as long as them.

'That's grand. Impressive, that.' Brewster coughed. 'So, we used a drone to survey the land surrounding Wadebridge and we discovered some interesting possible anomalies in the topography of—'

'The land looks as if it has been disturbed in one of the fields at some point,' Price provided.

'Disturbed?' Irene raised an eyebrow.

'Well, it's hard to tell. The field is ploughed, not grassed. Was that something Michael would have overseen?'

She nodded. 'I rent some of the fields out to local farmers for arable land, have done for years.' She stared out of the window towards the very area they were discussing.

Brewster unfolded an aerial photograph and pointed out an area outlined in red. 'This is the field in question.'

Irene reached for a small wooden box. Opening the lid only slightly she pushed in her hand, making a satisfied sound before pulling out her reading glasses. Slipping them on, she peered down at the photograph before taking them off again.

'Oh yes, I kept that field,' she said. 'It isn't one that's rented out.'

'Well, we'd like to investigate the land further,' Brewster said. 'Is that something you'd be happy for us to do, Mrs Wadebridge?'

'Certainly,' Irene said without hesitation. 'You must do what-ever it takes to bring that young boy's mother back. If the fields might hold some clue, although I dread to imagine what, then go ahead with my blessing.'

FORTY-ONE

NOTTINGHAMSHIRE POLICE

'Well, that was easier than I anticipated,' Brewster said as they walked back to the car. 'The old dear seemed quite open to the dig.'

'It was also interesting that *the old dear* defined a drone in far more eloquent terms than you'd have managed,' Helena teased. 'Best not to underestimate our Mrs Wadebridge, I reckon, Brewster. She finds it convenient to pass everything off as Michael's responsibility, but in my opinion, she's far too canny and curious not to keep up to speed on what's happening on her own land.'

Helena stared at the row of cottages as they approached their vehicle. They were all empty now, the only movement being yellow police tape that fluttered in the light breeze, the breadth of the fields serving as a barren backdrop to their damp, dark stone and shadowy vacant windows.

She shivered and got into the passenger seat of the car. She was a pragmatic woman, who unswervingly based all her theories and assumptions on fact. But she'd bet a year's salary that something bad had happened in this place.

She felt it in the chill on her face, in the eerie silence of the land.

She could swear she felt it in her very bones.

Next, as they'd planned, even if they got Irene Wadebridge's approval, they headed back to the station to apply for a warrant. 'Just in case our Mrs Wadebridge changes her mind,' Brewster murmured.

'Once the warrant comes through, we've got what we need to go ahead,' Helena agreed.

Brewster thought aloud as he navigated the roads. 'I know you don't rate gut feeling as a method of detection, boss, but what's your feeling about Kate Shaw? Do you think she knows anything about what her husband may have done ... his likely involvement in the disappearances of Suzy Baros and Jakub Jasinski?'

Helena grimaced, considering the question, as Brewster stopped at traffic lights.

'Honestly, Brewster? I'm not sure yet. I couldn't come down on a definite yes or no. How about you?'

'Same, I suppose. If it turns out Shaw did away with one or both of them, I can't believe his wife would be so gullible and unobservant as to not notice at least some odd behaviour. Stuff wasn't quite adding up.'

'I'm pretty sure she would,' Helena said as they set off again. 'The question is, would she confide any of that to us, or is she simply keeping it to herself in the hope that we won't reach a damning conclusion about her late husband?'

'Perhaps she might show her true colours when we tell her about the excavation plans,' Brewster suggested.

Helena nodded. 'I guess we'll soon find out.'

Later, on her way home from the station, Helena pulled up outside a small semi-detached house in Hucknall, the nearest town to Lynwick, where Brewster had arranged her an appointment.

'The Hansons are an experienced foster family that social

services use for difficult or unusual temporary placements,' Brewster had explained to her following his chat with Aleks Baros's social worker. 'Their own children are grown up and they only take one child at a time so all their attention and focus can be applied. They thought it was the ideal solution for Aleks to come here.'

The middle-aged woman who answered the door had very long brown hair that was parted like curtains over a wide, friendly face. 'Hi, I'm Janet Hanson,' she said with a smile. 'Come on in. Aleks is drawing at the kitchen table. Turns out he's quite a talented artist.'

She led them down a short hallway into a bright, airy extended kitchen with French windows and a seating area. A balding, wiry man with a moustache, and wearing Birkenstocks and loose linen trousers, stood up and stepped forward. 'Bill Hanson,' he said.

'Hello. I'm DI Helena Price. Thanks for agreeing to me calling at such short notice.'

'It's no trouble,' Janet said pleasantly. 'I'll make some tea. Camomile or green leaf ... or English breakfast?'

'The English breakfast would be great, thank you.' She walked over to the table. 'Hi, Aleks.' She bent forward to inspect the detailed drawing he seemed engrossed in. 'That looks great. A tractor.'

'It's a plough,' Aleks said. 'Bill took me to see one in a field.' He pointed to a complicated-looking roller at the front. 'This part rakes the soil and breaks up the lumps.'

He looked over at Bill, who gave him an approving thumbs-up. 'He's bright, this lad. Applies himself.'

Helena sat down next to the boy. 'Looks like you're doing a great job there.' It was good to see the boy engaging with people around him without having to be coerced, like had happened last time, at Kate Shaw's house.

'I like drawing,' he said. 'I had an art set at my house in Poland. There were six pencils in it, all with different types of lead. They were very good for drawing.'

Helena raised an eyebrow. Aleks seemed like a different boy.

Take a kid who felt vulnerable and nervous and make them feel secure, and they bloomed like a flower. The Hansons were obviously doing a great job with him.

Janet placed a glass of juice in front of him and he paused in his drawing to thank her. Helena saw her chance. 'Aleks, do you think you could stop what you're doing just for a few minutes so we can talk?'

He put his pencil down carefully and reached for the juice. He turned slightly in his chair to look at her. 'Have you found my mummy yet?'

'I'm afraid not,' she said. 'But we're hoping you might be able to help us. Last time we spoke, we talked about life back in Poland and the things you missed about it. But now I'd like you to think back to the days before your mum went missing. How did she seem to you? Was she happy here in England?'

Aleks thought for a moment, then said, 'She was happy in England but she was worried about stuff too. She said soon, we could find a nicer place to live.'

'Did she mean nicer than Wadebridge?'

He nodded. 'I think so.'

'I know your mum got on well with Irene, didn't she? And Michael, too. Why do you think she wanted to move away from the cottage you rented there?'

'She didn't like Michael,' he said, touching the side of his glass absently. 'But she said she had to be nice to him.'

'I see,' Helena said. 'And did she say why?'

'No. She liked Kate but not Michael.'

'She got on well with Kate, didn't she?'

Aleks nodded. 'She said Kate was nice. She also said that if I was ever in trouble and she wasn't around, someone would be looking out for me.'

'Who do you think she meant, Aleks?'

He looked down. 'I don't know.'

Helena felt a sharp pang in her chest, as if she might have hit on something. She needed to pursue the possible lead, but there was a risk attached. The boy could either crack open or close right down. 'I'm wondering why your mum might have said that.' She paused and looked at Aleks.

Aleks stared down at the table.

'Perhaps she was worried you might be upset so she kept some things a secret.'

'My mum didn't keep secrets from me,' Aleks said, his face darkening.

'It's OK if she did, Aleks,' Helena said calmly. 'Perhaps she thought you were too young, that you'd get upset.'

'She told me everything. She said I was old enough to know everything.'

Helena nodded. 'That's good. She told you everything but she didn't tell you the real reason she left Poland and she didn't tell you why she didn't like Michael Shaw.'

There was a tense silence, and then suddenly, just as Helena had decided the boy wasn't going to say any more, he stood up, his fists balled, two spots of colour flaring in his cheeks. 'She was looking for her friend Jakub!' he yelled, the buried anger and frustration pouring out of him. 'Michael knew where Jakub was but wouldn't tell her. He was talking to her at the Christmas lights and he made her cry. Then Mummy went away.' Tears ran unchecked down his cheeks. 'But she hasn't come back and it's been ages!'

'It's OK, Aleks,' Helena said kindly. 'Don't get upset about it. You've done nothing wrong and you've helped us so much. We're going to do our very, very best to find your mum.'

FORTY-TWO

2 DECEMBER 2019

KATE

The day after the funeral, I'd arranged with the school to return to my part-time teaching assistant role this Monday. I'd so missed the children and the contact with the other staff but after the delivery of the sinister letter and with several of the school staff living in or close to the village, I also felt more than a bit on edge.

Our routine had always been that on the mornings I worked, I dropped Tansy off a little early in the library – with Miss Monsall's permission – so I could meet with the teaching assistant who organised our hours and the reading rota.

I sat in the staffroom now, teachers milling around me, collecting their mail from pigeonholes, chatting about planning and grabbing a quick coffee before the start of class. One or two people smiled and nodded. I knew their faces, but I was only friendly with the teachers in Years 5 and 6 because it was those classes I worked in. My attention was caught by a small group of staff in the corner. I felt certain I'd seen a couple of furtive glances darted over towards me before the low hum of voices resumed.

Was I becoming paranoid because of the letter? For all I knew, it was just a handful of spiteful people trying to make trouble for me. I'd always got on well with my school colleagues and I was sure I'd done the right thing coming back here, despite my initial doubts. I just needed to relax and get used to being around people again, that was all it was.

The staffroom door opened and Jill Chiltern came in. I'd worked with Jill for the last three years, since the last teaching assistant who organised the class rotas retired. Jill did a great job and was friendly and approachable. She scanned the room and saw me, coming straight over to where I sat.

'Kate,' she said, sitting down next to me and smiling. 'How are you? I was so, so sorry to hear about Michael. How are you and Tansy bearing up?'

'We're just trying to get through each day, I suppose,' I said, not wanting to linger on Michael's death. 'Tansy is being so brave and Miss Monsall says she's trying really hard in class.'

'That's good to hear,' Jill said, glancing over at the group in the corner. 'Really good.'

There were a few moments of silence that I felt moved to fill. 'I'm looking forward to getting back into the swing of things,' I said. 'Will I be working in the same class, or—'

'That's exactly what I've come over to talk to you about,' Jill said, pressing her lips together. 'We've had a bit of a rejig of the reading rotas in your absence, and actually … well, we've realised we don't really need you for the rest of the term. We thought you might appreciate the break, with so much happening.'

'Honestly? Time on my hands is the last thing I need.' I gave a nervous laugh. 'I'm looking forward to working with the kids again, Jill. I've really missed it.'

'You've been such a valued member of our rota team. We're so grateful for what you've done for the children.'

Her placatory words definitely had the ring of the past tense about them. What was she trying to tell me exactly? This was more than a 'rejig', as she put it.

'I get the feeling decisions have already been made,' I said slowly. 'I just wonder why.'

'I'm so sorry, Kate. It's ... out of my hands.' Jill had the grace to look embarrassed. She was obviously the messenger for a decision that had been made at a higher level. 'We can review it again next term, OK?'

My heart was racing and I felt sure my cheeks must be flushed, but I kept my voice level. 'Look, I'm here now. Can I be of some use, at least? It doesn't have to be reading.' I looked around the room, suddenly aware that the hum of conversation had dropped to virtually nothing. More glances were definitely being sent my way.

'I really appreciate your offer, but that won't be necessary,' Jill said. It was obvious from her tapping foot and restless hands she was cringing inside, but her manner had become a touch more formal. 'I apologise that you've had a wasted journey. I think they could have decided all this before your first morning back.'

I stood up, angled my body away from the staff so they couldn't see my face.

'When you say "they", who do you mean exactly?'

She hesitated, as if she was considering whether to say something. Then, as if she'd resigned herself to the fact I wasn't going to be fobbed off, said, 'The head teacher and the governors. The official line is that it's no longer appropriate for you to be working in school. I'm sorry, Kate.'

I heard whispers behind me and wheeled around, suddenly furious that they were acting like kids out in the playground.

'What?' I said loudly, looking around. 'If you've something to say, then have the guts to say it to my face at least.'

Everyone seemed to suddenly find their own feet and hands fascinating. Eyes swivelled away from me. People turned back to their mail and planning sheets.

'She's got some front,' I heard someone murmur close by.

Then I knew. Somehow they'd heard about the police interest in Michael's involvement in Suzy Baros's disappearance and possibly Jakub Jasinski's. More worryingly, they seemed to think I was somehow involved in that, too.

I got back home just as Tansy would be starting her first lesson of the day.

I felt as though my chest had caved in. I shut the front door behind me and sat down on the stairs, dropping my head low to try and stave off the nausea I'd felt sure would knock me off my feet on the walk home.

Everything Jill had said to me had seemed on the face of it to be perfectly reasonable. They'd had a reorganisation. They didn't need me to work in class until at least next term.

Both she and I knew the real reason that was swimming under the calm surface of her patter. Rumours were lurking in school and on the streets about Michael. About me. They didn't want the hassle that would inevitably come from parents concerned about a suspected criminal's wife having unsupervised contact with their children.

The author of that letter might well have been one of the school governors themselves.

I had no means of fighting back. I was a temporary, part-time classroom reading assistant with a zero-hours contract. I hadn't got a leg to stand on.

The sound of the doorbell made me spring to my feet, my heart lurching in my chest.

I didn't look through the peephole. I just opened the door.

'Morning, Mrs Shaw,' DI Price said briskly. 'Sorry to turn up like this, but can we have a minute?'

Wordlessly I stepped back so they could enter the hall. As I closed the door, I saw two mums I knew from school craning their necks and whispering their theories out on the pavement.

I didn't offer drinks or ask the detectives to sit down. I just wanted them to say what they'd come to say and leave.

'I'm not feeling too good,' I said. 'Will this take long?'

'No, no. It won't take long at all,' Price said, glancing at her colleague.

'It's a courtesy call really,' Brewster said. 'To let you know that we'll be carrying out an organised forensic procedure up at Wade-bridge tomorrow afternoon.'

I looked blankly at him.

'Essentially it's a screened dig by trained officers,' Price added.

'You're digging for bodies?' I said faintly, leaning back against the wall.

'We carried out an exercise with the police drone and identi-fied what looks like disturbed ground on one of the Wadebridge fields,' Brewster explained. 'It might be something and nothing, but we've had clearance to investigate further.'

'And we have the approval of Irene Wadebridge,' Price added.

I looked up at that. Irene knew what they were doing and hadn't told me?

Something washed over me. A sort of panic. My decision to stay quiet gave way to a damage-limitation exercise in the face of such a serious police exercise, the dig. 'Wait here,' I said and rushed upstairs. Two minutes later I was back again.

'I found this. In Michael's toolbox.' I thrust the item forward. 'It's Suzy Baros's phone. It has Polish writing on it and I've seen her with it before.'

Neither of them reacted for a moment. DS Brewster looked at the phone and calmly took a plastic evidence bag from his pocket. 'Pop it in there please, Mrs Shaw.'

I dropped the phone in and wiped my hand on the side of my trousers.

'When did you discover this piece of evidence and where, exactly?' Price said curtly.

'I found it this morning. Just before I took Tansy to school. I was just going to ring you guys when you turned up at the door.'

'There's a coincidence,' Brewster said.

'I was! I swear. I needed to change a fuse and ... I went in

Michael's toolbox for a screwdriver and it was there. The phone was just lying there at the bottom of the toolbox.'

'And you're saying you knew nothing about it until then?' Price frowned. 'You didn't know Michael had Suzy Baros's phone?'

'No! Of course I didn't.' I saw Price glance down at my hands and I realised I'd balled them into tight fists. My armpits were damp and I kept blinking rapidly. My eyes felt dry and sore. 'I didn't know. I swear. It was a shock to find it there.'

'Mrs Shaw. We'll need to search these premises,' Brewster said, taking out his own phone. 'Are you in agreement for us to do that?'

'Yes! I mean, it will look bad if I say no, won't it?' The detectives glanced at each other. 'There's nothing else here, I'm sure of it.'

'You didn't know Miss Baros's phone was here until this morning, though, is that right?' Brewster said.

'Yes. I mean, no. I didn't know but there can't be anything else. There just can't.'

The detectives stood up.

'Can we ask that you don't leave the premises, Mrs Shaw?' Price said. 'We'll contact headquarters now and the search and forensics teams should be here shortly.'

'Of course,' I said, my heart battering my chest wall. 'That's fine. Thank you.' I felt sick with relief they hadn't arrested me. When they stepped out into the hallway, I rushed forward. 'Can I be there tomorrow?' I blurted out. 'Can I come to the dig, or isn't that allowed?'

'We'll be screening the forensic excavation from view and the field itself will be out of bounds. I'd advise you to stay away,' Brewster said shortly.

'There's a public footpath running close to the field, so you won't be able to stop anyone who wants to watch,' I said. My heart sank at the idea of word getting out and half the village turning up.

'As DS Brewster has said, it's best if you stay away, Mrs Shaw. But if you're determined to attend, then best to let us know beforehand,' Price said carefully. 'We can arrange for someone to accompany you to and from the site.'

'That's not necessary, I don't need you to ...' My words petered out when I saw their faces and understood what they'd been getting at.

'It might be for the best, Mrs Shaw,' Brewster said quietly. 'Emotions can run high in situations such as this.'

They were offering me protection from my own friends and neighbours.

FORTY-THREE

3 DECEMBER 2019

I stood at the edge of the field, flanked by two uniformed police officers. We were up at the Wadebridge estate, three acres of fields with a main house with a large garden and a row of five stone cottages.

The place my husband, Michael, had worked for more than twenty years.

A sheet of freezing rain arrowed down the back of my neck, trickling down my spine. My jeans were already soaked through and the raindrops dripped from the tip of my nose and my earlobes. I thought longingly of home, our house being just a fifteen-minute walk from here. The warmth of the log burner, curtains closed against the weather, and Tansy snuggled into my side as we read *The Ickabog* together for the umpteenth time this week.

In front of me was a different scene. My new reality. White tarpaulin sheets stretched high and wide across the middle section of the field, stark and clinical against the sludge and the moody skies.

Behind the screen, I could hear the guttural roar of the yellow digger, its dull black bucket plunging into the depths, forcing the earth to reveal its grim secrets. Powerful spotlights illuminated the area of police interest and the wide circle of land around it. The smell of damp, clogged earth stuck in my nostrils and throat, and I fought the urge to gag.

I turned away from the field to look at the people who were standing along the track – a public right of way that ran directly behind the row of cottages. They meandered in and out of their small, curious groups, standing and chatting for a minute or two before moving on. I recognised most of the faces that stared boldly back at me without acknowledgement. Locals who knew exactly what was happening here. People I used to consider friends and acquaintances who now found themselves unable to express their condolences. People we had lived peacefully alongside for years.

Now they'd braved the elements to come and watch our lives crumble as the drama unfolded, the small points of light cast from their phones dancing like sprites in the gloom.

Behind me: the press. The constant flashes from the cameras were distracting, and every few seconds I'd hear my name being called with a jarring, unwanted familiarity.

'Kate! Do you know what they're going to find here?'

'Who's looking after your daughter, Kate? Where's Tansy?'

My life was now an open book to these people, a free-for-all. I was no longer a human being. In their eyes I was subject matter. I was a headline, the star of a grim and gory story everyone wanted to read.

I didn't look their way. I didn't give any sign at all that I heard them calling out. I pulled up the collar of my old waxed jacket and shoved my bare hands into the pockets. The fingers of my right hand closed around a soft ball and my heart squeezed. Tansy's woollen mittens, left in my pocket from a few weeks ago, when we'd walked over here to bring her daddy his sandwiches and to forage for some yarrow for her flower press.

Stomach acid bubbled up into my throat and I closed my eyes against what was to come, what my six-year-old daughter would have to face.

'Mrs Shaw? *Daily Mail*,' a man's voice called out, closer than the others. He sounded friendly, sympathetic. 'Did you have any clue at all about what your husband did? We can help you tell your side of the story. Put an end to all the speculation. What do you say?'

I didn't turn around.

Yesterday the police had searched the house. I called Donna and asked her to pick up Tansy from school and to keep her last night so I could get things straight after the disruption. It had taken hours. They'd gone through every inch of the house, even lifted carpets and floorboards. They'd emptied the garden shed and virtually dismantled the garage.

A huge group of press gathered outside the house, blocking the road and inflaming passing drivers. I didn't leave the house. I sat in a corner of the kitchen and stared out at the garden. I went into the living room twice to peek around the curtains. There were villagers out there, standing around in groups, some with a takeaway coffee from the Larder. They talked and looked towards the house with twisted expressions and sneering faces.

The police found nothing. They took away items of Michael's clothing and shoes and the family laptop. But there were no startling revelations, no more of Suzy Baros's items. I'd felt relieved but wounded. I'd felt exposed and under fire from the obvious hostility outside the house.

The rain pelted down harder now, the biting wind scalding my cheeks, but I welcomed the discomfort. The sound of the digger filled my head with its relentless drone, every second bringing me closer to facing the horror that I dreaded and they all craved.

Then ... a splutter, the powering-down of an engine and the noise suddenly stopped.

For a moment or two there was perfect silence. Then someone shouted from behind the tarpaulin sheet, a sound of alarm.

The gaggle of headline-hungry reporters behind me erupted, surged forward. Cameras flashed so rapidly it almost felt like daylight. Voices rose in unison, all shouting my name and vying for attention. Demanding answers.

Several officers formed a loose chain behind us to restrain the press.

'What's happened?' I whispered hoarsely to my escorts. 'Does this mean they've found something?'

Neither of the officers responded.

A few feet away, DI Price talked animatedly on her phone in a low, confidential voice. Before I could get her attention, she ended the call and dashed behind the screen. My sinuses were blocked solid and I had to drag air in through my mouth.

A hum of chatter rose up. 'Have they found something?' a man shouted from the track. 'Is it human remains?'

The radio of the officer to my right crackled and he stepped away to speak into it. Another spurt of crackling, but I couldn't decipher what was being said. I found myself praying silently: *Please God, don't let them have found her.*

But the air seemed drenched with a dark foreboding, and I knew it would be bad. Very bad.

The officer with the radio returned and whispered something to his colleague. The second man gave a low whistle. 'Jeez,' he said, shaking his head, clearly appalled.

'What is it? What have they found?' A wave of panic shunted up and gathered in my chest, choking me like smoke. 'I have a right to know.'

The officers looked at each other, and then one of them turned to me, his face impassive.

'You'll find out soon enough, Mrs Shaw. Don't you worry about that,' he said coldly, glancing at the reporters behind him. 'I can guarantee that by tomorrow morning, the entire country will be talking about it.'

FORTY-FOUR

4 DECEMBER 2019

The morning after the forensic excavation, I woke to everything hurting. My head, my stomach, even my fingers and toes ached. I lay there feeling like I needed to move but knowing I couldn't. Not yet. Despite resenting what Paul had said about Michael having a girlfriend in Ellie's earshot, I had to thank my lucky stars yet again for Donna and Paul, who'd also kept Tansy yesterday afternoon and overnight.

The telephone rang and I picked the call up within seconds on autopilot. 'Hello?'

'Mrs Shaw, this is the *Mansfield Sentinel*. Have you any comment about the police findings yesterday up at—'

I slammed down the phone. Within seconds, it rang again. I unplugged it at the wall. When I checked my mobile, I had dozens of missed calls, and it was only just after eight in the morning.

Reporters. The police officers had predicted that the results of the police excavation work would be all over the newspapers today.

I could hardly remember coming to bed last night. My head was still full of the droning police excavator, the accusatory shouts of the press and the villagers. I'd called around at Donna's house afterwards and dissolved into tears on the doorstep. Donna had ushered me inside.

I hadn't realised Tansy was watching from the kitchen, her little face wearing the kind of worried and pained expression that did not belong on the face of an innocent six-year-old child. In the space of three weeks, her ordered, dependable family life had disintegrated into utter chaos. And now this ... What effect would it have on her in the future?

She'd rushed over and we'd hugged. 'I love you so much,' I whispered into her clean, soft hair.

'Mummy, what's wrong?' she'd whimpered, her little hands clutching at my own.

'Mummy's fine,' I'd said, kissing her cheek. 'I'm just not feeling well. I'll be OK after a rest.'

'Go and play with Ellie, sweetie, and I'll make Mummy a cup of tea,' Donna had said.

After studying my fake smile critically for a moment, Tansy did as she was told.

I could not fault Donna's support in this, our time of need. She was the only person I could really rely on, and I felt infinitely grateful to her.

She'd made tea and brought it through.

'Is Paul home?'

She'd nodded. 'He's upstairs, which is unusual. He never seems to be home just lately!' Her dark eyes betrayed her flippant reply.

'He's been so good, though, taking time off work to look after Tansy.'

Donna had pulled a face. 'That's what I thought too, but he's been out and about, coming up with excuses why he needs to be out of the house. Like I said, I recognise this behaviour from when he's strayed before. Tell me what happened up at Wadebridge.'

I'd talked her through the forensic excavation: the awful sounds, the smell of the damp earth, the spectators. 'I swear half the village turned out to come and have a look. The press were baying like wild dogs, and then when the digger stopped and it was obvious they'd found something, the police just escorted me away and wouldn't say a word.'

'Do you think they found a body?'

'They must have done. The police were scurrying around and they couldn't wait to get me out of the way and disperse the crowd.'

'Do you think it's ... Suzy Baros?'

I'd looked down at my hands and nodded. 'I can't think about it, Donna. I can't get my head around the fact that Michael had anything to do with something happening to Suzy. I just can't. One of the police officers made a comment that it would be all over the press tomorrow.'

Now I opened my call list and rang Donna.

Her first question was 'Did you manage to get some sleep?'

'I'm not sure. I feel like I've been awake most of the night, but I was so exhausted when I got back from your house. How's Tansy?'

'She's fine. They've had breakfast and now they're ready for school. Paul's going to take them in and have a word with Miss Monsall about the police excavation work in case anyone says anything to Tansy. I've had a little chat to her about letting Mummy rest, and she understands perfectly, so you mustn't worry.'

'Thanks, Donna, I don't know what I'd do without you.' Paul was another matter. I couldn't work out where his loyalties lay. Then, 'How's things your end?'

She knew what I meant. 'He's in the shower as we speak. He had a few errands and places he needed to call yesterday, apparently,' she said, her words dripping with sarcasm. 'When I ask where, he answers me like a politician. Saying quite a lot but telling me nothing at all. I'm at the Larder all day today, but Paul's stuck at home in Zoom meetings so at least I have peace of mind where he is. We can chat when I bring the girls over later. Anyway, enough about me. I'm more worried about you. Have you looked online?'

'No, but ... I'm scared to,' I confessed. 'I wanted to call you first, and then I'm going to take a look. I'm just terrified of what I might find.'

'I've looked,' she said. 'Do you want to know?'

'OK,' I said, unsure.

'I think it's safe to say people think they've found something … most likely Suzy Baros's body. People are starting to talk about Jakub Jasinski's disappearance, too. But everyone seems to be waiting for cast-iron evidence.' She went quiet. 'It brings it all back. I can't bear to think of what happened to Matilda. But I wanted to look online for you … to save you the anticipation of what you might find.'

'I'm so sorry, Donna,' I said. 'Please don't make yourself feel worse by trying to help me. I've got to face the truth. But I won't talk to the press and I'm avoiding social media for now.'

'I think you need to be aware, though, Kate. The villagers can be hostile. I hear things and I'm worried you might be tried and convicted behind closed doors.'

'I know people are speculating that Michael may have killed Suzy Baros and that I've known about it all along.'

She looked taken aback at my candour. 'It's the stuff of TV crime drama.'

I felt panic begin to stir. Our own people had turned against us. Everyone believed Michael was guilty. Now they were trying to drag me into the lion's den. There just wasn't enough space in my head to deal with it.

'I can hear Paul on his phone upstairs,' Donna said urgently. 'I need to listen.'

'I'll let you go. I'll call you soon about picking up Tansy.'

'No worries, they're playing nicely. Gotta go. Speak soon.'

I ended the call and swiped down for notifications. My phone screen filled with missed calls and Facebook alerts. I ignored them and went straight to the *Sentinel*'s page. I found what I was looking for in seconds.

REMAINS FOUND IN SEARCH FOR MISSING WOMAN

Forensic officers have unearthed human remains from an area of land known locally as Wadebridge, located on a hillside about a mile from the centre of the historic village of Lynwick.

Nottinghamshire Police have been searching for missing Polish woman Suzy Baros, who came over to the UK with her young son over six months ago. Baros disappeared after attending the popular Christmas lights turn-on.

DI Helena Price, who is leading the Wadebridge investigation, told the *Sentinel*, 'It's too early to comment on our findings yesterday. For now, I can confirm that the search for Suzy Baros will continue.'

I scrolled down and, against my better judgement, I read the comments under the article.

BookClubStar55: The missing Polish woman lived in a rented Wadebridge cottage and now the police have found human remains on Wadebridge land. Everyone knows who managed that land for the owner. Michael Shaw! Come on, Notts Police, use your common sense!!

FootieFan_MU: Probably topped himself to avoid justice.

SarahJ1968: Someone must've known what he was up to. Maybe his wife?!

ThomasSkinner: She was at the dig yesterday. Wouldn't look at anybody. Wonder why!!!

My online viewing was cut short by an incoming call. The

screen lit up with *DI Helena Price*, and I remembered I'd saved her number when she'd left me her card a while ago.

'Mrs Shaw?' she said when I answered. 'DI Helena Price here. I'm calling because I wanted to let you know myself that we sadly found human remains at the forensic excavation yesterday.'

'Yes, I just read about it online on the *Sentinel*'s website,' I said frostily. Shame they couldn't have told me what to expect.

'I wonder if you'd be able to come into the station this afternoon, say four p.m.? We have some questions we'd like to ask that could help our investigation.'

I sighed. Would this never end? 'I can be there for four.'

'Thank you. I also wanted to let you know some confidential information that the press aren't party to. I must ask you to keep this strictly to yourself for now.'

'I understand,' I said, holding my breath.

'As I said, we found human remains yesterday. Of two bodies.'

'What?'

'A recently deceased male with Polish identification papers, and the remains of a female—'

'Oh my God, no,' I gasped, clamping my hand over my mouth. So they *had* found Suzy Baros's body. My heart filled with pain for young Aleks.

'The forensic anthropologist has confirmed the remains of a female child who died some time ago.'

The line fell silent as her words rang in my head. The remains of a female child. There was only one child gone missing in Lynwick twenty-three years ago and that was Matilda. Matilda Spencer. Donna's lost sister.

FORTY-FIVE

I put down the phone, trying and failing to digest what DI Price had told me. I was questioning myself, what I thought I knew about Michael, about Irene Wadebridge. The stories he'd told me about life growing up in the village. I knew memories of what happened to Matilda remained vivid to him. Michael would have been young when Matilda went missing. He'd have been fifteen. Old enough to do her harm if he'd wanted.

I'd noticed Donna seemed to be fading every day. She was losing weight, her face paler than usual. Even her red hair seemed less vibrant, as if she was slowly turning into a shadow of her former self. It was the product of constantly fretting what Paul was up to. But what would this latest blow do to her? DI Price hadn't confirmed that the remains were Matilda's, but there weren't any other missing children that I knew of. It was obvious the male was Jakub Jasinski, but the police would not be drawn until they'd had official forensic confirmation, which could take several days if not longer.

I couldn't possibly tell Donna what I now knew. In the unlikely event that it wasn't Matilda after all, it would finish her off. For the sake of a few more days until the police findings were certain, I couldn't risk blowing her life out of the water.

I was swimming, trying my best not to drown in grief for the husband I thought I'd known. Worrying for my daughter's future. And in the middle of it all, Donna was slowly suffocating in her own past horrors.

'I went to see the doctor and he's put me back on tablets for anxiety. He's also given me some strong sedatives to try and get me back into the routine of sleep,' she'd told me a few days ago when I'd asked how she felt.

'Have they helped?'

'The last couple of nights they've worked brilliantly, but I can't drive while I'm on them, so I won't be taking them for long. I feel trapped.'

Suzy's disappearance had plunged her into the nightmare of twenty-three years ago, when her beloved sister went missing. The tendrils of that time had always touched her present life and although she didn't realise it yet, the tragedy was set to claim her once again.

I fell into a restless nap on the sofa, waking up in a sweat, my heart beating twice as fast as before. I had to go to the shop. I'd neglected everything at home and had no food in for when Tansy came back later.

As I came out of the supermarket car park with a bag full of goodies for the girls' tea later, I joined a short queue waiting to turn right at the junction. I saw a familiar-looking silver BMW and watched as Paul sailed by, singing to some tune he was listening to. Contrary to what Donna had said about him taking Michael's death badly, he looked as if he hadn't a care in the world.

Intrigued, I swapped lanes and turned left to follow him. There was one other car between us, and I slid in behind it. Donna had told me Paul was stuck at home, in Zoom meetings all day, but it didn't look that way to me.

He headed out towards the motorway. A couple more cars tucked in behind him. I could still easily see him but my cover was improved. I pulled down my visor even though it was dull outside and I could have done with more light in the car.

He took the M1 north and immediately put his foot down. I increased my speed to the legal limit, but he was soon exceeding 70 mph as he sailed ahead in the fast lane. I had no choice but to go to 80, which made me uncomfortable and strained the car. But I was aware we were approaching an exit, and if I wasn't close enough, I might lose him. In the event, though, he didn't take the exit, instead continuing north.

I kept my foot to the floor and hoped for the best. I disliked motorway driving at the best of times, and I hated going too fast. My little Ford Fiesta was starting to shake, and I knew I couldn't keep it up for much longer. Then, to my relief, Paul started to move back across the lanes, decreasing his speed in readiness for exiting the motorway at Junction 29.

I followed two cars behind him. He took the A617 for about a mile and then turned off onto a side road. There was only one vehicle between us now, and my heart pounded when the driver turned off and it was just me and Paul. I didn't want to blow my cover. I wasn't so close I was worried about him recognising me in his rear-view mirror, but I didn't know how observant he was about cars. Although he knew I had a red Ford Fiesta, it was hardly an unusual model.

I watched as we passed streets packed full of houses. This was unfamiliar territory. I didn't know Chesterfield well, had only been there a handful of times, to restaurants on nights out and to a good retail park on the outskirts. But we were off the beaten track here, on a housing estate.

Was Paul going to visit someone? Donna was adamant she'd seen the signs of more infidelity. My heart started galloping. What would I do if this was it – the other woman's house? If she came to the door, would I get out of the car and start shouting? Of course not. So why had I come here? Paul had suggested they divorce in the heat of an argument, but still, if I found out he did have a mistress after all, it might be useful to Donna legally.

I'd followed him here of my own volition, and now I felt nervous about what I might discover. I didn't like the thought of my friend being betrayed, but in her fragile state, this new knowledge could send her over the edge. But I was too far in to turn back now. I'd see it through, and if there was something untoward happening, then I'd sleep on it and decide what to do.

I expected Paul to slow down at any moment and pull onto the driveway of one of the smart new-build detached properties we were passing, but he kept on going. He turned left, turned right, drove straight on, and presently I sensed the area beginning to change. The houses were older semis, ex-council houses, and then, when he turned in to yet another street, run-down terraces peppered with 'To Let' signs. Some properties had several signs, which meant they had probably been converted to bedsits.

We approached another junction, and then, unexpectedly, Paul slowed quickly and pulled over to the right, stopping the car outside a grubby-looking Chinese takeaway with a red 'Closed' sign hanging in the window. I hit the brakes, spotting a narrow side street to the left and turning in. He hadn't got out of the car yet, and I did a quick three-point turn so I was facing the right way to observe him. I turned off the engine and waited, glancing at the dashboard clock. It was 12.12.

After a moment, he climbed out, smoothed a hand through his hair and walked around to the back of the car. He opened the boot and took out a couple of bags of shopping and a supermarket bunch of flowers, then closed the boot and locked the car.

It looked as if he was headed to the takeaway, but then he pushed open a peeling green gate at the side of the shop and disappeared down an alleyway. I looked up and down the street and saw lots of similar gates. It seemed we were in bedsit central. I reached for my phone, opened the camera and zoomed in as closely as I could, snapping a photo of the gate. When I pinched the picture to zoom in, I saw there were two numbers painted on the gate: 13a and 13b.

I waited. 12.22. And waited. 12.29.

What if he was planning on spending the whole afternoon here? I wasn't going to wait around forever, and at least I had something for Donna if she needed to contact the other woman. Yet I couldn't quite bring myself to leave just yet.

12.38.

The minutes ticked by slowly when you were waiting on someone with nothing else to do. I had my Kindle in my handbag and debated getting it out. Then at 12.52, Paul emerged from the green gate. I snapped a pic or two for posterity as he stepped out onto the street. When he turned around, I saw there was someone else standing in the shadow of the alleyway.

Paul said something, holding out his hands in a sort of 'what can I do?' gesture, and, briefly, the woman stepped forward into the light.

A small noise escaped my throat and my hand flew to my mouth. With shaking fingers I managed to snap a couple of photos, then I dropped the phone. I pressed my head back into the neck rest as I made sense of what I was witnessing.

The woman in the alleyway was Suzy Baros.

FORTY-SIX

I felt dazed. When Paul had driven away and Suzy had disappeared back inside, closing the gate behind her, I sat in the car and just stared into space.

I started to itch all over. All this time, all this upheaval of everyone looking for her. I'd started to fully believe Michael had done something terrible and now here she was. She'd been hiding away, laughing at us.

And all this time, Paul knew.

I glanced at the clock. Tansy and Ellie had a dance and drama after-school club until half past four, so I still had some time before I had to be at home. Donna was picking up the girls and then, after I'd been to the police station at four, Ellie was coming back to our house for tea.

But the girls' pizza was far from my mind right now. I wanted to call Donna and tell her everything. I wanted to ring the police and witness them hauling Suzy out under a charge of wasting police time. I thought bitterly of the way they'd hounded Michael because they'd suspected he had something to do with her disappearance. I wanted to go in there and wring her skinny neck for putting Aleks through torture while she enjoyed a torrid affair with Paul Thatcher.

I didn't do any of that in the end. I just sat there, thinking everything through, until I felt I'd made the right decision.

I got out of the car and locked it. Hooking my handbag over my arm, I crossed the road and approached the green gate.

13a and 13b.

Which one? I pushed open the gate and walked down the dark, dank passageway. My footsteps echoed in the narrow space and I shivered, more in anticipation of confronting Suzy than because I was cold. At the end of the passage there were two weather-worn brown doors leading off a tiny yard. Weeds sprouted up through the cracked concrete, and pizza boxes and beer cans lay in a sodden heap in the corner.

I looked at 13a on my left and 13b on my right. Both looked equally drab and neglected. There were no doorbells, so I rapped on 13a. No answer. I tried again, but nobody came. I did the same with 13b, and a young man appeared holding headphones in one hand and a phone in the other.

'Yeah?' He looked to be in his early twenties. He had dark shadows under his eyes and was dressed in a grubby white T-shirt covered in stains, and baggy cotton shorts. He peered at me blearily.

'Sorry. Wrong door,' I said. Before I'd even finished speaking, he'd stepped back and closed it.

I took a breath, pushed my shoulders back and knocked again on 13a. I knocked and knocked and knocked. If I hadn't just seen her, I'd have left. But I knew she was in there, hiding away from a police investigation and from a very upset little boy.

'Suzy, I know you're in there. Answer the door. I'll stay here all day if I must. Maybe I'll just call the police.' *Bang, bang, bang.*

I had questions and she had to answer them whether she liked it or not. It was time for her to be accountable for her selfish, deceitful actions.

As I raised my fist again to batter the wood, the door opened and Suzy stood there. She looked scraggy and pale. Her hair had been cut, short and badly. The groomed image was gone. She wore torn jeans and a baggy jumper that was at least three sizes too big. We looked at each other. I clenched my jaw.

'Leave me alone,' she said, her voice fearful. 'You have no right to come here.'

'I have every right to come here.' I stepped forward and she tried to slam the door shut, but I got my foot over the step and jammed it open.

'Go away! Go away or I'll ... I'll ...'

'You'll what, Suzy? Ring the police? I think they'll be delighted to learn you're safe and well. And what about little Aleks? Will you speak to him too, remind him he's got a mother? Maybe he'll be able to go to bed happy instead of crying himself to sleep.'

'Stop!' She covered her face with her hands.

I stepped inside and she moved back, away from me. I closed the door, my nose wrinkling as I smelled damp and a sour, unclean odour. I was in a large, dirty room, a sink, oven and table-top fridge on one side, with a sagging two-seater sofa and an upright dining chair arranged in front of a three-bar fire. The place was freezing, the carpet covered in dark stains that had hardened the pile.

'Why are you here?' I demanded. 'What happened?'

She balled her fists and opened her mouth ready to have another go at me.

'I'm not leaving until you tell me why you'd choose this hole above living in the cottage with Aleks, who is suffering and missing you more every day.'

She just sort of deflated in front of me, as if all the stuffing inside her had dissolved. Then she sat down heavily on the sofa and pressed her face into her hands again.

'I don't know where to start,' she wailed. 'Paul wouldn't let me leave. He said I couldn't yet or I'd go to prison.'

'Start from the beginning.' I sat on the chair. I had to somehow let go of my obvious anger or we'd get nowhere. 'Start with why you came over to England and this time, let's have the truth.'

'I met the love of my life at school,' she said. 'I was known as Ana back in Poland, short for Zuzana. We were together from the age of thirteen. We lived in the same village, our families knew each other and … well, it was always just assumed that one day we'd marry and have children. But when I was eighteen, my head was turned by another local man, Oskar. He had an air of excitement about him. He'd been living in another part of the country and he was a bit flashy. I liked it. He made the other men look boring. Anyway, I ended up marrying him instead, and then we had Aleks.'

It all sounded fairly standard to me, but her face looked troubled.

'Years passed and I realised Oskar wasn't who I thought he was. His smart image covered up a troubled man who liked to use his fists rather than talk. And he had some very dodgy contacts. His flash car and house had not been earned by working in a car factory as I'd thought. It was through other dealings of which I did not ask details.' Suzy glanced at me, then looked away again as though she felt ashamed to meet my gaze. 'I was trapped in a violent marriage. I wanted to leave with Aleks, but Oskar said he would hunt us down, and when he'd finished with me, he would make sure no other man would want me.'

'But you managed to get yourself to the UK?' I tried to keep my tone reasonable so I could get information out of her. But I wasn't sure I believed a thing she said. After all, this was a woman who had lied to everyone, including myself and her young son, when she staged her disappearance at the Christmas lights event.

'I never forgot my sweetheart and as each year passed, I regretted more and more my decision to leave him and marry Oskar. I went to see his family to ask for his contact details and they told me they had not heard from him for six months. His mother said she was going to file a missing person's report with the UK police. I had this crazy urge to travel here, to try and track Jakub down.'

'Without having any idea where this guy was?' I said doubtfully.

'Yes! It was … I don't know, just a feeling I had that it was now or never. I knew I might be too late, that something had happened to him but I felt convinced I must try.' She looked down at her hands. 'I would never forgive myself if I did not try.'

I might have felt sorry for her if it wasn't for the image of Aleks, sitting forlorn in his borrowed pyjamas with tears rolling silently down his face.

She looked at me and said faintly, 'Did you know Jakub?'

'Not exactly,' I said. 'I said hello to him a couple of times. Michael had hired him as a labourer up at Wadebridge ...' My words faded away as I made the connection. She'd come to Wadebridge to try and track down Jakub. 'He didn't turn up for work one day and that was that. Michael said the foreign labourers often did that. They moved around. Sometimes they went back home.'

She nodded. 'Aleks and I did a moonlight flit – I think you'd call it that here. Oskar was with his friends, drinking at some out-of-town bar. They had rooms booked and he was due home in the morning. I'd known about the event for a few weeks, so I got everything ready for our escape. My parents had both died, and I couldn't tell anyone else we were leaving because I didn't want them to have to try and hide information from Oskar.' She looked down at her hands. 'He can be a very persuasive man. In the worst possible way.'

'Jakub's parents did not know you were coming out?'

'No. I was careful to tell them I wanted his details for a mutual friend who wanted to get in touch from school. The last thing I wanted was for Oskar to pressure them for information.' Suzy nodded slowly. 'I made contact with several online Polish forums before I left for the UK. That was how I tracked Jakub down to the East Midlands. Everyone I spoke to, I asked them not to discuss our conversations with anyone. I explained I was fleeing a violent home situation with my young son. I was not the only one. Lots of women had done the same. I headed here and started my search, trying to find Jakub ... Sorry, I need a breath.'

She stopped talking for a moment and closed her eyes. I wanted to hurry her along, ask her if there had been anything going on between her and Michael. She'd obviously moved on to Paul now, but I needed some questions answered about my own husband. I glanced at my watch. I was still OK for time.

'I had not been in the UK long before I heard from friends back home. Everyone asking where I was and saying that Oskar suspected we had gone to the UK. He was determined to hunt us down,' Suzy continued. 'I was terrified. I kept moving around, which was not good for Aleks and I was worried about his education. He became withdrawn and nervous. I could not make progress no matter who I asked. Jakub seemed to have vanished into thin air. Nobody had heard of him, nobody knew where he might be.'

I thought about the first time she'd visited our house. Her nervous demeanour, the feeling I had she was hiding from something or someone in her past.

'Then I got a breakthrough,' she said. 'Someone I'd been talking to on a forum emailed me with the name of a bed and breakfast establishment where he'd heard Jakub had stayed. I went there the same day. All the residents were Polish, but I hit yet another brick wall. Nobody could help me. I sat in the lounge there and just began to cry with frustration and sadness, and also fear that something very bad had happened to him. I thought maybe Oskar, in his jealousy, had paid someone to kill him. He is crazy enough, believe me.'

She offered me a glass of water, but I declined. She fetched one for herself and sat down again.

'Then a lovely man called Pawel came downstairs on his way out. I'll never forget his kind words. "My dear, why are you crying?" All my frustration about trying to find Jakub poured out. He took off his cap and jacket and sat down. He told me that Jakub had been his roommate, and that when Pawel had returned from a short trip home to Poland, Jakub had already gone without leaving any message or contact details. I asked him why no one else around there knew anything about him, and he said it was the way the Polish community did things. See nothing, hear nothing, he said.

He said the police had been sniffing around but his stock answer was always to say he knew nothing.' She looked at me, seeing my confusion. 'There are people in our community who need to hide, people who are working illegally. We protect each other.'

'But he told you about Jakub?'

Suzy nodded. 'He said he felt sorry for me when he saw me in tears with my small boy. Thank God for that man. He told me Jakub had been working at a place called Wadebridge at the edge of a small village about nine miles away, and that was all he knew.'

'So that's why you came to Lynwick. You came looking for Jakub.'

'Yes. Pawel found out through his contacts that Irene Wade-bridge used an agency for home help. The agency employed many Polish workers. I registered with that same agency and stayed in a local B&B, very close to the village. The manager swapped out one of the other workers who she had to pay travel expenses to and put me on Irene's rota. When I started work there, I found that Irene and I got on well together. She's a nice lady and I genuinely liked her, liked working for her. She was brilliant with Aleks, too. She offered me a cottage at low rent if I agreed to work for her directly. She was sick of having lots of different people coming from the agency. But when I asked about Jakub, she said she left all that to her land and property manager. That she had nothing to do with the hiring and firing of labourers.'

'And that's when you decided to get to know Michael.' I couldn't say much more without wanting to choke her. But I had to keep her talking, had to find out everything I could.

'Yes, I got chatting to Michael. I tried to find out about Jakub, but—'

'Hang on! You can't just scoot over Michael. I believe he died because of what he was about to be accused of. He was confused, panicked. He swore he was innocent but the evidence was stacking up against him that he had something to do with your staged disappearance.'

'I am sorry, Kate. I just wanted to find out why he would not talk about Jakub.'

'It was more than that, though, wasn't it?' I felt my breaths shorten as I remembered all the 'evidence' stacked up against Michael for a woman who was not missing at all. 'When you supposedly went missing, the police found his keys in your cottage. I found your phone in his toolbox! I feel terrible that I doubted him for a while, but now that I've seen this' – I swept my hand around the room – 'the extent of your deceit, I'm asking myself ... did you frame him? Did you want the police to think he had something to do with your disappearance?'

'Yes!' she cried out, then clapped her hand over her mouth. 'Please, just listen to me. I tried asking Michael about Jakub and he would not discuss it with me. Ever. Irene had confirmed that Jakub had worked at Wadebridge, although she didn't know how well I knew him.'

'Irene also told me you had cosy afternoon tea breaks with Michael, and that you helped him by ringing suppliers. Irene told me you had a soft spot for *my husband*.'

'No! It is true I set up as many opportunities as I could to talk to Michael. That's the only reason I did these things. I had to find ways to speak to him, to try and get information about Jakub. Irene was mistaken. She thought my willingness to spend time with him was something else. My heart belongs to Jakub – now I realise it always has. He's the only man I care about.'

I laughed out loud, a harsh, bitter sound. 'Looks like it when you're now having an affair with Paul Thatcher. Always somebody else's guy with you. Donna used to say you were sly and one to watch, and my goodness, was she right!'

'It's not ... it's not what you think,' she stammered, knotting her fingers together. 'I tried to get information out of Michael because I knew something was wrong. He was holding stuff back about Jakub, I could tell. One day I tried to talk to him again and he got annoyed. He said if I didn't stop bothering him about it, he'd speak to Irene and convince her to fire me and to throw me out of the cottage.'

'So there was nothing going on between you?' I said faintly.

'Truthfully, Michael could not stand the sight of me. But ... that made me angry and sad and ... I ended up confiding in Paul. He fancied the pants off me, that much was obvious. I'd been friendly but had not encouraged him, but this particular day, I bumped into him down in the village and he asked what was wrong and I ended up explaining that I was looking for my Polish friend and I was absolutely certain Michael knew something but wouldn't tell me. And Paul came up with the plan.'

'Which was ...?'

'Kate, I'm sorry. If I'd known what was going to happen to—'

'What was the plan?' I clenched my teeth.

'Paul suggested I went missing for a short time. Just for a few days. I'd leave some clues, enough for the police to interrogate Michael. Paul, in the meantime, would send an anonymous tip-off to the police saying that Michael knew where Jakub was. He wouldn't be able to just ignore the police like he did me, you see. It would force him to talk.' She eyed me cautiously. 'I'm sorry, Kate, I—'

'And the night you went missing ... how did you do it?'

'I'd packed a bag with a change of clothes and a dark wig. Paul left them just inside the trees where I was standing. At the right moment I dashed back into the trees, got changed and waited at the other side until Paul picked me up to take me to the bedsit he'd rented. To all intents and purposes it seemed I had vanished into thin air. But I still had second thoughts. I caught Michael as he was leaving the event.'

'After Irene had rung him about the potential flood?'

'Yes. I told him I would give him one last chance to tell me what he knew about Jakub. I pleaded with him for ages and at one point I really thought he would spill the beans but then he told me to get lost and stormed off.'

Michael must have explained that delay by saying he'd popped home first. The Ring video footage had proved otherwise.

'And Aleks? What would happen to your son while you did your disappearing act?'

'I told him that Mummy might have to go away for a short time, but that whatever happened, I would come back. No matter what people said, he had to remember that but to keep it our secret. He was used to saying nothing about Poland in case Oskar got to hear about us being in the vicinity, so this was just an extension of that. Paul assured me that he'd convince Donna to take Aleks in, and that it would only be for a few days anyway.'

'I still can't believe you did that to him. Do you realise you could have done long-lasting damage to his mental health?'

In a second, the mild-mannered Suzy I knew had gone. 'Not as much damage as living in a house where a brute regularly hit his mother and on occasion raised his hand to Aleks too!' She sneered. 'You people see everything in black and white. You don't do this, you don't do that ... In the real world, you do what it takes to survive. Aleks having to lie about his past is a small price to pay to help us find a safe place, a life where we are not abused.'

I'd had every intention of giving her a piece of my mind, but her words were powerful. My own childhood had been damaging, and I'd done what I needed to survive. I understood what she was saying but her selfishness still staggered me.

'Tell me about you and Paul,' I said quickly, to move on. 'Are you together?'

Suzy pulled a face. 'No way. But he thinks we will be when this is over. I haven't slept with him, I told him I wanted it to be special, not in this dump. But I kiss him. I have to. He says he's never met anyone like me and that he loves me. I had to say the same. Plus he is caring so well for Aleks while I am away.'

'Is that what he's told you?' I gave a bitter laugh. 'You've been duped. Aleks has been in foster care for some time now. Your son is heartbroken without you.'

She let out a small noise like a distressed kitten. 'No!'

'I took Aleks in for a few days and then when Michael died, Donna and Paul cared for him for a short time. Then social services insisted on finding him a temporary foster family.'

A tear traced its way down her pale cheek.

'You haven't been the first woman Paul's lied to and you won't be the last,' I said archly. 'Do you know he's told Donna he wants a divorce? Admittedly it was in the heat of an argument but you'd do well to remember there's a marriage and other people's feelings involved here. What you want is not the only consideration.' I looked at her. She looked so thin, pale and vulnerable but I couldn't forgive her for what she did to Michael and to Aleks.

Her jaw dropped. 'I swear I didn't know any of this.'

'So you're saying Paul has got himself involved in all this because he's got the hots for you?'

'Not quite. He told me he hates Michael, that he will never forgive him for telling tales about him to Donna. He's been waiting all this time to get revenge.'

'Telling tales as in revealing yet another one of his extra-marital affairs.' I blew out air. 'It sounds totally over the top to go to all this trouble. For both of you to lie and plan your disappearance ...'

'It wasn't supposed to go wrong,' Suzy groaned. 'Michael dying and the massive police and press interest ... We never thought it would blow up like this. Suddenly I was trapped. I've had no phone or computer here; I get all my information about what is happening in the village from Paul.'

'Come back with me now,' I said. 'I'll go with you to the police. It's time for all this to end.'

'But ... Jakub. I need to find Jakub.'

I took a deep breath. 'I'm not sure how to tell you this, Suzy,' I said quietly. 'Yesterday, the police found two bodies buried at Wadebridge. They think one of them is Jakub.'

FORTY-SEVEN

I helped Suzy get some stuff together. She had agreed to come back to the house with me.

'This has gone on too long,' she said. 'If Jakub is dead, there is no point in me being away from Aleks. It is time to come back.' Her face was tear-stained, and she looked beaten. So many people had been hurt, and for what? 'Can we go straight to pick him up?'

I shook my head. 'It doesn't work like that. The police are the first people you need to speak to. They'll have to call off their investigation and you need to be aware you may be in trouble for wasting police time.'

'I have done wrong and I know I must pay for that. But I need to see Aleks.'

'The police will alert social services. They hold the key to you getting Aleks back. One step at a time.' She'd managed this long without seeing him and my sympathy was in scarce supply.

On the way back in the car, Suzy carried on talking. 'Pawel at the B&B has been good to me. He has been working to put out requests in the Polish communities throughout the UK to locate Jakub. Now I must tell him the sad news together with Jakub's mother. She will be heartbroken.'

'And what about Paul?' I asked.

'I'm not interested in him. My heart must heal from Jakub. He was the love of my life.' She looked so forlorn and sad, I almost wanted to stop the car and console her. But then I remembered the hell Michael had had to go through because the police had thought he had something to do with her disappearance. And the anonymous letter I'd got from villagers who believed the same. Poor Aleks, whose suffering could stay with him for life. I kept on driving. We needed to sort this mess out, and fast.

I pushed thoughts of Donna from my mind. On top of learning about Paul's treachery, there was the possible discovery of Matilda's body after all these years. I was seriously worried about her mental state. Now that I knew about Paul's involvement, I wanted to get Tansy back home as soon as I could. Ellie would probably need to stay with us, too, while her parents sorted out their mess.

We parked up outside the house. I immediately noticed a battered old Ford Escort parked further up the road. We got out, and I squinted to try and get a better look. There were two men sitting in the car and I suspected they might be press.

'Let's get in the house,' I said to Suzy. 'I've had reporters hanging around outside before.'

Inside, I made us drinks, and then, with a very nervous Suzy by my side, I called DI Helena Price.

There was no answer and the call went to voicemail.

'Hi, it's Kate Shaw here. I can't now come to the station at four p.m. There's been a big development and I've just got back home. Please come to the house as soon as you can. It's important.'

Before Suzy and I could sit down to talk, there was a knock at the door. I looked through the peephole and saw one of the men from the car up the street.

'Go away. I'm not interested in speaking to you,' I shouted through the closed door. 'The police are on their way.'

'I am here to speak with Suzy,' a man's voice called out. 'Tell her it is Pawel from the hotel.'

'Please, let him in!' Suzy begged.

I opened the door. The second man stepped forward, and I gasped as I immediately recognised him. Suzy let out a shocked noise and staggered back. Then she rushed at him and embraced him.

'Jakub! They told me you were dead!'

The older man looked at me. 'I think we should leave them for a few minutes,' he said in heavily accented English. 'It is a long time since they were together. My name is Pawel.'

I shook his hand. 'Kate Shaw,' I said. I hesitated a moment, keen to ask my own questions then reluctantly led him into the kitchen. 'How did you find him?'

'It has taken many months. I first put out a trace when the first lot of police came to the B&B about six months ago. Then when Suzy came, I tried much harder to find him. He had been working in Scotland, but he'd heard on the grapevine that Suzy was over here and had made his way back to the area. He told me he'd even been to the woods near Wadebridge on the lookout for her after hearing she'd come over to the UK to search for him.'

I suddenly remembered the mystery man in the woods ... sounded like Tansy had been right after all, for all my doubting her.

'I had to wait to see if this was confirmed before contacting her.'

'Why didn't you go to the police?'

He shook his head. 'That is not the way we do things when there is a problem.'

Jakub and Suzy walked into the kitchen, hand in hand. The look of bliss on their faces at finding each other was so obvious, even I melted a touch, despite all the mess and heartache they'd caused. I felt a deep longing for Michael and I swallowed it down with the rest of my grief.

'The police should be here soon,' I said. 'Let's sit down and try and make a bit of sense of what's happened.'

FORTY-EIGHT

NOTTINGHAMSHIRE POLICE

Helena and Brewster walked along the corridor and stood outside Detective Superintendent Della Grey's office.

'Ready, Brewster? We got all the facts, you reckon?' Helena reached out and straightened his tie.

'Ready, boss.' He nodded.

Helena knocked at the door and opened it. Grey looked up sharply and put down her pen. Her desk was placed in front of the window, but she sat with her back to the view of the open fields behind the station. Her ultra-short silver hair glinted in the light as she leaned back in her chair and folded her arms.

'Take a seat, both of you. Where are we up to, Helena?'

'As you know, the remains of two bodies were found at the forensic excavation, ma'am. An adult male and a young female, possibly a teenager.'

Grey gave a curt nod. 'But still no sign of Suzy Baros?'

'Sadly not. We're expecting fast-tracked results in forty-eight hours, but we're expecting that the remains are those of Matilda Spencer, a local girl, and Jakub Jasinski, who was reported missing six months ago but hasn't been seen for about a year.'

'Matilda disappeared after leaving school twenty-three years ago?' Grey frowned, picking up a piece of paper and reading the hand-written notes.

'That's right,' Helena said.

'And Jasinski disappeared without a trace also. Followed by our latest vanishing resident, Suzy Baros.' Grey put down her notes. 'Unusual for a small village, to say the least. Any connection between the two victims?'

'Not that we can find,' Brewster said. 'As you know, Michael Shaw, the land and property manager up at Wadebridge, died in a road traffic accident three weeks ago. He's the only obvious link so far.'

'Shaw would have been just fifteen when Matilda went missing,' Helena remarked. 'That doesn't preclude him from taking her, but it would be unusual for someone to wait that length of time before abducting another victim, this time a fully grown man.'

'Hmm.' Grey picked up her pen and tapped the desk with it. 'Families been told yet?'

'That's our next job,' Helena said, dreading the task. In circumstances like this, particularly in the case of children, families were usually told about the discovery to prepare them for the worst. Full confirmation would come when pathology results were received.

'And Shaw's wife ... Kate, is it? She was at the excavation, I understand.'

Helena nodded. 'We advised against it but she turned up anyway. She's coming into the station at four today. After her admission she knew Jakub Jasinski, we'll be questioning her under caution.'

'Married to Michael Shaw for fifteen years and knew nothing about what he might have been up to,' Grey said cynically. 'Do we believe her?'

Brewster spoke up. 'If Shaw is the killer of both people, then it's hard to believe Kate didn't have her suspicions at the very least. But we've nothing solid as yet to connect her to the crimes apart from possibly withholding evidence.'

'What about the owner of the land, Irene Wadebridge?'

'We're also speaking to her this afternoon,' Helena confirmed. 'She also claims to not know much about what went on in the running of Wadebridge. A bit more believable given her age and health concerns.'

'Let's meet again tomorrow morning. Eight o'clock,' Grey said, picking up a document from her desk. 'Good luck this afternoon. Won't be easy for the Spencer family.'

'There's only Matilda's sister left, ma'am,' Helena said as she and Brewster stood up. 'Their father died five years after Matilda's disappearance, and the mother is in a nursing home suffering from advanced dementia.'

'Sad, sad,' Grey murmured, then pointedly went back to her paperwork.

Walking back down the corridor, Brewster checked over his shoulder before saying, 'I reckon the super has a rock where her heart used to be.'

Helena grinned. 'She's all right. It's an act, I reckon. She's soft as grease underneath. Someone in uniform told me he saw her out with her two little pugs. They had pink ribbons in their fur and everything.'

'What? No way!' Brewster gave a hearty laugh and Helena joined in at the unlikely picture forming in her head.

'By the way, Helena?' They both visibly jumped as Grey called after them. 'Make it eight thirty tomorrow. I have to walk my dogs.'

'No problem, ma'am,' Helena said, swallowing hard.

Grey's flinty eyes locked with Brewster's and she gave a curt nod before ducking back into her office.

'Do you think she heard?' Helena hissed, her eyes wide as she quickened her pace.

'Nah, it's just coincidence, boss. Don't worry about it,' Brewster said unconvincingly. 'Like you said, she's probably soft as grease at heart.'

. . .

Brewster collected the pool car and Helena met him out front.

'The Thatchers live on Main Street, in one of the larger houses leading into the village,' she said, climbing into the passenger seat. 'Donna Thatcher runs the village tea room, so if she isn't home, she'll probably be there. Though I hope not.' The news they had to impart was best done in private, at Donna Thatcher's home.

'I would think she expects the news to come at some point,' Brewster said sadly. 'She must've known for years that her sister isn't coming back.'

Helena sighed. 'In my experience, Brewster, people never stop hoping. Hope is one of the most powerful human traits, but in a situation like this, it can add to someone's suffering. Until you get the worst news, there's always a chance, I suppose. No matter how slim.'

Brewster flicked a switch, and a track from *The Best of Neil Diamond* filled the car. At first Helena was about to complain, but then she sat back and got lost in the music, trying not to think of the way she was about to wreck Donna Thatcher's day, her week – probably her whole year and beyond.

Ten minutes later, Brewster turned in to the sizeable driveway and parked behind a silver BMW. Helena got out of the car and took a moment to admire the traditional house, which had been built in the Arts and Crafts style. Probably constructed towards the end of the nineteenth century, it boasted an asymmetrical roof and gable details that added a certain charm.

It was the kind of house that she herself dreamed of owning when she met the right person and settled down. For now, though, she headed back each night to her two-bed terrace, with its leaky roof and small, soulless garden that she had tried to pretty up with a few pots. She sometimes indulged herself with imagining how things might be in a few years, when she met her life partner. One could dream, she always thought.

'Ready, boss?' Brewster tipped his head as if he was trying to guess what she was thinking.

'Sure.' She pushed her shoulders back and stepped forward. 'Let's go.'

Brewster rang the bell, and a short woman with reddish-brown shoulder-length hair and freckles answered the door. The smile slid from her face when he held up his warrant card.

'DS Brewster and DI Price from Nottinghamshire Police. Are you Donna Thatcher?'

'Yes. I ...' She looked back into the hallway. 'I'll step outside and we can—'

'We'll need to come inside to talk, if that's OK, Mrs Thatcher,' Helena said quietly.

'Oh! I ...' Her eyes dimmed. 'This isn't about the dig yesterday, is it? This isn't ...'

'If we could just step inside, Mrs Thatcher,' Brewster said and put a foot over the threshold.

'Course. Sorry, come in.' She glanced at her watch. 'Just so you know, I'm doing the school run today but I've got some time. Come through.'

It seemed to Helena like someone had wound Donna Thatcher up like a clockwork toy and she was scurrying around with no direction in mind. She led them into a bright, airy kitchen with modern grey Shaker units and a wall of bifold glass overlooking the garden.

'Is anyone else home with you now?' Brewster asked. 'Or is it just you?'

'My husband is upstairs in his office on a work call. He sells kitchens. Travels a lot. This is one of his.' She waved a hand around. 'He's good at what he does. He just ... Well, the job takes a lot of him. Oh, I'm so sorry, you must think me rude! Would you like tea? Or water? Or—'

Helena stepped forward and placed a hand on Donna's arm. 'We're fine. Please, sit down for a moment, Mrs Thatcher. We have something important to tell you.'

'No! Don't tell me ... What is it? Is it about that dig? Is there any news on Suzy?'

Helena spoke slowly and calmly. 'Yesterday we carried out a forensic excavation on the Wadebridge land. We found human remains, and—'

'No!' Donna croaked. 'It's not her, is it? It's not ...'

'I'm so sorry, but we believe we may well have found the remains of your sister, Matilda Spencer.'

Donna Thatcher opened her mouth and tipped back her head, and a chilling wail emerged. The hairs on the back of Helena's neck bristled, and she noticed that even Brewster, who seemed immune to noise, shrank back slightly. Donna cut off the wail and looked to the door, perhaps worried she'd disturb her husband's call. Helena watched as she took a breath and gathered herself.

'Forensic tests are currently being carried out using DNA comparison,' Brewster said. 'We can't confirm one hundred per cent until we have the results of those, but the remains are consistent with a young female matching Matilda's details.'

'What did you find after all this time?' Donna's hands flew to her mouth. 'What's left of her?'

'Don't do this to yourself, Mrs Thatcher,' Helena said softly. 'Best to remember Matilda as she was.'

Helena had seen photographs and read descriptions of Donna's sister and it was clear that her most prominent feature had been her vibrant red hair.

When Helena had peered into the dank, deep hole at yesterday's excavation, only small, dirty bones remained of a young girl who was raised with love and tender care by a sister who clearly still grieved her as badly as the day she disappeared.

FORTY-NINE

Back in the car, Helena and Brewster sat in silence for a few moments, waiting until the negative energy finally began to flake away.

'Christ, that was tough,' Brewster said, blowing out a long breath.

'Very tough,' Helena agreed. She took a breath. 'Onwards and upwards, Brewster. Time for us to speak to Irene Wadebridge.'

Brewster started the engine and reversed back down the driveway, pausing at the bottom to check the traffic.

'Clear this way,' Helena said, and he swung the car out into the road and accelerated.

'I could pick us up a coffee and a muffin on the way if you fancy it,' he said hopefully. 'Helps to keep the blood sugar up, see. Useful when we're doing this sort of work.'

'Luckily I've got an apple in my bag,' Helena said, reaching in to check her phone. 'But it was a nice thought, Brewster.' His face dropped and she heard his stomach growl. 'Let's get the Wadebridge visit over, then you can pick something up to scoff before we go to see Kate Shaw. How's that sound?'

'Sounds super,' he responded glumly.

Helena tapped on a notification and listened to the voicemail message.

'Great!' She tossed the phone back in her handbag. 'That was Kate Shaw. She isn't coming into the station at four. Says there's been a "big" development and could we call at her house.'

'Out of order.' Brewster scowled. 'Wonder what she classes as a big development.'

'Well, now we're almost here, we'll speak to Irene Wadebridge and we'll swing by the Shaws' house on our way back to the station.'

Up at Wadebridge, they knocked at the door and waited. When there was no answer, Brewster knocked again.

'Doesn't look like there's anyone—'

'Hang on.' Helena inclined her head and turned her ear towards the door. 'I thought I heard something.'

A voice called out, 'Nearly there, one moment!'

They heard a bolt sliding and a key turning on the other side, then the door opened slightly and Irene Wadebridge's face peered out.

'What can I ... Oh, it's you, Detective Inspector Price! Come in, come in, dear.' She glared at Brewster, at the food stain on his lapel. 'You too, if you must.'

Helena grinned at Brewster's exaggerated expression of offence as she walked past him and stepped inside the house. The air was fusty in here. Not damp, just old and stale from lack of ventilation. Filled bin bags and piles of folded newspapers lined the hallway, reducing the ample floor area down to a narrow strip.

'Come through to the kitchen,' Irene said, shuffling ahead with the aid of a stick. 'My arthritis is playing me up today, so I'm afraid I'm not up to making drinks.'

'Would you like a cup of tea?' Helena said when they got to the kitchen. 'Brewster will do the honours.' She flashed him a smile.

'Oh, how kind. That would be lovely.' Irene looked at him.

'Half a teaspoon of sugar, please, and I'm a little particular about the milk. Just a splash, but don't make it too strong. Oh, and milk in first for me. Semi-skimmed. Can you remember all that?'

'I think I can just about manage, Mrs Wadebridge,' he said drily.

Helena looked away and smothered the laugh that bubbled up into her throat.

'Let's sit down,' Helena said, extending her arm. 'Do you need any help?'

'No, no. I'm fine getting around, just slow.' Irene frowned. 'Doris should have been here this morning, but she's had to take her cat to the vet. The poor creature has had hairball problems yet again. But she's coming over later.'

'Well, if there's anything we can do for you in the meantime, just let me know,' Helena said. She waited until the elderly woman had sat down in a worn but comfy-looking armchair, before taking a seat next to her on an equally ragged sofa. 'Now, Mrs Wadebridge, as you know—'

'Please, call me Irene.'

'As you know, Irene, we carried out a forensic excavation in a field here yesterday afternoon.'

'Yes, and nobody said a word to me afterwards, you know,' Irene said, looking rather put out. 'I expected to hear all about what was found, but you lot just cleared off, sticking a notice through my door telling me not to go near the excavation site. Only the reporters were any help.'

'Oh, really?'

'Yes, a nice man from the *Mansfield Sentinel* came to the door. He said the police had found something, possibly Suzy Baros's body. It's most upsetting.'

'Did he now?' Brewster said from over by the kettle. 'It's best not to speak to the press, Mrs Wadebridge. They'll tie you up in knots with their theories.'

'I only spoke to him because he reminded me a bit of Michael, that sort of kind, sensible air he had about him.' She stared at her hands and fell silent.

Brewster brought the tea over and placed it in front of Irene on a low table.

'You must miss Michael,' Helena said softly.

'I miss him terribly,' she said, without looking up. 'I've known him since he was a young man, you know. Amos, my late husband, he always thought highly of him too. With us not able to have any children of our own, Michael became sort of an adopted son. Then I lost my Amos, and now Michael's gone too.'

Helena nodded. 'I understand.'

Irene looked up, and Helena saw that her eyes were full. 'Michael took care of everything, you see. He sorted out the cottages and the land, and in his own way, he took care of me too. Sometimes he'd just sit and have a chat over a cup of tea, but it made such a difference to my day.'

Helena took a breath. Often the antidote for loneliness in older people was simply a matter of a few minutes of chat, a smile. Maybe passing the time of day on the street. If only people with busy lives understood that kindness, however brief, could linger and get a soul through a long, quiet evening.

Helena forced her attention back to the job in hand. This next bit wasn't going to be easy, but it was very necessary. 'Irene, I'm so sorry, but we're here today to inform you that we did indeed find human remains on your land.'

Irene clamped a hand over her mouth. 'Oh, that poor girl. How awful.'

'It's not Suzy Baros,' Helena said. 'We believe we may have found the remains of Matilda Spencer, who lived in the village and went missing one day after school twenty-three years ago,' Brewster said.

Irene cried out, 'I thought you were going to say it was Suzy. That's terrible, truly terrible.' She took a tissue from her sleeve and dabbed at her eyes. 'The poor girl's family ... I'm outraged that whoever did this chose to bury her on Wadebridge land!'

'We also found the body of a Polish man who we believe to be Jakub Jasinski,' Brewster continued. 'The man who worked here for two years who you claim not to remember.'

'Goodness, yes!' Irene raised an index finger into the air. 'The shock of it must have jogged my memory. Michael was annoyed because he'd given Jakub a chance and then he'd just gone off like that.'

Helena watched her carefully. It seemed Irene had miraculously recalled all the details now that she'd realised they'd uncovered Jakub's remains and could no longer deny he'd been there.

'Irene, I have a question that's going to be difficult to hear, but I'm hoping you understand it has to be asked,' Helena said earnestly. 'Do you think Michael Shaw had anything to do with the deaths of Matilda Spencer and Jakub Jasinski? Do you think he may have abducted Suzy Baros?'

Irene opened her mouth to answer, then hesitated. 'I loved Michael like a son, you know. I've protected him when I shouldn't have. He had a terrible temper that showed itself sometimes. Nobody would have believed it, the way he could blow up over this or that.'

'Can you give us an example?' Brewster prompted.

'If someone irritated him, or didn't do something he wanted them to, he could get quite annoyed.' Irene fell silent before speaking again, her voice low and serious. 'So in answer to your question, I'd say yes. I would imagine Michael could be responsible for those deaths. Only he had access to the land. Nobody else could bury two bodies out there without his knowledge.'

'Matilda has been there a long, long time,' Brewster reminded her. 'Michael would have been just fifteen years old.'

Irene frowned. 'He was a strapping lad at that age. His father knew Amos. Michael used to come up here regularly with his dad.'

'And Suzy Baros?' Helena added.

'Between you and me, I have my suspicions Michael had something to do with her disappearance, too,' Irene said faintly.

'Why were you suspicious?'

'Well, he was always talking to her, acting shifty when I asked what they'd been chatting about. I've known him long enough to see when he's trying to hide something.'

'And yet you've never mentioned any of this to us or any of the police officers who've been working up at Wadebridge.' Brewster frowned.

'Hindsight is the perfect science,' she said softly. 'I have what you might call an old-fashioned trust in people.' Irene pulled a tissue out that had been tucked under the cuff of her cardigan. She dabbed her eyes.

'It seems I was harbouring a monster here in Michael ... and I didn't even realise.'

'There was something very off about her reaction, if you ask me,' Brewster said when they were back in the car. 'There wasn't a single tear there when she dabbed at her eyes. And she seemed to be thinking a lot before she answered your questions.'

'She might just be nervous,' Helena said, clicking on her seat belt. 'But I tend to agree. She wasn't remotely as upset as I thought she might be. Next stop, Kate Shaw. Let's see what this earth-shattering development is that can't wait.'

FIFTY

KATE

We were all sitting talking in the living room when the doorbell rang.

'One second,' I sighed as I left the room. I opened the door and Donna fell into my arms in floods of tears.

'They've found her, Kate,' she sobbed. 'They've found Matilda after all these years.' We stood in the hallway as she blew her nose noisily into a handkerchief. 'I knew. When they came to the door, I just knew.'

'They're certain it's her?'

'As certain as they can be. They're doing tests, but ... everything matches, apparently. It's a young girl and ... Oh God, I can't believe it. It's what I wanted and yet I can't bear to think about it. Can't bear to think she's been in that cold, dark place just a stone's throw from where I live. So close to Mum and Dad, too, when they were still in the village.'

That did feel like an unbearably cruel twist.

'I'm so, so sorry, Donna.' She buried her wet face into my shoulder. 'Has Paul got the girls?'

She nodded, her words muffling into my sleeve. 'He picked

them up from school and kept them while I came to—' Donna stopped crying and listened. 'You've got people here?'

I nodded. 'Suzy is in there, Donna.'

'*What?*'

'Yes. She's safe and well. She's been in hiding. Jakub Jasinski is here too. They're just about to explain everything.'

'I want to stay and listen,' she said, straightening up, wiping her eyes with the back of her hand. 'I want to know what happened, after all this trouble she's caused.'

'Donna, you're too upset after getting the awful news about Matilda. Please, go home and—'

'I don't want to go home. The girls are fine and I need to get out of the house for a while to try and clear my head.'

'I'm warning you now, it won't be what you expect. What Suzy will say ... it will hurt you.'

She made a disparaging noise. 'I can assure you, nothing she could say would even touch the news I've just had.'

I thought for a moment. 'Listen, I need to tell you something. Let's go into the kitchen first.'

Donna shook her head. 'I'm going in there now.' She marched towards the living room.

As I turned around to close the front door, the two detectives, Price and Brewster, pulled up in their car. It had taken them long enough. They'd probably discounted my 'big development'. Well, they wouldn't be expecting *this*.

The look on the detectives' faces when I greeted them at the door with 'I'm glad you've come over. Suzy Baros is here' was a picture. 'You'd better come through,' I said.

Everyone looked up as we walked in, and Suzy gripped Jakub's arm when I announced the detectives' arrival.

I introduced the two Polish men and Suzy, who they'd been working flat out to find but never actually met. Brewster let out a low whistle, a cool glare fixed on her. 'Well, this is quite the little gathering.'

Donna looked daggers at Suzy and I hovered by the door, feeling that somehow this was all my fault. I was the one who'd followed Paul and brought Suzy back here when I could have just called the police and let them deal with it.

DI Price cleared her throat. 'Miss Baros, have any of the men sitting here done you harm, prevented you from returning home or coerced you in any way?'

Suzy gave a weak smile and laid her hand on Jakub's thigh. 'No, of course not.'

Price, who usually had an easy, pleasant manner about her, suddenly showed her mettle. 'Then can you tell me where you have been for the past three weeks while your son has been placed into foster care and Nottinghamshire Police have been conducting a major investigation as to your whereabouts?' Her tone sounded dangerously reasonable.

Suzy's eyes widened. 'It wasn't my fault, it was ... it was someone else's idea.'

'I see. And who was this person?'

Suzy glanced at me and then at Donna. She hung her head. 'I'd rather not say.'

'I'm sure.' Brewster folded his arms. 'Unfortunately, you have no choice but to tell us the truth, otherwise we will be entirely within our powers to arrest you for wasting police time.'

The colour drained from Suzy's face, but she sat very still, her lips pressed wordlessly together.

I looked at Donna. 'I'm sorry to be the one to say this, but the person who helped her to hide away is Paul.'

Donna's mouth dropped open. 'What the hell?'

'I saw him earlier today, Donna. You'd said he was on calls all day at home, and because of all the other stuff you'd told me, your suspicions, I decided on a whim to follow him.'

'And where did your travels take you, Mrs Shaw?' Brewster asked.

'A bedsit in Chesterfield,' I said. He went inside with bags of food, and I waited. I thought ...' I shot Donna a regretful look. 'I thought he was having an affair. When he came out again, I saw Suzy standing in the shadows behind him. I waited for Paul to drive off and then I went to confront her.'

'I am sorry, Donna,' Suzy said quietly. 'I assure you nothing happened between us. I am not having an affair with your husband. He said he wanted to help me and then he stopped me from leaving because he said Michael was dead and everything had blown up here. He said if I didn't stay hidden, I would go to prison.'

'I think you'd better explain yourself,' Donna said. I knew my friend well enough to spot the seething fury beneath her relatively calm exterior. It was as though when she looked at Suzy, she saw all Paul's infidelities, all the women he'd cheated with.

'On the contrary, I think it's best if we calm down a bit,' Price said firmly. 'We can do this two ways. We can arrest everyone here and take you all to the station, or we can talk like adults and get to the bottom of exactly what's happened.'

'I would like to speak for myself here,' Suzy said.

'Then let's start from the beginning,' Brewster said, taking out his notebook.

'My name is Zuzana Baros, and although people here know me as Suzy, I was known as Ana back home in Poland. Jakub and I grew up together. We were childhood sweethearts.'

Jakub squeezed her hand. 'I was a fool. I let Ana fall in love with someone else and she married him. His name was Oskar Krol.'

'Oskar swept me off my feet, and we got married quickly. But he was a cruel, uncaring man, and a few years into the marriage, I fled Poland because of a domestic abuse situation.' Suzy stopped talking and seemed out of breath. Jakub nodded, encouraging her to carry on. 'He told me many times that if I left him, he would hunt me down and kill me and my son. I came to the UK to try and find Jakub, and word somehow leaked out into the Polish community. I got word he was coming to England to try and find me.'

'That's why you seemed so nervous whenever you were out in the village,' I murmured. That at least made sense now.

'Yes. I had to explain to Aleks that he must forget about Poland, at least for a while, until we found Jakub. He is young but he said he understood.'

'He kept his word,' Price said sadly. 'We had trouble getting any information out of him when you disappeared.'

'I hoped Oskar would tire of his quest to find us, but he would not be beaten. Last year, using one of his dodgy contacts, he traced Jakub to the Devonshire bed and breakfast where he stayed, and Pawel here protected Jakub.'

'I lied and said he'd already moved on,' Pawel said. 'Oskar roughed me up a little but I swear I did not tell him about Wadebridge.'

'When I finally found Pawel, he told me that Jakub had been working at Wadebridge,' Suzy said. 'I rented a cottage from Irene and – I'm not proud of this – I put pressure on Michael to tell me what had happened to him. I got a bad feeling that he was lying to me, holding something back. He got sick of me and said he would tell Irene to ask us to leave. I was afraid he would do it and so I said that if he did not tell me the truth about Jakub, I'd tell his wife he had made advances towards me. Sorry, Kate,' she said, but she didn't meet my eyes. 'I started to believe Michael had hurt Jakub in some way. Donna's husband, Paul, was always hanging around trying to talk to me. If I went down into the village, he'd suggest we go for a drink somewhere. It was one of these times I ended up confiding everything to him.'

'You could have spoken to me, to Kate,' Donna snapped. 'Instead you flirted around my husband.'

'No! It was not like that,' Suzy pleaded, but I could see Donna was closed off to her. 'Paul insisted so I came up with this idea that if I went missing, the police would look closely at him and Wadebridge and I'd find out at last what had happened. He said he'd put me in a safe place and that Aleks could join me in a short time.' She looked at each of the detectives in turn. 'Paul said he and Donna were caring for Aleks and that he wanted revenge on Michael because he told Donna some time ago that Paul was having an affair. He said that me going missing and the police finding the clues we'd left – his keys in the cottage and my phone in his toolbox – would force them to investigate Michael, and if he'd had anything to do with Jakub's disappearance, it would surely come out then.'

'But Kate Shaw found out about your little ruse today and it came to an end,' Price remarked. 'Why wait so long to come back, though? It's been three weeks your young son has been without you. It's caused him so much trauma.'

'I had no phone, no television. Paul said Aleks was fine and being cared for at his home by him and Donna. Everything had gone wrong, he said. Michael had probably taken his own life because the police were blaming him for my disappearance and Paul said we would both go to prison.'

'Jakub, your family reported you missing six months ago. Initial investigations came to a stop as there were no leads. Now we know why,' Brewster said sternly. 'We had recently resumed a missing person inquiry to search for you again. Would you care to tell us where you cleared off to a year ago without telling anyone, not even your family?'

Jakub sighed. 'It is a long story, I'm afraid.'

'Another one. Well, it's your lucky day, Mr Jasinski,' Brewster said caustically. 'We have plenty of time.'

FIFTY-ONE

AUTUMN 2018

JAKUB

Things got better for Jakub at Wadebridge. It had taken a long time but he felt part of the team at last. Irene started bringing him a cup of tea when she made one for Michael. Before, he'd had to make do with water from the outside tap. Things quickly escalated so he was included in a mid-morning slice of toast or perhaps a biscuit in the afternoon.

He suspected such gestures meant little to Irene, but to him, they made a world of difference. He felt valued and part of the estate, the closest thing he had to his family life back in Poland.

He and Michael had an understanding. Jakub stayed out of Michael's way and got on with the job. Michael soon stopped barking out orders and would take the time to discuss matters with him, sometimes even asking his opinion on planting an area of grass or retiling part of a roof.

Jakub was not a clock-watcher. Besides, he had nothing to get back to the soulless B&B for, apart from to listen to his roommate, Pawel, spouting plans for the future that never seemed to materialise. He knew that Michael valued the fact that he would stay until the job was done.

One evening, they'd been working late out on the driveway to replace some cracked water pipes.

'We'll call it a day,' Michael had said. 'How early can you get here in the morning? We need to take advantage of the dry weather to finish it, and it's going to rain in the afternoon.'

'I would happily come early but I will have to see what time the earliest bus is.'

Irene offered him a room for the night. 'Seems silly you going all the way back to your B&B when you'll be back a few hours later.'

'Thank you, Irene.' Jakub had beamed. 'I'm most grateful.'

That had been the first time, and they'd sat up talking later than Jakub wanted to. Irene had been fascinated to hear about his life back in Poland. Soon, staying over when he'd worked late became a regular thing.

'After New Year, when the holidaymakers have gone, you can have one of the cottages for a small rent,' she'd promised, and Jakub was over the moon.

Irene had explained she was on a waiting list for a hip replacement, and finally she was called into hospital. Michael agreed to move into the house for a week to look after everything. His wife, Kate, and their child would stay in the family home and Irene said that Jakub could stay in one of the spare cottages.

About halfway through her hospital stay, Jakub woke up hearing scuffling noises outside the cottage. He'd had an uncomfortable sensation for a while that he was being watched, but this was something else.

He got out of bed and padded to the window. Seeing lights on in the main house, he got dressed quickly and ran outside. As he approached the house, he saw that the back door was open, and he heard Michael shout out. A tall, broad man stood with his back to Jakub, brandishing a shotgun at Michael.

Jakub rushed in and launched himself at the powerfully built man from behind. As the man turned, striking Jakub on the head with the barrel of the gun, Jakub caught sight of his face. Those wild eyes, the hatred etched on his features. He felt his knees shaking and the world began spinning.

Then time seemed to stand still as Oskar Krol, his old adversary, the man who had married his beloved Ana, made to shoot him at point-blank range. That was when Michael Shaw fired his own gun and Oskar slumped to the floor.

Jakub explained to Michael who Oskar was, and how he suspected he'd come over to England to kill him when a friend told Jakub Ana had left him. Together they buried him on Wadebridge land and cleaned up the kitchen.

'If the police somehow trace him here and you're still around, they'll definitely suspect you had something to do with his disappearance,' Michael said. 'Much as it pains me, Jakub, we're both better off if you disappear.'

The next day, Jakub left Wadebridge for good. He smashed his phone, waited until Pawel was out, then collected his belongings and headed up to Scotland.

Too ashamed to return to Poland or contact his family after what he'd done, he'd been running ever since.

FIFTY-TWO

KATE

The detectives took Suzy and Jakub to the police station.

'We'll want to talk to you again, Mrs Shaw,' Price told me. 'We still have the suspected abduction and murder of Matilda Spencer to solve, and we'll need to investigate whether Michael had any part in that.'

I nodded. I felt so tired of it. I couldn't defend Michael any more. The police had to do their job and clear him of any wrongdoing. I realised I had to absolve myself from responsibility and let justice take its course. My shoulders suddenly loosened; my jaw relaxed.

They turned to Donna.

'We'll also want to speak to your husband today,' Price said. 'Did you say there are children at the house?'

Donna nodded. 'I'll go back home now.'

'I wish you could stay and talk,' I said.

'My head is spinning,' she said quietly. 'I've learned that Matilda's body has been discovered, and now all this stuff about Paul ... I can't think straight. Maybe tomorrow.'

I couldn't imagine how bad she was feeling.

When she'd left, I decided I'd go up to Wadebridge and see Irene, tell her everything that had happened. It had been too long. I'd been so taken up with my own problems, I'd forgotten that apart from her new home help, Doris, she was largely alone.

I drove up there, my heart heavy and aching with loss when I saw Michael's cottage office. I tapped on the door before walking into the hallway.

'Irene? Hello?'

No answer. I popped my head around the living room door and saw her there in her armchair, fast asleep.

The kitchen was a bit of a mess. Doris tried her best, but she was in her late sixties herself and I suspected she found the work quite hard going. I put the kettle on and loaded the dirty dishes into the dishwasher. After I'd emptied the bin, I took out the recycling. It felt good to lose myself in a bit of housework. My brain had been working overtime now for ages.

I made Irene's tea and took it through to find she was still sleeping. I was worried that she'd left the door open and hadn't a clue I was in the house. It was chilly in here without the fire, so I took a blanket from the floor and draped it over Irene's legs. I looked down and saw that the blanket had been covering the small, ornately carved wooden box she seemed so fond of.

I glanced at her now, but she was still fast asleep. Obviously all the drama with the police presence had taken its toll on her. I picked up the box to move it away from her feet and it slipped. The lid opened and one or two items fell out. I carried it over to the sofa and replaced Irene's reading glasses and a packet of mints.

That's when I saw all the folded newspaper cuttings. I pulled out the topmost one. These were old newspapers, that much was obvious from the dated layout and faded print ... I opened it out, careful not to rip along the deep, aged creases. I read the headline

LOCAL   GIRL   STILL   MISSING   AFTER THREE DAYS

Thirteen-year-old Matilda Spencer, who went missing at the end of school last Friday, has still not been found, despite extensive police and community searches and door-to-door enquiries in the village of Lynwick. Matilda is five feet tall, with pale skin and striking long red hair that she often wore in ringlets. She was last sighted at the end of school, heading towards the student library.

Police are appealing for witnesses.

Something bulged in my throat. My breathing slowed. I unfolded the next cutting.

MATILDA STILL MISSING

Missing girl Matilda Spencer, who vanished after leaving school one day last September, has still not been found over six months later.

'It's been a torture no parent could understand unless they've been through it,' a spokesman for the Spencer family said. 'We just want Matilda home. If someone has her, just drop her off anywhere near the village. If anyone knows the slightest piece of information that could help bring her back, then please, please, contact the police.'

Nottinghamshire Police are appealing for anyone with information to come forward confidentially.

There were other articles, roughly two or three a year. They all repeated the circumstances of Matilda's disappearance, together with a renewed plea from Nottinghamshire Police for information.

I lifted out the last cutting and stared at what lay underneath, nestling on a piece of black velvet. I picked it up and laid it against my pale palm. Hair. A rich red in colour, it had been delicately tied with thin pink ribbon at one end.

I shivered with sudden cold. This wasn't just a few strands. It was a thick ringlet that had been cut bluntly at one end. I felt strange. Very strange. My skin began to crawl, as if an army of insects were marching across it, burrowing into the creases of my body, the hidden places where I might never be able to get them out.

I knew without the slightest shadow of doubt that this was Matilda Spencer's hair.

FIFTY-THREE

My first instinct was to call the police. But then what? Although every bone in my body knew I'd found something very bad, there was still a slight chance the newspaper cuttings and Matilda's hair were just a macabre curiosity Irene had. If I summoned the police and Irene clammed up, we'd never find out what had happened to Matilda. Donna would never have true peace. I had to be cleverer than that. I had to play Irene at her own game. She pretended to be a defenceless old lady when underneath she was keeping secrets at the cost of a grieving family and a young girl's life. Even if she'd been protecting Michael in some way, I had to find out the truth. I'd finally realised the time for protecting my husband's integrity was out of my hands. Whatever he might have done, that had no bearing on my own character or the pure innocence of our daughter.

In a minute or two, I had my plan. I put the box back on the floor next to Irene, then clomped around a bit, pretending to tidy up, and she stirred.

'I came to see you and made you some tea,' I said. 'Sorry if I woke you.'

'No, I'm glad you did. If I sleep too long in the afternoon, I'm often awake in the night.'

I took my phone out of my pocket, tapped at the screen and put it down on the table next to Irene. Then I sat down opposite her. 'We've been friends for a long time now, haven't we?'

She looked at me over the rim of her cup. 'We have, yes.'

'I want to be completely honest with you. Is that OK, Irene?'

'Yes, of course!'

I stood up, walked over to her and picked up the box.

'Oh! What are you ...' She looked down, glanced at the blanket on her lap and made the connection. 'You found my box.'

'I did more than that, Irene. I looked in it.'

Her mouth sagged. 'It's just some newspaper cuttings about things that have happened around here.' A shadow passed over her face. 'You shouldn't have looked in there. It was my private property.'

'I'm sorry. It's just ... Well, I saw the red hair, Irene. Matilda's hair.'

'Who? It's not Matilda's hair.'

'Whose hair is it?'

'That's not really your concern.' She made an unsuccessful attempt to get up out of her chair.

'I know it's Matilda's hair, Irene. But I wanted to be honest with you and to say I understand. It's your own business.'

Her eyes narrowed. 'What are you playing at?'

'Nothing. Look, before Michael died, I would've panicked seeing that. But now, I'm a widow like you and I know some things about Michael that I don't want other people to know. They're things I wish he hadn't done, but they don't make me love him any less.'

'Things like what?' Irene said, interested.

'You first,' I said. 'I found the box, so you tell me what happened to Matilda Spencer, and I'll tell you what happened to Suzy Baros.'

Her eyes widened, hungry for gossip, and I thanked my lucky stars she didn't yet know Suzy was back safe and well.

'It was a long time ago,' she said grudgingly. 'I can barely remember.'

'I can understand that. And I think when we don't want to remember, it's harder. I know it's been that way for me.'

She nodded slowly as she regarded me. I knew she was weighing up whether she trusted me or not.

'I mean, for me, it wasn't as if Michael meant to hurt Suzy. I know he was a good man. He treated Tansy and me so well. People see a victim and they think that person was perfect, innocent. You know?'

She nodded. 'I *do* know. People aren't interested in whether someone pushed you too far. They don't know how it feels until they find themselves in that situation.'

'The police want to speak to me again. I don't care if they lock me up, or interview me another thousand times, I will not betray Michael. I won't betray his memory. Do you understand?'

She sat forward a little. 'I do, Kate. I do understand. But most people wouldn't. Most people haven't lost the person they love most in the world.'

I thought of Donna, and the irony of Irene's words struck me.

'Michael was a good man and no matter what he did, I'll always love him.'

We sat in silence for a moment, and I felt she was deciding whether to tell me the truth. Finally, she spoke.

'You see, what people around here didn't realise was that Matilda Spencer was a madam. She might have only been thirteen years old, but in reality she was a conniving young woman, make no mistake about that.'

'Just like Suzy Baros, then.' I was getting into my stride now and she was responding. Her confidence in me was growing, I could feel it. 'Suzy was Miss Sweetness and Light on the face of it, but she badgered Michael. As you said, she was attracted to him, and when he shunned her, she threatened to tell me he'd made a move on her. Did you know that?'

'No!' Irene said, shocked. 'I confess I was taken in by her

charm offensive, but … That little weasel Matilda, she threatened to go to the police. She … she accused my Amos of touching her inappropriately.'

'Never!'

'Oh yes. He broke down in tears and told me he'd accidentally brushed against her. He'd apologised, for goodness' sake. It was an accident. But she wouldn't have it, she was adamant she'd go to the police and Amos … well, he'd have been ruined! His father would have disinherited him. The villagers would have hanged him on the green.'

'Poor Amos. What an awful thing to happen.' I creased my face in mock concern. 'So what did he do?'

'It was my idea,' she said, pleased with herself. 'I saw her in the village and told her to meet me after school the next day. There was a track by the school, shielded by a few trees. I told her I'd give her some money, if only she would consider not going to the police. But if she told anyone at all then the deal was off. The next day, Matilda was waiting where we agreed. You should've seen her greedy little eyes light up when she saw me. She demanded five hundred pounds there and then. She raised her voice, backing out of the trees when I said that amount was out of the question. "I'm going straight to the police!" she hissed. We'd anticipated trouble from her, so Amos was waiting in the trees just in case with a chloroform-soaked rag. I've never seen someone go down so fast. We bundled her in the car and brought her up here.'

I forced a poker face. The horror of it, the sheer terror Matilda must have felt.

'Then what happened?'

'It was her own fault. We only wanted to speak to her, to offer her a reasonable amount of cash and have her sign something to say Amos had never touched her. He was a pillar of the community, a governor of the school. It would have ruined him. We planned to talk some sense into her up at Wadebridge, you see.'

'Of course,' I agreed.

'She came to, but before we could make her an offer, she

sprang up and ran for it. Amos grabbed her, and the nasty little cat bit his hand. I lashed out more as a reaction ... I didn't even think about it.'

'You hit her?' I pressed.

'Yes, I hit her.' She hesitated. 'I had a poker in my hand at the time, ready to stoke the fire. I knocked her out cold, and when she went down, she hit the cast-iron hearth.' She nodded to the fireplace with its buffed iron fender in front of my feet, and I pulled my legs tighter into the seat. Matilda had met her end here, in this very room. All the years we'd sat in here. Tansy had played in here, sat down there on the floor to do her drawings, her crafts. It was ... unthinkable.

'What did you do, when she fell?' I battled to keep my voice level.

'It was obvious she was a goner. Her eyes were open wide, staring. While Amos went for a tarpaulin sheet from the shed to wrap her in, I had a few minutes alone with her. In death she looked so young, so defenceless, just the kind of daughter I'd have loved, that we could have given a good life to.' Irene had alluded before to the fact that she'd have loved a child, but that it wasn't meant to be. 'I remember touching her pale skin, and it felt so smooth, and that hair ... that glorious hair! I snipped a pretty ringlet off to keep, to remember her by. Amos never knew about the hair. He wouldn't have understood. In death, I forgave her, you see. For trying to ruin us.' She stared into the middle distance, a gracious expression settling over her face.

I had to keep her moving on. 'Then Amos came back with the sheet?'

'Yes. I helped him roll her up in it and drag her outside. He dug until midnight. It seemed never-ending. He waited until dark and used a spade, didn't want to draw attention with any noisy machinery or lights.'

'Was Michael working here then?'

'No. It was a good few years before Michael came to Wadebridge, he never knew what had happened to Matilda. But he would have helped us if we'd asked him, I know he would.'

The disgust and fury whipped dangerously together in my gut. 'How did you cope, seeing Matilda's family in the village? Everyone must have been so upset, searching for her.'

'We made ourselves part of it,' Irene said simply. 'We sent food and donations to the family like everyone else. One day in the village, I spoke to young Donna. She was beside herself for not meeting her sister as planned to walk home from school. I told her it wasn't her fault, that she shouldn't feel guilty. I tried to help her, but she wouldn't listen, of course. We were saddened too, in our own way.'

'And that was it? Amos buried Matilda's body, you cleaned up and lived happily ever after?' I tempered my tone quickly, fighting to keep the anger out of it until I had all the information I needed. 'You and Amos are good people. It must have had some negative effect on you.'

'Of course it did! This is what I'm talking about, Kate. We *were* good people, living a perfectly happy life, until that bare-faced little liar came along with her threats to ruin us. It all got out of hand, but nobody would have been interested in that if she'd gone to the police. No. Amos would have been branded a pervert and we'd have been drummed out of the village. We'd have been outcasts.'

'But the police must have questioned everyone when she disappeared, come up here …'

'They did. But in those days, things were far more civilised. We knew our local police. Some of them lived among us. Amos would go for a drink with the chief inspector, so when those jumped-up detectives came from the city, he knew their movements before anyone else and he knew they had no leads. Nobody ever asked to start digging up here. Nobody remotely thought of us.'

'Did you never doubt Amos?'

'What do you mean?' She frowned, and I knew I had to be careful not to overstep the mark.

'Did you ever, even for a moment, wonder if what Matilda had said was true?'

'Never!' she snapped, clenching her fists. 'Amos loved me. We were devoted to each other. As he said, something about him must have made these young women tell lies and try and ruin him.'

'There were others?' I said faintly.

'Just a couple, as far as I know.' Irene folded her arms. 'Amos offered them money to keep their mouths shut and they took it. They had more sense than Matilda Spencer.'

'So ... you knew that he touched girls?'

'For goodness' sake!' Her face flushed scarlet. 'Of course he didn't! They were all liars, every last one of them! That's why Amos came to me for help. Me! I was always the strong one. I always knew what to do.'

She began rocking slightly, wrapping her arms around herself as if she were unravelling from the inside out. I sensed I hadn't got much time left.

'One more question, Irene. Why keep the hair, the newspaper cuttings? Why not get rid of all that in case it incriminated you?'

The rocking ceased and she grew suddenly very still, contemplative almost. She didn't answer right away, and then she said softly, 'It was something about those few minutes I had alone with her, I suppose. I felt close to her, if you can understand that. When I stroked her face and saw her as a young girl, it was almost as if we bonded. Amos and I could not create a child of our own, but we took her life together.' She seemed to come to her senses and shook herself. 'It might sound mad to you, but it was special. Very special. And I had to keep something to remember her by.'

'And you collected the newspaper articles too.'

She nodded. 'It was like watching a drama unfold while I held the delicious secret inside me. I'd go down into the village, and everyone would pour their hearts out, and then I'd come back here and hold Matilda's hair in my hand.'

I couldn't breathe. I stood up, reached for my phone.

'Hang on!' She shuffled forward in her seat, grimacing as the arthritis bit back. 'You can't go. You must tell me all about Michael and what happened with Suzy. She wouldn't leave him alone, would she?'

'There's nothing to tell,' I said sharply. 'Michael didn't hurt Suzy. She's safe and well and is talking to the police as we speak.' I couldn't spend another minute with this woman and I had no intention of telling her the story of Suzy and Jakub.

'What? How ... you have to tell me what happened. You said you would. Help me up,' she demanded. I ignored her and walked towards the door.

'I'm going straight to the police to tell them about what happened to Matilda, so you should prepare yourself.' I couldn't bear to look at her.

Irene threw back her head and laughed. 'I don't think the police will be coming, Kate. All that stuff I just told you, nobody will believe it. It will be painfully obvious you're making it up simply to defend Michael, just like I'm still defending Amos.'

'I wouldn't have defended Michael to this extent,' I said, my stomach turning at the sudden change in her. The glee on her face at the thought that she'd won. No remorse. No feelings for Donna, for Matilda, whose life she'd snuffed out without a second thought. 'I loved him, but there's a point beyond which decency cannot survive. I've seen the years of misery and grief in Donna, the result of what you did. It's time for the truth to be told so Matilda can be truly laid to rest.'

She fixed her dark, beady eyes on me, her features screwing up in disdain.

'They won't believe you,' she hissed. 'Nobody will believe you. I knew there was a chance they'd uncover Matilda's bones and I already told them I suspected Michael had killed Suzy and Jakub.'

'Oh, but they will. They'll all believe me when they hear this.' I tapped my phone, rewound the recording, then pressed play and held it up.

Irene's voice rang out clear as a bell.

I had a poker in my hand at the time, ready to stoke the fire. I knocked her out cold, and when she went down, she hit the cast-iron hearth.

Her mouth dropped open. 'What did you do? You conniving little—'

'And I'll need this.' I bent down and picked up the box containing Matilda's hair and the newspaper cuttings, snapping down the lid and locking it.

'No! That's mine, give it back!' she gasped, and started coughing, pulling out a hanky and spluttering into it. When she pulled the hanky away, I saw a flash of scarlet. She was coughing up blood.

For a second, I saw a frail old lady who needed my help, but then she started ranting.

'You didn't love Michael, not like I loved Amos. I am proud to be his widow, proud that my loyalty did not die with him. It will last forever.' She slumped back in her chair, her eyes dull.

It was time to finish this once and for all.

'It doesn't matter what you say, how you try and justify it to yourself,' I said calmly. 'It's time to tell the truth. It's time to give Matilda and her family the peace they deserve.'

And then I left the house.

FIFTY-FOUR

ONE WEEK LATER: 11 DECEMBER 2019

Donna and I sat by the glass doors in my kitchen with our coffee, looking out at our two girls in their coats, hats and scarves, squealing happily and running around in the snow.

The silver tinsel they'd draped in the trees that bordered our small garden glittered as the weak sunlight forced its way through the clouds. The girls' ruddy cheeks and sparkling eyes were a tonic in what had been a very challenging time.

'I need more of this,' Donna said, putting down her cup. 'More of seeing our girls enjoying their life. I want to watch Ellie grow, happy and safe, doing what Matilda couldn't do because it was taken away from her.'

I nodded and reached to squeeze her hand. 'And you will, Donna. I'm certain of that.'

Donna had surprised me by leaving Paul immediately when she'd learned of his involvement in Suzy's story. 'Ellie and I will check into a B&B or something. Just until the fog clears in my head.'

'You'll do no such thing. There's plenty of room at our house, and Tansy would never forgive me if I didn't offer. The girls will be in heaven. Sleepovers together every night.'

Donna had looked doubtful. 'Kate, I don't want to put even more of a burden on your shoulders. I don't know ...'

'I don't see it like that. I see it as *sharing* our joint burdens. We can get through this together. It's Christmas soon, and there is no way you and Ellie are going to be spending it in a B&B. So you might as well stop arguing.'

And that was that. We hugged, we shed a few tears and then we sealed the deal. The girls were delighted, and Donna and I provided mutual therapy for each other, getting it all off our chests each night over a gin and tonic and home-baked cookies we made regularly with the girls.

'When Matilda was found it felt like a switch had been flipped inside me. I felt a sense of responsibility to make mine and my daughter's life count. To live for Matilda, as well as myself,' Donna told me. 'It was as though someone shone a light on my life and I saw Paul for what he was. A selfish, controlling, disloyal man who gave me constant pain and grief.'

After leaving Irene's house a week ago, I'd headed directly for the police station. It was only two hours since Suzy and Jakub had left my house with DI Price and DS Brewster, so I knew there was a good chance the detectives would both be there. I'd been prepared to wait if necessary, but I insisted to the desk clerk that I had to speak to one of them. Price appeared within minutes and took me into an interview room, where I revealed the truth about Matilda. I sent a copy of the recording to her phone and she took custody of Irene's macabre box.

'Playing you Irene's confession was the hardest thing I've ever done,' I told Donna. 'But I knew it couldn't come from the police. I didn't know if it would set you free or send you into a terrible downward spiral.'

It took us three goes to get through it. I had to keep stopping to allow Donna to gather herself, to soak up her tears with handfuls of tissues. The expression on my friend's face was unbearable. I would never forget the pain, the fury and finally, the reluctant relief that she knew the final piece of the terrible puzzle.

'It did both,' Donna said quietly. 'But it had to be done. If you hadn't cornered her, she'd have happily let the blame for Matilda's death lay on Michael's shoulders.'

I nodded. DI Price told me she'd already told them he was capable of it, that he had a vile temper.

'Michael wasn't perfect,' I said. 'But he was a good man and the burden of Krol's death must have lain heavy on him. A secret he hadn't even told me. He knew Krol's body was buried up at Wadebridge and so the police searching around there for Suzy would have added immeasurable stress.'

All that time I'd suspected Michael was hiding his guilt because he was involved in Suzy's 'disappearance'. At the same time, I'd felt a compulsion so strong to take on the mantle of responsibility for whatever had happened. Just like I had as a kid, covering up for Mum's drinking, trying to pre-empt disaster and continually failing. Trying to be the adult in our screwed-up relationship. The day she took the car out after swearing to me she was sober, she hit a wall head-on and was killed instantly. And I'd blamed myself for her death my whole life. I tortured myself: Why did I believe her? Why didn't I realise what would happen? So many wasted years believing if I tried hard enough, I could stop bad things happening to me, to the people I loved. So many years of feeling responsible for things out of my control.

Now, I'd finally realised I could be a good friend, a reliable and loving mother and, if bad things happened, then I trusted I was strong enough to support others. I could leave those very heavy burdens of my childhood by the roadside and move on.

We sat in companionable silence for a few moments before Donna spoke again.

'I don't miss Paul, not like I thought I would. I never realised how much I worried about where he was, who he was seeing, until that burden lifted. It's helped not seeing him, even though I do want him to remain close to Ellie. To me, he's poison.'

Together, we'd fixed an arrangement whereby Paul called at

my house and I handed Ellie over at the appointed time. Then I'd meet them both at the door when he returned her. That way Donna was kept out of the equation completely.

Paul could barely meet my eyes, but that was OK. I could easily live with that.

FIFTY-FIVE

NOTTINGHAMSHIRE POLICE

Standing at the end of the corridor of doom, as the team called it, Helena braced herself for the final debrief of the Wadebridge case with Detective Superintendent Della Grey.

'Ready, Brewster?' She turned to her colleague and gave his tie, shirt and jacket lapels the once-over. Remarkably, they appeared to be stain-free.

'Ready, boss.'

She tapped on the door and walked in.

'Morning, ma'am,' she said brightly.

'Morning,' replied Grey, standing up to close the window. 'Take a seat.'

Helena looked in admiration at the violet trouser suit and crisp white blouse that Grey wore with such panache. Aside from a pair of small diamond stud earrings, the super sported no other jewellery. Nobody seemed to know if she was married or had a partner. All Helena had heard about her was her two pugs. The dread that Grey might have overheard her and Brewster laughing about the dogs made a reappearance, and she pushed it away.

Grey sat down and regarded them both. 'So. Where are we on the case ... all wrapped up with a bow?'

'Pretty much,' Helena said confidently. 'As you know, the forensic results are back, with no surprises thanks to Kate Shaw's amateur sleuthing. The remains of Matilda Spencer and Oskar Krol were confirmed as we expected.'

'And Irene Wadebridge?'

'It's a bit messy,' Helena said. 'We arrested her on suspicion of murder and interviewed her at the station with her solicitor present. After hearing the recording of Kate Shaw's chat with her, Wadebridge made a full confession. In view of her age and the historical nature of the incident, we deemed her not to be a threat and released her pending further investigation.'

'When do we get to the messy bit?' Grey prompted her.

Helena indicated for Brewster to answer. 'Unfortunately, after we'd charged Irene Wadebridge with the murder of Matilda Spencer, her health took a nosedive. Everyone knew she suffered with arthritis and sciatica, but it transpires she also has advanced lung cancer and hadn't told a soul.'

'I see.' Grey frowned.

'The team are preparing a file of evidence to submit to the local Crown Prosecution Service for advice on potential charges. We're hoping for manslaughter and preventing the lawful burial of a body, ma'am, but of course the final decision rests with the CPS.'

'Let's hope that case reaches fruition for Matilda Spencer's family's sake,' Grey said, consulting her notes. 'And what are we doing about Suzy Baros and Paul Thatcher? Their little ruse had consequences.'

'It looks like they might get away with a caution due to mitigating circumstances,' Brewster provided. 'Just before we came up, we heard about a new lead in the death of Michael Shaw.'

Grey raised an eyebrow. 'Really? Tell me more.'

'A new witness has come forward with dashcam footage captured on his way to the airport. He's been working abroad and only checked the footage when he returned home and heard about the accident. It's being enhanced and analysed as we speak but it looks very much as though Shaw trips up on the pavement and careers into the road, his arms windmilling as he tries to stop himself falling. He doesn't appear to consciously throw himself into the road at all, although it may well have looked that way to the advancing truck driver.'

'My, my, quite a twist in the tale,' Grey murmured. 'Anything else?'

'We're consulting with the CPS regarding the death of Oskar Krol,' Helena said. 'Although Jasinski claims it was self-defence when Michael Shaw shot Krol, both Shaw and Jasinski failed to report the death and took it upon themselves to prevent the lawful burial of a body. We have therefore interviewed Jasinski under caution.'

'Again, the CPS will review the evidence,' Brewster added. 'They may well decide, due to his previous good character and remorse, that it isn't in the public interest to proceed with any charges in which case no further action will be taken.'

'Very good. Well, still one or two details left, but generally, well done.'

'Thanks very much,' Helena said, beaming.

'Thank you, ma'am,' Brewster added.

'Warms the cockles of my heart, seeing my officers get the job done.' Grey smiled thinly and Helena's own heart missed a beat. She looked from Helena and back to Brewster. 'Contrary to popular rumour, I do have a heart, you know.'

'Yes, ma'am,' they said in innocent unison.

FIFTY-SIX

CHRISTMAS DAY 2019

KATE

Donna and I had risen early, even earlier than the girls, who had exhausted themselves with excitement the night before and were still sleeping soundly.

By 5.30, we'd already got the log burner going and put on a Spotify Christmas playlist on low volume. It was still dark out, but the lamps gave out soft pools of light and our eight-foot tree, which had had us almost wetting ourselves laughing as we battled to get it in the room, looked resplendent in the corner with its five hundred twinkling lights and its glitter and sequin decorations hand-made by the girls.

'Bit early for an eggnog, but this will do just fine for starters.' Donna laughed, handing me a mug of tea. 'Cheers!'

'Cheers.' We clinked mugs. 'To the start of the rest of our lives,' I added.

'Definitely cheers to that,' Donna said. 'Thanks to you, Kate, I'm in a better place now than I've ever been. I feel like I can really start to steer my own ship.'

'That's great, but don't sell yourself short. You got yourself out of a toxic situation by leaving. That took real courage.'

.   .   .

Later, Suzy, Aleks, Jakub and Pawel arrived for Christmas lunch. For the three kids' sakes, Donna and I had decided between us to put aside our feelings and just plan a good day to underline a very difficult time. I'd been shocked by Suzy's selfishness and we were both far from ready to forgive her. But we also didn't want to see Aleks spending his first Christmas in the UK shrouded in misery, plus Suzy had insisted she had a final part of the story she wanted everyone to know.

'Even I can put our differences aside for one day,' Donna had said magnanimously. Then, with the mischievous twinkle in her eye I'd missed so much, added: 'I can try, anyway.'

We did a buffet lunch with there being so many of us. Pawel brought some Polish delicacies for us to try and halfway through the meal, Suzy stood up.

'I have a Christmas surprise for everyone,' she said, looking nervously at Jakub, who smiled and winked at Aleks. 'I wanted you all to know that Aleks is Jakub's son. This is why it was so important for Aleks to come with me to find Jakub.'

Everything made more sense now. The way Suzy was willing to go to extreme lengths to find out the truth of what had happened to Jakub. Aleks himself had paid a high price to find his father and Suzy had trodden on a lot of people to get where she was today. My heart squeezed. We would all bear the scars of her quest.

Suzy's upbeat voice continued.

'Once we have put all this behind us and we know Jakub is a free man, we are going back to Zalipie in Poland to resume our life as a family there.'

Everybody clapped and raised a glass. 'You didn't know you were a father, Jakub?' Donna asked.

'No. When Ana left me for Oskar, we saw each other once more in secret when I visited home in 2012. I was hoping that after that she would change her mind and come back to me, but it wasn't to be. My mother never told me that Ana had a child, I don't know why.'

Suzy nodded. 'When I found out I was pregnant, I was very worried. Aleks looked like Jakub and I think somehow Oskar sensed that he was Jakub's son, because he forced me to get a parental DNA test done. For years he kept me like a virtual prisoner and treated my boy badly. But now that is all behind us. The three of us are reunited.'

We were twenty minutes into a game of Trivial Pursuit when there was a knock at the door. I left the others playing the game and looked through the peephole before opening up.

'Hello, Paul,' I said stiffly. 'You're not supposed to collect Ellie until tomorrow.'

'It's Donna I want to see. I have something to say to her.'

'Wait here,' I said before fixing my eyes on his. 'Ellie's having fun with Tansy and Aleks. Don't ruin her Christmas.'

'I won't. I'm not here to cause trouble. I just need to speak to my wife.'

I went back to the living room and managed to signal to Donna to come through without Ellie or Tansy spotting me and jumping up to see what was happening.

Donna came out into the hallway smiling. 'I just answered a question that I didn't even know I knew! Can you—' She stopped in her tracks. 'Oh, it's you,' she said.

'I'll be in the other room,' I told her. 'Just let me know if—'

'No! I want you to stay,' Donna said firmly. 'Whatever it is Paul needs to say, he can say it in front of you.'

I shifted awkwardly, but stayed put, pulling the living room door closed.

Paul took a breath. 'Donna. I've come here today to tell you how much I love you. I've been such a fool. I didn't realise what I had until I woke up this morning without you both.'

Donna folded her arms but said nothing. When Paul had left

her last time, she'd told me how he'd won her back with a fancy speech, and here it was again, almost word for word.

'I know you've heard this before, but this time I really mean it. I swear to God, I can't live without you and Ellie.'

'Suzy told me you said you loved her like you'd loved no other woman. That you wanted to be with her for the rest of your life,' Donna said. 'I think if Jakub hadn't come back, you'd still be trying to win her over.'

'That's not true! I said those things to her because I wanted her to believe I'd divorce you. I wanted to get my revenge on Michael and I needed her to buy into the disappearance scam.'

His voice was getting louder, and I worried Ellie would hear. Then Christmas music started up in the other room and I could hear the girls laughing and dancing around. Someone in there had had the sense to disguise what was happening in the hallway.

'See, that's what I can't stand about you,' Donna said. 'That's what I don't miss one bit. The way you use people for your own ends, manipulate them. Pick them up and put them down as it suits.'

'I just want a chance, Donna! I deserve that, don't I? We've been together too long to—'

'You used up your chances a long time ago, Paul. I told you that when I took you back like a fool last time. It's over. I'm done with your lies, your games.' She turned to go back to the living room and he lurched forward, grabbing her arm.

'Donna, I beg you. It's Christmas Day and I'm all alone! I want to be with you and Ellie. Come home. Please, just come home and we'll talk.'

She shook him off. 'I've nothing to say, Paul. It's all been said a thousand times. Now go home, please, and don't come back. I don't want to ring the police, but I will if necessary.'

'Donna! You don't mean that. Please, I ...' Tears began rolling down his cheeks, but Donna turned on her heel and went back into the living room, closing the door behind her.

Paul turned to me. 'Can you help, Kate? Please? Try and make her listen at least.'

'I'm not getting involved, Paul,' I said dispassionately. 'For what it's worth, I think she should have done this years ago. You were slowly killing her. Sucking the very lifeblood from her. Get some help, that's my advice. Admit you've got a problem.'

He wiped away the crocodile tears and sneered. 'Do you know what, I'm glad Michael's gone. He was a thorn in my side. You deserved each other.'

He stormed out of the house and slammed the front door so hard, I felt the vibration of it under my feet.

'Good riddance to bad rubbish,' I murmured under my breath.

I stood in the doorway and watched everyone smiling, laughing and chatting together. My Christmases with Michael and Tansy flashed before my eyes and I felt a longing and a dark space that could never be filled. I said a silent prayer for my husband, who had turned out to be exactly the kind of man I'd believed him to be. Loyal, good and the best father. The police had allowed me to view the unexpected dashcam footage. I watched again and again as Michael tripped and stumbled into the road. He hadn't taken his own life. He'd tried to right himself, to stop the accident happening. Michael had wanted more than anything to be with us, his family, and now his daughter would know that. She'd know how much he loved her.

And here we were, despite everything, enjoying a great Christmas after such a sad and traumatic year.

Our best life was ahead of us now. I really believed that.

I knew we would both do Michael proud.

A LETTER FROM K.L. SLATER

Thank you so much for reading *The Widow*, and I really hope you enjoyed it. If you did and would like to keep up to date with all my latest releases, just sign up at the following link. Your email address will never be shared and you can unsubscribe at any time.

www.bookouture.com/kl-slater

It was my interest in the clash of family morals and loyalties that prompted the writing of *The Widow*. We all usually know the right thing to do, the moral way to react when something terrible happens. But life often isn't that simple. Relationships and loyalties get in the way, clouding the issue. Past wounds can reappear and force us to react from a place of fear, guilt or anger.

Like so many before it, the story began with a 'what would *you* do?' scenario: what would you do if someone you'd known for nearly twenty years, the father of your child and a loving, caring man, turned out after his death to be a monster? Would you default to denial? Would you make excuses? Would you lie yourself in order to protect your child? This is the dilemma our protagonist, Kate Shaw, faces.

Kate must battle painful memories of her own mother's alcoholism and the feelings of insecurity and distrust the past brings with it. Her overriding concern is for her daughter's future and how her life will be impacted by her father's actions. Will she allow her daughter to suffer so she can do the right thing?

This book is set in Nottinghamshire, the place I was born and have lived all my life. Local readers should be aware I sometimes take the liberty of changing street names or geographical details to suit the story.

I do hope you enjoyed reading *The Widow* and getting to know the characters. If so, I would be very grateful if you could take a few minutes to write a review. I'd love to hear what you think, and it makes such a difference helping new readers to discover one of my books for the first time.

I love hearing from my readers – you can get in touch on my Facebook page, through Twitter, Goodreads or my website.

Thank you to all my wonderful readers … until next time,

Kim x

https://klslaterauthor.com

 facebook.com/KimLSlaterAuthor

 twitter.com/KimLSlater

 instagram.com/klslaterauthor

ACKNOWLEDGEMENTS

Every day I sit at my desk and write stories, but I'm lucky enough to be surrounded by a whole team of talented and supportive people.

Huge thanks to my editor at Bookouture, Lydia Vassar-Smith, for her expert insight and editorial support.

Thanks to *all* the Bookouture team for everything they do – which is so much more than I can document here. Everyone is a pleasure to work with and special thanks to Alexandra Holmes, and the publicity team especially Sarah Hardy.

Thanks, as always, to my wonderful literary agent, Camilla Bolton, who is always there with advice and unwavering support at the end of a text, an email or a phone call. Thanks also to Camilla's assistant, the wonderful Jade Kavanagh, who works so hard on my behalf. Thanks also to the rest of the team at Darley Anderson Literary, TV and Film Agency, especially Mary Darby, Kristina Egan, Georgia Fuller and Rosanna Bellingham.

Thanks as always to my writing buddy, Angela Marsons, who has been a brilliant support and inspiration to me in my career. We have even supported each other through our recent house renovations ... anything that affects the writing, we devise a plan!

Massive thanks as always go to my family, especially to my

husband and daughter, who are always willing to put outings on hold and rearrange to suit writing deadlines.

Special thanks to Henry Steadman, who has worked so hard to pull another amazing cover out of the bag. Thank you to copyeditor Jane Selley and proofreaders Becca Allen and Lauren Finger for their work in making the book the best it can be. Also, many thanks to Stuart Gibbon for his expertise in police procedural matters. Any mistakes made during the transfer of this information are most definitely my own!

Thank you to the bloggers and reviewers who do so much to support authors; to everyone who has taken the time to post a positive review online or who has taken part in my blog tour. It is always noticed and much appreciated.

Last but not least, thank you *so* much to my wonderful readers. I love receiving all your comments and messages and I am truly grateful for the support of each and every one of you.

Printed in Great Britain
by Amazon

74487290R00194